THE AYODHYA ALLIANCE

BOOKS IN THE BHARAT COLLECTION

The Rozabal Line
Chanakya's Chant
The Krishna Key
The Sialkot Saga
Keepers of the Kalachakra
The Vault of Vishnu
The Magicians of Mazda
The Ayodhya Alliance

Praise for the Bharat Collection

The Rozabal Line (2008)

'In *The Rozabal Line*, Ashwin Sanghi does a Dan Brown by mixing all the ingredients of a thriller—crusades, action, adventure, suspense—and pulling off, with dexterity and ease, a narrative that careens through cultures and continents, religions and cults.' ~*The Asian Age*

'*The Rozabal Line* by Ashwin Sanghi is a kickass thriller that forces you to re-examine our histories, our faiths.' ~Pritish Nandy

'Sanghi's flair for religion, history and politics is clearly visible as he takes the reader across the world, spanning different decades. A mixture of comparative religion, dangerous secrets, and a thrilling plot makes for an esoteric read.' ~*The Statesman*

'Sanghi has got the sure-fire formula right.' ~*The Times of India*

'A provocative, clever and radiant line of theology ... Sanghi suggests that the cult of Mary Magdalene has its true inspiration in the trinity of the Indian sacred feminine, thereby out-thinking and out-conspiring Dan Brown.' ~*The Hindu*

Chanakya's Chant **(2010)**

'With internal monologues and descriptions as taut as a-held-by-the-thumb sacred thread, we have Ashwin Sanghi's cracker of a page-turner, *Chanakya's Chant*. Two narratives flow like the Ganga and Yamuna ... a brisk technicoloured thriller.' ~*Hindustan Times*

'I am utterly enthralled. A delightfully interesting and gripping read. The historical research is deeply impressive.' ~Shashi Tharoor

'A gripping, fast-paced read, the novel is a true thriller in the tradition set by Dan Brown.' ~*People*

'Political grooming and conspiracy remain at the core of Ashwin Sanghi's historical thriller. Bloodshed, legal trials, betrayals, murders, assassination attempts make this into a page-turner.' ~*Sakaal Times*

'Released in India to wide acclaim, *Chanakya's Chant* is a political page-turner.' ~*Business India*

The Krishna Key (2012)

'Why should racy historical thrillers or meaty fantasy sagas come only from the minds of Western writers? Ashwin Sanghi spins his yarns well and leaves you breathless at every cliffhanger. No wonder his books are bestsellers!' ~*Hindustan Times*

'While the plot is set in today's world, one can expect to travel back and forth in time with generous chunks of history and nail-biting action.' ~*The Telegraph*

'An alternative interpretation of the Vedic Age that will be relished by conspiracy buffs and addicts of thrillers alike.' ~*The Hindu*

'Rocking story and incredible research. Loved it!' ~Amish Tripathi

'Sanghi manages to blur the line between fact and fiction and give a whole new perspective to history and the Vedic Age.' ~DNA

The Sialkot Saga (2016)

'*The Sialkot Saga* moves at a breakneck pace, hurtling through time and space, uncovering ancient secrets and burying modern ones.' ~*The Hindu*

'The book spreads across decades and centuries, till it reaches present-day India and will sure have both historic and thriller readers in for a treat.' ~*The Times of India*

'There are books that take time to develop an interest and then there are books that grip you from the very first page. *The Sialkot Saga* is one such book that hooks you from the start.' ~*Hindustan Times*

'There's never a dull moment in the book. In fact, the story takes on such a pace that the overwhelmed reader is compelled to put the book down and take a deep breath on many an occasion.' ~*The Financial Express*

'Sanghi weaves a masterpiece building up the readers' involvement in the novel with every turn of the page.' ~*The Pioneer*

Keepers of the Kalachakra (2018)

'The book can't be put down till all pieces of the jigsaw puzzle are put together.' ~*The Financial Express*

'The author packs a powerful punch … spicy and saucy, a survey of the past and the present … without a dull moment, without a dull page.' ~*The Sunday Standard*

'Science and spirituality collide in Ashwin Sanghi's latest thriller.' ~*India Today*

'Spread over a vast canvas, the novel has an engaging plot laced with mythology, history and legends.' ~*The Hindu*

'Ashwin Sanghi's *Keepers of the Kalachakra* is as explosive as a time bomb ticking in your hand. Every chapter springs an unpredictable surprise.' ~*Deccan Chronicle*

'*Keepers of the Kalachakra* has it all: political characters that remind you of real-life politicians, a racy, complex plot and enough improbable twists to keep you hooked.' ~*Hindustan Times Brunch*

The Vault of Vishnu (2020)

'In an enthralling alchemy of myth and science, Ashwin Sanghi gives us the sixth book in his Bharat Collection. As with all of Ashwin's books, the research is meticulous and the technical(ese) leaves one gasping as *The Vault of Vishnu* takes the reader through the highs and lows of history, myth, physics, warfare technology, artificial intelligence and biochemistry.' ~*The Times of India*

'*The Vault of Vishnu*, like all of Ashwin's books, is a heady mix of history, myth, science and thrills.' ~*The Hindu*

'A very interesting and intriguing thriller, thanks to the author's storytelling gift and painstaking research on Hindu metaphysics.' ~*The New Indian Express*

'Sanghi's latest work uses his favourite tool—mythology—and blends it with history to deliver some edge-of-the-seat action.' ~*Hindustan Times*

The Magicians of Mazda (2022)

'*The Magicians of Mazda* is a deft blend of imagination, history and thrills.' ~*Deccan Herald*

'An excellent cocktail of a thriller that has lessons for the present time too.' ~*The New Indian Express*

'Hold your hearts and reading glasses in place, readers! *The Magicians of Mazda* promises to be Sanghi's best thriller yet!' ~*The Times of India*

'Ashwin Sanghi has an extraordinary talent for bringing ancient wisdom alive, then whipping up a fast-paced thriller by blending fact with fiction … he doesn't disappoint.' ~Firstpost

'Sanghi's fascinating style of storytelling ensures that readers find a comfort spot on the very edge of their seats.' ~*The Telegraph*

THE AYODHYA ALLIANCE

ASHWIN SANGHI

**HARPER
FICTION**

An Imprint of HarperCollins *Publishers*

Published in India by Harper Fiction 2025
An imprint of HarperCollins *Publishers*
HarperCollins *Publishers* India, Cyber City,
Building 10-A, Gurugram, Haryana – 122002, India
www.harpercollins.co.in

2 4 6 8 10 9 7 5 3 1

Copyright © Ashwin Sanghi 2025

P-ISBN: 978-93-6989-644-8
E-ISBN: 978-93-6989-786-5

This is a work of fiction and all characters and incidents described in this book are the product of the author's imagination. Any resemblance to actual persons, living or dead, is entirely coincidental.

Ashwin Sanghi asserts the moral right
to be identified as the author of this work.

All rights reserved. No part of this publication may be reproduced, stored in a retrieval system, or transmitted, in any form or by any means, electronic, mechanical, photocopying, recording or otherwise, without the prior permission of the publishers.

Other than the official Indian boundaries depicted on the map, few boundaries are as per author's own findings and study. The author and publisher do not claim them to be official/legal boundaries of India. The map is neither accurate nor drawn to scale and the international boundaries as shown neither purport to be correct nor authentic as per the directives of the Survey of India.

Without limiting the exclusive rights of any author, contributor or the publisher of this publication, any unauthorized use of this publication to train generative artificial intelligence (AI) technologies is expressly prohibited. HarperCollins also exercise their rights under Article 4(3) of the Digital Single Market Directive 2019/790 and expressly reserve this publication from the text and data-mining exception.

Typeset in 10.5/14.2 Minion Pro
by HarperCollins *Publishers* India Pvt. Ltd

Printed and bound at
Replika Press Pvt. Ltd.

This book is produced from independently certified FSC® paper
to ensure responsible forest management.

HarperCollins *Publishers*, Macken House, 39/40 Mayor Street Upper,
Dublin 1, D01 C9W8, Ireland

शिवाय विष्णुरूपाय शिवरूपाय विष्णवे ।
शिवस्य हृदयं विष्णुः विष्णोश्च हृदयं शिवः ॥
यथा शिवमयो विष्णुरेवं विष्णुमयः शिवः ।
यथान्तरं न पश्यामि तथा मे स्वस्तिरायुषि ॥

śivāya viṣṇurūpāya śivarūpāya viṣṇave |
śivasya hṛdayaṁ viṣṇuḥ viṣṇóśca hṛdayaṁ śivaḥ ||
yathā śivamayo viṣṇurevaṁ viṣṇumayaḥ śivaḥ |
yathāntaraṁ na paśyāmi tathā me svastirāyuṣi ||

To Shiva, the form of Vishnu; to Vishnu, the form of Shiva.
Vishnu dwells in Shiva's heart, and in Vishnu's heart dwells Shiva.
As Vishnu is filled with Shiva, so too is Shiva imbued with Vishnu.
As I perceive no difference between them,
May that vision grant me peace and a life of well-being.

— Skanda Upanishad of Krishna-Yajurveda

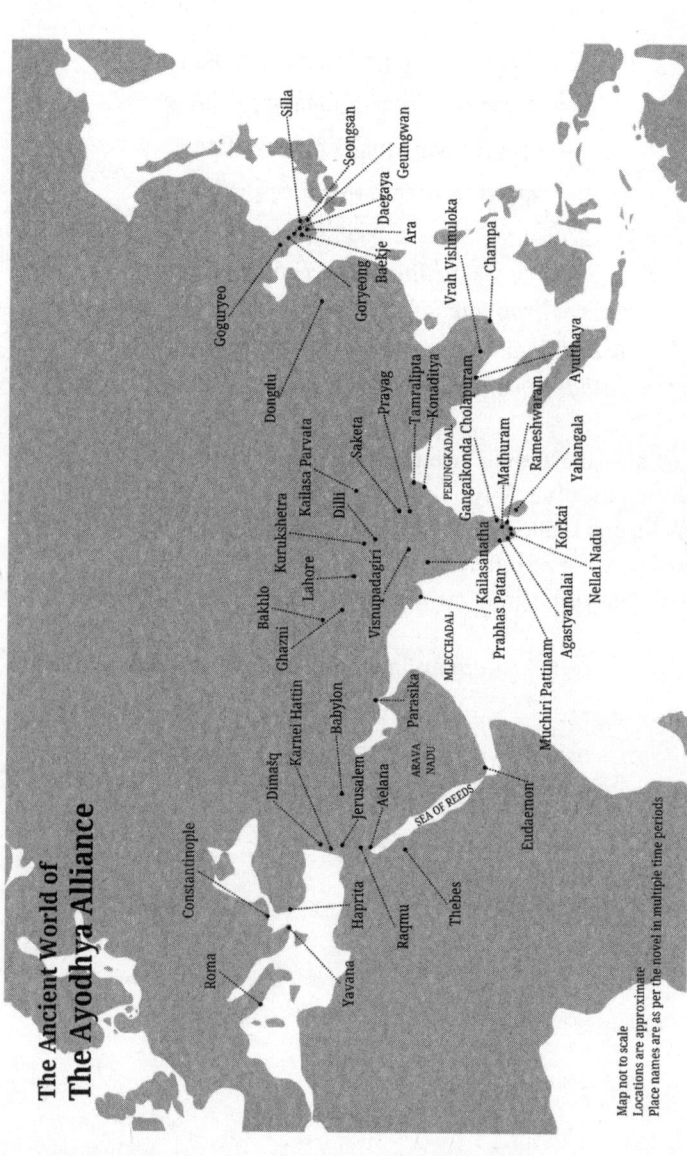

DISCLAIMER

This is a work of fiction. All names, characters, organizations, incidents, dialogues and locations—whether historical, mythological, political, religious or contemporary—are either products of the author's imagination or used fictitiously in an artistic and narrative context. Any resemblance to actual persons, living or dead, or to actual events, places or institutions is entirely coincidental and unintentional.

References to religious, historical, mythological, political, scientific, or cultural figures, scriptures, texts, places, doctrines, practices or events are made solely to enhance the thematic and dramatic fabric of the story. These references are fictionalized, speculative and interpretative in nature. The author explicitly disclaims any intention to assert, imply or represent accuracy. These portrayals are not intended to question, challenge, endorse, criticize, or validate any faith, ideology, belief system, political viewpoint or cultural position.

This book does not purport to present authoritative or scholarly perspectives on any field of study, including but not limited to: religion, mythology, theology, history, archaeology, science, anthropology, sociology, psychology, philosophy, literature, geopolitics, political science, military affairs, strategic studies, cultural studies or jurisprudence. The contents are presented strictly as a fictional narrative and should not be interpreted otherwise.

All quotations, verses and imagery—whether textual, visual or symbolic—should be understood as narrative devices within the fictional structure of the book and not as accurate or authenticated references. Any resemblance to real scripture, canonical text or doctrinal literature is coincidental or creative in nature and does not reflect any claim to authenticity or endorsement.

Design elements such as internal images, section breaks, cover artwork and maps, if included, are purely illustrative and are not intended to be geographically, historically, politically or scientifically accurate.

Wherever appropriate, the author has provided notes, references and citations at the end of the book for readers who may wish to explore contextual inspirations. These references are intended solely for background interest and are not necessary for the understanding or enjoyment of the story. The author makes no representations or warranties as to the accuracy, reliability, completeness or credibility of any such sources and disclaims all responsibility for how they are interpreted or used by readers.

The author unequivocally disclaims any and all liability—legal, civil, criminal or reputational—arising from interpretations, misinterpretations or actions based on this work of fiction. Readers are strongly advised to treat all content in this book as fictional and to exercise discretion in drawing conclusions or forming opinions based on this work.

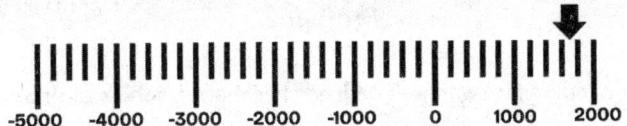

PROLOGUE

Mughal Sultanate

Present-day Mehrauli, Delhi, India

Around 300 years ago

As the Mughal Empire gasped in its twilight, chaos engulfed the land. It was no surprise that Dilli crumbled under the assault by Nadir Shah, the ruthless Persian warlord and self-declared Shah of Iran. Silence, heavy and absolute, gripped the once vibrant metropolis, broken only by the desperate screams of the innocent and the cries of the injured. A thick, choking curtain of smoke and dust hid the carnage. Now a wasteland of rubble and ash, Dilli lay utterly broken.

Nadir Shah stood atop the high ramparts of the Red Fort, admiring this macabre dance of death with an emotionless, impersonal stare. Dilli, the city beneath him, was under siege. The streets were clogged with lifeless bodies, and the agonized cries of survivors filled the air. Many of the city's magnificent buildings were ablaze, the flames reaching towards the heavens.

Nadir Shah exuded authority and dominance. His powerful, muscular frame attested to his years as a fighter. He had a strong, commanding face with well-defined cheekbones, a thick, dark beard and a prominent nose. His unusual turban was adorned with a jewelled plume. A long, flowing cloak of silk and brocade, detailed with gold thread, completed the ensemble. Sharp and merciless, his gaze conveyed the iron will of a conqueror devoid of empathy.

∾

After subduing Persia, Nadir Shah had launched a full-scale attack on his adversaries in Afghanistan. He had pursued his enemies all the way to Hindustan, conquering Peshawar, Lahore and the Khyber Pass in quick succession. Then, after his brutal victory over the Mughal army at Karnal, he ransacked the Mughal treasury.

With the Mughal emperor rendered powerless and the Persian army openly flaunting its conquest, resentment simmered beneath the surface. Fear turned to rage. Hunger, humiliation and helplessness choked the streets. When Nadir Shah visited the Golden Mosque in Chandni Chowk, a mob—driven by desperation and defiance—attacked. Enraged by what he saw as treachery, Nadir Shah ordered a mass slaughter and pillage.

Acting on his orders, his men razed the city with merciless efficiency, their swords dripping with the blood of innocent citizens. They destroyed temples and seized every possession in sight. Bodies lay in gruesome heaps in the streets, their lifeless eyes fixed on the unfolding disaster.

Dilli's Iron Pillar, the Vishnu Stambha, stood as an unwavering sentry in the midst of this nightmare, a symbol of the city's enduring power. The relic caught Nadir Shah's eye as he made his way from the Red Fort towards the Qutb Minar. He stared at the ornamental bell-shaped capital at the top of the Iron Pillar, which had once supported a figure of Garuda, Vishnu's transport

PROLOGUE

of choice. 'Is what they say about this Iron Pillar true?' he asked General Ahmed Khan, his voice piercing the smoky air.

'Difficult to say, Shahanshah,' Ahmed Khan answered. 'It is said to have been here for seven hundred years and may have stood elsewhere for a millennium before being placed here. Legend claims it to be the very nail holding Dilli together because it has withstood both corrosion and splits.'

Ambition flashed in Nadir Shah's eyes. 'I want the bell-shaped capstone of the pillar,' he declared. 'Fire a cannon and bring it down. I will use it as a platform in Mashhad.'

'Shahanshah, the Quwwat-ul-Islam Mosque's structures surround it,' Ahmed Khan cautioned delicately. 'Our cannonballs could damage them.'

'The Muslims of Hindustan are a corrupt lot, like the Hindu infidels,' the Shahanshah retorted. 'They deserve no special consideration.'

As soldiers hurried to place a cannon through a hole in the mosque's northwest wall, tension crackled in the courtyard. The gigantic weapon was aimed at the upper half of the pillar, the target being the base of the embellishment that crowned it.

Nadir Shah moved to a position from where he could observe the explosion from afar. His generals watched silently. There was little they could say in the face of the emperor's obstinacy.

'Fire!' Nadir Shah roared.

The cannonball hurtled towards the pillar and smashed into it with a deafening crash. Mountains of dust flew into the air. The soldiers nearby coughed as the soot settled.

The pillar's strength was evident to all present. It continued to stand though it bore the mark of the blast. The impact zone was dented, revealing the force of the projectile. The crash erased the original inscription honouring Rama. Beneath it, a symbol with two fish swimming in a circle—forever intertwined—met the same fate, their dance silenced forever.

Instead of breaking off the bell capital as intended, the cannonball had ricocheted off the pillar and smashed into the southwest wall of the Quwwat-ul-Islam Mosque. This severely damaged what had been Qutb ud-Din Aibak's pet project that commenced in 1193, tauntingly built by tearing down many Hindu and Jain temples.

Nadir Shah's annoyance was obvious, his eyes narrowing. 'Once more!' he bellowed, but Ahmed Khan intervened. 'Your Majesty, one side of the mosque is already damaged. Further attempts might destroy the structure completely.'

Nadir Shah scowled at the pillar, at its insufferable durability. 'Leave it alone,' he said as a concession to Islam. 'If we cannot break the pillar, we can destroy everything else.'

The emperor turned away and the looting of Dilli resumed with even greater fury. The Mughal treasury, amassed over decades, was completely emptied, its wealth transported to Persia. The legendary Peacock Throne, an emblem of Mughal grandeur, was among the loot, disassembled and readied for shipping. The estimated value of Nadir Shah's plunder at the time, including the prized Koh-i-Noor diamond, was seventy crore rupees, a staggering sum in the eighteenth century.

Nadir Shah's forces stormed through the city—no one was safe from the emperor's fury. Temples were demolished, homes were ransacked and the streets ran red with blood. Within a few days, almost 350,000 people lay dead.

At the heart of the city, in Mehrauli, the Iron Pillar watched the destruction unfold, a silent witness to the carnage. Its surface would forever bear the mark of Nadir Shah's depravity. Yet, its survival stood as a testament to the skill and technology that had created it.

1

Saketa, Kosala
Present-day Ayodhya, Uttar Pradesh, India
Around 2,000 years ago

Sweat dripping from his brow, the man dug furiously into the earth around the iron pillar, his shovel biting into the packed soil of the peaceful grove. It lay just a short walk—a few hundred yards—from the palace.

The pillar itself was imposing: twenty-three feet tall and sixteen inches wide with its surface polished to a mirror-like sheen, it was crowned with an impressive sculpture of Garuda, Vishnu's mythical mount. Known as the Vishnu Stambha, it had stood for countless years without a trace of rust. Engraved just below the Garuda, a Sanskrit shloka in Brahmi script proclaimed:

sa-anukrośaḥ jitakrodhaḥ brāhmaṇa-prajā-pūjakaḥ
dīnānukampī dharmajñaḥ nityaṁ pragrahavān śuciḥ

The inscription, taken from a celebrated work by the sage Valmiki, described the virtues of an ancient king named Rama, an avatar of Vishnu. Valmiki's words meant:

He possessed empathy, having conquered rage.
He revered the learned and showed kindness to the weak.

He remained steadfast in his duty.
He practised self-control and purity in conduct.

Beneath the inscription was a depiction of two fish swimming clockwise.

Many who saw this symbol assumed it represented the fish, Matsya, Vishnu's first avatar, who, as the legend goes, saved King Manu and his kingdom from a devastating flood towards the beginning of the Satya Yuga. But the symbol's true meaning remained a mystery.

It had been five thousand years since Rama had reigned. Since then, Kosala's *Ayodhya-nagari* mentioned in Valmiki's narrative had begun to be called Saketa. Yet, the profound impact of Rama's rule resonated in the secluded grove even after millennia.

On most days, it remained peaceful, its perimeter surrounded by majestic banyan trees. But every year on the ninth day of Chaitra, the grove throbbed with activity as virtually all of Saketa gathered to make offerings in commemoration of Rama's birth anniversary—his Navami. Once, it had been Queen Kaushalya's palace, the birthplace of Rama.

There had been discussions about constructing a temple there to honour Rama but for now his Janmabhoomi—the spot marking his birth—remained open to the sky, punctuated only by the imposing pillar. Legend held that the pillar had been placed there by Sheshanaga, the king of serpents. The primordial being of creation, said to bear the universe's planets upon his many hoods, was believed to guard the grove. Sheshanaga's earthly incarnation had been Rama's brother—Lakshmana.

The labourer's heart pounded with anticipation as he dug on. What if his master's hunch proved correct? Could what they sought truly lie buried in such a prominent location? His nervous excitement intensified with each clod of earth he scooped out, until his shovel struck something unyielding. Heart hammering, he clawed away the mud to reveal what lay beneath. But before he could take a closer look, he was thrust face-first into the ground. His shovel clattered into the pit he had dug, striking the hard surface it had unearthed.

He managed to turn and, looking up, saw a hulking figure standing over him. The man was clad entirely in black—dhoti, uttariya and turban—and he held a glimmering sword. Moonlight reflected off the polished steel, revealing intricate patterns etched into the blade. The labourer froze, staring in terror at the weapon. The swordsman's face was veiled by the tail of his turban, only his blazing eyes were visible. He advanced, lowering the sword until its tip rested against the fallen man's throat. In a low growl, he demanded in Prakrit, 'To eim kao pathao? Who sent you here?'

Terror choked the digger's voice as he pleaded. 'Th-they... they will k-kill me if I s-say anything ...'

'You have until the count of three to answer,' the swordsman stated coldly. 'Ekam ...'

'I am b-begging you ...'

'Dve ...'

'P-please ...'

'Trini,' the swordsman intoned. 'Do not worry. The slash itself will not hurt.' *But choking on your blood is a given*, he thought, the unspoken threat hanging heavy in the air.

The frightened man continued to plead for his life, but his attacker was no longer listening. In a blink, the sword slashed the man's throat. The motion was quick, clean, almost surgical, like one of the precise incisions of the famed physician Charaka.

As dawn broke over Saketa, painting the ancient trees in hues of gold and crimson, the swordsman dragged the corpse away from the site. He worked swiftly and efficiently, replacing the unearthed soil and smoothing the ground until no trace of the disturbance remained. As soon as the task was completed, he sheathed his sword and carried the body deeper into the dense thicket surrounding the clearing.

He soon reached a familiar spot—a grassy patch fragrant with damp earth and blossoming jasmine. The pre-dug pit gaped in front of him, a chilling reminder of the bodies he had disposed here before. He pushed the lifeless form into the crater, leaving it as a feast for the jackals, hyenas, vultures and beetles that prowled the night. Then, fading back into the shadows, he murmured a shloka:

śivāya viṣṇurūpāya śivarūpāya viṣṇave

Shiva is in the form of Vishnu, and Vishnu is in the form of Shiva …

2

Chennai, Tamil Nadu, India

Present day

The atmosphere inside the conference room was sombre, the air thick with tension. The Defence Research and Development Organisation—or DRDO—team was still grappling with the previous week's events. The room, lined with polished wooden panels, was dominated by a large oval table surrounded by high-backed chairs. A projector hummed softly, casting a flickering light on the serious faces of the assembled engineers and military officials.

On the screen, Indian tank regiments could be seen positioned along the Line of Actual Control—or LAC—in eastern Ladakh. India's Fire and Fury Corps had deployed these mechanized forces at 16,000 feet, making it one of the few army units worldwide to operate at such extreme altitudes. Jagged, snow-capped peaks loomed in the distance, the treacherous terrain a constant challenge. Temperatures regularly plummeted to minus 35 degrees Celsius at night, worsened by high-speed winds—the soldiers battled daily for survival.

The video that was playing showcased twenty newly inducted tanks. Known as the Bharat Primary Battle Tank, or BPBT, these machines were the pinnacle of Indian engineering. This latest indigenous design was intended to eventually replace all other tanks in the Indian arsenal—the Arjun MBT, the T-90S Bhishma and the T-72 Ajeya, each a symbol of India's evolving military prowess.

In recent years, India had prioritized indigenous defence manufacturing. Decades of complacency had handed China a significant military advantage and the government was now striving to redress that imbalance. The BPBT was a key element in this strategy. Its success was a matter of national pride and security. The previous week's footage showed a contingent of twenty BPBTs lined up along the LAC. The crew appeared confident, having witnessed the tank's performance during trial runs. They had excelled in a series of mobility tests on progressively challenging terrain, proving the BPBT's speed, manoeuvrability, stability and climbing ability. DRDO engineers had scrutinized its firing accuracy and effectiveness, and conducted survivability tests simulating battlefield conditions—gunfire, artillery and explosions. The BPBT had performed remarkably well, embodying hope and resilience. No one could have anticipated the attack that had lurked moments away.

China was, of course, displeased with these developments. They preferred to build up their side of the LAC unchallenged, while expecting India to remain passive. The recent spate of activity in India was perceived as a threat by Beijing, an unwelcome opposition to their uncontested dominance.

A bloody war in 1962 over a border dispute had resulted in a 1996 agreement: neither side would use firearms or explosives within 1.24 miles of the LAC. While fistfights, clubs, swords and axes were permitted, resorting to firepower was strictly forbidden. The previous day's explosion had shattered both a tank and this fragile understanding—and the tense peace was ruptured.

The group in the conference room watched, frame by agonizing frame. The explosion had come suddenly. Dense clouds of smoke and fierce flames engulfed the sky as one of the BPBTs was violently torn apart. The attacking missile itself had been a blur, impossible for the eye to catch. Shockwaves rippled across the desolate landscape, scattering debris. The surviving soldiers ran for cover, their screams swallowed by a deafening roar. The wreckage of the once-powerful machine burned against the barren backdrop. The scene was ghastly.

The BPBT unit was designed to have an active defence system capable of stopping Anti-Tank Guided Missiles—ATGMs. It was supposed to detect and intercept approaching rockets before they hit, safeguarding both the crew and vital equipment. It was clear now that this system had failed. The loss was not merely a technical setback; it was a blow to the nation's confidence, a stark reminder of the challenges that lay ahead.

Indian intelligence analysts had reviewed the footage and confirmed to the DRDO what leaked data from Tsinghua University had suggested: the invention of China's next-generation ATGM, the HJ-12E. This latest model, equipped with a fibre-optic wire guidance system, was immune to jamming and could penetrate 43 inches of armour even from a distance of 9.3 miles. The BPBT, in light of this new threat, appeared alarmingly vulnerable. A punch to the gut for India's defence establishment.

'The Tsinghua data necessitates a change in the BPBT's specifications,' explained Dr V.K. Reddy, DRDO's seasoned chairman. 'The Prime Minister's Office was briefed yesterday and is now demanding armour capable of withstanding even the deadliest ATGM.' Reddy, a brilliant strategist and an alumnus of the Indian Institute of Technology Madras, had risen through the ranks by virtue of his expertise and his unwavering commitment to India's autonomy in defence technology.

'We spent months experimenting with various grades of High Hardness Armour steel,' explained Director General Vinay Kamat, 'engineered to offer exceptional projectile penetration resistance. We added nickel and chromium to high-carbon steel, dramatically increasing its strength and toughness in the BPBT.' His voice was steady, but the underlying tension was palpable.

'But it's obviously not worked,' said the chairman. 'Any alternatives that we should consider?' Reddy's usually calm demeanour was replaced by an intensity that had pervaded the mood of every meeting over the last couple of days. For a man dedicated to India's self-reliance, the loss was a personal affront.

'We explored high-strength, low-alloy steel,' Kamat explained, 'along with strengthened carbon fibre and military-grade stainless steel. None of them proved adequate. Frankly, we are at an impasse.' Kamat was visibly frustrated. The technical challenges were daunting, but it was the race against time and the potential cost of military lives that truly weighed on him.

'Perhaps it's time to seek external assistance,' Reddy suggested, a hint of desperation in his normally purposeful eyes. He understood the gravity of the situation. Every decision they made would have profound implications on India's future defence systems.

'What do you have in mind?' Kamat asked. The room fell silent. Every eye was on Reddy, every ear strained to catch his next words.

'Get Aditya Pillai on the line,' Reddy commanded, his voice slicing through the stillness. 'It's time to play our wild card.'

3

Geumgwan, Garak Confederacy
Present-day Gimhae, South Korea
Around 2,000 years ago

The city of Geumgwan, nestled in a verdant valley with the mighty Nakdong river coursing through it as a vital artery of commerce, was the Garak Confederacy's political and cultural hub. Thatched cottages, modest in design, lined the city's narrow streets. Their nooks were alive with the joyful laughter of children and the city itself seemed to breathe with the natural world. Small, terraced paddy fields covered the landscape in patches, dotted with farmers labouring over their crops. A light wind, fragrant with earth and blossoms, blew in from the river. Beyond these fields, lush forests cloaked the hills, threaded with paths to nearby mines and villages.

But the rhythm of Geumgwan's days was set by the constant clanging and hammering from its forges. Here, expert blacksmiths, emblematic of the region's famed iron culture, toiled relentlessly, crafting ceremonial objects, tools and weapons.

In the heart of the city rose the grand dwelling of Kim Seok—its size a fitting symbol for the tribal chief's power and fame. Seok was no ordinary leader. Renowned as Garak's most skilled blacksmith, he drew the wealthy and powerful, monarchs and merchants alike, all eager to avail of his exceptional craftsmanship.

'Watch closely, Soju,' Seok instructed his adopted son, Kim Suro, while working in the forge one day. Soju, as the boy was affectionately known, was just twelve years old, but his eyes, wide with curiosity, absorbed every detail. 'Ironworking is more than a craft—it is an art requiring both strength and finesse.' The heat from the forge enveloped them as Seok, sweat glistening on his brow, demonstrated to his son the rhythmic dance of his hammer against the glowing iron.

'How do you know when the iron is ready to be shaped?' Soju asked with genuine interest.

'Ah, that knowledge comes with experience,' Seok's response was measured. 'The colour of the iron tells its own story. As it heats, it transforms through several stages. First a dull red, then a vibrant cherry. But the crucial moment is when it reaches a brilliant, luminous orange, like the heart of a sunrise trapped in metal. At this point, it is at its most malleable, ready to be moulded like clay in a potter's hands.'

Seok selected a hammer and handed it to the boy. 'Now you try, Soju.' He guided the boy's grip. 'Hold it firmly. Keep your wrist supple. Feel the rhythm of the hammer striking the metal and you will know when it responds.'

A wave of excitement crashed over Soju as he took the hammer, only to be followed by an undertow of fear. He watched the orange glow of the iron, felt its heat radiating outwards. As he struck, he began to grasp the delicate interplay of force and precision, the iron yielding to his will under the dancing flames. 'Good!' Seok said approvingly. 'Now, find the rhythm. Each strike should be like a beat in a drum dance.'

With focused determination, Soju replicated Seok's movements, the clang of metal echoing through the forge like a symphony. 'It is harder than it looks,' he admitted, his young muscles straining with the unfamiliar effort.

'Indeed, it is,' Seok said, his voice brimming with pride and encouragement. 'But remember, even the greatest blacksmiths were once beginners.'

Soju paused, his gaze shifting from the glowing iron back to Seok. 'Will I *ever* be able to do what you do?'

Seok smiled, his words carrying the weight of prophecy. 'I believe you have the potential to forge not just swords but a kingdom, Soju. But remember—power should always be tempered with compassion. I hope you will become the Iron King ... but one with a soft heart.'

Finishing the day's work, they headed to their home's backyard. The forge's heat lingered on their skin and they stood under the cool water from the bathing tank to wash it away, along with the day's fatigue. 'Wash properly, else your Eomeoni will be cross,' Seok warned his son regarding his mother.

∽

Later that evening, Soju, accompanied by Kim Seok's trusted manservant Minjun, headed to a friend's home for dinner, while Seok sat down with his wife, Kim Hwa, for their evening meal. Steamed rice, bowls of kimchi and mixed greens, a perfectly grilled fish and fragrant vegetable stew graced the low wooden table. As Hwa poured her husband a bowl of nuruk makgeolli, the fermented liquid frothed invitingly. She asked, 'How was it teaching Soju today?'

'He has a natural talent,' Seok replied, savouring the familiar flavours. 'He replicates my movements flawlessly. I have no doubt he will become one of the finest swordsmiths in the land.'

'But can he ever be more than a blacksmith?' Hwa asked, concern straining her voice. 'He is not our blood, after all. Will you truly make him the chief one day?'

'The tradition of Geumgwan, and indeed the Garak Confederacy itself, has always been to elevate the most capable individual, regardless of lineage,' Seok explained patiently. 'If Soju proves himself to be strong, competent, fair, honest, compassionate and wise, he will naturally rise up to the position. And if another surpasses him in those qualities, it is only right that they lead instead. Our present concerns, however, must lie elsewhere, Hwa. All is not well between the seven principalities … There are more pressing matters to be addressed.'

Geumgwan was not a kingdom in its own right. It was simply one of the seven small principalities that comprised the Garak Confederacy, the others being Daegaya, Seongsan, Goryeong, Bihwa, Bangam and Ara. Although each tiny principality was independent, governed by its own chieftain—like Kim Seok—and local administration, they were united on matters of defence. Recent times, however, had seen more squabbling than cooperation between them. Kim Seok was not just the chieftain of Geumgwan but also the elected chairman of the Confederacy. Maintaining unity on defence matters was vital. The Garak Confederacy was surrounded by powerful rivals— Silla to the east, Baekje to the west and Goguryeo to the north. Known as the Three Kingdoms, these mighty neighbours— with no need for any confederation—had long coveted Garak's iron mines and the skill of its blacksmiths.

Kim Seok stared at the dancing glow of the lamps in his home. He drained his makgeolli, the flames triggering a memory of a fateful day some years ago …

A blaze had erupted from Chang Bakery's oven, sending fiery sparks showering through the street. Thick smoke billowed out, obscuring the chaotic scene as workers scrambled to escape the inferno. The fire, triggered by a moment of carelessness, had claimed several lives, including those of the bakery's owners. It had also consumed half of the orphanage behind it, leaving only six of the seventeen children alive. Kim Suro—Soju—was one of the survivors. Eventually, all the orphans found homes with families scattered across the Garak Confederacy. Seok and Hwa, who had lost their only child to smallpox the previous year, readily welcomed Soju into their family. Another surviving child, Talhae, was adopted by the chieftain of Seongsan.

The tragedy, and the resilience of the six surviving orphans, had been immortalized in a painting by a local artist named Adokan. His *Yeoseot Gaeui Dalgyal*—The Six Eggs—depicted the children emerging from six magical eggs tossed about on turbulent seas.

Hwa nodded, knowing her husband's words were true. 'The person you choose to become is ultimately the one you are meant to be,' she said, her tone soft yet firm. 'Let us see what path Soju chooses.'

4

Dimašq, Roman Empire
Present-day Damascus, Syria
Around 2,000 years ago

The streets of Dimašq—a city that the Romans called Damascus—teemed with traders. Spices from Korkai and Muziris, Mediterranean pottery, and silks from the Far East jostled for space along the column-lined Decumanus Maximus, the main east–west street in the city. A dozen languages mingled in the air, redolent with exotic aromas and the vibrant spirit of commerce. Under Rome's watchful eye, Dimašq was a medley of cultures.

Governor Baruchus Philippides stood on the balcony of his palace, looking contemplatively over the city. His eyes followed the line of the Via Recta, the straight road slicing through the old city to connect the imposing eastern gate with the distant western wall. Philippides had always loved Dimašq—its unique blend of Roman order and Eastern mystique had captivated him since childhood. The city's bustling streets thrummed with the energy of its historical and strategic importance. Yet, today, he could sense a simmering discontent beneath the surface.

The Roman Empire typically controlled its provinces through appointed officials. However, local leaders like Philippides often played vital roles in governance. Pragmatic to the core, the Romans understood the value of influential figures, especially those hailing from powerful families, in maintaining order. These individuals, Romanized and integrated into the Empire's fabric, were instrumental in the functioning of the local government, collecting taxes and maintaining loyalty to Rome.

Philippides knew that the region's traders were becoming increasingly frustrated with Rome. The high taxes levied by the Empire were cutting into their profits and making it harder to maintain the lifestyles they were accustomed to. The Nabataean traders in particular were openly discussing the possibility of an uprising. This was not mere fantasy—there had been a marked rise in local pride and growing resentment against Roman rule. The Nabataeans, renowned for their wealth, were busy reinvesting their profits into building a magnificent city in the desert—Raqmu, known to the Romans as Petra. The escalating Roman taxes in Damascus meant that there was less money to send back for Raqmu.

Philippides was a seasoned leader, yet the situation in Dimašq troubled him. Emperor Tiberius's recent demands for increased taxes to fund distant military campaigns were placing a heavy burden on the province. Philippides was acutely aware of the impact these levies would have on the already fragile economy and he felt caught between his duty to Rome and his responsibility to the people he governed.

As he watched a crowd gather in the bustling square below, he sensed an undercurrent of tension. People argued heatedly, their voices rising in a crescendo of anger. In the throng, Philippides spotted the tall figure of Barakat, a Nabataean merchant respected in the community and known for his outspoken nature. Philippides realized that this gathering was more than a simple protest—a storm was brewing. He turned abruptly and walked back inside, the sound of his footsteps echoing across the marble floors.

Cornelius, his lieutenant, was in the study poring over tax records. Philippides's twelve-year-old son, Mithradates, sat beside him. When the boy looked up, his eyes widened with worry. 'Father,' he said, his voice hushed, 'they say the city is on the verge of revolt.'

'It does appear that way,' Philippides replied equably, though his heart was pounding. 'But do not worry, Mithra. We will handle it.' He paused, glancing at Cornelius. 'It appears the Nabataeans are leading the charge. They resent these ridiculous taxes—and Roman rule itself.'

Even as he tried to maintain a calm appearance for his son, a nervousness gripped the governor. At the sound of a commotion outside, he and Cornelius rushed to the balcony. Below, the crowd pressed forward, overwhelming the Roman guards stationed at the eastern gate, shoving and yelling, their rage palpable.

'We must act quickly,' Cornelius urged. 'I will summon reinforcements before the situation escalates.'

But Philippides hesitated. He looked at the crowd, taking in the desperation and anger etched on their faces. These were not merely subjects; they were *his* people. For the second time, he found himself ensnared in a painful conflict—his unwavering devotion to Rome clashing with the deep, personal obligation he felt towards the well-being of his people. 'Cornelius,' he said, his voice strained, 'surely there is another way? Could we not speak with their leaders and find a compromise?'

Cornelius considered the governor's suggestion. 'Perhaps you are right, My Lord,' he conceded. 'Rome's strength lies not just in its legions, but also in its capacity for diplomacy. Shall we extend an invitation to Barakat and the other trade leaders to discuss the matter?'

Within the hour, the leaders stood before the governor in the palace, their faces defiant though their eyes betrayed a flicker of doubt.

'We have maintained peace in this land for many years,' Philippides said, his tone measured. 'Rome desires nothing more than the continued prosperity of Dimašq. Let us find a way to ease your burdens without causing upheaval within the Empire.' His words conveyed both power and sincerity.

The hours stretched into the night as they negotiated. Though the discussions were tense and protracted, the two sides eventually reached common ground. The merchants agreed to maintain order while Philippides promised to intercede with Rome on the matter of the taxes. As the city was touched by the first light of dawn, the tension in the room began to wane. Hope flickered in Philippides's chest as the merchant leaders departed. The revolt had been averted without bloodshed. Mutual respect, it seemed, had won the day. But Philippides was also aware that he had only bought time. He knew that significant challenges remained and the future of Dimašq hung precariously in the balance. For the moment, an uneasy peace settled over the city under the watchful eyes of Roman soldiers. He needed to think of something that would guarantee future peace ... In that instant, he made up his mind.

Mithradates, who had been with his father all day, taking in his initial lessons in governance, walked beside him now as they returned to their quarters. 'Do you believe the problem is truly resolved, Father?' the boy asked, his young voice laced with uncertainty.

'A temporary reprieve, Son,' Philippides replied, weariness colouring his tone. 'Greater conflicts loom on the horizon ... But a true leader does not rule with fear or force. He listens. He protects. He builds a future for those who cannot build one themselves. But for now, you must focus on other matters.'

'What matters, Father?' Mithradates pressed, ever eager to grasp the complexities of the world he was inheriting.

'Knowledge, Mithra. Knowledge is power.' He paused, his eyes locking with his son's. 'I will be sending you far away for a time. To a place where you can acquire the knowledge you need to navigate the challenges that lie ahead. The education you gain will be vital—not to claim a title, but to uphold a legacy that may one day call upon you.'

Mithradates nodded silently, his father's words settling heavily on his shoulders. Yet, as the shadows deepened around them, he could not shake the feeling that the path ahead would demand more than knowledge—it would demand sacrifices.

5

Kailasa Temple, Ellora, Maharashtra, India

Present day

Dr Bala Ramaswamy stood in awe before the magnificent Kailasa Temple. In real-life, its grandeur was more imposing than any photograph could convey. Sweat trickled down his face and neck, drenching his linen shirt. He gulped water from his bottle, even feeling the need to pour some over his head. He and his team of scientists, archaeologists, geologists and historians had arrived a week earlier to study the ancient marvel.

Over the past several days, the team had spread out across the ancient temple complex, each member equipped with state-of-the-art scanning devices and sample-collection kits. The air hummed with the sounds of digital beeps and clicks as they moved slowly, eyes trained on their equipment, looking for even the faintest traces of chemical residue that might hint at the use of an ancient technology. But it was like finding a needle in a haystack, and today was their last day on the site.

Unlike other temples that were built up from the ground, this one was built down from the top—the shikhara emerging first—and had been carved out of a single monolithic rock. It covered twice as much area as the Parthenon in Athens, its construction requiring the removal of 200,000 tons of rock.

'Just imagine the sheer audacity of our ancient builders,' Ramaswamy remarked, wiping his forehead with a drenched kerchief. 'There isn't a single joint or building block. Everything within the complex is part of one giant sculpture.'

In his late fifties, Ramaswamy cut a distinguished figure. Of average height and lean build, his tousled, greying hair and neatly trimmed beard framed his intellectual authority. But a veil of sadness softened this forbearing demeanour. Things hadn't been the same for Ramaswamy since the passing of his wife a decade ago.

He wasn't really an archaeologist. The Chennai-born scientist was renowned for his advanced research in quantum chromodynamics at the European Organization for Nuclear Research, or CERN, but what set him apart was his ability to connect ancient and modern science. His seminal work, *Forgotten Science of the Vedic Age*, explored ancient Indian scientific knowledge, drawing parallels with contemporary advancements. Kailasa was the object of his study, its construction techniques a mystery he was determined to unravel. As an expert in ancient technologies and an avid historian, he had seen many marvels, but Kailasa was something else entirely.

Dr Satheesh Jayaraman, a renowned archaeologist borrowed by the team from the Archaeological Survey of India, or ASI, had explained on their arrival, 'To build this top-down, three massive trenches were dug vertically through the basalt. There were no jackhammers or earthmovers then, just hammers, chisels and hundreds of men carting away debris. Only then could the artisans have begun their work, slowly descending on precarious ropes to sculpt the individual structures—the shikhara, pillars, statues, shrines. As they went lower, they would have added the lifelike sculptural details.'

Ramaswamy wasn't convinced. The temple defied modern understanding, not just in its scale, but also in the precision and skill involved in its planning and construction. It was this gap in their scientific understanding that he wished to address.

On the third day, Ramaswamy had addressed the team. 'As you know,' he began, 'Kailasa was built in the eighth century by the Rashtrakuta king Krishna I. What is astounding is its scale and the intricate details of the sculptures, all carved out of a single rock. It is as if the builders possessed tools that could soften and mould stone as easily as if it were wax.'

The team nodded, their eyes reflecting wonder. They had gathered various theories over the years, but none could fully explain the precision and speed of the temple's construction.

Ramaswamy had continued, 'My hypothesis involves an ancient technology—rock melting. This suggests the builders possessed instruments or substances that could soften rock, making it malleable enough to carve easily.'

He had led them deeper into the temple complex, pointing out features that would have been nearly impossible to achieve with conventional tools. 'Look at this Ravananugraha scene, depicting Lord Shiva bestowing his favour upon Ravana, the king of Lanka,' he said in awe. 'Notice the detailing! And these elephants? Each is unique, with perfectly captured muscles, skin folds and expressions. It's as if their chisels could transform every surface they touched.'

They moved to the central shrine, where a massive lingam was the focal point, surrounded by intricate carvings of deities and scenes from Hindu texts. Dr Lukas Müller, a Swiss geologist who was a part of the team, examined the rock closely. 'If this technology existed,' he reflected, 'it would have had to alter the rock at a molecular level. A process that could temporarily disrupt the crystalline structure of basalt, making it pliable without fracturing.'

Ramaswamy nodded. 'It could have been a combination of thermal, chemical and possibly ultrasonic treatments,' he had agreed. 'Such treatments would have made the rock behave more like clay at the point where the chisel touched it.'

'Before we depart,' Ramaswamy said, 'we must try to locate any residual traces that might indicate the use of ancient technology: chemical residues, unusual weathering patterns, anything that might provide a clue for future research.'

The team spread out, armed as always with their advanced scanning equipment. Ramaswamy moved to a secluded alcove where a particularly detailed carving had caught his eye. He ran his hand over the smooth surface, musing, 'If only these walls could talk.' Wiping his brow, he turned to watch his team from a distance. Adjusting his portable scanner, he took a deep breath before stepping into the next shadowy alcove of the temple. His mind raced as he pondered the challenge before them. 'The answer has to be here,' he whispered to himself. *We're missing something. And it is hiding in plain sight.*

Around him, the team moved silently, focused yet growing increasingly frustrated. Müller crouched by a section of the temple wall, his face tight with concentration as he ran his scanner over the intricate carvings. Nothing. 'I am not picking up anything abnormal here,' he reported, his voice heavy with disappointment. 'It's just ordinary basalt.'

Hours passed, the sun casting long shadows across the temple complex. Reports similar to Müller's trickled in from other members of the team. Jayaraman, the team's archaeologist, was pacing along the boundary of a pillar, muttering under his breath as he checked his readings. The enthusiasm that had fuelled them earlier was beginning to wane, replaced by a palpable tension in the air. They had come so far, studied every inch of the temple, yet its secrets eluded them.

Ramaswamy felt the weight of their failure pressing down on him. 'All right, everyone,' he called out. 'Let's take a break. We'll regroup in twenty.'

The team gathered under a canopy outside, exchanging weary glances. Ramaswamy knew they were all thinking the same thing: What if there was nothing to find? What if the technology they sought had simply left no trace?

But something in Ramaswamy refused to give up. He scanned the temple's towering facade once more, eyes narrowing at the smallest of details. He took a deep breath, steadying his resolve. 'One more sweep, everyone. Focus on the edges. The edges of intricate sculptures would have had maximum contact with ancient tools. Müller, let us check that alcove again, where you thought the rock looked different.'

An hour later, Müller's voice rang out excitedly. 'Over here!' he shouted. He was pointing to a section flagged as unusual— the elephant sculptures. 'There's a distinct chemical signature, different from the surrounding rock. It suggests an altered molecular structure on the surface, possibly traces of an agent that could have facilitated the rock's temporary softening.'

Ramaswamy's eyes sparkled. *Could this be it?* They found matching signatures across the structure, capturing spectroscopic readings from specific areas with handheld X-ray Fluorescence devices. Then they swabbed the surfaces meticulously, hoping to extract trace residues for lab analysis. The evidence was finally trickling in.

As the sun set, Ramaswamy called the team together. 'In the past few days, we've made significant progress,' he announced. 'What we have found could change our understanding of ancient technology. But this is only the beginning. We must conduct further tests, analyse these samples closely and compare our findings to ancient texts.' The team responded enthusiastically, excited by the prospect of solving a puzzle that had baffled researchers for centuries.

Ramaswamy turned back towards the temple, its tall form now gleaming in the golden light. 'Kailasa has kept its secrets safe for over a thousand years,' he said softly. 'But today, we have taken a step closer to uncovering them. Now we must wait and see what CERN's tools can reveal.'

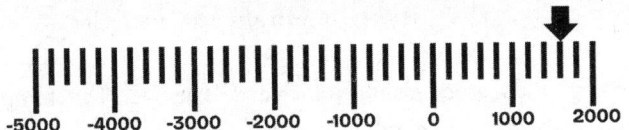

Mathuram, Nayak Desam
Present-day Madurai, Tamil Nadu, India
Around 400 years ago

King Tirumala Nayak sat in the grand dining hall of his lavish palace in Mathuram, awaiting the chiming of bells. A devout follower of Vishnu, he would not break his fast until the morning puja at the distant Srivilliputhur Aandal Temple was complete. Bell towers, spaced every 3 miles between the temple and his palace, ensured the news would reach him swiftly.

Today, he was sharing breakfast with his chief architect, Varunan. As they waited, the king drummed his fingers impatiently on the exquisitely carved tabletop. 'Why is the temple taking so long?' he demanded. His frustration was evident. He was not referring to the ceremonies in progress, but to the grand restoration and expansion of the Meenakshi Temple a mere mile away. 'The threat from Bijapur, Golconda, the Dutch and the Portuguese is constant,' he declared. 'As long as Meenakshi's blessings are upon Mathuram, our kingdom will prevail. But I find the pace of the renovation frustrating. I am pouring lakhs into it, yet it merely crawls forward.'

'Apologies, Your Majesty,' Varunan replied. Though a senior man, his age had not diminished his dedication. He had served the king faithfully, overseeing countless grand projects, including this very palace, often hailed as the Deccan's most resplendent. 'Each gopuram will be adorned with hundreds of sculptures, depicting gods, goddesses and celestial beings. The temple will be a labyrinth of chambers and corridors, each detail on its pillars, walls and recesses intricately carved. We have massive refurbishments in progress—the Hall of Thousand Pillars, the sacred tanks, the bustling marketplaces. And I have not even described the sanctum sanctorum which is bound to create an overwhelming sense of spiritual connection. A project of this magnitude is unprecedented.'

The bells chimed and bearers entered carrying trays laden with food. Ven pongal, soft idlis, spiced tamarind rice, fresh plantains and an assortment of chutneys and buttermilk were placed before the king and his guest, but Varunan's appetite had vanished. How could he convey to the king that the restoration and expansion of the temple would consume many more years?

'Why are you not eating?' the king asked sharply, helping himself to coconut chutney.

'I am ashamed by the delays, Your Majesty,' Varunan admitted. 'Our ancestors achieved incredible architectural feats in Kailasa, Konark and Angkor. But they had a significant advantage.'

'What advantage?' Tirumala Nayak inquired, curiosity flickering in his eyes.

'The fish eyes of Meenakshi,' Varunan responded cryptically.

'What are you talking about?' the king demanded. 'Speak plainly, Varunan!'

'There was an ancient technology,' Varunan explained, choosing his words carefully. 'Known only to a lineage of ironsmiths called the Dvaitalingam Rakshaks. It allowed them to create tools of extraordinary strength and sharpness—tools that could almost melt stone. With such tools, vast projects could be completed quickly. Sadly, that knowledge is lost to history.'

'And what do the eyes of Meenakshi have to do with this?' the king questioned, still bemused.

'As you know, Your Majesty, Meenakshi translates to the "fish-eyed one",' Varunan said. 'Derived from the words *meen* for "fish" and *akshi* for "eyes". The blacksmiths marked their creations with a symbol with two fish, representing Meenakshi's eyes.'

'I am familiar with the legend,' the king stated, chewing his food thoughtfully. 'Stories tell of her eyes, wide and watchful, representing her omnipresence and benevolence. But there seems to be more to the symbolism of the fish-eyes.'

Varunan smiled faintly. 'Meenakshi is an avatar of Parvati, the wife of Shiva. That is all I know. Maybe it is related to the tantra of duality?'

'That is all very well, Varunan,' the king said, impatience creeping into his voice now, 'but the Meenakshi Temple is not meant to be just a place of worship, it is also a vital economic hub for Mathuram. We need the expanded temple completed quickly to revive the local economy. The pilgrims who come bring significant revenue to our markets and guest houses. Do you understand?'

'I understand my duty, Your Majesty,' Varunan assured him. 'I will review all plans and schedules again. We must find ways to accelerate the work and regain your trust.'

The king nodded absently, his fingers moving restlessly in the basin of rose-petal water, his gaze unfocused, as if he was lost in a flurry of thoughts. Was it truly possible to uncover the lost technology their ancestors had possessed? If the secrets of the technicians who marked their creations with Meenakshi's eyes could be rediscovered, he mused, the temple could be completed in half the time. But those were matters for another day. Right now he needed to motivate Varunan and his men to find ways to complete the expansion, with whatever tools were currently at their disposal.

Yet, deep within, the king felt a flicker of hope: the secrets surrounding the fish-eyes would not remain hidden forever.

6

Saketa, Kosala
Present-day Ayodhya, Uttar Pradesh, India
Around 2,000 years ago

No one knew precisely when Saketa had come into existence. Valmiki's Ramayana indicated that Manu had established the city on the banks of the Sarayu river thousands of years before Rama. Even five millennia after Rama's era, the town overwhelmed its visitors with its size, scale, sophistication and splendour.

Built as a perfect rectangle following the precepts of Vastushastra, it was 60 miles long and 15 miles wide—almost four times the size of that other magnificent ancient city, Rome. A deep moat encircled Saketa, its waters routinely replenished from the Sarayu. Hundreds of highly territorial hippopotamuses populated the moat, deterring any trespasser from attempting to swim across. Beyond the moat lay dense sal forests, planted during the reign of Rama's father, Dasharatha. Sentinels in tall turrets could quickly observe imminent threats. Each turret was equipped with a powerful catapult, capable of hurling massive stones at any approaching intruders. Saketa was unconquerable, hence the alternative name bestowed on it during Dasharatha's time was *a-yuddha*—'that which could not be battled'.

Today, those very sal leaves rustled softly, the sound composing a symphony with the gentle flow of the Sarayu as

Padmasen took a quick dip to wash his bloody sword, his clothes and himself. The river's gentle currents seemed to whisper secrets of the ancient ages, stories of heroes and gods, battles won and lost. As he emerged from the river, the first rays of the sun appeared, bathing the city in a golden hue and making the stone structures shimmer as if coated in gold dust.

The streets were quiet except for the workers sprinkling water on them at dawn. Saketa's arterial avenues and main streets intersected at right angles to one another in a perfect grid, making the cleaning and watering process remarkably efficient. The same workers scattered flower petals on the streets for special occasions.

Padmasen crossed two more streets before reaching his destination. He quietly entered a kiln-fired brick house with an open courtyard. He knew that his family would be asleep, which meant he would be able to get through his morning regimen uninterrupted. The courtyard provided a sense of calm at this hour, making it the perfect spot for his workout that would otherwise have to be done at an akhada in the vicinity.

He paused for a moment to worship Harihara, a deity split down the middle, with one half representing Shiva and the other representing Vishnu. Facing east, Padmasen poured water containing flowers and rice from a kalash onto the ground as he chanted:

śivāya viṣṇurūpāya śivarūpāya viṣṇave
śivasya hṛdayaṁ viṣṇuḥ viṣṇóśca hṛdayaṁ śivaḥ

'Shiva is in the form of Vishnu, and Vishnu is in the form of Shiva
Vishnu resides in Shiva's heart, and Shiva resides in Vishnu's heart.'

Prayers complete, he discarded his dhoti and uttariya. Now clad only in his loincloth, he picked up a heavy shisham-wood mugdar and swung the heavy club in various patterns, working his shoulders, arms and wrists. Then he switched to his gada and completed a swing, press and rotation sequence. His movements were precise and fluid, his routine designed to keep him flexible, forceful and fast. The rhythmic motion of his practice was a dance of discipline and strength, exemplifying his warrior spirit. He worked through a series of exercises, each demanding more from his body than the last.

Lost in the flow of his training, he did not notice the slight figure slip into the courtyard. It was not until he heard the familiar voice, clear and sweet, that he realized he was no longer alone. 'Udaye, Pitaha,' said Suriratna, his daughter, bending down to touch his feet as he wiped the sweat from his torso. He smiled and gently touched her head to bless her. 'How many times have I told you that girls do not touch people's feet to seek blessings?' he chided. 'How can an embodiment of Lakshmi do that?'

The eleven-year-old was the apple of his eye, and she knew it. 'And allow all your blessings to go to Bhadraketu?' she asked, with an impish smile. Padmasen's son, Bhadraketu, was Suriratna's elder brother. But Padmasen's gaze rarely strayed from his daughter.

By now, the household was abuzz. Padmasen held Suriratna's dainty hand and accompanied her to the kitchen where his wife, Indumati, had prepared warm turmeric milk for both father and daughter. 'The one who finishes last is a donkey,' Padmasen declared, swiftly downing his milk. Out of the corner of his eye, he watched Suriratna, gauging her reaction.

Unperturbed, she drank leisurely. Setting down her shiny black earthen tumbler and wiping her mouth, she calmly announced, 'Now I am done.'

'But I won the contest,' Padmasen said in a sing-song voice, clearly relishing the playful competition.

Suriratna looked up at him. 'But you have always said I only need to compete with myself. Were you lying? And is the donkey not the favoured mount of Goddess Kalaratri?'

Caught off guard, Padmasen stared at her in amazement before bursting into laughter. Suriratna, too, giggled. Her infectious laughter was melodic. Her creamy caramel skin glowed with youthful vivacity. Dark brown eyes, deep and expressive, sparkled with unbridled curiosity and joy. When she smiled, her pearl-white teeth seemed to brighten her surroundings. To Padmasen, she was a magical child.

'What use is competition to girls?' Indumati interjected. 'Focus on becoming a beautiful and talented maiden who will attract the finest husband in the land.'

'Nonsense,' scoffed Padmasen. 'There are thirty rishikas listed in the Rig Veda. Think of the accomplishments of Gargi, Maitreyi and Lopamudra. Our people would not exist without the might of Sarasvati. And which family does not seek Lakshmi? The sky is the limit for my little Suriratna!'

Indumati sighed, shaking her head as Suriratna left the kitchen. 'You fill her head with these grand ideas. What if the world does not see her the way you do?'

Padmasen's face softened as he looked at his wife. 'The world will see her strength and wisdom because we will nurture them in her. She will be prepared to face any challenge. We owe her that much, Indumati.'

Indumati nodded, a small smile forming on her lips. 'You always know how to reassure me,' she said gently. 'But remember, it is a harsh world out there.'

'I know,' Padmasen replied firmly. 'But she is part of a legacy, the legacy of the city that cannot be conquered—Ayodhya.'

7

Seongsan, Garak Confederacy
Present-day Seongju County, South Korea
Around 2,000 years ago

The clang of wooden swords echoed through the misty training yard as dawn broke over Seongsan, a principality like Kim Seok's Geumgwan, of the seven-member Garak Confederacy. Thirteen-year-old Talhae sparred fiercely with his mentor, Hwan. His small frame belied surprising agility as he dodged the older man's attacks. Talhae was one of the six children—like Soju—who had survived the fire that had engulfed his orphanage. Each swing of his sword channelled the anguish of that night—the flames, the screams, the loss— fuelling a determination far beyond his years.

'Focus, Talhae!' Hwan barked, parrying a quick jab. 'Do not just strike blindly—read your opponent's intentions.'

Talhae's brow furrowed in concentration. He adjusted his stance, feinting left before whipping his sword right in a deft arc. Hwan stumbled, surprised by the move, and then chuckled. 'Nicely done. True strength is not just physical—it is here.' He tapped his temple. 'Your mind is as crucial as your muscles. Predict, adapt and counter—that's the key to victory.'

As they paused to catch their breath, Min-ho, another pupil, strode into the ring. He squared his shoulders and locked eyes with Talhae. 'Let me take you on next,' he declared, his tone sharp with challenge.

Talhae did not flinch. 'If you insist. Let us see what you are capable of.'

The bout began with Min-ho charging recklessly, his moves telegraphed and lacking finesse. Talhae sidestepped the wild attacks effortlessly, countering with precision and economy of movement. Curious passers-by stopped to watch them and soon a small crowd had gathered, cheering and shouting out advice. Tension grew as the skirmish intensified and Min-ho's thrusts became increasingly desperate and sloppy in the face of Talhae's superior technique and calm demeanour. Then, with a final, decisive manoeuvre, Talhae sent Min-ho's wooden sword clattering to the ground.

'Up for round two?' Talhae goaded, his triumphant grin unmistakable. 'Or have you had enough embarrassment for one day?'

'Plenty of fire, Min-ho,' Hwan interjected, resting a hand on the flustered boy's shoulder, 'but you lack control. You charge like a bull, leaving yourself wide open. Try to anticipate actions—like Talhae. See how far he has come.'

At that moment, Jangsu, the chieftain of Seongsan, strode into the yard. Unlike Kim Seok, the chieftain of Geumgwan, who was loved more than feared, Jangsu's presence commanded immediate respect, bordering on fear. The morning sun glinted off his ornate chest plate as he surveyed the scene.

'Abeoji, did you see me disarm Hwan?' Talhae grinned, eager for his father's approval.

Jangsu watched as his adopted son resumed sparring with Hwan, clapping sharply when Talhae scored a skilful hit. 'Well struck. You have clearly been practising.' He beckoned Talhae closer. 'But brute force alone will not secure our borders. Walk with me.'

They walked along the high battlements, the view showcasing the valley below—a green expanse sloping towards far-off mountains. Each turn unveiled fresh bursts of colour from wild blossoms, their fragrance mingling with the birdsong that filled the flower-scented air. 'Tell me, Talhae,' Jangsu asked, 'what do you see when you look upon our lands?'

Talhae's eyes swept the panorama, keen and assessing. 'I see territory ripe for unity, Father—not just our Garak Confederacy's seven fractious principalities, but also the Three Kingdoms. All brought under a single, centralized rule.'

'And whose rule would that be?' Jangsu probed.

'Mine,' Talhae replied without hesitation, standing up straighter. 'I shall be the one to unite them, putting an end to the squabbling once and for all.'

A ghost of a smile tugged at Jangsu's lips, betraying his pride at his adopted son's boldness even as he maintained an appraising air. 'Unification is an ambitious dream for one so young. But remember, even the greatest conquerors understand that moderation tempers bravery. Building partnerships through diplomacy is just as vital as outright conquest.'

∼

As an interminable council meeting droned on in the stifling hall, Talhae's keen ears pricked up at a Daegayan diplomat's suggestion of joint training exercises between their kingdoms' forces. Leaning towards his father, Talhae murmured, 'Such cooperation could solidify ties and trust between our peoples. But how can we ensure they value the alliance as we do?'

Jangsu nodded approvingly at the youngster's perceptive observation. As they exited the chamber, he leaned in close to Talhae. 'Your strategic insight is commendable,' he whispered.

'But remember, subtlety in discourse is key. Overplaying your hand alerts others and weakens your stance.'

'Of course, Abeoji.' Talhae's mind raced with possibilities and contingencies. 'One day, our supremacy over these petty kingdoms will be unquestioned.' *Especially over that snivelling Kim Suro*, he added silently, his fists clenching at the thought of Soju.

Their history was complicated.

∼

That night, Talhae slipped out of his bedroom and made his way to Seongsan's battlements. As he sat down beneath a star-studded sky, his eyes lingered on the distant horizon. Dreams of empire, war and conquest consumed him. He barely registered the chill night air, so absorbed was he in visions of martial glory.

The crunch of armoured footsteps behind him heralded Hwan's arrival. 'What are you doing here out of your bed at home? Trouble sleeping?' the ageing warrior asked, walking up to stand beside his protégé.

'Too much on my mind,' Talhae confessed.

Hwan's eyes followed Talhae's focus across the shadowy expanse of the valley. 'Grand ambitions can weigh heavily, especially on the young,' he said at last. 'But a great leader needs more than just physical might and strategic cunning.' He placed a calloused hand on the boy's slight shoulder. 'Wisdom, and yes, even compassion, are equally vital to ruling over men and building an enduring legacy.'

Talhae nodded, his jaw clenched. In his mind, swords clashed and armies marched. He saw himself leading the charge, a conqueror's crown upon his brow. He was certain that history's pages awaited his name.

8

New Delhi, India

Present day

Inside one of the conference rooms in the majestic South Block in central New Delhi, the imposing sandstone structure that houses the Ministry of Defence, framed photographs of former defence ministers lined the walls, their austere gazes seemingly scrutinizing the proceedings. The meeting, convened to address urgent matters of national defence, had lasted for over an hour, drawing together some of the most powerful figures in Indian defence: the DRDO chairman, the national security advisor (NSA) and the defence minister.

And then there was Aditya Pillai.

They sat around a massive oval table, crafted from rich mahogany and embellished with brass. The polished surface of the table gleamed, illuminated by the diffused light from the chandeliers hanging above. Worn by time, the table had been witness to decades of pivotal decisions.

A usually unflappable Aditya felt a knot of uncertainty tightening in his stomach. Why this unexpected summons? As a businessman, Aditya had spent years courting the defence establishment, hoping to cater to their steel requirements, only to be repeatedly turned down. In their view, he was a wildcard, often experimenting with improbable techniques and fanciful materials, and so he wondered why his presence was suddenly deemed necessary. Aditya's eyes darted between the stern faces in the photographs and the equally grim countenances around the table.

The defence minister, a seasoned politician known for his no-nonsense attitude, was the first to speak. His voice was low and measured. Folding his hands on the table, he said, 'Pakistan might collapse. Should that happen, we believe areas like Punjab, Sindh, Balochistan, PoJK and Gilgit–Baltistan could disintegrate. The result? Displaced populations flooding into Punjab and Jammu and Kashmir, triggering a refugee crisis. The same could happen in Bangladesh.'

Silence descended as the imagined scenario took hold of people's minds. Aditya shifted in his seat, wrestling with the inevitable implications. Devendra Thakural, the NSA, a man with keen features and a razor-sharp intellect, took over. 'We have gamed this scenario. In the event of a fragmentation, the Chinese will likely exploit the situation, instigating border conflicts along the LAC in areas like Arunachal Pradesh to divert our attention.' He paused, letting the ominous suggestion of his words hang in the air. 'Imagine managing multiple fronts—against Chinese troops, Pakistani infiltrators and Bangladeshi jihadi groups. It could have happened during Operation Sindoor ... hence India's cautious and calibrated approach.'

The defence minister leaned forward, his expression grave. 'We're witnessing a global realignment of powers,' he said, 'reminiscent of the pre-World War II era. Ukraine–Russia, Israel–Hamas, Armenia–Azerbaijan, HTS–Syria ... multiple conflicts that are reshaping the world.'

He paused, his eyes scanning the room. 'True we've strategically avoided rigid alliances.' The minister's tone became more pointed. 'But make no mistake, the United States—in particular, their deep state—would find it advantageous to see India cornered, irrespective of who occupies the Oval Office.' He concluded firmly, 'They'd prefer to see us compelled to align subserviently and unconditionally with their bloc.'

Aditya felt a sense of uncertainty weighing down on him. Here he was, seated in a room steeped in decades of national policy and difficult choices, a space where powerful men grappled with matters of global significance. He, however, was a businessman. His comfort zone was the realm of toplines, manufacturing costs, commercial research, production schedules, profit margins and market share; a world he thought was far away from this intricate dance of national security and foreign relations. Politicians and bureaucrats had lofty ideals … businessmen like him only had business ideas, some of them commercial failures. As the NSA and the defence minister laid out the geopolitical landscape, a single question reverberated in Aditya's mind: *Why am I here?*

Finally, DRDO Chairman V.K. Reddy, known for his directness, turned to Aditya. 'Ten critical military initiatives outlined by the prime minister must be expedited in response to these escalating threats,' he stated, his gaze unwavering. 'One of them is the new BPBT. We need that upgraded tank—and we need it fast. And we need you to deliver the steel for it.'

'And what, precisely, do you mean by "fast"?' asked Aditya. *And why give me an opportunity when you've always considered me an oddball?* He left the question unasked.

'These ten projects must be completed within a year,' the chairman stated.

The air in the room thickened further still. Aditya was wide-eyed in disbelief. One year to re-engineer a tank? What would be the materials schedule for such a project? He suddenly realized why he was here. No one else in the industry would be crazy enough to take up the challenge.

Aditya was no stranger to wild swings between glory and failure. Over the years, he had dabbled in ventures most would not touch with a ten-foot pole—from designing pressure-resistant alloys inspired by forgotten Rasayanic metallurgy to trying to replicate sound-hardened metals based on the sonic resonance described in the *Samarangana Sutradhara*. The latter project had failed spectacularly but had won him a cult following on tech forums. Others—like a lightweight, corrosion-proof composite developed after decoding texts from a Takshashila archive—had returned unexpected profits. He was a gambler in a world of industrial pragmatists, chasing the glimmers of genius buried in dusty manuscripts and rusting relics.

'The current steel standard is inadequate,' the chairman continued. 'It leaves the upgraded BPBT vulnerable. We need a variant strong enough to withstand the latest Chinese ATGMs. Mere hardness is not enough. We need something resilient, something that can not only deflect, but also destroy. We need your full cooperation to expedite this process. We have to pull out all the stops. Do whatever it takes. That's why we've asked you to come here.'

Aditya drew a breath, steeling himself. 'How long do I have?'

Reddy's response was swift and decisive. 'Eight weeks.'

Eight weeks? To develop a new steel variant with unknown specifications? The sheer absurdity of it threatened to overwhelm him. No discussions about compositions, quantities, performance benchmarks, delivery schedules—not even a written brief or payment clause. It was as though he were expected to conjure metallurgy from thin air.

He wanted to protest, to point out the ridiculousness of such a deadline, but he knew it was futile. Then there was the maverick in him who loved taking risks; unpredictability held an irresistible appeal. Aditya realized that this was the opportunity of a lifetime; exactly what he had been hungering for.

He nodded, his face a mask of reluctant acceptance. He stood up and walked towards the exit; clearly, time was of the essence. South Block's hall of ministerial portraits closed behind him.

Miniature missiles of rain bombarded the windscreen as he drove off. Storm clouds gathered, mirroring his growing anxieties. Had he been too quick in accepting an unreasonable challenge?

And then the solution hit him. *Somi Kim.*

Though he had always kept his ventures domestic, this situation called for unconventional measures. As he dialled her number, apprehension coursed through him, the shadow of his task looming large.

'Hi Somi, it's Aditya,' he said, his tone urgent. 'I need your help. I may have bitten off more than I can chew.'

9

Saketa, Kosala
Present-day Ayodhya, Uttar Pradesh, India
Around 2,000 years ago

Padmasen rode towards the palace, his horse's hooves clopping on the dusty road. Raja Vidushika's summons had been urgent, demanding his immediate presence.

Dressed simply in a white dhoti and a saffron turban with a matching uttariya, Padmasen stroked his generous moustache. He was a handsome man, with chiselled features and a prominent forehead accentuated by a long vermilion teeka. His golden earrings shone against his long dark hair, curling beneath his turban. His toned body and bronzed complexion completing the picture of a seasoned warrior. A shadow of concern clouded his face. Why had Vidushika summoned him? He left his horse with a palace attendant and strode quickly towards the ruler's chambers.

The last few decades had brought political upheaval to Kosala. After the fall of the Maurya and Shunga dynasties, brief periods of Datta and Mitra rule had flickered, only to be extinguished by the Kushan king Kujula Kadphises who brought Saketa—along with several other regions—under his control, with Vidushika as his puppet.

Vidushika was the brother-in-law of the previous king—Padmasen's cousin—and had also served in his army as a commander. He had shrewdly switched sides in the final days of the Dattas and Mitras. Kadphises rewarded Vidushika's cunning move and appointed him governor while allowing him to retain the title of Raja due to his royal connection. Padmasen should have felt jealous; instead he pitied Vidushika.

Everyone knew that true power rested in Bakhlo, 930 miles away.

~

'Pranaam, Prabhu,' said Padmasen softly, catching the scent of rosewater from a basin near the entrance. A large window, usually framing the garden for Vidushika's peacock-gazing pleasure, was today covered with drapes. *This governor is no better than a strutting peacock himself*, thought Padmasen.

The room, dimly lit by a few strategically placed oil lamps, was filled with opulent furnishings: heavy silk curtains, intricate wooden carvings and luxurious cushions. Padmasen sat down on a low chair as Vidushika took his place on a higher settee with golden handles, a symbol of his power and influence. Vidushika's pale complexion, droopy eyes and rotund figure gave him a deceptive air of lethargy, but Padmasen knew better than to underestimate him.

'I called you to find out if everything is ... normal,' Vidushika said, dispensing with preliminaries. His eyes, usually half-lidded with apparent disinterest, were now focused sharply on Padmasen, scrutinizing his every move.

'Nothing out of the ordinary,' Padmasen lied, his heart pounding. Had spies alerted the governor to the incident at Rama's grove? Or had the dead man been Vidushika's agent? Or was this summons entirely unrelated?

Vidushika sighed, a weary sound laced with feigned patience. 'When will you trust me, Padmasen?' he asked. 'I only want what is best for Saketa. Why do you refuse to work with me?'

'There is no point of difference, Prabhu. All who love Saketa are on the same side.' Padmasen knew Vidushika saw through his deception. Like dancers circling each other, wary of a misstep, they navigated the conversation with cautious, calculated movements.

Padmasen, the 157th Dvaitalingam Rakshak, was bound by ancient oaths and traditions. Though political realities demanded he show deference to the ruler, his true loyalty lay with the secret he guarded—the Dvaitalingam buried in Rama's grove beneath the Vishnu Stambha. Should a conflict arise, he knew his path was clear. His royal lineage gave him the standing to resist Vidushika's demands, to stand firm in his duty.

Vidushika leaned back, his fingers tapping a rhythmic beat on the golden handles of his settee. 'Imagine what we could achieve together,' he said in a silken whisper. 'A word to Emperor Kujula ... and untold power would be yours.'

Padmasen knew this dance of words would soon end, replaced by a more dangerous contest. His fears were justified. The Kushans, a branch of the Yuezhi alliance, were a tribe that had migrated from Cheen and settled in Bakhlo. Their king, Kujula Kadphises, was ostensibly a patron of Greek art, a follower of Shaivism and a benefactor of Buddhism, but his ultimate goal was clear: to expand his influence throughout Bharatvarsha.

'Perhaps you are right, Prabhu,' Padmasen conceded. 'Perhaps we should work together—for the sake of Saketa.'

'Splendid,' Vidushika purred, a thin smile on his lips. 'But allies must be transparent.' He fixed Padmasen with a steady look, his drooping eyes no longer concealing the sharp intelligence within. 'They must not keep secrets from one another.'

Vidushika's intention was clear: he wanted the Dvaitalingam.

Padmasen knew he needed to buy time. To protect the secret, he needed to keep its location hidden. 'Indumati has been unwell,' he said, hoping to deflect the king's scrutiny. 'My mind is preoccupied, Prabhu. Perhaps I could return in a day or two?'

Vidushika rearranged his features in an expression of concern, but the intensity in his eyes remained. 'Give my regards to your wife,' he said smoothly. 'I am concerned for her health. But please, Padmasen, give my proposal due consideration.'

'Thank you for your kindness, Prabhu,' Padmasen responded, exhaustion tinging his voice. His every word was being assessed and he felt the weight of the charade slowly engulf him.

'Of course. Tend to your wife, Padmasen,' Vidushika urged. 'For weary men, even death can seem a welcome respite.' A subtle edge of steel underlay his seemingly gentle tone.

The doors to the chamber shut behind Padmasen. The hairs on his neck prickled. Eyes—unseen but felt—followed his every move. The grand palace hallways seemed to close in around him. His footsteps echoed, each one a thunderclap in the oppressive silence. A warning. Indumati's face flashed in his mind: warm eyes, gentle smile. His stomach twisted. *Using her name as a pawn in this deadly game ... What have I done?*

The first stars were emerging in the night sky as he mounted his horse. The familiar winding path home stretched long before him. The cold evening wind whipped against his face, steeling his resolve. Ahead lay a battle, and he would have to fight to protect everything he held dear.

He needed to urgently speak to one man: Kulasekara, Indumati's brother.

10

Bakhlo, Bactria
Present-day Balkh, Afghanistan
Around 2,000 years ago

The area around Bakhlo—the kingdom's capital—was proof of the resilience of both the land and its people. The wider region—Bactria—exemplified the delicate balance between nature's raw power and human determination. Rolling steppes and arid fields stretched out beneath a vast sky, punctuated by tough grasses and vibrant clusters of wildflowers. Farmers carved furrows through parched soil that resisted the plough, coaxing harvests from a land where drought and duststorms were routine adversaries. In the distance, the towering mountains stood watch, their snow-capped peaks a stark contrast to the clear blue above.

The spirit of Bakhlo was palpable even in the small town at its centre. The air, a melange of scents—smoke from cooking fires, the earthy aroma of animals and the freshness of newly tilled soil—buzzed with anticipation. In this town's heart stood the grand palace of Kujula Kadphises. The massive structure, a fusion of Hellenistic grace and Tokharian strength, symbolized the far-reaching authority of the emperor. Its sturdy walls and elaborate carvings stood as silent reminders of his power.

Excitement thrummed through the town that day. A relay messenger from Kosala had arrived, completing his journey in a record thirty-two days. The Kushan relay system, with its regular replenishments of men and horses, was renowned for its speed and reliability. The messenger's horse, covered in sweat and caked in dust, thundered through the palace gates, alerting everyone to his arrival, the urgency of his mission apparent to all.

Once he dismounted at the main entrance, the messenger was swiftly escorted by royal guards to the grand audience hall. It was a vast space filled with an air of solemnity and magnificence. Hundreds of torches blazed, their flames casting flickering shadows that danced across the soaring pillars and high-vaulted ceiling. The sheer scale of the chamber dwarfed everyone within, reducing them to mere specks beneath the watchful eyes of the emperor, Kujula Kadphises, seated upon his raised platform.

In the torchlight, Kadphises's silk shirt shimmered, its elaborate needlework catching the light. A fur cape was draped over his broad shoulders, adding to his imposing appearance. His features were sharp, his acute gaze piercing. His well-groomed beard, framed and complemented by a golden circlet studded with precious gems, spoke of power; his every gesture—the deliberate tap of a finger against the throne, the almost imperceptible nod of agreement—conveying a sense of carefully controlled authority. This was a man who commanded respect and instilled fear, a leader whose very presence demanded obedience.

'Any news from Vidushika?' Kadphises asked, his question echoing through the hall. As the young courier bowed deeply, the question hung in the air, amplifying the tension in the room. The messenger quickly presented a scroll to the emperor's footmen, who in turn passed it up to their ruler.

Kadphises did not bother reading it, passing the scroll to his prime minister instead.

The prime minister studied the message before reading it aloud to his lord, his thin Kong Qiu moustache quivering as he did so. The king's expression shifted from curiosity to irritation as he heard once again the excuses that Vidushika had mastered.

'What is your counsel?' Kadphises asked, impatient, when the prime minister came to the end of the message. 'I sent my army to conquer and rule Kosala and installed Vidushika as my governor in Saketa. Since then, several intelligence operatives have searched everywhere without success—the place is littered with palaces, temples, groves and wells. Many of the operatives have gone missing too. Vidushika's attempts at diplomacy have yielded nothing. What should I do?'

The prime minister, a seasoned administrator who had stood by the king through countless conquests, understood the delicate balance of diplomacy and force. He had been instrumental in bringing many lands under Kadphises's rule, including Balkh, Gandhara, Kuru, Panchala and Kosala. Only a few in the court possessed the courage to speak truthfully to the emperor; this man was one of them.

The prime minister carefully smoothed his moustache, considering his words. He understood the potent weight of the message, the thin line that separated measured persuasion from decisive action. 'O Emperor,' he began, 'your wisdom in matters of power is renowned. As you well know, a silk glove often conceals an iron fist.'

The answer, typical of the Kushan philosophy, reflected their masterful blend of strength and diplomacy. It was a strategy that had served them well, helping to forge a vast and ever-expanding empire. A wave of murmurs, like a ripple across a still pond, passed through the court as the assembled lords and officials considered their ruler's next move.

Kadphises leaned back in his throne, his fingers tapping on the armrest. 'Vidushika has served his purpose,' he conceded, 'but this delay is unacceptable. We cannot allow this opportunity to slip away.'

He turned to the prime minister. 'Send a message back to Vidushika. Quiet stealth and gentle diplomacy have failed. Now brute force must prevail. Remind him of the consequences of failure ... and the rewards of success.'

The messenger stood at attention, awaiting the prime minister's response. All eyes followed his departure, the emperor's command hanging heavy in the air. Kadphises then motioned his prime minister closer, his voice a low murmur. 'Prepare our special forces. We must be ready to act, should Vidushika prove incapable of fulfilling his task.'

'Your will shall be done, O Emperor,' the prime minister bowed. 'Your plans will be executed with utmost efficiency.'

Kadphises surveyed the assembled dignitaries, his eyes lingering upon each man. His voice, though quiet, held a power that resonated throughout the chamber. 'Remember this,' he stated. 'Our empire is built on the strength of our will. But sometimes ... a sharp sword is needed to enforce it.'

Kadphises knew that the sharpest of those came from something called the Dvaitalingam.

Konaditya, Mahodadhi
Present-day Konark, Odisha, India
Around 400 years ago

The heat was sweltering in Konaditya—also known as Konark—that day of May 1610. Down by the shore, activity abounded. A group of Portuguese sailors and local labourers, their bodies slick with sweat, struggled to haul a huge lodestone away from the ruins of the Sun Temple. The massive 52-ton stone had tumbled from the temple complex to the harbour years earlier, its magnetic field disrupting the navigation of passing ships ever since.

Captain Rodrigues, a seasoned sailor with a salt-and-pepper beard, oversaw the operation. Beside him stood Binayak, an Indian guide famed for his local knowledge and wisdom. Rodrigues had recruited him to locate the lodestone and oversee its removal.

'This stone is the root of all our problems,' Rodrigues muttered, wiping perspiration from his brow. 'Every time we sail these waters, our ships lose their way. Our compasses spin wildly. We cannot allow it to remain here and wreak havoc on our voyages.'

Binayak nodded solemnly. 'I understand, Captain. But this lodestone is part of a grander story. It belongs to the ruins of the Sun Temple built by King Narasimha Dev I of the East Ganga dynasty some three hundred and sixty years ago. This temple, Captain, was built to honour Surya, the sun god.'

Rodrigues's interest was piqued. 'Why place such a powerful magnet near the harbour then, where it interferes with navigation?'

Binayak gestured towards the crumbling ruins in the distance. 'The lodestone was never meant to reside in the harbour,' he explained. 'The temple was constructed with an array of magnets. Artisans carefully placed iron plates between each stone, culminating in the lodestone at the apex, creating a powerful magnetic field. This arrangement, Captain, allowed the statue of Surya—crafted with a high iron content—to levitate.'

'Levitate? For what purpose?' asked Rodrigues.

Binayak smiled. 'The secret lies within the name itself. "Konark" is a fusion of two Sanskrit words—"kona", meaning angle, and "arka", meaning sun. Konark, therefore, translates to "the angle of the sun".' He paused, his voice filled with pride. 'The temple was constructed with such astronomical precision that, during certain times of the year, the first rays of the morning sun would strike the sanctum directly, said to reflect off a diamond embedded in the navel of Suryadev's idol.'

Rodrigues eyed Binayak sceptically. *Could this tale be true*, he wondered. But as Binayak continued to point out the remnants of the temple's structure, Rodrigues eventually found himself marvelling at its grandeur.

As the sailors continued their labour, Binayak led Rodrigues towards the ruins. 'The temple was designed to resemble Surya's chariot,' he explained. 'Drawn by seven horses, its twelve pairs of exquisitely decorated wheels are, in fact, exceptionally accurate sundials.'

'But why is it in ruins?' Rodrigues asked, gesturing at the crumbling stonework as they neared the temple complex.

'The main sanctum collapsed forty years ago,' Binayak replied. 'Destroyed by Kalapahad, a general serving the Bengal Sultan,

Sulaiman Khan Karrani. He dislodged the lodestone at the top, disrupting the temple's delicate balance. Without its magnetic anchor, much of the structure collapsed.'

'Who possessed the skill to create such a marvel?' Rodrigues asked in wonder.

'The king commissioned a master builder named Bisu Maharana. He possessed tools and knowledge lost to us now, passed down through generations of blacksmiths known as the Dvaitalingam Rakshaks,' Binayak replied, his features softening with a touch of sorrow.

'But architects and masons—not blacksmiths—build temples,' Rodrigues countered.

'True, but Bisu Maharana's knowledge was not limited to metal,' Binayak said. 'He was a master of magnetite, a swordsman, and a craftsman skilled in the use of chisels and other tools. Legends speak of him as the 208th Dvaitalingam Rakshak.'

Rodrigues paused, absorbing the intricate details of the project and the expertise required to bring such a vision to life. 'And now the structure lies in ruins,' he murmured. 'What use is advanced technology against barbarians?'

'What became of this Bisu Maharana?' he finally asked, leaning in with interest.

'His is a tragic tale, Captain,' Binayak said softly. 'The temple's construction fell behind schedule. Few understood the secrets of his craft. Then, before its completion, Bisu Maharana died. The king, swayed by jealous rivals, forced Bisu's son, Dharmapada, to continue the work. The son—well-versed in Bisu's methods completed the project against a near-impossible deadline, but perished soon thereafter. Some say he died of exhaustion and dehydration; others whisper of suicide.'

'And the secrets of his craft, the tools, the technology?' Rodrigues probed.

'Their fate remains a mystery,' Binayak replied. 'Perhaps the knowledge perished with him, or was passed on to others. The magnificent levitating lingam at Somnath, the intricately carved temples of Angkor and Kailasa—all point to a shared knowledge, a mastery of materials that allowed for such feats of engineering. Perhaps the technology survives, scattered, hidden, waiting to be rediscovered.'

As the sun dipped towards the horizon, the Portuguese crew finally secured the lodestone, hauling it onto a barge. They prepared for their arduous journey, towing the heavy stone behind their ship. Rodrigues and Binayak, their conversation revolving around history, legend, art and science, continued to explore the ruins, the fading light casting long shadows upon the remains of a lost world.

As they neared the shoreline once more, Rodrigues stole a glance at the barge. For the first time since the operation had begun, doubt crept into his mind. The stories, the reverence, the sheer brilliance of the structure—they were not merely myths, were they? Perhaps this stone was more than just a navigational nuisance.

Rodrigues felt a shiver run down his spine. The lodestone was aboard, but the land itself seemed to hum in silent warning. Some forces, he realized, were never meant to be disturbed.

11

Seongsan, Garak Confederacy
Present-day Seongju County, South Korea
Around 2,000 years ago

Talhae retreated to his room, sinking into the bed and closing his eyes as his mind hovered between wakefulness and slumber. He stared at the blazing torch on the wall, observing the dance of the flame. Memories of the fire that had ravaged the orphanage flickered through his mind—a relentless loop of terror-stricken shouts, the acrid scent of smoke, the crackling roar of the flames. The memory then shifted, replaying his hollow victory over Min-ho earlier that day—a meaningless triumph that offered no consolation. His thoughts drifted to his parents—faces he could barely recall, blurred by time and the trauma he had suffered in the fire. He recalled only fragments: a gentle smile, the warm cadence of a lullaby, and then flashes of fear, a scream and silence. Finally, his mind returned to the orphanage, memories of which had long been buried beneath years of survival.

The Chang Bakery, just beyond the orphanage walls, had been a source of both comfort and anguish. He remembered the intoxicating aroma of fresh bread and delicious pastries that sometimes wafted into the orphanage, a tantalizing reminder of the kindness the proprietor occasionally showed, sharing his unsold goods with the children. The fire had changed everything, its merciless flames consuming not only the bakery but also half the orphanage. Only six of the seventeen children had escaped the inferno, their carefree lives irrevocably shattered.

Talhae and Kim Suro, two of the surviving children had initially found solace in their mutual experience of parental loss. In the first few weeks at the orphanage, they had clung to each other, sharing meals, whispered memories and silent grief. It had been a fleeting but intense closeness. But their bond had begun to unravel as time passed in the orphanage. Their paths diverged entirely when they were adopted. Kim Suro, affectionately known as Soju, was taken in by Kim Seok, the chieftain of Geumgwan. Talhae was adopted by Jangsu, the chieftain of Seongsan. Their new lives were vastly different, but their common past, the time at the orphanage, continued to shape them both.

The days before the inferno had been a mixture of joy and sorrow, the youngsters finding comfort in the orphanage's regime despite the tragedies that had brought them together. Talhae, with his quick wit and agile reflexes, often dominated their games. He was a natural leader, deft, creative and fiercely competitive. But it was Soju, with his innate charm and easy-going nature, who seemed to effortlessly win the hearts of everyone around him.

One crisp morning, the youngsters gathered in the courtyard for their daily chores. Soju, his infectious smile brightening the day, was busy assisting the younger children. Talhae watched from a distance, his jaw clenched. He had spent the previous day repairing a section of a damaged fence, expecting at least a nod of approval from the strict headmaster. But, as usual, the charmer Soju and his 'good deeds' had eclipsed Talhae's efforts. Intense resentment surged through Talhae. He longed to scream, to demand recognition, but he swallowed his anger. This, he realized, was just another battle in a war he was bent on winning.

Soon, the tensions extended beyond daily tasks. Soju, quick to absorb and retain knowledge, with a mind like a sponge, excelled in their lessons, his effortless grasp of knowledge a source of constant frustration for Talhae. Even their literature teacher, a wise old shaman monk, frequently held Soju up as a shining example. Talhae, though equally driven, had to work twice as hard to keep pace. The constant comparisons and the casual praise heaped upon Soju fuelled a simmering hatred within Talhae's heart.

One day, the youngsters were pitted against each other in a test of agility and strength—a race through a challenging obstacle course. Talhae's eyes, burning with determination, locked onto the finish line. This was his chance, his opportunity to prove his superiority, to finally outshine Soju. As the starting gong sounded, he pushed himself to the limit, his heart pounding with exertion, each hurdle cleared, each haystack scaled a testament to his grit and tenacity. He crossed the finish line, his chest heaving, his face flushed with victory.

But as he turned to savour his triumph, a bitter taste filled his mouth. Soju, he saw, had stopped midway through the race to help another child who had fallen and whose leg was bleeding. The cheers were not for Talhae's victory, but for Soju's compassion. Talhae forced a smile, congratulating Soju with feigned enthusiasm, but inside him, envy and fury raged. Victory had never tasted so unpleasant.

That night, Talhae lay awake in the stifling darkness of the dormitory, Soju's rhythmic breathing a constant reminder of his presence. *I am the hero*, Talhae thought hotly, *not him*.

The next day, as Talhae worked the school's vegetable patch, his anger found release in the vicious force of his spade. His frenzy attracted the attention of his teacher. The old man, sensing the turmoil within, rested a gentle hand on his shoulder. 'Talhae,' he said softly, 'I see the struggle in your heart. Do not allow envy to consume you. Each of you possesses unique abilities. There is no space for comparison.'

Tears stung Talhae's eyes. 'But why is he always the favourite? Why am I never deemed good enough?' he asked, his voice choked with emotion.

The monk sighed, his gaze penetrating Talhae's tormented soul. 'It is not about being better than another, Talhae,' he said. 'It is about embracing your own path, your own strengths. Soju's light does not diminish yours. Find your own light, and it will shine brightly.'

Talhae's jealous heart rejected the monk's words. His resentment for Soju grew with each passing day, rooting itself in his determination to surpass his rival.

With time, the smouldering embers of envy within him would flare into an unrelenting blaze—just like the inferno that had once scorched away his childhood.

12

Geumgwan, Garak Confederacy
Present-day Gimhae, South Korea
Around 2,000 years ago

Kim Seok, chief of Geumgwan, leaned against the railing of the anchored ship. The Nakdong river stretched before him, its waters mirroring the evening sky. Beside him was Kadalan Cheliyan, the most famous merchant of Pandya Desam. His iron ingots, forged with materials from Saketa, were prized above all others. His alliance with Padmasen and Kulasekara had made their partnership unbeatable.

There was a stillness about Cheliyan that drew every gaze—a quiet strength that needed no proclamation. A bushy beard framed his strong jawline, adding to his imposing aura. Years at sea had honed his posture and lent a natural confidence to his every movement. His deeply tanned skin was evidence of countless voyages under an unforgiving sun. His attire—a traditional mundu and angavastram, with a woollen blanket draped over his shoulders—spoke of both his heritage and his practical nature. From his simple clothes to his worn leather sandals, Cheliyan exuded dignity, but the glint of a sheathed blade at his waist indicated his readiness for and skill in battle.

His weathered vessel on the Nakdong river, having braved numerous storms, was a silent witness to Cheliyan's diplomatic and commercial exploits—a fitting extension of the man himself: merchant, sailor and warrior. The vessel had docked at nations far and wide: Roma, Yavana, Suvarnabhumi and Parasika, from Haprita to distant Cheen. The ship carried a diverse cargo: pearls, black pepper, cardamom, precious stones, earthenware, ivory, iron ingots, copper, gold, oilseeds, silk and cotton, all vied for space within its hold. On its bow, proud and defiant, was emblazoned the emblem of the Pandyan Empire: two fish, side by side.

Cheliyan had embarked on his journey at Korkai, a bustling port renowned for its global trade. His knowledge of the world was as vast as the oceans he traversed. 'My friend,' he remarked to Kim Seok, keeping his tone low and steady, 'your thoughts seem more turbulent than these waters.' He spoke in Gaya, one of the many languages he had mastered. Noting Kim Seok's furrowed brow, he added, 'What troubles you?'

Kim Seok sighed. 'It is Soju,' he confessed, his voice full of concern. 'He is still young, yet every passing day brings him that much closer to donning the mantle of leader. This land, with its endless skirmishes and fragile alliances, offers little peace. It is no place for a future ruler to learn the ways of harmony and leadership.'

Cheliyan nodded, understanding the reason behind his friend's distress. He reclined against the enormous ballast stones piled at one end of the deck, their rough surfaces offering a moment of grounding on the gently swaying ship. 'Perhaps,' he suggested, 'it is time to consider a sanctuary for young Soju, a place where he can thrive—far from the shadow of war.'

'A sanctuary?' Kim Seok echoed, intrigued.

'Yes,' Cheliyan said. 'Near Korkai in my homeland, there is a gurukul—a school—run by the Harihara sage Satyamuni. It is where knowledge and virtue shape young minds. Soju would study the stars, mathematics, ancient texts, governance and warfare strategies. The wisest mentors guide the students there. My business partner Kulasekara is Satyamuni's disciple. He could look after Soju.'

Kim Seok pictured his son amongst the Pandyan scholars, learning logic and philosophy, strategy and astronomy. 'Will he be safe there?' he asked, his question thick with a father's love.

'Safer than anywhere else,' Cheliyan assured him. 'Pandya Desam is a land of prosperity and peace, shielded by its geography and fortified by its alliances. Soju will not only be safe, but he will also thrive. Six months ago, I was in Dimašq. The governor—Baruchus Philippides—has already sent his son, Mithra, to the very same gurukul.'

As the first stars pricked the twilight, the two men found themselves discussing not Soju's but Kim Suro's future. They spoke of the man he would become, the contributions he would make to the world. The cool night air seemed to hold the weight of their hopes.

Dawn painted the sky over Geumgwan in hues of rose and gold. Kim Seok, having disembarked, watched Soju play by the shore, his laughter carrying over the water, tugging at his heart. The decision was made. He walked up to his son and knelt before him, a smile softening his features.

'Soju,' he began, 'how would you like to go on an adventure?'

Soju perked up, his words tumbling out. 'An adventure? Where to, Abeoji?'

'To a faraway land where the ocean meets the sky at every end. A place where wisdom flows deeper than our mighty river.'

Kim Seok could see that his words were painting images in Soju's mind.

The boy glanced towards the sea, where the faint curl of smoke from a distant ship caught his attention. 'Why is that ship smoking?' he asked. Kim Seok smiled. 'They are burning *ssuk*, mugwort. It is a sign of peace—our way of letting others know we come with no swords drawn. You must learn more about these ways too to understand our culture.'

Soju nodded. 'Will I learn to read the stars and speak new languages besides Gaya?' he asked.

'Yes, my son. And so much more. You will learn about the world, the art of peace, and even war strategies. You will learn to be a wise and just leader.'

Cheliyan, who had followed Kim Seok ashore, clasped Soju's shoulder. 'I will be your guide and protector on this journey.'

Kim Seok nodded, swallowing the lump in his throat as he prepared himself to send his beloved son on the long voyage that awaited him.

∼

It was several weeks before they could set sail. On the day of departure, Soju bid a tearful goodbye to the parents who had taken him in and treated him as their own.

As the Pandyan ship shrank on the horizon, Kim Seok's whispered prayer mingled with the sea breeze. Nearby, Minjun, Kim Seok's trusted manservant, wiped his eyes, watching his master's solitary figure against the fading light.

On the ship's deck, looking out into the vast, blue expanse, Soju felt the first stirrings of destiny. With each wave that broke against the bow, he felt he was sailing not just towards Korkai, but towards his fate as a future ruler of the Garak Confederacy.

13

Ayodhya, Uttar Pradesh, India
Present day

Somi Kim gazed out of the chopper window, taking in the sprawling landscape of Ayodhya. Believed to be where Lord Rama was born, Ayodhya was a fertile region—both literally and culturally—where history, legend, philosophy, religion and civilization had taken root and blossomed over millennia. Numerous temples and shrines dotted the city, each structure more elaborate than the last—testament to Ayodhya's ancient heritage and its deep association with Rama.

As Somi observed the city below, the low-rise buildings seemed to form a gigantic mosaic—temples, narrow streets and bustling marketplaces tessellated in a vibrant array of colours and shapes. The Sarayu river snaked through the city, its banks flanked by sugarcane fields. A smile flickered across Somi's face. A split second later it was gone, like a spark from a dying fire. She inhaled deeply, held her breath for a moment, then let out a slow, controlled exhalation.

The Ram Mandir's golden shikhara pierced the sky, the grand temple itself standing on the long-disputed Janmabhoomi site; a powerful symbol of faith built on centuries of controversy. Its gleaming surface caught the afternoon sun, drawing the eye to it despite the scaffolding clinging to unfinished walls. As she took in the imposing structure, her gaze drifted towards the riverside, settling on her destination: Queen Heo Hwang-ok Memorial Park. The *Samguk Yusa*, a thirteenth-century Korean chronicle, recounted the story of a princess from Ayodhya who had journeyed across the seas to marry a Korean prince in 48 CE. The Queen Heo Memorial Park was a living reminder of that ancient alliance.

This was the location chosen for the signing of the momentous agreement between Somi's company, GISCO, South Korea's largest steel producer, and India's Pillai Group. The partnership would see them collaborate on the manufacturing of a new steel variant—one designed to meet the stringent requirements of India's DRDO for their next generation of battle tanks. The Pillai Group, with its iron ore mining concessions in Odisha and Jharkhand and its massive steel mill in Angul, Odisha, stood to gain immensely from GISCO's cutting-edge technology—a leapfrog into the future of steel production.

Fascinated by the legend of Queen Heo Hwang-ok, hundreds of Korean tourists visited Ayodhya each year to pay their respects. In Korea, the queen was revered as a matriarchal figure, believed to be the ancestral grandmother of several Korean clans. Her story was not only taught in schools but also commemorated with shrines and ceremonies. In 2001, a simple stone memorial—an 8-ton block shipped from Korea—was placed in her honour in a quiet corner of the Rama Katha Park. By 2018, the site had transformed into the independent 4-acre Queen Heo Hwang-ok Memorial Park, where Korean and Indian architectural elements met gracefully along the Sarayu riverbank. The Uttar Pradesh government's official name for the site was Queen Huh Memorial Park. *A clumsy attempt to reconcile the name 'Heo' with everyone's bewilderment about the legend,* Somi thought in amusement.

From above, the park resembled a geometric puzzle embedded in a swathe of lush green lawns. As the helicopter descended, Somi focused on the most striking element of its design—two gazebos, one distinctly Korean, the other unmistakably Indian, linked by an arched bridge spanning a tranquil lake. The Korean gazebo's polished wooden pillars and sloping grey-shingled roof with upturned corners evoked memories of Changdeok Palace, one of the five grand palaces of Korea. The Indian one, a vision in white marble, featured intricate carvings, multifoil arches and a temple-shaped cupola.

The helicopter landed on a helipad close to the park. As Somi emerged, she was greeted by a delegation of officials from the district and the state. They ushered her along a red-carpeted walkway towards a massive air-conditioned canopy specially constructed for the occasion. Traditional Rasiya musicians and folk dancers lined her path. The sounds of dholaks and harmoniums harmonized with the jingle of dancers' ankle bells, their spirited movements celebrating her arrival. Young girls clad in crimson saris scattered flower petals before her. Somi responded with a namaste, her hands folded respectfully, and strode briskly towards the waiting tent.

Her attire—a simple beige Chanel pantsuit—was elegant, its sharp lines highlighting her petite frame. A Banarasi silk scarf provided a vibrant splash of colour against the neutral fabric, adding a touch of Indian flair. Her ivory complexion and flowing auburn hair complemented the sophisticated ensemble. Entering the tent, she spotted Aditya Pillai waiting on stage. He was already surrounded by an entourage of executives and assistants. Somi raised her hand in greeting and, with a confident stride, approached him, her smile warm and genuine, radiating an undeniable charisma.

She could not help but recall the flurry of late-night conversations and meticulous planning that had followed Aditya's initial phone call, the magnitude of their impending agreement looming over her. The deal they were about to finalize was poised to transform the industry, but it was more than just a business transaction.

Underneath her carefully constructed facade of calm, a lingering uncertainty remained. They still lacked the crucial element—the specific steel variant that could meet Aditya's key client's demands. Aditya had, she knew, taken a significant risk by trusting her with this project. He'd shared his plans with his superiors at the DRDO, and Somi was certain that Indian intelligence agencies, ever vigilant, would have scrutinized every aspect of her life before granting their tacit approval.

Somi Kim was, after all, a trailblazer. She had shattered glass ceilings and climbed the corporate ladder to become one of the youngest CEOs in a nation still dominated by old men. This partnership with Aditya Pillai was a calculated gamble, a bold move in a game being played for the highest stakes. And in which both players were equally matched.

In Somi's mind, this deal transcended mere commerce. She sensed it was the beginning of something transformative—a catalyst that could reshape the future. As Somi smiled for the cameras, she could not help but feel that—like the silence before a storm—something momentous was approaching, something none of them were prepared for.

14

Saketa, Kosala
Present-day Ayodhya, Uttar Pradesh, India
Around 2,000 years ago

It was the fifth muhurta of the day; the noonday sun beat down relentlessly. Indumati, ever the doting sister, served another generous portion of rice to her brother, Kulasekara. He tried to protest, but it was a futile gesture. She would feed him until he burst.

It had been a long journey—four months—from Korkai on the banks of the Thamirabarani river to Saketa. The trek on horseback had been arduous, traversing five rivers and two mountain ranges, crossing the borders of numerous kingdoms. But seeing his beloved sister again and meeting his niece and nephew after a three-year absence had made it worthwhile.

'I cannot eat another bite,' Kulasekara complained. He was a short, stocky man with a bald, leathery head, his long shikha—a lock of hair—at the back at a clear right angle to the three parallel sandalwood streaks that adorned his forehead.

They sat in a circle on the floor of the paakshala, their lunch—rice, dal and vegetables served in copper vessels—spread out on banana leaves.

'But you have not even tried the sweet kshirika,' Indumati argued. 'You have travelled so far. You need to replenish your energy.'

'Feeding me to death is not the solution,' Kulasekara retorted playfully, a twinkle in his eye. He turned to his niece and nephew. 'Why do you not tell her to stop?'

Suriratna giggled. 'Come more often, Matalu, and she will starve you like she does us. You only visit once every few years, so you always see her best side!'

Bhadraketu chuckled at his sister's quip.

'Insolent children,' Indumati muttered. 'No respect for their elders.'

Padmasen entered, having completed his morning appointments. 'I see she has already begun her culinary assault,' he remarked to Kulasekara. He settled down before a banana leaf and sprinkled a few drops of water around him before serving himself from the shared dishes. 'Children,' he asked, 'are you ready to impress your matalu with your skills this evening?'

~

Padmasen and Indumati were a devoted couple, but they came from very different worlds—separated by geography, language, customs and cuisine. Their union, unlikely in the normal course of events, had been orchestrated by fate itself.

Twelve years earlier, the planets had aligned in a rare and auspicious configuration—Brihaspati in Vrishabh, Surya-Chandrama in Makar during the month of Magha—a celestial signal for the sacred congregation that convened every twelve years at the confluence of three sacred rivers in the ancient city of Prayag, an event dating back to Satyug that would in later years be called the Mahakumbh.

Satyamuni, a revered Harihara sage from Pandya Desam, had decided to undertake the pilgrimage, accompanied by a hundred disciples. Indumati and her family were among them. In

Prayag, they had been joined by disciples from Kosala, including Padmasen and his parents. Padmasen had been seventeen then; Indumati, a mere fifteen.

The Rajasnaana—a ritual bath at the confluence of the Ganga, Yamuna and Sarasvati rivers, believed to wash away one's past karma—was the most auspicious event of the forty-eight-day festival. Pilgrims gathered before dawn, their chants rising with the mist as they awaited the sacred hour. But when the sun crept over the horizon, Indumati was nowhere to be found. She had vanished during the night, leaving behind only a faint imprint on her sleeping mat and a half-folded shawl. Her disappearance was as sudden as it was silent.

Her family was frantic. Kulasekara, aided by other youths, scoured the crowded festival grounds. Hours passed with no sign of her. Finally, a young man, seeing their desperation, offered the services of his father's hunting hounds. The dogs followed her scent to a hill along the riverbank. There they found her, sitting by a thicket, her ankle twisted, unable to move. Her rescuer was Padmasen, the young huntsman.

Within the safety of their tent, Satyamuni the sage declared that this was no accident. He proclaimed it was destiny that had brought Padmasen and Indumati together. He swiftly consulted their horoscopes, confirming his intuition. They were a match made in heaven, he announced triumphantly.

Both families, deeply devout, found common ground in their faith. Padmasen's family, devotees of Rama, also held the Jyotirlinga at Rameshwaram in high regard in their reverence of Shiva. Indumati's family, though rooted in the worship of Shiva at Rameshwaram, also paid their respects to the Vishnu Stambha at Rama's Janmabhoomi when visiting the north. Both families saw the two great deities as different facets of the divine, a single force manifested in two forms. Both families were bilingual, their shared knowledge of Sanskrit bridging the linguistic divide between Padmasen's Prakrit and Indumati's Tamil.

Their marriage was sanctified by the saptapadi, a simple ceremony on the banks of the Ganga—seven steps taken around the sacred fire, with vows exchanged with each revolution.

Kulasekara, overjoyed at his sister's happiness, ordered his wife, Vishnupriya, to arrange a grand feast for hundreds of the poor. Overwhelmed with gratitude, Padmasen and his father joined in by distributing clothing and blankets to the needy who had gathered. Among them was a frail, wide-eyed boy named Somadatta. His ribs showed through the thin cotton tunic clinging to his frame and his lips were tinged blue from the morning chill. Hardship had etched deep lines into his young face.

Moved by the sight, Padmasen paused beside him and gently draped an extra woollen blanket over his narrow shoulders. The boy flinched at first, unfamiliar with kindness, then clutched the warmth close to his chest.

'Th—thank you,' he stuttered, his voice barely more than a whisper.

Padmasen gave a nod and moved on, unaware that this small gesture had planted a seed—a debt of gratitude that would grow many times over and come to his aid when he would need it the most.

Charitable works complete, the newlyweds received Satyamuni's blessings and embarked on their life together, unaware of the challenges that awaited them.

∽

Kulasekara snapped out of his reverie. His attention drawn back to the present, he realized the sun had begun its descent.

The central courtyard of Padmasen's home, bathed in the golden light of the setting sun, was filled with the playful sounds of children sparring. Long shadows stretched across the cow-dung-plastered floors, the subtle scent of incense from the evening prayers lingering in the air. Suriratna and Bhadraketu, their wooden swords a blur of motion, were demonstrating their skills. Suriratna, fluid and graceful, moved with a dancer's precision. Each movement was deliberate, perfectly choreographed.

Bhadraketu, his skin a deep, rich mahogany, was lean and agile, his shoulder-length curls framing a face that held a youthful confidence. Despite his simple white dhoti, he had the presence of a prince.

Kulasekara observed their practice, his expression unreadable. Suriratna whirled, her sword arching through the air, her feet kicking up dust as she battled imaginary foes with the bravery of a seasoned warrior. As she completed her routine, her weapon pointing forward in a final powerful stance, a hush fell over the courtyard. Kulasekara clapped his hands, a single sharp sound that echoed against the walls.

'Very impressive, my children,' he said, a smile creasing his weathered countenance. 'Both of you possess hearts of warriors ... and the discipline of masters. Continue to hone your skills. One day, you will defend our land with real swords.' The children's faces glowed with pride as they bowed deeply before their matalu and their father.

'You have trained them well,' Kulasekara said, turning to Padmasen.

'I had no choice,' Padmasen replied. 'As the 157th Dvaitalingam Rakshak, I am obligated to ensure that the next generation of Rakshaks is prepared, whether they are my own descendants or someone else's. Both Suriratna and Bhadraketu possess equal potential. I have never favoured one over the other.'

Kulasekara chuckled, his smile genuine. His simple attire and unassuming demeanour belied his shrewd business acumen. Along with his partner Cheliyan, he controlled the most successful trading enterprise in Pandya Desam. 'The Ramayana teaches us that Ma Sita's power rivals that of Rama,' he said, his voice softening. 'They are two sides of the same coin.' His expression turned serious. 'The Dvaitalingam is indispensable. We must ensure its safety.'

'It is safe for now,' Padmasen assured him. 'Hidden as it has always been. But recent events ... they trouble me. Kujula Kadphises and Vidushika pose a grave threat. I am considering relocating it.'

'The Dvaitalingam is capable of protecting itself,' Kulasekara said. 'Have you forgotten its journey, its history? It has survived far greater threats.'

'But never have so many lusted for it,' Padmasen said, his shoulders slumping slightly. 'We are guardians of ancient wisdom. Benefits from that knowledge should be shared with all humankind. But sharing fruits, ironically, requires maintaining strategic secrecy. For now, its protection remains my responsibility. And that is why,' he continued, looking at Kulasekara, 'I need your help ...'

'Anything,' said Kulasekara. 'You have only to ask.'

Padmasen hesitated for a moment, then said gently, 'There is something I hope you can do ...'

15

Ayodhya, Uttar Pradesh, India
Present day

Ascending the steps to the podium within the specially erected canopy in the Queen Heo Memorial Park, Somi shook hands with Aditya as press cameras clicked all around them. The LED backdrop flashed animated versions of both companies' logos alongside two motion graphics of their fluttering national flags. Somi and Aditya stood at attention behind a large Gothic desk as the national anthems of South Korea and India were played, followed by the lighting of a massive oil lamp by their officials. Then, taking their seats on ornate chairs, they signed the agreements, each stroke of their pens greeted by a flurry of flashbulbs and the whirring of cameras. Aditya was beaming. Securing this deal was a major coup.

Every CEO of GISCO who had come before Somi had been a fifty-something man. She, however, had been catapulted to the top job in her forties to take up the task of rescuing the company from the brink of financial ruin some years earlier.

GISCO, established in 1968, had become a global leader within a few decades in the steel industry, its reputation built on the manufacture of cutting-edge steel variants. Headquartered in

Gimhae, in South Korea's South Gyeongsang Province, GISCO was a behemoth with subsidiaries and joint ventures spanning the world.

The Pillai Group, headquartered in Chennai, was no less formidable. A large Indian multinational corporation with diverse holdings in energy, mining, metals and infrastructure, it had been founded in the 1990s by Aditya's father. Under Aditya's leadership, it had grown exponentially, establishing itself as one of India's leading business conglomerates.

At forty-five, Aditya was a man of slender build, but his muscled physique hinted at an underlying strength. His honey-toned complexion accentuated his chiselled features and his easy charm, and the way he carried himself commanded the attention of those around him. Yet, beneath his composed exterior, an undercurrent of melancholy seemed to pulse, barely perceptible yet unmistakable. *You would have been so happy to see this day, Lakshmi,* he thought, his chest tightening with a familiar ache.

After the ceremony, the two CEOs fielded questions from the press, their answers confident and concise, before retreating to a luxurious mobile office specially stationed within the park. Inside, shielded from the clamour of the crowd and the watchful eyes of the media, they were finally alone, the entrance guarded by Pillai's security detail.

Outside, in the sprawling gardens of the memorial park, a sculpture of a golden egg gleamed in the sunlight—a tribute to the legend of the six kingdoms of Korea, whose rulers were said to have emerged from six such eggs. Nearby, an abstract model of a ship represented the vessel that, according to legend, had carried a princess from a distant land across the high seas to her future home. Tucked away in the southeast corner of the park, on the ground, was a circle enclosing a twin-fish symbol—the royal crest of the princess of yore.

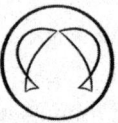

Symbols, Aditya thought, his eyes drawn to the design.

Like badges of honour, worn with pride.
Often concealing secrets deep inside.

And no one understood symbolism better than Somi. Born in Pohang, South Korea, in the late 1970s, she had known adversity from an early age. Her mother had succumbed to leukaemia when Somi was just fifteen. Later, while applying for a scholarship to study in the US, her initial acceptance had to be heartbreakingly withdrawn due to the Asian financial crisis. When she finally graduated from the University of Chicago—her studies delayed by two years—tragedy struck again. Her father suffered a stroke, slipping into a coma for ten long months before passing away. Despite these hardships, she had remained resilient, facing each challenge with unwavering determination.

She had first encountered Aditya at the university, where he was pursuing an MBA at the Booth School of Business. She was an undergraduate then, immersed in her Materials Engineering studies. Despite their different academic paths, they were drawn together by a shared passion for music—both were members of the Chicago Blues Ensemble, a student interest group that celebrated the city's vibrant music scene. Though they enjoyed a comfortable camaraderie within the group, their one attempt at dating each other had been awkward, an excruciating two hours of strained silences and stilted conversation, after which they had mutually decided to stick to group outings.

Then, at a Chicago Blues Festival concert at Millennium Park, fate had intervened. As Buddy Guy's electrifying guitar riffs filled the air, they found themselves alone, their friends having drifted away unnoticed. Fuelled by the music, the energy of the crowd and perhaps a few too many Coors, Aditya ended up spending the night in Somi's apartment. Nothing had happened. At least, nothing beyond a shared bed and a tangle of limbs in the morning. They had laughed it off, dismissing the incident as a drunken indiscretion. But the memory lingered, a tantalizing 'what if' echoing in Somi's mind.

Soon after, Aditya had returned to India to join his father's burgeoning business empire. Somi, meanwhile, embarked on her own career trajectory at GISCO, starting as an engineer and steadily working her way up to head their operations in Brazil. It was a position she relished until a corruption scandal engulfed the company. Dozens of senior executives back home were charged with bribery, sending shockwaves through the organization. The company's stock plummeted; lenders demanded their money back.

Thrust into the role of CEO—a position no one else dared to take—by circumstance, Somi faced a seemingly impossible challenge. It took two years of relentless effort—restructuring the company and negotiating with government officials and creditors—to revive the ailing giant. But Somi's unwavering commitment and sharp business acumen paid off. With market confidence returning, GISCO's stock soared to dizzying heights.

Her success, however, came at a price, particularly for her relationships. A whirlwind affair crumbled quickly. Subsequent romantic entanglements, though initially promising, faltered under her demanding schedule and towering success. It seemed the men she met could not withstand the force of her ambition. Frankly, she was relieved. Work provided a sense of purpose and control that her personal life—and the men in it—could not match.

Under Somi's leadership, GISCO continued its global expansion, moving into new markets—Australia, France, South Africa, Canada, Sweden and the United Arab Emirates. The company now boasted the world's largest steel plant in Gimhae, annually producing a staggering 85 million tons of steel. But Somi was not content to rest on her laurels. She poured billions of the company's profits into research and development, determined to push the boundaries of steel technology, exploring new possibilities in diverse sectors: automobiles, construction, defence, railways, shipping, petrochemicals and energy.

In addition to these, GISCO had one product that was still under wraps, not yet fully developed. But Somi sensed that something extraordinary was taking shape—something that had been waiting for the right moment and, perhaps, the right person. Aditya, with his unique blend of insight and conviction, seemed less the architect of and more the vessel for its emergence. A gnawing certainty settled in her chest: they had just opened a door neither of them could close.

Lahore, Delhi Sultanate
Present-day Androon Shehr, Lahore, Pakistan
Around 800 years ago

Qutb ud-Din Aibak, the governor of Hindustan, sat upon his opulent throne in Lahore, his eyes gleaming with the steely resolve of a man destined to rule. Intricate carpets adorned the floors of his court, while the walls bore exquisite engravings of Islamic calligraphy and geometric patterns. Tall, arched windows filtered the sunlight, casting elaborate patterns across the chamber. The air was rich with the fragrance of oud and rosewater, symbolic of a subtle blend of power and piety.

News of his master Muhammad Ghori's assassination had reached Aibak swiftly. Based in the Hindu Kush province of Ghor, Muhammad Ghori had ruled vast swathes of lands on both sides of the Indus. The Ghurid network of relay messengers, spanning the length and breadth of the Punjab, ensured that any messages that needed to be conveyed travelled as rapidly as the rivers that crisscrossed the land. The news while eliciting a pang of sorrow also ignited a spark of triumph in Aibak. Ghori, attacked near the Jhelum river, had met a treacherous end. Now, it was Aibak's turn to ascend. And what a remarkable ascent it would be.

Born into a Central Asian Turkic tribe called Aibak, separated from his family and sold into slavery in a bustling market in Nishapur, Qutb ud-Din had been purchased by a qazi—Fakhruddin—a man of learning who had instilled in him a love for the Quran, and taught him archery and horsemanship. Fate, however, had intervened once more. Aibak had been resold to Sultan Muhammad Ghori. His innate military prowess and strategic brilliance had propelled Aibak through the ranks, ultimately earning him a position as a trusted general and governor at the sultan's court.

Aibak's wazir, Ziauddin, shuffled towards the high throne, his head bowed low. 'My Lord,' he said respectfully, 'with the passing of your mentor, the territories of Dilli, Ajayameru, Lahore, Kannauj, Gwalior and Sindh now await your command.' These regions, once ruled by Rajput kings, had been wrested from them through Ghori's relentless campaigns. A shrewd strategist, Ghori had secured a series of victories, culminating in the decisive defeat of the mighty Prithviraj Chauhan in the Second Battle of Tarain. Prithviraj Chauhan, the ruler of the Chahamana dynasty, had governed a vast territory that extended across the regions of Sapadalaksha, Hariyana and Dilli, with Ajayameru—which later came to be known as Ajmer—as its capital.

Aibak nodded, his face a mask of determination. 'Let it be known,' he declared, 'that I, Qutb ud-Din Aibak, am now Sultan of all lands once ruled by Prithviraj Chauhan. From this day forward, Dilli, Ajayameru and all our territories shall acknowledge my rule.'

'Zafar Sultan!' his courtiers roared in unison, their words echoing through the chamber. *Victory to the Sultan!*

Ziauddin, ever the pragmatist, nodded sagely and, after a pause, brought up another matter. 'My Sultan,' he said, his voice hushed, 'there is a matter ... of some concern. In Dilli, there is an iron pillar, surrounded by Hindu and Jain temples. It is said that as long as this pillar stands, Hindu rule over Dilli can never be truly terminated.'

Aibak leaned back against his opulent throne, a wry smile playing on his lips. He cut a formidable figure—his tall, conical turban, embroidered with gold and encrusted with diamonds, accentuated a strong jawline and prominent nose. A thick, well-groomed beard framed his face and a string of large emeralds at his neck rested against his silken robes. 'I have ruled Dilli for thirteen years as my master's trusted general and governor,' he said dismissively. 'That pillar did little to hinder my reign. But tell me, Wazir, what is it about this pillar that troubles you?'

'The temples surrounding the pillar represent the faith of the non-believers,' Ziauddin explained. 'They believe their gods protect the city. They call the land "dhilli"—the loose, fragmented one—hence Dhillika or Dilli. They say the pillar is the nail that binds the land together, preventing it from breaking apart. They say it is centuries old, forged in honour of one of their countless gods—Vishnu. Many believe the pillar has defied the ravages of time because it is a product of magic, and that it should be uprooted and destroyed.'

Aibak let out a deep, throaty chuckle. 'If it is temples that give them hope, then it is temples we shall destroy. The pillar itself will remain. Let it stand as a reminder of our power, a symbol of their defeat—a final nail in their coffin.'

'As you command, My Sultan.' Ziauddin bowed low. 'What are your orders?'

Aibak rose, his posture commanding. 'Send word to Dilli,' he declared. 'The temples surrounding the pillar are to be dismantled. Use the recovered stones, pillars, doors, beams and arches to construct a grand mosque in the heart of our new capital. I shall call it the Quwwat-ul-Islam—the might of Islam. And within this mosque we shall erect the tallest minaret in the land—it shall be called the Qutb Minar. Let the call to prayer echo across Dilli. Let the infidels feel the bitter sting of humiliation each time they hear the adhan.'

The hall erupted with cries of triumph, the assembled courtiers roaring their approval. Aibak's vision resonated with them, fuelling their dreams of an Islamic Dilli. The wazir dispatched messengers to convey the sultan's orders. The courtiers, their conversations buzzing with excitement, began planning the grand construction project.

A new era had begun—one in which Islam would dominate the landscape of Dilli.

16

Saketa, Kosala
Present-day Ayodhya, Uttar Pradesh, India
Around 2,000 years ago

The karagara of Saketa—a prison shrouded in whispers and prophecy—lay buried beneath the bustling streets, a stark contrast to the vibrant life above. The air grew damp and musty as one descended the rough-hewn steps into its depths that contained untold suffering.

Inside, the dungeon was a labyrinth of darkness—narrow passageways paved with cold, unforgiving stone. The scant light from smoky torches wavered, casting grotesque shadows that danced and writhed across the walls. Each laboured breath drew in the stench of mildew, sweat, excrement and the metallic tang of rusting iron.

Tiny, airless cells lined the passageways, their heavy iron bars a constant reminder of confinement. Inside, inmates huddled in misery, their threadbare clothes offering little protection against the damp chill that seeped into their bones. Echoes of distant groans and the clinking of chains created a haunting symphony of torment. Even the hardiest rats shunned the muddy, filth-ridden floors, preferring the hollowed crevices of the walls, where their frantic scurrying added a scratchy percussion to the prisoners' mournful chorus.

At the heart of the dungeon lay the interrogation chamber, a place of terror that paralysed the soul. Bare stone walls devoid of comfort or compassion displayed an array of torture instruments: whips, branding irons, shackles, pliers, pokers and manacles. Each tool had borne witness to countless confessions, brutally extracted from broken bodies and shattered spirits.

Padmasen's naked form was suspended from the wall, his limbs stretched wide, bound by chains and tethers. His genitals, exposed for all to see, added to his humiliation. The flickering torchlight illuminated his battered body, highlighting the strained muscles and the exhaustion etched upon his face.

Deep purple and blue bruises marred his skin, their edges crusted with dried blood. Open cuts slashed across his torso and back, some still oozing, others sealed by dark, flaking scabs. His fingertips were a mess of raw flesh and clotted blood—his fingernails, torn away by pliers, leaving behind swollen, mangled stubs. Shallow breaths rattled in his chest, each one a struggle. His bright eyes had dulled, mirroring his pain. Cracked lips, parched from thirst and hunger, formed a grim line across his face. His hair, matted with sweat and grime, clung to his head. Yet, despite the agony, a flicker of satisfaction burned within him. He would never betray the sacred trust, never reveal the secret he guarded—even if it meant death within this fetid hellhole. For the oath of a Dvaitalingam Rakshak was older than kings and deeper than blood, forged not in ink, but in the fire of duty.

~

Kadphises's message had been received. Its impact had been immediate and brutal. While a contingent of soldiers had scoured the city, searching for Padmasen's family and the Dvaitalingam, another squad had stormed his home, their orders clear: capture Padmasen alive.

The house was quiet when they arrived—too quiet. As the soldiers burst through the bedroom door, their armour clanging, Padmasen had jolted awake, his heart hammering. For a breathless instant, panic gripped him—where was his family? Had the soldiers already taken them? Then it hit him: they were gone. Relief flooded his chest, swift and sharp—but it was laced with anguish. They were safe, for now, but far from him. He was alone.

Padmasen sprang to his feet and reached for his sword, defiance blazing in his eyes. A fierce struggle had ensued—metal clashing against metal, shouts and moans resounded in the close confines of the room. Despite being outnumbered, Padmasen fought with the ferocity of a cornered tiger, his sword deflecting blows and striking with lethal precision. But fatigue, compounded by the sheer number of his attackers, slowly overwhelmed him.

Overpowered and bound, he had been thrown into a chariot that sped towards the karagara. His thoughts, a whirlwind of fear and anger, raced as the chariot pounded over the rough road. Each jolt sent waves of pain through his body. The relentless rhythm of the wheels seemed to mock his powerlessness. He knew the soldiers would be searching four locations—the Janmabhoomi grove, Hanuman Garhi, Treta Ke Thakur and Sita's palace, Kanak Bhawan—seeking his family and the Dvaitalingam. But the secret, he knew, remained safe—*for now*.

~

When informed that Padmasen had indeed been captured alive but without his family, Vidushika erupted, furious. 'Find his family! Find them, I say, no matter the cost! And make that bastard Padmasen talk. He will reveal the secret, even if I have to break every bone in his body.'

Padmasen's body sagged against the unyielding bars of his oppressive cage. In the darkness, he clung to his ancestors' lessons and the sacred duty entrusted to him. He would never betray their faith in him. This unshakeable conviction, he knew, would accompany him to his pyre. His heart seeking solace, his thoughts drifted towards Indumati's loving gaze, her gentle smile and the laughter of his children. It was these memories that sustained him, giving him the fortitude to endure the unbearable.

Above, the search for his family and the Dvaitalingam continued.

'Tell us where it is!' his interrogator demanded with a menacing growl.

Padmasen summoned the last vestiges of his strength and spat out blood onto the floor between them. 'You will never find it.' His voice was raw with pain but still combative. 'It is protected.'

His captor leaned in closer, eyes narrowed with fury. 'Do you think your intransigence will save you?' he hissed. 'You will break, Padmasen. You will beg for death.'

The ghost of a faint, weary smile appeared on Padmasen's lips. 'You may break my body, you pathetic excuse for a man,' he whispered, 'but my spirit ... my spirit remains unbroken.'

17

Korkai, Thamirabarani, Pandya Desam
Present-day Thoothukudi District, Tamil Nadu, India
Around 2,000 years ago

'I miss Pitaha,' Suriratna said, her voice thick with unshed tears. She sat gazing at the bustling harbour of Korkai, the scent of fish, sea salt and spices a stark contrast to the dry, earthy fragrance of Saketa.

'I miss him too, Putri,' Indumati replied, her eyes glistening. 'I know his absence weighs heavily on your heart. But can you imagine my pain—leaving him behind in Saketa knowing the dangers he faces? He taught us to be strong. We must honour his wish.'

Suriratna nodded, though her heart ached. She could still hear her father's reassuring voice, see the kindness in his eyes, feel his unwavering belief in her strength. None of them had wanted to leave Saketa without Padmasen, but he had been adamant. There would be no discussion. Kulasekara had been ordered to escort Indumati, Suriratna and Bhadraketu to safety 1,400 miles away. Eight horses, two attendants and a precious, heavy cargo—all entrusted to his care.

Kulasekara's own journey to Saketa had taken four months; his return, under Padmasen's strict instructions, was to be completed in half that time. It had been a gruelling trek, their days a relentless cycle of riding, brief rests and ever-present risk.

For the most part, they rode in silence, the only constant sound the rhythmic beat of hooves against the dusty road. The menace of wild beasts, dacoits, venomous snakes or sudden storms paled in comparison to the fear of Vidushika's soldiers, on the prowl to capture them, to seize Padmasen's sacred possession. Outside Kosala, the presence of Kushan spies added another layer of danger. Known for their reach and ruthlessness, these agents thrived in the borderlands, intercepting messages, shadowing emissaries and turning the tide of wars with information rather than brute force. Kulasekara knew their kind—faceless watchers who struck when least expected. He stayed alert, eyes sweeping the horizon, every shadow a possible threat.

Memories of Padmasen sustained Indumati. She recalled his last words, a reminder to stay resolute in the face of peril. His courage had propelled them forward, urging them towards Korkai even as dread nipped at their heels.

Korkai, positioned strategically on the banks of the Thamirabarani river, was a bustling port city. Its natural harbour accommodated ships from far-flung corners of the world—Roma, Yavana, Suvarnabhumi, Parasika, Haprita and Cheen. Merchants, drawn by the lucrative pearl and ingot trade, flocked to this vibrant metropolis, its thoroughfares teeming with a rich blend of local and international traders.

The city thrummed with life. Its lanes, bursting with the scents of the sea, vibrated with the sounds of commerce—a symphony of languages and dialects, the clang of hammers—as well as the rhythmic chiming of temple bells. Stalls overflowed with exotic wares, and their merchants, draped in brilliantly coloured robes, engaged in spirited negotiations. Korkai was, after all, driven by its famous pearl market. Beneath palm-thatched awnings, traders displayed their glittering treasures, pearls of all sizes and hues, carefully sorted and meticulously graded. Iron ingots, their raw material imported from the north, were another prized commodity. Majestic ships, loaded and unloaded their exotic cargoes at the bustling docks: spices, wine, silks, perfumes, pearls, ingots, iron and bronze tools, and gemstones—a tantalizing blend of goods, some locally sourced, others brought from distant lands.

Indumati, despite her heartache at leaving Padmasen, felt a sense of homecoming as they neared her childhood house—one of the grandest in the harbour district, its walls echoing with the music of family life. For the children, raised in the heart of Saketa, the sight of the sea was a revelation, a magical expanse that filled their eyes with wonder.

'Look, Bhadraketu!' Suriratna exclaimed, pointing towards a ship adorned with the twin-fish emblem. 'It is massive!'

'A Pandyan vessel,' Bhadraketu added, his eyes wide with excitement. 'I have read about them!'

Indumati, observing their youthful enthusiasm, smiled, though her heart ached with concern for her beloved spouse. In the twelve years since her marriage, she had not returned home—her life with Padmasen and their two children had left her with little time for long journeys back home. Her only connection to Korkai had been through her brother, Kulasekara, whose business partnership with Padmasen and Cheliyan brought him north to Saketa every few years.

Indumati's father had succumbed to a tropical virus in her absence. She had not got the chance to bid him farewell. But Kulasekara and his wife, Vishnupriya, had kept the house alive, its usual rhythms a comforting balm against grief. Sadly, they had no children of their own. Vishnupriya had suffered multiple miscarriages and eventually they had decided they would not try further—they had each other and that was enough. This, Indumati knew, had only deepened Kulasekara's affection for Bhadraketu and Suriratna, and he had drawn them into his heart as his own.

The house itself, a grand structure of local sandstone and granite, embodied the rich heritage of Pandya Desam. Its walls, painted in earthy hues derived from natural pigments, glowed warmly in the afternoon sun. Shaded by a roof of ochre-red terracotta tiles, the courtyard was an oasis of tranquillity, its paved floors decorated with intricate tilework. The scent of jasmine mingled with the salty tang of the sea, creating a familiar, comforting fragrance. Lush greenery, both within the courtyard and on the outer walls, added to its serene beauty.

As they arrived, Indumati spotted her mother across the courtyard. 'Amma!' she cried, rushing towards the older woman, tears streaming down her face. She embraced her mother tightly, unwilling to let go.

Her mother disengaged gently, her eyes filled with compassion. She beckoned to the children to come closer and enveloped them in her loving arms. She was seeing them for the first time but it felt like she had known them forever. 'All is well, Kanna,' she whispered to Indumati. 'Destiny took you to Saketa, and destiny has brought you home. Have faith. Padmasen will be safe. The sun always follows a storm.'

The children, captivated by the novelty of the seashore, quickly adapted to their new environment. Their youthful enthusiasm and their eagerness to explore helped ease the ache of their father's absence. As they adjusted to their new home, Indumati found reassurance in the ordinary rituals of shared meals and evening prayers, while the lively markets and fragrant spice-laden air of Korkai diverted her troubled thoughts. For now, at least, the shadows of the past seemed distant, the challenges that lay ahead veiled by the warmth of their homecoming.

But even as the waves whispered peace along the shore, somewhere beyond the horizon darker tides were beginning to rise.

18

Safed Koh Mountains, Afghanistan
Present day

A modern fortification lay hidden in the Safed Koh mountains. Khalil Ghaznawar's hideaway was a place where ancient mysteries coexisted with modern technological marvels. Crafted from mountain wood, the exterior blended seamlessly with the natural environment, rendering it nearly invisible.

Inside, however, cutting-edge technology reigned—real-time global news feeds flashed across screens, encrypted communication lines hummed softly and sophisticated security systems maintained constant vigilance. Underground generators ensured a continuous twenty-four-hour power supply—a rarity in war-torn Afghanistan. This level of organization was in stark contrast to the chaos of the nation.

The atmosphere within this contemporary grotto was one of purpose and danger. Ghaznawar stood over a sleek, glass-topped table illuminated by recessed lighting. Before him lay a fragile yet perfectly preserved page from an antique palm-leaf manuscript. It contained a Sanskrit verse accompanied by a circular emblem of two fish swimming clockwise. The artwork, rendered with elegant simplicity, hinted at mysteries that lay beyond the surface.

Ghaznawar's gaze was fixed on the emblem as he addressed the lone shrouded figure standing just outside the circle of light. 'Do you see this?' he asked, gesturing towards the palm leaf. 'This emblem represents a technology I must possess. An age-old power.'

Reza, Ghaznawar's most trusted operative and a man of few words, stepped forward at that, his features still cloaked in shadow. Though his curiosity was stirred, he held his tongue. Ghaznawar's eyes gleamed with ambition and reverence as he continued in a hushed voice, 'This power has capabilities beyond our comprehension. It could unleash unimaginable terror, ensure that our enemies fall before they even face us.'

The walls around the two were adorned with a collection of historical artifacts: antique weapons, ancient texts—each piece carefully preserved beneath protective glass and illuminated by focused beams of light. Ghaznawar's passion was gathering knowledge—harnessing the secrets of these forgotten fragments of history. His fingers traced the lines of text on the old manuscript even as he began reciting from the Quran. 'Remember Al-Baqarah 2:258,' he intoned. '"My Lord is the One who has the power to give life and cause death." This primeval power—it rightfully belongs to Allah. And with it we shall be supreme.'

Reza listened intently, absorbing every word. Sensing the import of his leader's expectations, he finally spoke, his voice a low murmur. 'What is your command?'

Ghaznawar's attention shifted to a lump of black stone placed near the manuscript. He ran his hand across its surface, a surge of adrenaline coursing through him at the contact. It was a piece of the Somnath lingam, a relic of a past victory, a symbol of authority that had been safeguarded within his family over the ages. 'Forty generations have passed,' he said with a quiet intensity, 'since my ancestors first ventured into India, seeking a lingam that purportedly held within it a remarkable power. Mahmud of Ghazni, my illustrious forebearer, led seventeen raids, seizing treasures and crushing the infidels who stood in his path. He even took the stone they worshipped, our Manat.'

'Manat?' Reza questioned.

'Mahmud attacked Somnath for a reason,' Ghaznawar explained. 'He believed the Prophet Mohammad himself had commanded the destruction of three pre-Islamic goddesses: Lat, Uzza and Manat. Two idols were destroyed, but it was alleged by Farrukhi Sistani, Ghazni's court poet, that Manat was hidden away in Gujarat, enshrined in a temple the infidels called *Su-Manat*, or Somnath. Mahmud, driven by faith, smashed the lingam into bits. His alchemists searched for the source of its power, but they could not find what he sought. Even today, my family carries the legacy of that quest within our name—Ghaznawar, the warriors of Ghazni.'

Ghaznawar's eyes burned with fierce determination as he caressed the stone fragment. 'Deploy the scouts,' he commanded. 'Infiltrate those places where the power might be hidden. Speak to our informants. I want updates around the clock. This is not just some old technology—it is the key to our future, the foundation of our dominance. We must retrieve it before its true nature is revealed to others.'

'As you wish,' Reza replied, nodding in assent.

Ghaznawar's hand lingered on the manuscript as Reza turned to depart. His eyes swept across the room, taking in the stark landscape visible through the windows. His lair, hidden from view yet wielding immense influence, mirrored the ancient force he sought to control. The twin fish on the parchment stared back at him, a silent promise of the power he was intent on possessing and then unleashing upon humanity.

The departure of his operative brought his attention back to the many screens that lined one wall. The flickering images displayed a world in constant flux—wars, political upheavals, economic turmoil—a chaotic stage upon which he was determined to play a leading role. His mind, a whirlwind of audacious plans and strategies, embraced the challenge. Though this fortified lair might be his sanctuary, the world was his battleground.

A millennium after Mahmud of Ghazni's conquests, Khalil Ghaznawar sought to carve his own name into history.

~

Ghaznawar was driven by the legacy of his ancestors. He recalled the many empires that had shaped this land: the Islamic culture fostered by Mahmud of Ghazni, the rise of the Ghurids, the Mongol attack that shattered Ghazni's glory in 1221 and the subsequent rule of the Timurids. The Mughals had followed, bringing with them grandeur and centralization, though their control over Afghanistan was often contested by rising tribal powers. Then came the Durrani Empire, which laid the foundations of a unified Afghan identity, and was succeeded by the Barakzais, who had struggled to hold the nation together amid growing foreign interference.

That era was followed by the British incursion in 1839 during the First Anglo-Afghan War and the Soviet invasion of 1979, the emergence of the Mujahideen, the bloody civil war of the 1990s and, finally, the Taliban's ascendance as American forces withdrew in 2021.

Ghaznawar's ascent had begun during the tumultuous 1990s. A teenage warrior when he joined the Taliban in 1994, he had quickly distinguished himself, his tactical brilliance and audacious leadership leading them to victory in Kandahar and, later, in Kabul. Mullah Omar, the Taliban's supreme commander, had recognized his potential and trusted him implicitly.

Ghaznawar had proven instrumental in negotiating the Doha Agreement with the United States in 2020—a deal that secured the withdrawal of American forces and paved the way for the Taliban's return to power. His understanding of the country's complex tribal dynamics, his ability to forge strategic alliances, and his unwavering commitment to the Taliban's cause had elevated him to a position of considerable influence.

The Ghaznawar lineage, forged in the fires of conflict and tempered by centuries of adversity, was defined by resilience and adaptability. Each generation, rising from the ashes of past struggles, had been more determined, more driven than the last. Now, thought Khalil Ghaznawar, his time had finally come.

As he stared at the twin-fish emblem, it no longer seemed to be pointed to destiny—it warned of its dangers. For in the silent curves of the symbol lay the shadow of a storm, and he was its chosen harbinger.

19

Agastyamalai, Pandya Desam

Present-day Agasthyamala Biosphere Reserve, Kerala, India

Around 2,000 years ago

Bhadraketu and Suriratna stood by the gurukul gates, watching the receding figures of Kulasekara and Cheliyan. Five days earlier, they had embarked on a journey—one that would irrevocably alter their lives.

They had left from Korkai as the sun rose, bathing the harbour in a morning glow. Their convoy had assembled, ready for the long trek to Sage Satyamuni's renowned gurukul, hidden deep within the tranquil Agastyamalai hills.

The siblings, each holding the reins of their horses, stood beside Kulasekara. The air, diffused with the briny scent of the sea and the lingering aroma of their mother's jasmine perfume, held the bittersweet ache of departure. Indumati adjusted Suriratna's light shawl over her shoulders, her eyes shining with unshed tears. 'Remember,' she said, her voice trembling as she embraced them one last time, 'the path to knowledge is the path to life.'

Kulasekara's longtime friend and business partner Kadalan Cheliyan stood by his horse. Weeks earlier, he had brought a young boy he called Soju—Kim Suro—from distant Geumgwan in the Garak Confederacy to be entrusted to Satyamuni's care.

Now, Kulasekara had informed him that his own niece and nephew were also bound for the same gurukul.

They began with hesitant steps, the children casting long looks at their mother's receding form—a solitary figure framed against the vast expanse of the sea. Sensing their sorrow, Kulasekara urged his horse forward, leading them into the sheltering embrace of the forest. As the dense canopy enveloped them, the sounds of civilization faded, replaced by the symphony of nature—the melodious calls of birds, the rustling whisper of leaves.

Cheliyan rode alongside, his tales of faraway lands and renowned scholars a welcome distraction. He spoke of Soju's journey—a sea voyage of many months—and of the gurukul itself, where children from across Bharatvarsha found sanctuary and community. 'We are headed to a place of great learning,' Cheliyan declared, his voice echoing through the stillness of the forest, 'where wisdom from all corners of the world converges. Satyamuni's gurukul is a melting pot—a vibrant tapestry of cultures and knowledge. Here, the trade is in ideas, not spices and silks.'

The path, winding through verdant undergrowth and across sparkling streams, led them ever closer to their new life. With each passing hour, the initial pain of separation softened, replaced by a tingling anticipation. On the fifth day after their departure from Korkai, the gurukul finally came into view—a harmonious cluster of red-tiled, sloping-roofed buildings made of sun-baked clay and stone, their walls adorned with hand-painted mandalas and sacred symbols.

Surrounded by a profusion of jackfruit, mango, banana and sal trees, their new home was a natural paradise. The fragrance of cardamom, turmeric and sandalwood lingered in the air that vibrated with the rhythmic chanting of students. At the entrance, Satyamuni, the sage, awaited them. To Kulasekara, he seemed unchanged since that auspicious day in Prayag when he had joined Padmasen and Indumati together in marriage.

A benevolent smile softened the sage's weathered features. The sun had caressed his bronze skin for decades, leaving a map of fine lines around his eyes and mouth. His long white beard cascaded down to his chest, mirroring the snowy white of his hair, which was neatly bound in a knot. He wore a simple white dhoti, his chest bare, his body seemingly impervious to the winter chill. A string of rudraksha beads encircled his neck. His posture, belying his age, was erect and strong and held the quiet confidence of a man who had spent a lifetime in the pursuit of knowledge.

'Welcome, children of Saketa,' he greeted them, his voice warm and amiable, his arms outstretched. 'This is your new home. Here, you will learn not only about the scriptures and sciences, but also about the art of diplomacy and the strategic thinking of kings.' The children, humbled by his presence, bowed their heads and touched his feet.

Satyamuni led them through the gurukul—a bustling complex of open courtyards and thatched study halls alive with the energy of young minds from across the land. At the entrance, stood a massive statue of Harihara—a divine fusion of Vishnu and Shiva. 'In the Vishnu Parva of the Harivamsha,' Satyamuni explained, 'Vishnu once appeared before Shiva in the guise of Mohini, the enchantress. When Shiva attempted to embrace her, Mohini transformed back into Vishnu. And thus, the two deities merged into the single form of Harihara.'

They continued their tour, marvelling at the scrolls and instruments, celestial globes and mathematical tools that filled the study halls—each a promise of knowledge and understanding yet to be gained. In one of the courtyards, a group of students sat in a semicircle around a sand-drawn astronomical chart, deep in debate. One of them, a boy with olive skin and keen, observant eyes, looked up and smiled.

'You are new,' he said, rising to his feet. 'I am Mithradates—but most people call me Mithra.' His Sanskrit was soft and lilting, yet hesitant, as though each word were being tested—new to his lips, unfamiliar in weight and cadence. 'I am from Dimašq. You will get used to everything sooner than you think.'

Before anyone could reply, he turned and gestured at another boy sitting a little apart from the group. 'That is Soju. He recently arrived from the Garak Confederacy.' The boy gave a shy nod, his hands fidgeting in his lap. His eyes, wide with uncertainty, flicked towards the newcomers.

Cheliyan stepped forward, crouching beside Soju and speaking to him in Gaya, his tone gentle and familiar. The boy's shoulders eased and the ghost of a smile appeared on his lips.

Mithra grinned. 'We come from everywhere. But in time, this place feels like it has always been ours.'

Suriratna, ever curious, turned to Mithra. 'What is a typical day like here?' she asked.

Mithra's smile was warm, his eyes sparkling with pride. 'Our days begin at sunrise, with morning prayers and lessons that cover a vast spectrum of subjects—from the ancient verses of the Vedas and the Buddhist Tripitaka to the intricacies of mathematics and alchemy. In the afternoons, we focus on the arts—painting, music, martial combat and dance. And, of course,' he added, 'there is always time for debate, for exploring the philosophies and sciences that shape our world.'

'Who will teach us here?' Bhadraketu asked.

'Our teachers are the wisest scholars from across Bharatvarsha and beyond,' Mithra replied. 'They bring with them a wealth of knowledge and stories of far-off lands.'

The time for Cheliyan and Kulasekara's departure having arrived, Kulasekara drew Suriratna aside, his gaze tender. 'The wisdom you gain here, my dear,' he said, gently touching her shoulder, 'will guide you through the darkest of times. Embrace it. Cherish it.'

Standing by the entrance, Cheliyan addressed Bhadraketu. 'Remember the bonds you forge here,' he said. 'They will endure. They will offer strength and guidance—for a lifetime.'

With final blessings and words of encouragement, the two men turned their horses towards the road, heading back to Korkai. The children watched as they rode away, their figures gradually swallowed by the vastness of the forest. As Kulasekara and Cheliyan vanished from sight, Suriratna and Bhadraketu, surrounded by their newfound friends, turned towards the heart of the gurukul. The rich, sonorous tones of a conch shell reverberated across the school, drawing the students to the central assembly hall for evening rituals.

A sense of profound awakening filled them. Standing amidst the ancient trees along with fellow seekers of knowledge, they knew that this place would shape their destinies in ways they had not yet dreamed of.

20

Ayodhya, Uttar Pradesh, India

Present day

The retreating beat of the nagada folk drums faded, leaving a gentle silence that settled over the mobile office. Inside, a bottle of champagne nestled in an ice bucket and two flutes rested on a table draped in starched white linen. Aditya pulled out the chilled bottle, feeling the condensation against his fingers. With a practised hand, he popped the cork, its celebratory hiss greeting the quiet space. He carefully filled the flutes with the effervescent liquid and offered one to Somi.

'To new beginnings,' he said, proud and relieved. 'Thank you for making this happen.'

He pressed a button on the remote and the familiar strains of 'Sweet Home Chicago' wafted in the air. It was a shared touchstone, a reminder of their time together at UChicago a lifetime ago. They clinked their glasses and settled into the plush armchairs on opposite sides of the table.

'This agreement was a foregone conclusion, Aditya,' Somi said, taking a sip of the champagne. Her words were light, yet a subtle undercurrent of something deeper and unspoken lingered in them.

They set down their glasses. Somi's hand reached across the table, her fingers resting lightly atop his. A wave of warmth coursed through Aditya, his pulse quickening at the unexpected contact. *It's just a gesture of friendship*, he told himself, his mind struggling to quell the unexpected flood of emotion. *This is the business deal of a lifetime. Nothing more.* But his heart, as always, refused to listen.

Aditya Pillai had been born into privilege. His father, Sriram Pillai, had started as a small-time cement dealer, but during India's economic liberalization of 1991, he had transformed himself into a powerful thermal power producer. Sriram Pillai possessed a unique talent—a knack for navigating the complex world of politics, bureaucracy and finance with ease. His charm and his ability to please had allowed him to build a solid foundation for their Chennai-based conglomerate.

'Do you ever think about the cost of all this?' Somi asked, her voice soft, breaking through his thoughts. She wasn't looking at him; her attention remained fixed on her glass, bubbles swirling like miniature galaxies within it.

'The cost?' Aditya echoed, momentarily puzzled.

'Of success,' she clarified, turning towards him, her eyes searching his. 'What we have had to sacrifice … to get here.'

The question, unexpected and poignant, struck a chord within him. No one knew the cost of success better than Aditya Pillai.

Eight years into his marriage to Lakshmi—a woman who had filled his life with joy—tragedy had struck. A truck, slamming into their car from behind on an interstate highway, had taken Lakshmi and their six-year-old daughter, Kavya, both sitting in the back seat. By a cruel twist of fate, Aditya had been miraculously spared because he had been up front, next to their chauffeur. The chauffeur too had been injured grievously as the right side of the car had smashed into a cement divider.

'I think about it ... every day,' he admitted, his voice barely a whisper.

For the longest time, Aditya hadn't been able to face his chauffeur. It was not that he was indifferent, but every thought of that day tore through him like shrapnel. He had buried himself in the cold comfort of routine, trying to outrun the guilt and the memories. But they had clung to him relentlessly. When he could no longer bear the weight of avoidance, he had finally made the journey many months after the accident.

Seeing the man—his trusted helper, his body now mangled, his right arm and leg permanently lost—Aditya had been overcome, no longer able to suppress the grief that plagued him. Despite the pain he was in, the chauffeur's eyes had crinkled with joy as Aditya greeted him and he reciprocated using the old term of endearment, 'Adi-kutty.' Aditya, his heart breaking, had embraced the man tightly. By the time they parted, he had ensured a generous pension for the driver—enough to support his family for the rest of their lives.

That visit had marked a turning point. Until then, Aditya had tried to wall off the past, drowning himself in work to avoid facing what had happened. But standing there, looking into the eyes of the man who had lost so much and yet bore no bitterness, only affection and quiet strength, something inside him shifted.

At one point, the chauffeur had smiled and said, 'I remember your mother used to narrate tales of ships and voyages to you. All of us staff members would gather around. Remember the ballast stones? Heavy chunks placed in ships—not to sink them, but to steady them in rough waters? Much of life's burdens are like that, kutty. They weigh on us, yes. But they also hold us upright.'

The encounter stripped away every excuse and every diversion he had clung to. He saw with searing clarity that survival came with responsibility—not just to the living, but to the memory of those lost. He could no longer hide behind distractions. From that day on, he did not work to forget—he worked with purpose. He became a karmayogi in the truest sense: driven not by ambition, but by duty, by the need to make each moment count. Nothing else mattered.

The quiet hum of the vehicle's engine brought Aditya back to the present. He blinked, the weight of memory slowly lifting. Somi sat opposite him, watching him with quiet understanding. 'Do you regret ... the sacrifices?' she asked softly.

He shook his head slowly. 'I regret ... not being there ... for them during the time that we were together as a family,' he said, his voice ripe with emotion. 'But I don't regret ... what I've done since. It's the only way ... I can honour their memory.'

Many years after the accident, Aditya had been attending a business conclave in New Delhi when a familiar face had caught his eye. Somi. By now Aditya had transformed the Pillai Group into an Indian multinational corporation with interests in energy, mining, metals and infrastructure. His unorthodox approach to business had earned him a reputation for being unpredictable—even eccentric—but he always delivered in the end, after making everyone around him think that he had failed.

When Aditya and Somi met for dinner that evening in New Delhi, the awkward pauses of their student days had vanished, replaced by a genuine connection. As they explored potential collaborations, they realized their business interests aligned. But there was no effort to actually lock a partnership. Their shared past—the brief friendship forged at UChicago—had made their equation one of dependable friends.

Then came the pressure of the DRDO deadline, and negotiations for a collaboration shifted into overdrive.

Now, seated in the mobile office at the Queen Heo Memorial Park, Somi said, 'This agreement—it wasn't signed today.' Her eyes were fixed on Aditya, and her voice was laced with a strange intensity. 'It was decided two thousand years ago. We're just ... finalizing it now.'

Her words, enigmatic and strangely compelling, hung in the air. Aditya, intrigued, searched for an explanation in her unwavering stare. 'What do you mean?' he asked.

'Perhaps ...' she said softly, 'some things transcend time and space. Maybe ... this is one of them.'

He longed to question her further, to understand the meaning behind her cryptic words, but he hesitated. Something held him back. Some things were best left unsaid.

As the last few soulful notes of 'Sweet Home Chicago' filled the interior of the mobile office, a sense of peace descended upon him. Despite the uncertainties, the sacrifices, the losses that had shaped his life, a promise of optimism remained—a glimmer of hope for a brighter future.

'To fresh beginnings,' he said, raising his glass.

'To fresh beginnings.' Somi's soft smile accompanied the words. Their glasses clinked again, sealing a wordless pact.

Nellai Nadu, Pandya Desam
Present-day Tirunelveli District, Tamil Nadu, India
Around 900 years ago

King Kulottunga Chola I scanned the battlefield, his discerning gaze evaluating the enemy's stance. The Pandyan forces, famed for their valour and combat prowess, held a formidable position. Their razor-sharp swords, crafted with mysterious techniques, were the stuff of legend. From a distance, they resembled a shimmering sea of shields and spears, rippling beneath the blazing sun. Across the battlefield, Kulottunga's own army stood ready, a vast force holding aloft banners emblazoned with the Chola tiger, their roars echoing on the wind.

The air thrummed with the sounds of war: clanging swords, the thunderous beat of war drums, shouts of command, and the anguished cries of the wounded. Kulottunga, mounted upon his grand warhorse, observed every movement, every shift in the tide of battle. Sunlight glinted off his armour, creating an aura of power about him, a divine sheen that his soldiers interpreted as a sign of the gods' favour.

Kulottunga had inherited the Chola throne upon his maternal uncle's death. He had quickly consolidated his power, quelling internal disputes and securing the loyalty of local chieftains. His next move—a strategic alliance with the eastern Chalukya kingdom—had significantly bolstered his resources. But his ultimate goal was the subjugation of the Pandyas, a final and decisive victory that would cement his position as the undisputed ruler of the south.

The Chola infantry advanced—a relentless, unstoppable machine. The soldiers moved in perfect synchronicity, shields interlocked, creating an impenetrable wall of iron and bronze. They pushed forward, their march a symphony of clanging metal rising to a crescendo as they collided with the Pandyan forces.

From his vantage point, Kulottunga directed the battle with meticulous precision, his orders relayed swiftly and accurately via a network of messengers. Behind the front lines, Chola archers unleashed a barrage of arrows, a deadly rain that fell upon the Pandyan soldiers, sowing confusion and terror. Kulottunga, a seasoned warrior, understood the importance of breaking the enemy's spirit before engaging in close combat.

Years of warfare had honed his strategic instincts. He watched as his most trusted general led a flanking manoeuvre, the cavalry sweeping in from the west, catching the Pandyan army off-guard. Their swords flashed, a whirlwind of iron, cutting through enemy ranks. A cloud of dust obscured the view, but even from afar Kulottunga could sense the tide turning. His heart swelled with pride as he witnessed the courage and skill of his soldiers. His gaze focused on the Pandyan king, his elaborate armour and the twin-fish standard that marked his presence.

Kulottunga knew that the Pandyas possessed a secret—a knowledge of metallurgy that allowed them to create the strongest, sharpest weapons. That secret was tantalizingly close, almost within his grasp. He spurred his warhorse forward, his own blade gleaming as he cut through the chaos, determined to confront his rival. Dismounting before the Pandyan king, he raised his sword, challenging him to a duel.

The two monarchs clashed, their blades a blur of motion, sparks flying as they parried and thrust. The surrounding soldiers paused, awestruck by the epic confrontation unfolding before them. Kulottunga, moving with deft precision, deflected a barrage of blows, his eyes seeking an opening in his opponent's armour. The Pandyan king, sensing vulnerability, unleashed a furious attack, his sword whistling through the air. Kulottunga twisted aside, narrowly avoiding a deadly blow. The two men circled each other, their eyes locked, acutely aware that a single misstep could mean death.

The Pandyan ruler lunged, his blade aimed at Kulottunga's throat. The Chola king sidestepped just in time and countered with a swift strike that landed on his opponent's shoulder. The Pandyan king cried out in pain, clutching the wound. It was the opening Kulottunga had been waiting for. He pressed his attack, forcing the Pandyan king into a defensive position. Then, in a flurry of movement, his blade found its mark, piercing the king's armour, drawing a crimson stain.

The Pandyan monarch crumpled, blood spilling from his lips as he crashed to his knees. The fight drained from him, his gaze locked with Kulottunga's for a final, silent exchange. Then his eyes glazed over and he slumped to the ground, defeated.

A roar of victory erupted from the Chola ranks, their raja's triumph echoing across the battlefield. Panic seized the Pandyan army. Their formations dissolved as they broke rank, fleeing in terror. Kulottunga, raising his sword, bellowed out an order to pursue, to hunt down the enemy. Inspired by their king's victory, the Chola soldiers pressed their advantage, savagely chasing the retreating Pandyan forces.

As the sun dipped below the horizon, bathing the field in an eerie red glow, the sounds of battle faded, replaced by the moans of the dying. The air, ripe with the stench of blood and smoke, felt heavy with the weight of victory and loss. Kulottunga surveyed the carnage, a wave of conflicting emotions washing over him—pride in his army's conquest but also sorrow for the lives lost.

His commanders, their faces flushed, gathered around him. 'We are victorious, Your Majesty,' one of them declared, bowing low.

Kulottunga nodded, acknowledging their triumph. 'See to the wounded,' he commanded, his voice weary, 'and honour the fallen. They have served with courage and distinction.'

He retreated to his tent, seeking solace from the slaughter. As his attendants removed his armour and washed away the blood and grime, his mind replayed the day's events, the thrill of victory tempered by the sobering thought of what it had cost. Seated by the flickering light from a lamp, he summoned his general. 'The Pandyans possess a secret,' he said, his voice low, 'forged with a power we do not yet understand. They call it the Dvaitalingam. Find the one who guards it. Bring him to me.'

21

Agastyamalai, Pandya Desam
Present-day Agasthyamala Biosphere Reserve, Kerala, India
Around 2,000 years ago

The dusty training yard buzzed with energy as fifty youngsters, including Suriratna, Soju, Bhadraketu and Mithra, sparred and practised, eager to demonstrate their prowess at martial arts.

Soju stepped forward, his bamboo staff held firmly in his grasp. He squared off against another student, their eyes locking as they circled each other in the Silambam ring. Tension crackled in the air. Soju struck first, his staff whipping towards his opponent's side. The other boy, skilled in the art of defence, blocked the blow expertly. A flurry of strikes and counterstrikes ensued, bamboo staves meeting with sharp, rhythmic clacks, until, with a deft feint, Soju unbalanced his opponent, forcing him to concede defeat. Acknowledging his opponent's effort with a light pat on the shoulder, Soju accepted victory with a grin. The boy bowed gracefully and stepped out of the ring.

'Well done, Soju!' Suriratna called out from across the yard as she entered the circle, ready for her own practise. Soju smiled back, his understanding of Sanskrit and Tamil growing stronger with each passing day. Those early weeks at the gurukul, when understanding every word had been a struggle, felt like a distant memory.

Suriratna faced her opponent—a strong, sharp-eyed girl—in the Kalaripayattu ring. Their swords clashed, each strike met with a swift parry. Suriratna's forceful approach, a blend of strength and agility, pushed her opponent back. Adrenaline surged through her veins with each successful block. Her heart pounded and her senses were heightened with the thrill of the fight. With a quick sidestep and a flick of her wrist, Suriratna disarmed her opponent, sending her sword clattering to the ground. Suriratna beamed, extending a hand to help her opponent up. 'You fought well,' she said sincerely. The girl smiled back, her eyes holding a spark of determination in spite of the defeat.

A circle gathered around Mithra and Bhadraketu, drawn by the anticipation of the final contest. 'Today's workshop concludes with a wrestling match,' Bhimashankar, the wrestling instructor, announced. 'A test of strength and skill, hand-to-hand.' A circle gathered around the two boys, drawn by the anticipation of the final contest. The air felt alive with excitement.

Mithra and Bhadraketu faced each other on the soft earth of the training ground, their bare feet grounding them. Bhadraketu, tall and powerfully built, moved with a dancer's grace. His open stance was deceptively relaxed, betraying a precision honed over months. Mithra, shorter and more compact, adopted a wrestler's crouch, his focus entirely on his opponent, calculating his every move.

Satyamuni, the sage, watched from the sidelines as the youngsters waited for his nod, a silent signal for the match to begin.

Initiating the contest, Bhadraketu lunged forward, his arms reaching for Mithra in a classic grappling hold. He aimed to trap Mithra's head under his arm. But Mithra was too quick. Twisting like a coiled spring, he countered the move, his hands gripping Bhadraketu's wrists, redirecting his momentum. They tussled, a whirlwind of dust and straining muscles, each trying to outmanoeuvre the other. Mithra, his style unorthodox and unpredictable, proved a challenging opponent. Momentarily gaining the upper hand, Bhadraketu pressed his advantage, but Mithra had anticipated his move. Using Bhadraketu's momentum against him, Mithra executed a swift leg sweep, sending his opponent sprawling. In a flash, he was on top of Bhadraketu, pinning his shoulders to the ground. Bhadraketu bucked and twisted beneath him, but Mithra was firm. The crowd stood gaping breathlessly as the seconds passed. Then came the call—Mithra had held him down long enough. The match was his.

Cheers and applause echoed across the yard. Mithra, extending a hand, helped Bhadraketu to his feet.

'Well done, my friend,' Bhadraketu said, clapping Mithra on the shoulder, a broad smile lighting his face. 'But next time, victory will be mine.'

Mithra chuckled, wiping sweat from his brow. 'There are a few cheats I learned from Cornelius in Dimašq,' he admitted. 'Because you are my friend, I shall teach them to you in due course.' They walked off the field together, their easy camaraderie a testament to their growing bond—now strengthened further by their spirited contest.

∼

As the sun dipped below the horizon, painting the sky in shades of orange and gold, the four friends gathered beneath a sprawling banyan tree, seeking refuge from the lingering heat of the day. They sat in a circle, the silence around them broken not by solemn thoughts, but by laughter.

'Did you see the look on Master Vishoka's face when Soju dropped his staff mid-spin?' Mithra asked, a grin tugging at his lips.

Soju groaned. 'Do not remind me. I nearly impaled his sandal with the butt end. I will be scrubbing the training yard for a week.'

'You should consider it a meditative exercise,' Suriratna said, smirking. 'Sweeping with purpose builds character.'

Bhadraketu chuckled. 'And muscles. Which you will need, Suriratna, when I beat you in tomorrow's match.'

'Bold words for someone who just ate dirt,' Mithra quipped.

The laughter faded gradually into a comfortable quiet, the kind that only came from being with those who truly knew one another.

Soju, his gaze fixed on the horizon, broke the silence. 'We have all grown so much since we arrived,' he said softly.

Bhadraketu nodded, his expression serious. 'We have, indeed. We came from different lands, different cultures, seeking knowledge and understanding. But we have also found something far stronger—friendships that will endure even after we leave.'

Mithra was usually reticent about his past, so the others were surprised when he said, 'I once believed I was alone in the world—my father rarely had time for me in Dimašq. I spent my days in the company of his lieutenant, Cornelius, for the most part. But here, with you, I have found another home ... a family.'

Suriratna had been twirling a blade of grass between her fingers. She looked up. 'We should make a pact. No matter what the future holds, no matter where life takes us, we will stand together—as equals, as warriors, as friends,' she said.

Soju smiled. 'A pact among warriors bound not by land or lineage, but by the strength of our commitment to one another.' They placed their hands over each others' in the centre, four hands stacked, a symbol of unity. 'Together,' they said in unison.

As they stood up to return to their quarters, the pact sealed, a sense of profound connection settled upon them. Each of them knew with a certainty that transcended words that this moment—this alliance—would be forever etched in their hearts.

Suriratna's eyes shone with emotion as she looked at the others. 'We are stronger together,' she said, her voice filled with conviction. 'Let us promise to stay connected.' Little did she realize that the promise would be a difficult one to keep.

22

Gimhae, South Gyeongsang Province, South Korea

Present day

It was a challenge to fully comprehend the sheer scale of the world's largest steel plant. It was not merely a plant—it was an entire city. Spread over 5,000 acres, the sprawling complex was a microcosm of industrial and community life, with storage yards, furnaces, office blocks, steel mills, a power plant, a water treatment facility, a railway junction, a cargo pool, residential quarters, a school, a hospital and even recreational grounds.

This was Aditya's second visit to Gimhae since finalizing the joint venture with GISCO. The initial shock of the plant's immensity had faded, replaced by a grudging respect for the quiet efficiency of the colossal operation. He was astounded by the logistical brilliance that kept this enormous machine functioning flawlessly.

Aditya had spent the morning touring the raw materials area, a vast space filled with mountains of iron ore, coal, limestone and scrap metal. The subsequent visit to the blast furnace had been an immersive experience, the air rank with the smell of molten steel and burning coal. The raw, elemental energy of the site resonated within him, connecting him to the ancient art of metalworking, refined and perfected over centuries.

Despite the industrial earmuffs he had been handed, the noise was relentless, a cacophony of pounding metal, hissing steam and the roar of the furnaces. Without the muffs, the din would have been unbearable. Even the protective gear—the heavy helmet, safety goggles and steel-toed boots—felt inadequate against the sheer intensity of the environment. Employees scurried about like ants—a tireless, organized collective—navigating a labyrinth of ladders and catwalks. Massive conveyor belts transported tons of coal and iron ore towards the hungry maw of the furnaces. Overhead, gigantic cranes controlled by unseen hands moved heavy loads with balletic grace. *Our Angul plant seems insignificant in comparison*, thought Aditya, feeling dwarfed by the scale of the operation.

The plant's output was staggering—enough steel to build a small town each day. Yet, amidst the constant activity and the overwhelming noise, an underlying order prevailed. Aditya watched the workers, their movements precise and coordinated despite the oppressive heat and noise. He admired their tenacity and quiet mastery of this volatile world. Each worker, focused on the assigned tasks, moved with clockwork precision, a cog in a vast and complex machine. Observing the harmony achieved within this harsh, unforgiving environment, Aditya could not help but think of Dante's *Inferno*. There was a strange beauty, a zen-like quality, to the organized chaos—a testament to human ingenuity and perseverance.

Standing near the furnaces, their immense heat a palpable wave against his face, Aditya felt a sense of awe. Each one was the size of an apartment building and roared with an infernal energy. The molten steel within, glimpsed through narrow openings, glowed blindingly—like a miniature sun, its power mesmerizing. Huge ladles remotely operated by skilled workers moved gracefully, carrying the molten metal with synchronized efficiency.

They left the furnace area, moving towards the steelmaking section where molten iron was transformed into slabs, billets and blooms. Further on, at the rolling mill, these rough shapes were moulded into sheets, bars, rods and wire. The final stages—finishing, coating and rigorous quality control—ensured that each product met the highest standards.

After leaving the factory floor, Aditya and Somi boarded one of the many electric shuttles that ferried people around the complex. Back in the conference room, roasted barley tea, honey-ginger cookies and bottled water awaited them. The executives who had accompanied them on the tour took their leave and a comfortable silence descended. Relishing the respite from the noise and heat, Aditya gathered his thoughts, preparing for the discussion ahead. He glanced at Somi, who was reviewing her notes, her brows creased in concentration.

With a click of her remote, Somi launched her presentation. 'You require a substance that does not yet exist,' she stated matter-of-factly. 'As of now, the most advanced steelmakers—GISCO's competitors in China, Japan, India and the US—have failed to create any material even close to what you need.'

He felt a wave of disappointment. 'We'll find a way,' Somi said quickly, sensing his mood. She was determined to figure out a solution, to help him realize his vision.

Aditya could sense her confidence, the relish with which she embraced this seemingly impossible challenge. He had seen the same passion in her eyes during their dinner in Delhi. It had been a key factor in his decision to partner with her.

'Do you have any ... starting points?' Aditya asked, taking a gulp of water. His mind raced, searching for possibilities, clinging to a fragile thread of hope.

'Ultra-high molecular polyethylene fibre-reinforced steel might offer a solution,' Somi said, 'though we'll need to reimagine the heat treatment process entirely. Polyethylene fibres degrade under high temperatures, so traditional annealing or surface hardening will destroy the composite. We'll need a workaround. Perhaps cryo-processing or layered post-fabrication reinforcement. It's a long shot—but it's a start.'

'After all that, will it meet the DRDO's requirements?' Aditya asked, remembering the heated debates he had had with the DRDO officials, their exacting standards and the pressure of the looming deadline.

'One variant is already used for body armour and bulletproof vests,' Somi replied. 'The energy of impact is absorbed and dispersed by the fibres, preventing penetration. We need to find a way to magnify those qualities.' Her mind, he could see, was already strategizing, searching for potential enhancements.

'But ...? There's a problem, isn't there?' Aditya asked, recognizing the unspoken hesitation in her voice. He watched as her brows furrowed and her mind focused on some distant thought.

'The current iteration, while incredibly tough, is not invincible,' she conceded. 'I believe another variation exists—one with the capacity to resist penetration more effectively, perhaps even with the scope to consume the projectile itself.' She looked at him, her eyes filled with a quiet confidence. 'We simply need to discover it.'

'*Discover* it?' Aditya echoed, the word hanging between them—a challenge, an audacious promise.

'Yes,' Somi replied with a warm, reassuring smile. 'It's out there. We just need to find it.'

'But how?' Aditya asked, his eyes fixed on hers, seeking answers in their depths. The path ahead seemed cloaked in uncertainty, the goal distant and difficult to grasp.

'We have a little time,' Somi said softly. 'Come. There's a place I want to show you. Once you've seen it, you'll understand.' She paused, her gaze unwavering. 'Remember, sometimes, the solutions we seek in the present were first dreamed of in the past.'

23

Saketa, Kosala

Present-day Ayodhya, Uttar Pradesh, India

Around 2,000 years ago

The air in the dungeon reeked of mildew and the unmistakeable scent of rusting iron. Padmasen's cell, a cramped hole deep within the dungeon's bowels, was perpetually shrouded in darkness. Light rarely entered this desolate space and hope was an even rarer visitor.

Padmasen lay on a pallet of stinking hay, its rough texture scraping against his raw, wounded flesh. The frequent beatings he was subjected to meant that his body ached constantly. Each day bled into the next, the monotonous routine of abuse punctuated only by meagre meals—watery gruel that tasted of decay—delivered with a contemptuous shove or a muttered curse. Loneliness and suffocating stillness were his only companions—except, of course, for the agony that accompanied the frequent interrogations.

One particularly cold morning, as the familiar clang of keys announced the arrival of his paltry breakfast, a shift in the air, a subtle change in the guard's demeanour, sent an unexpected ripple of anticipation through the prisoner's chest. A new guard, a hulking figure silhouetted against the dim torchlight, stood at the cell door. His movements were measured, his steps deliberate.

He placed the tray on the floor, his touch surprisingly gentle. Instead of departing, he lingered. 'Padmasen ...' His voice was barely audible. 'Listen carefully. I have been sent by Kulasekara. We are going to get you out.'

Padmasen's heart skipped a beat. Hope, an emotion forgotten over nearly two years of confinement, weakly stirred within him. 'How?' he managed to say, his voice hoarse and weak from disuse.

'Not tonight,' the man whispered, his eyes darting nervously towards the entrance. 'Three days from now—on the night of the new moon. Be ready. I will come for you.'

'Why are you risking your life for me?' Padmasen asked, squinting to discern the guard's features in the dim light. He needed to understand the motivations of this unexpected saviour.

The guard's voice, though hushed, was firm. 'I am Somadatta. Years ago, at the Maha Maghamela, your brother-in-law offered me food when I was starving. You gave me an extra blanket when I was shivering in the cold. Your family showed me kindness when I desperately needed it. Without that, I would surely have perished. I owe you a debt—it is a karmic obligation.' With that, he turned and departed, his footsteps fading into the distance.

Padmasen, left alone in the silence, contemplated the guard's words. A simple act of compassion, a random gesture of kindness, so far back in the past that he hardly had any memory of it, had borne fruit in the most surprising way.

∼

The following days were a torment, each sound magnified, each sensation amplified within the confines of his cell. The incessant drip of water from the damp ceiling measured the passing of time, each drop a hammer blow against his frayed nerves. Rats scurried about, their beady eyes gleaming in the scant light. Every sound, every movement served as a reminder of his precarious position.

He pushed himself to eat the stale food, to exercise his cramped muscles within the limitations of his shackles. A whirlwind of possibilities and contingencies blew through his mind as he prepared for Somadatta's plan. When the time came, he would be ready.

The night of the new moon arrived; a night of impenetrable darkness. Padmasen waited, his heart pounding in his chest, his senses on high alert. Finally, he heard footsteps approaching—slow, deliberate. A key rattled in the lock; the heavy cell door creaked open.

'Are you ready?' Somadatta whispered as he unshackled Padmasen, his face barely visible in the faint glow of a tiny, hooded oil lamp.

'Yes,' Padmasen said, his voice trembling as he struggled to his feet.

Somadatta urged him forward. 'Quickly! We must make haste!'

Guided by the flickering lamp, they moved silently through the labyrinthine corridors. As they neared the exit, the oppressive stench of the dungeon gave way to the fragrant aroma of earth and jasmine, a reminder of the world beyond the dank walls. With each step, the air grew fresher, lighter. But anxiety, a constant companion, tightened Padmasen's chest.

Suddenly, a shout pierced the night. 'Halt! In the name of Raja Vidushika!' A squad of guards, swords drawn, emerged from the shadows, blocking their escape.

Somadatta reacted instantly, shoving Padmasen towards a narrow side passage. 'Go!' he hissed, drawing his sword. 'Follow the path to the Sarayu. A boatman waits. Give him this message: "Dharmo rakṣati rakṣitaḥ." Dharma protects those who protect it.'

Padmasen did not hesitate. He plunged into the darkness, his weakened legs driven by adrenaline, his lungs burning. He ran, his breath a ragged wheeze in his throat, until the sounds of pursuit faded and he reached the forest's edge. The cold night air filled his lungs as he paused and the weight of his escape settled upon him. He offered a silent prayer for Somadatta's safety and heartfelt thanks to Kulasekara, whose loyalty and courage had paved the way for this desperate flight.

Though the river was further ahead and the path forward remained uncertain and fraught with danger, Padmasen felt a wave of optimism. He had tasted freedom. He would survive. He would find his family. And he would continue to guard the sacred secret entrusted to him—the legacy of the Dvaitalingam.

In his veins ran fear, hope and fire—and, above all, purpose.

24

Gimhae, South Gyeongsang Province, South Korea
Present day

Aditya and Somi passed through the gates of the peaceful sanctuary, the tomb and pagoda rising before them. A board at the entrance proclaimed it to be the final resting place of Queen Heo Hwang-ok, the queen and consort of the king who had united ancient Korea's Garak Confederacy.

The board further detailed the queen's origins—a princess from the distant kingdom of Ayuta, sent by her parents on a divinely ordained mission to marry a prince of Geumgwan in Garak. In 48 CE, she had travelled across the sea, arriving in the Garak Confederacy to wed the prince. The union, blessed by the heavens, produced ten sons and two daughters.

'It is said that six million Koreans are descended from the royal couple,' Somi explained, her voice tinged with reverence. 'That includes the Gimhae Kim, Gimhae Heo and Incheon Lee clans—some of the most prominent families in Korea.'

When he finished reading the inscription, Aditya turned to Somi. 'It's hard to imagine what would compel a princess to undertake such a long and arduous journey two thousand years ago,' he mused, his mind struggling to grasp the magnitude of such an undertaking—a voyage of more than 4,300 nautical miles at a time when few dared to venture so far from home.

'Perhaps ... love,' Somi offered, her eyes reflecting an unwavering belief in the timeless power of that emotion.

'Love can certainly be a motivator,' Aditya conceded—thoughts of Lakshmi, his beloved wife, surfacing. 'But to embark on such a crossing to marry a complete stranger? There's something ... unusual about that.' He recalled his marriage to Lakshmi—an arranged union, yet one preceded by a year of courtship, a time for them to discover each other, to nurture their connection. 'How could Queen Heo have summoned the courage, the faith to commit to such a leap of faith?'

'Perhaps the Indian princess was tougher than we give her credit for,' Somi said. 'Shall we?'

They followed a cobblestone path, arriving at a grassy mound enclosed by a low stone wall. The mound itself was unremarkable—16 feet high and 50 feet in circumference—but the air here hummed with a palpable tranquillity. It was a sanctuary, removed from the relentless clang and heat of GISCO's furnaces. The breeze felt fresh and clean, scented with dew and wildflowers, the gentle rustling of leaves mingling with the distant songs of birds and the soft buzzing of insects. Time seemed to slow down, past and present existing side-by-side in harmonious balance. Aditya felt the serenity seep into his bones. He glanced at Somi, who seemed equally captivated by the sanctuary's quiet beauty.

A gazebo with an ornate roof stood beside the mound. Inside, a stack of rough-hewn stones arranged in six tiers formed a curious structure. A nearby placard identified it as the Pasa Stone Pagoda, built, according to local legend, with 'heavenly stones' brought by the princess to calm the turbulent seas during her voyage to Korea.

Ballast stones, Aditya thought, recalling his mother's tales of ancient seafaring. He knew that skilled mariners often used large stones to stabilize their vessels. 'Do you think this is a genuine historical account?' he asked Somi. 'Or is it just a fanciful tale?'

'It depends on the location of Ayuta,' Somi replied. 'Was it Rama's city of Ayodhya? Or perhaps a region in south India, like Kanyakumari, which was also called Ayuta? Or could it be the Ayutthaya kingdom of Thailand?' Her voice, laced with intellectual curiosity, hinted at a love of history, a fascination with its unsolved mysteries.

'What do you think?' Aditya asked, genuinely intrigued.

Somi smiled. 'Do you know the Korean words for "father", "mother" and "sister"?' Without waiting for his answer, she said, 'Appa, amma and anni.'

'You're kidding!' Aditya exclaimed, astonishment lighting his features. 'Are they really the same as the Tamil words?'

'There are remarkable similarities between the two languages,' Somi explained. 'Over two thousand words sound alike and share similar meanings. For instance, both Korean and Tamil use the word "pul" for grass. The word for day is "naal" in both languages. And both use "onnu" for one.'

'Amazing,' Aditya said, his excitement growing. 'So … the princess must have come from southern India?' He was captivated by the linguistic connection, the possibility of tracing the journey of language and culture across vast stretches of time.

'Not necessarily,' Somi countered. 'These linguistic overlaps could also be attributed to ancient trade routes, the cultural exchange that flowed between the Chera, Chola, Pandya and Pallava kingdoms of southern India—and China and Southeast Asia. History is rarely straightforward. These relationships were often complex, multifaceted.'

'Are there any other clues that might help pinpoint her origins?' Aditya asked, eager to delve deeper into the mystery.

'There's another tomb nearby,' Somi said. 'King Suro's final resting place. His tomb is marked with his royal insignia. Do you recall what symbol he used?'

Aditya shook his head, admitting ignorance.

Somi quickly pulled up a picture on her phone. 'A twin-fish symbol,' she said, pointing to the image. 'The sangeomun. Does that motif seem familiar?'

Aditya's eyes widened in recognition. 'It's the same symbol we saw at the Queen Heo Memorial Park in Ayodhya.' The connection, tenuous at first, solidified in his mind.

'Exactly,' Somi said. 'The twin-fish emblem adorns several historic royal buildings in Ayodhya. It's certainly plausible that the symbol travelled from India to Korea. But do you know what Suro was often called?'

'What?'

'The Iron King,' replied Somi. 'Do you now understand why we need to examine the past?'

Aditya nodded as he contemplated the long journey of symbols and stories across the centuries. He felt a strange connection to this place, a sense of the past reaching out and intertwining with the present. The sanctuary's serene beauty, its quiet energy, filled him with a sense of gratitude.

He offered a silent prayer, seeking guidance.

Two dancing fish, tangled in the sea.
Swaying in the current, wild and free.

25

Goryeong, Garak Confederacy
Present-day Sangju City, South Korea
Around 2,000 years ago

The Seongsan army's encampment hummed with anticipation. Campfires burned low, their light barely reaching the edges of tents as the men silently readied for battle. Talhae, though young in years, sat with the demeanour of a seasoned warrior, meticulously polishing a sword once wielded by a fallen commander of Seongsan. It had been passed down to him by his father, Jangsu—a symbol of trust, and perhaps of possession. Though Talhae had not yet led men into any major conflicts, the sword, now reborn in his younger, hungrier hands, bore the memories of blood and war.

He wore a jeogori, its layers of fabric offering a semblance of protection. A sleeveless, quilted vest gave him extra defence against strikes. His baji pants were cinched tight, allowing for ease of movement. His boots—scuffed, creased, disciplined—were built for the long march, not glory. At his waist hung the sword, its jewel-encrusted hilt gleaming under torchlight.

It had been three years since he had first sparred with his mentor, Hwan. Sixteen now, Talhae had grown into an imposing figure—tall and lean, his body honed by tireless drills and border skirmishes with factions loyal to Goryeong. His bronze skin bore the marks of blade and toil, but it was his eyes that had changed most. The warmth was gone, replaced by something harder. A cold, calculating fury burned within—an inheritance not of blood, but of betrayal.

He had loved Hwan—his teacher, his compass, the only man in Seongsan who had ever spoken to him with unfiltered honesty. But that bond had been cruelly severed. Jangsu had ordered Hwan's execution, branding him a traitor for questioning the path laid out for Talhae. With that Talhae had lost his last protector.

Talhae had learned the lesson well. Affection made one vulnerable. Attachment was weakness. In the years since, he had buried his grief beneath layers of discipline and disdain. While Soju, away in distant Agastyamalai, flourished with the warmth of camaraderie and acclaim, Talhae sank deeper into isolation, the wounds of his youth calcifying into cruelty. He would not be forgotten, he would not be overlooked again.

'Tomorrow, we march.' Jangsu's voice, deep and resonant, rolled through the camp. Clad in iron and leather, the chieftain radiated conviction. 'We shall reclaim our destiny from Goryeong,' he said. 'We shall be the strongest pillar of this fractured Garak Confederacy.'

The Garak Confederacy—once a promising union of allied clans—had long since splintered into bickering strongholds, each led by chiefs claiming the right to autonomy. Goryeong, a rival clan to the north, had recently allied itself with traders from the coast and begun consolidating power—challenging Seongsan's influence in the region. For Jangsu, this campaign was more than retaliation; it was reclamation. His divine mandate. He saw himself as the rightful heir to the mantle of Garak's unifier.

A murmur of agreement scattered through the ranks. But Talhae stood apart. His reserve spoke not of fear, but of purpose. Of a boy who had been shaped into a weapon.

Across the firelight, Jangsu met his gaze and gave a slow, deliberate nod. Talhae returned it—impassive, unreadable. His wait had finally ended.

∼

As darkness fell, cloaking the encampment in a tense silence, Talhae, the designated leader for the immediate assignment, moved through the shadows, a phantom among the tents. He had gathered a small band of men, chosen for their loyalty and their capacity for stealth. They melted into the night, guided only by the pale glow of the moon. Talhae's every step was purposeful, his every action designed to inflict maximum damage. A cruel smile tugged at the corners of his lips.

They approached Goryeong's outskirts, their movements swift and noiseless. Up ahead, a solitary farmer was guiding his cattle back to the village, unaware of the peril lurking just beyond sight. Talhae and his men surrounded him, cutting off his escape.

'Spare me! I beg of you ...' the farmer pleaded, falling to his knees, his face contorted with terror as he looked up at the circle of grim warriors.

Talhae stood before him, his sword gleaming in the moonlight. 'Help us,' he said, his voice deceptively calm, 'and you will live. Betray us and you will be flayed alive.' He traced the tip of his blade across the farmer's cheek, a chilling reminder of his promise.

The farmer nodded mutely, fear rendering him speechless.

'You travel in and out of the walled city. There must be a way to enter—one that avoids the main gate.' Talhae's voice, though soft, held an undeniable threat.

After a few moments, the farmer, his lips trembling from fraught nerves, pointed towards the hills that lay between them and the city. 'There is an old path, long forgotten,' he whispered. 'Used by shaman monks in ancient times. It leads to a weak section of the wall that is rarely guarded.'

Talhae smiled, his eyes shining in triumph. 'Show us,' he commanded.

Guided by the terrified farmer, they navigated the winding path through the hills, their soft footsteps barely discernible even in the stillness of the night. As they approached the city walls, a dark gap in the ancient stone became visible. Talhae sent one of his men racing back to the camp to inform his father.

Gradually, the sky began to lighten, casting a pale silver hue over the slopes. A faint glow crept across the horizon, revealing the jagged silhouette of Goryeong's ramparts. Then, with a suddenness that stole the breath, the heavens ignited—streaked with copper and rose, heralding the day. As dawn spilled over the battlements, Jangsu's warriors surged forward, launching a fierce assault on the main gate. It was a calculated feint, meant to pull any defenders away from the gap. The silence shattered, metal clashed, war cries rang out and the battle roared to life.

Meanwhile, Talhae and his men, stealthy as shadows, sneaked in through the opening, and disappeared into the maze of narrow streets within. Talhae had divided his men into smaller units, each with a specific target. He led his own group towards the palace, eliminating any guards they encountered with ruthless efficiency. As they approached the palace gates, a rush of anticipation coursed through him. He ordered his men to fan out, securing all exits. Then, sword drawn, he led the charge inside. The palace guards, taken by surprise, fell swiftly to the onslaught.

The chief of Goryeong stood in the magnificent hall, surrounded by his terrified advisors. Talhae strode towards him, his presence filling the space, his gaze cold and unwavering. 'Your reign ends now,' he declared, his voice echoing against the stone walls.

~

The success of the carefully orchestrated attack shattered the already fragile unity of the Garak Confederacy. By virtue of the cunning and ruthlessness of Jangsu and Talhae, Seongsan was now its most powerful member.

Exhausted and exhilarated all at once, Talhae stood atop the palace walls, gazing at the conquered city. Jangsu approached him and, placing a hand on his shoulder, said proudly, 'You have done well, my son. You have secured our future.' His face hardened. 'Now we shall devour the rest of the Confederacy, piece by piece.'

'This is merely the beginning,' Talhae replied, his eyes burning with ambition. 'Our destiny is far greater than this.'

As the setting sun bathed Goryeong in a golden light, casting long shadows across the ravaged city, word of its fall reached Seongsan, setting off a wave of jubilation. But in distant Geumgwan, Kim Seok received the news with a heavy heart. While grateful that he had sent Soju away, he also knew, with a chilling certainty, that war—one that would engulf the entire peninsula—was now inevitable.

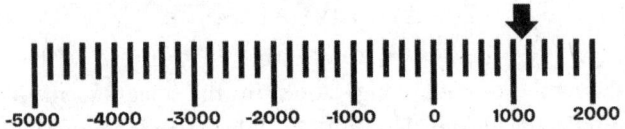

Karnei Hattin, Kingdom of Jerusalem
Present-day Horns of Hattin, Israel
Around 900 years ago

From his vantage point atop the hill, Sultan Saladin surveyed the parched plains below. The Crusader army was encamped near Karnei Hattin, their banners fluttering in the dry wind. The atmosphere at the summit was stiff with anticipation, thick with the charged stillness that precedes a storm. Below, the heavily armoured Crusader knights and weary footmen shifted restlessly in the brutal sun and an unforgiving heat they were ill-equipped to endure. To the sultan, they looked like pawns scattered across a scorched board, preparing for a battle they did not yet realize they had already lost.

Saladin's voice was low, measured, yet laced with fervour as he turned to his trusted commander and said, 'Their hubris will be their undoing.' His eyes closed briefly. 'The desert is our ally. We strike tonight.'

The Crusades—the Holy Wars—launched by Pope Urban II, represented the ultimate test—a clash of civilizations, a bloody struggle for dominance between Christianity and Islam. They had a singular purpose: to reclaim Jerusalem and other sacred sites in the Holy Land that had fallen under Muslim control. The Crusaders were a diverse lot: seasoned soldiers, ambitious noblemen, devout clergymen, farmers seeking a better life and skilled artisans. All were driven by religious zeal, fuelled by the promise of eternal salvation and the lure of riches.

Saladin's commander, a veteran who had served his master for many years, was familiar with the sultan's reputation as a cunning tactician, a leader respected even by his enemies. He stood next to Saladin, eagerly waiting for a brilliant strategy to unfold. 'The archers are ready, My Lord,' he said, a confident smile stretching his lips. 'They await your command.'

With the sun's retreat, a dusky veil settled over the land, accompanied by the persistent whisper of movement from the Crusader encampment below. Understanding the debilitating effects of thirst, Saladin moved his troops into position, surrounding the enemy and cutting them off from the vital spring that was their sole source of water.

The heavy armour of the Crusaders, which offered protection on the battlefields of Europe, was fast becoming a liability under the relentless desert sun. Each man wore a tunic emblazoned with a cross—a symbol of their sacred mission—over chainmail and a padded surcoat. But here, in the arid furnace of Hattin, the weight of their gear became suffocating. Sweat pooled beneath helmets. Blisters appeared on scorched lips. Soldiers clutched at their cracked throats as though that might soothe the burning within. Horses stumbled from exhaustion, their flanks heaving. The Crusaders' canteens had long run dry and Saladin had denied them access to the springs, blocking their only sources of water.

'Patience, my brothers,' Saladin had instructed his men. 'Let the desert weaken them. Let thirst and heat become our allies.'

The first wave of arrows whistled through the air and rained down upon the parched and weary Crusaders. Caught off guard, they scrambled for cover, their shields—designed for close combat—barely effective against the relentless barrage. Arrows blackened the sky like a swarm of deadly insects, their razor-sharp tips hunting for gaps in the Crusaders' armour. Dehydrated and disoriented, the soldiers faltered. Coordination dissolved. Horses reared and bucked.

Saladin watched with satisfaction as the enemy's once-impenetrable formation began to crumble—broken not just by iron, but by the desert itself.

His horsemen, wielding Damascus swords forged with meticulous care, were a formidable force. Each blade, its surface rippling with a distinctive watery pattern, bore an emblem—four crossed swords etched near the hilt—a mark of their exceptional quality.

These swords, crafted in Dimašq from the legendary wootz ore of India, were renowned for their strength and sharpness. They were more than weapons—they were symbols of Saladin's might, instruments of Allah's will.

Sensing the enemy's weakening resolve, Saladin raised his hand—a silent signal. The noose tightened with his archers increasing their tempo, forcing the exhausted Crusaders into a desperate, last-ditch attempt to break through his lines. They were met with an unyielding wall of iron. Turning to his commander, Saladin said, 'The time has come. Unleash the cavalry.'

The order, relayed swiftly down the ranks, was met with a roar of approval. Saladin's riders, their hooves pounding down on the parched earth, thundered towards the enemy. The sound of their approach, like a gathering storm, was soon drowned out by the clang of metal against metal, the screams of the wounded, the cries of the dying.

Saladin, at the head of his troops, charged into the heart of the battle. His sword flashed, a deadly silver arc against the dust-filled air. He locked eyes with a weary Crusader knight—a man whose courage was undeniable, but whose strength was waning. The knight swung his broadsword, but Saladin blocked the blow effortlessly, his sword, a whisper of death, slicing through the knight's armour, shattering his blade. With a final, merciful thrust, Saladin ended the man's suffering.

All around him, the tide of battle had turned. The Crusaders, their formations broken, their spirits crushed, were falling back in disarray. Saladin's eyes searched the battlefield and spotted King Guy of Lusignan surrounded by his remaining guard. He urged his horse forward, pushing through the throng of desperate men. He could sense Guy's exhaustion, his thirst, the weight of his armour dragging him down. 'Your campaign ends now, King,' Saladin declared, his voice carrying over the din of battle. 'Surrender, and Allah may yet show you mercy.'

Guy, his chest heaving, his face pale with fatigue, roared in defiance. He rushed forward, but his movements, sluggish and ill-timed, were easily countered. Saladin's sword flashed once more, disarming Guy, sending his weapon to the ground. 'Surrender,' he commanded, the point of his blade resting lightly against the king's throat.

The Crusaders had marched into the Holy Land with an air of divine entitlement. Cloaked in the righteousness of their cause, they believed their victories were preordained—sanctioned by God and history. Their banners bore the cross, but their eyes gleamed with conquest. However, they had underestimated the terrain, their enemy and the cost of arrogance. Saladin had watched their manoeuvres for weeks, noting how they pressed forward without caution, how they dismissed local warnings, how they believed sheer will could bend the desert to their purpose.

Now, the sands told another story.

As Saladin fixed him with an unyielding expression, King Guy's defiance began to crack. The heat, the thirst, the relentless assault—they had broken through his pride like water eroding stone. He sank to his knees, a gesture of surrender. Around him, the remaining Crusaders—witnessing their leader's collapse—threw down their weapons, yielding en masse.

Raising his hand, Saladin signalled for the fighting to cease. A heavy silence settled over the battlefield. Dust hung in the air like the breath of the fallen. He gazed at the once-mighty king, his eyes brimming with both pity and respect.

'You fought well,' he said, lowering his sword. 'But pride ... pride was your downfall. You thought the land would yield because your God willed it. But the desert does not kneel to arrogance.'

Then he turned to face his men, raising his blade high, its metal catching the light like a beacon. 'Today, we have proven our resolve,' he thundered. 'The Christians coveted our symbol. But the fish—and the sword—are ours. And Jerusalem? She will follow!'

26

Geneva, Switzerland
Present day

The CERN hallways were always abuzz with scientific discoveries. Among CERN's most respected researchers was Chennai-born physicist Dr Bala Ramaswamy. His landmark study, *Forgotten Science of the Vedic Age*, was inspired by his visits to historic locations like Kailasa. Colleagues intercepted Ramaswamy as he navigated CERN's corridors, seeking his opinion on varied subjects, aware that his viewpoint was priceless.

Books, research papers, equipment and historic texts vied for space in his office. Modern equipment buzzed in the background. Ramaswamy stood before a camera setup in the heart of his laboratory. The red recording light blinked steadily as he adjusted the focus. 'Good afternoon,' he began, his calm, authoritative voice projecting a sense of confidence to the remote audience in science laboratories around the world. Within the laboratory, around ten chairs were occupied by local scientists.

'Today, we are exploring the fascinating properties of a substance hypothesized to act as a catalyst for both attraction and repulsion at the quantum level. This material—referred to in ancient Indian texts by various names—exhibits unique characteristics that could influence quantum interactions. We have recovered trace elements of this substance from rock surfaces at Kailasa. Similar traces have been found at Konark, Angkor, Petra—and even in swords from Damascus.'

He moved to a bench where a complex apparatus had been assembled. 'Here we have a sample extracted from the stone at Kailasa. We're attempting to measure its impact on quantum entanglement and superposition states.' Ramaswamy carefully placed the sample in the cryostat and began cooling it till it reached absolute zero. 'Lowering the temperature minimizes thermal noise, allowing quantum effects to dominate. The superconducting magnet will generate a controlled magnetic field and our sensors will capture any changes in the quantum state of entangled particles.'

He glanced at the camera. 'Our hypothesis is that this substance can modulate the gauge fields, influence the coupling constants and effectively alter particle interaction strength.'

As the apparatus hummed to life, a series of images and data streams appeared on the computer screen.

'We are monitoring the behaviour of qubits within this magnetic field,' Ramaswamy explained. Then, with a small grin, he added, 'Qubits are the basic units of quantum information—think of them as bits that can be in two states at once. Simply put, they're like coins spinning in the air, rather than just lying flat with heads or tails revealed.'

He manipulated the controls, his attention fixed on the real-time data. 'Any significant deviation in their entanglement or coherence times will indicate catalytic properties.' He paused, then glanced at the camera. 'What I mean to say is ... if the qubits start behaving differently—like dancing better together or staying in sync longer—it means the compound is doing something powerful.'

'Our initial findings suggest that the compound enhances entanglement entropy, producing a more robust quantum state,' he said. Then added, almost reflexively, 'In other words, the system's becoming more complex—but also more stable. It's like upgrading from a solo flute to a full orchestra where every instrument plays in perfect harmony, even across great distances.'

A frown creased his forehead. 'Ancient Indian texts offer tantalizing glimpses into early scientific thought—thought that is remarkably advanced for its time. It's hardly surprising that the likes of Niels Bohr and Erwin Schrödinger found inspiration in the Upanishads.'

Warming to the theme, he continued, 'Frankly, these texts could hold the key to understanding many of the architectural and engineering wonders of ancient India.' He chuckled softly. 'Simply put, maybe our ancestors were messing with quantum coherence long before we had the language to describe it.'

'We are on the brink of a breakthrough,' he concluded. 'If we can harness the properties of this substance, we could unlock new pathways in our understanding of the quantum world—bridging the gap between ancient knowledge and modern science.'

As he ended his lecture and walked to his desk, his mind lingered on the intricate Sanskrit verses he had studied. These texts spoke of materials and technologies far beyond their time—lost knowledge he was now striving to bring back to life. The laboratory, usually bustling with activity, gradually emptied as the other researchers departed for the evening. Hours later, Ramaswamy, was still engrossed in his work, oblivious to the growing silence in the building.

∼

A sleek black van pulled up outside the CERN facility. Inside sat Reza, Khalil Ghaznawar's agent, his dark eyes focused on the entrance of the building. He checked his watch, his every movement radiating menace. His mission was clear. 'We're in position,' a voice crackled through his earpiece. 'Security systems are compromised. You have ten minutes.'

'Understood,' Reza replied.

He exited the van with his team of operatives, disguised as maintenance workers, following close behind. Hours of meticulous planning had led to this moment. They moved like clockwork, their pre-programmed biometrics granting them access.

Inside his lab, Ramaswamy glanced at his watch and sighed, rubbing his tired eyes. He was about to pack up when the door suddenly swung open. He looked up, startled, into the faces of Reza and his men. 'Can I help you?' he asked, apprehension twisting in his gut.

Reza smiled thinly, stepping forward. 'Dr Ramaswamy,' he said, his voice smooth, 'we need you to accompany us.'

Before Ramaswamy could respond, his eyes fell on the silenced handgun in Reza's hand. 'No sudden movements, Doctor,' Reza said, his voice soft yet intimidating. 'None of us want ... complications.'

Heart pounding, Ramaswamy raised his hands in surrender. 'What is it you want?'

'You,' Reza replied plainly. 'And your immense knowledge.' His men moved swiftly, binding Ramaswamy's wrists, covering his head with a hood.

Ramaswamy's world went dark.

They walked quickly, avoiding the sections of the building where the few remaining employees worked. Within minutes, they were gone, exiting unnoticed through a side door. The waiting van sped away, swallowed by the night.

They headed through deserted streets towards a remote safe house nestled in the peaceful suburb of Chêne-Bougeries. Ramaswamy, trapped within the suffocating darkness of the hood, battled his fear, his mind a whirlwind of conflicting thoughts. His work—his lifelong pursuit of knowledge—had always felt worthwhile, but now a chilling realization dawned.

It had also attracted the wrong kind of attention.

~

The van screeched to a halt, its sudden silence amplifying the throbbing in Ramaswamy's head. As he was dragged out, he stumbled on loose gravel. When the hood was removed, he found himself facing a secluded villa, its windows dark, no signs of life within it. Reza, his grip tight on Ramaswamy's arm, propelled him forward.

The interior of the villa was just as forbidding, its bare walls and sparse furniture further heightening the sense of isolation, of impending danger. Ramaswamy was shoved into a chair, his wrists roughly unbound. He rubbed his chafed skin, scanning the room, searching for escape routes. There seemed to be none.

Unnervingly still, Reza studied him, like a predator assessing its prey. 'Dr Ramaswamy,' he said, his voice flat, devoid of emotion, 'your research ... it has piqued my employer's interest.'

Ramaswamy, stalling for time, said, 'You have no idea what you're meddling with. My work is dangerous. If applied incorrectly, it could be disastrous.'

'Cooperate, Doctor,' Reza said, eyes cold. 'Or I could be disastrous for you.'

His thin smile promised pain.

27

Agastyamalai, Pandya Desam
Present-day Agasthyamala Biosphere Reserve, Kerala, India
Around 2,000 years ago

The forest was alive, the gentle breeze carrying the sounds of nature—birdsong mingling with the rustling of leaves. In a sun-dappled clearing, beneath the sheltering canopy of trees, several children sat in a semicircle, their gazes fixed on their teacher.

Satyamuni, the venerable sage, his beard as white as the Himalayan snow, sat upon a raised platform, a palm-leaf manuscript open before him. The *Arthashastra*—an ancient treatise on statecraft, law and economics—was his text for the day's lesson. His strong voice carried across the open space.

'Listen carefully, children,' he began. 'Today we explore the duties of a king as outlined by Kautilya in the *Arthashastra*. A true king, it is said, must be wise, just and ever vigilant.' His keen eyes, sharp and knowing, scanned the young faces before him.

'Rājadharmeṇa dharmajñaḥ, nītijñaḥ vinayānvitaḥ,' he intoned, reciting a Sanskrit verse from the ancient text. The children repeated the verse, their voices blending harmoniously with the sounds of the forest, eyes closed in concentration as they recited each memorized word perfectly.

'A king must be learned in his responsibilities, grounded in ethics and possess humility,' Satyamuni explained.

The Ayodhya Alliance

Suriratna, seated cross-legged, her brow furrowed in thought, raised her hand. 'Acharya, these are noble qualities. But what, specifically, are the duties of a ruler?' Her thirst for knowledge was evident, her mind eager to absorb his teachings.

Satyamuni smiled, his eyes twinkling. 'A ruler must ensure the prosperity of his kingdom, maintain law and order and protect his subjects from external threats, always promoting ethical governance.' He paused, looking around the group of students. 'He must be a master of diplomacy, skilled in negotiation, a builder of alliances. He must strive to balance power with righteousness.'

Suriratna imagined a wise king presiding over bustling markets and peaceful villages. Bhadraketu, who had been listening with attention, frowned. 'Acharya,' he asked, 'if a king wields so much power, how can he resist the temptation of tyranny? Does absolute power inevitably corrupt?'

'That, my son, is why the *Arthashastra* emphasizes the importance of self-discipline—and wise counsel,' Satyamuni replied. 'A king must surround himself with advisors who are unafraid to speak the truth no matter how unpleasant it may be. Remember, one wheel alone cannot move a chariot.' He then guided the children through another verse.

'Aprāptāni ca kāryāṇi, prāpyāṇi ca viśeṣataḥ, kartavyāni manuṣyaiś ca, bhidyante rakṣaṇena vā,' he chanted, and proceeded to explain. 'Tasks not yet achieved—especially those within reach—should be entrusted to men who are loyal, protected from dissent.'

Mithra, sitting upright, said, 'In my homeland, it is the Romans who choose the ruler. When there was trouble in Dimašq, the most powerful trader in the city—a Nabataean merchant called Barakat—accused my father of being a Roman puppet. What are the qualities of someone appointed to rule?'

'The power of a king—inherited, elected, appointed or anointed—is irrelevant,' Satyamuni replied. 'A true king upholds justice, regardless of the status of those involved. He must lead by example, demonstrating that no one is above the law—not even the king himself. This is especially important when a ruler is perceived as an outsider, an appointee.'

A lively debate erupted, the youngsters' faces animated as they engaged in a spirited exchange of ideas. Bhadraketu argued passionately for a compassionate ruler, one who prioritized the welfare of the underprivileged. Suriratna, however, countered that while compassion was essential, in times of conflict, strength and decisiveness were paramount.

Satyamuni, listening with a smile, occasionally interjected, guiding their thoughts, nurturing their understanding. Their voices, echoing through the clearing, showcased a rich array of ideas—a vivid demonstration of the diversity within the gurukul.

'Remember, children,' Satyamuni said, gentle yet firm, 'some of you may become rulers, while others will become merchants, monks, scholars, or warriors. The path to power is fraught with challenges. But our texts offer guidance, they show the way.'

As the lesson concluded, Satyamuni shared a final thought. 'Whether you become advisors or rulers, carry these lessons with you, and you will find your way.' His words lingered in their minds long after he had uttered them.

Suriratna, rolling up her straw mat, glanced at her companions. 'A wise king,' she mused, 'should rule like a skilled gardener—tending his kingdom with care, nurturing its growth.'

'But even a gardener,' Mithra countered, 'must know when to prune, to cut away that which prevents the garden from flourishing.'

As they walked towards their dormitory, Satyamuni's voice called out, halting their progress. 'Remember, children,' he cautioned, his tone grave, 'even the wisest ruler must be ever vigilant. The darkness conceals unseen dangers. Be alert. Your journey has just begun.'

The youngsters exchanged nervous glances, the weight of his words settling upon them. They continued walking, their youthful energy tempered by a newfound awareness that their path in life would be paved with challenges.

The forest, silent and watchful, seemed to envelop them, a guardian of their dreams and a silent witness to their journey. The leaves whispered secrets as they walked away, unaware that the next test awaiting them would not be from any text, but in the shadows that stretched from Saketa to Korkai.

28

Korkai, Thamirabarani, Pandya Desam
Present-day Thoothukudi District, Tamil Nadu, India
Around 2,000 years ago

As the sun dipped below the horizon, the Thamirabarani river shimmered in the golden light. The gentle lap of waves against the hull of the sturdy Pandyan vessel marked the evening's rhythm. Onboard, Padmasen, weary yet alert, scanned his surroundings. His once muscular frame was marked by dark bruises, and his wrists were raw and chafed from the relentless bite of shackles. After escaping from Saketa's karagara, the boat had become his sanctuary, a fragile promise of hope against the torment he had left behind.

The journey to Korkai had begun at a small riverine port on the Sarayu. The boatman—a trusted friend of his liberator, Somadatta—had navigated the winding waterways, past serene villages and dense forests until the river had broadened dramatically at the confluence with the holy Ganga, its waters a lifeline to several kingdoms. Though the onward journey had been perilous, the boatman had expertly negotiated treacherous currents and bustling river towns. As they ventured eastward, hours melting into days, the landscape had shifted from fertile plains to the edge of the sprawling delta.

At the busy port of Tamralipta, under a shroud of secrecy, Padmasen had been transferred to a Pandyan seafaring vessel bound for the southern kingdom.

One day merged into the next, until weeks had passed. Though the vastness of the ocean seemed daunting, hope filled Padmasen's lungs with each breath of salty air as the vessel rode the waves. Each night, under the expanse of the starry sky, he wondered if he would ever see Indumati and his children again. Rationed food and water made the days and nights long and demanding, but the thought of his family sustained him.

Eventually, land appeared on the horizon—the lively harbour of Korkai. Children frolicked at the water's edge, merchants bartered with patrons and fishermen hauled in their catch. Laughter and the vibrant symphony of life mingled with the distant cries of gulls. Mustering his remaining strength, Padmasen sat up, his heart pounding. He searched the faces on the shore, desperate for a glimpse of the family he yearned for. As the captain steered the ship towards the port, Kulasekara's informants spotted its occupant and immediately sent word to the house only a few yards away from the harbour.

Indumati ran out from the house into the harbour. Her eyes widened in disbelief, her hand trembling as it flew to her mouth. Padmasen, though battered and weary, was home! As the vessel grazed the dock, he struggled to his feet. His legs nearly gave way when he stepped onto solid ground, but Kulasekara's strong arms caught him just in time. Indumati embraced him fiercely, tears of relief streaming down her face.

'My love,' she whispered, overcome with emotion. 'You are home at last.'

Padmasen clung to her, drawing strength from her presence. 'By the gods, Indumati ... I missed you every single day.'

Then, as if her touch had unlocked something held too long behind a dam, his breath hitched. A sob escaped—raw, involuntary. His shoulders began to shake, and he collapsed into her arms, the weight of years of vigilance, pain and fighting for survival crashing through the armour he had so carefully worked to keep intact.

Indumati held him tighter, her hand cradling the back of his head as he wept into her shoulder. 'You do not have to be strong now,' she said softly. 'You are safe. You are home.'

She pulled back slightly, her eyes sweeping over his battered form, taking in his injuries. 'You are hurt. We must get you inside.'

'The hope of seeing you again, seeing our children, kept me going,' Padmasen replied, his voice trembling with gratitude. 'That, and Kulasekara's help. Where are Suriratna and Bhadraketu?'

'At a gurukul some days' journey from here,' explained Indumati. 'They are safe, my love. Have no fear.'

Kulasekara and Indumati led him to their home, the grandest house on the harbour, always alive with activity. The aromas of spices and the warmth of the hearth greeted him like a cherished embrace. Indumati's mother guided him to a seat with a touch that was both gentle and firm. Vishnupriya hurried to fetch cool water and fresh bandages for his wounds.

'You have come back to us,' Kulasekara said, his voice cracking with emotion. 'We feared the worst.'

'Tell us everything,' Indumati urged, her fingers working deftly as she cleaned his cuts and bruises. 'How did you escape?'

Padmasen winced but began to recount his harrowing tale. 'I barely did. The guards were close, but I managed to evade them and reach the river, thanks to Somadatta—Kulasekara's friend. The boat was waiting, just as promised. It was frightening, facing those unpredictable waters, but here I am.'

Kulasekara, who had been listening intently, said, 'What matters now is that you are here. You will be guarded, Padmasen. We will keep you safe.'

Vishnupriya offered Padmasen a steaming bowl of fragrant rasam. Her brow creased with worry as she said. 'You must be famished. Please, eat. You need to regain your strength.'

As he ate, a feeling of contentment settled over Padmasen. After the turmoil and peril of his escape, the loving presence of Indumati and her family and the taste of homecooked food anchored him.

'We were so worried,' Indumati confessed. 'Each hour, I beseeched Harihara for your safe return.'

Padmasen reached for her hand, his touch reassuring. 'Your prayers guided me back. It was your love, along with the blessings of Harihara, that brought me home.'

The evening deepened. Above them, the stars twinkled, bearing witness to Padmasen's return and the start of a new chapter in Korkai. But in the heart of his relief, unease lingered. The journey back had been risky, the dangers he had narrowly escaped were still a threat. Vigilance was paramount.

'We must be cautious,' he said gravely, his eyes meeting Kulasekara's. 'Vidushika and Kadphises will not be easily deterred. We need to be prepared for whatever comes. Tell me, have you found a secure location for the Dvaitalingam?'

29

Dimašq, Roman Empire
Present-day Damascus, Syria
Around 2,000 years ago

The moon, yet to rise fully above Dimašq, cast long shadows over the ancient city's cobblestone lanes. A secret gathering of men was in progress in a courtyard, hidden from the eyes of Roman soldiers. Sitting at the head of the table, Barakat wore a grim expression that reflected the gravity of the situation, the burden of his people's dreams—and their fears.

'We cannot endure this any longer,' he began, his voice harsh, commanding authority. 'The taxes imposed by Rome are crippling our businesses. The governor's Roman masters have reneged on the promises made years ago. Our people starve while the Romans grow fat from our toil. The work on the treasury in Raqmu has stopped because Nabataean merchants like me have no coin left to send home. There is a limit to the duty that can be extracted from frankincense.' He stopped speaking and looked at the faces of his companions, at the pain and frustration that marked them.

Murmurs of agreement rippled through the group comprising traders, artisans, influential members of the local community. Each had suffered under the heavy hand of Roman rule, each was desperate for change. The lines of worry on their faces spoke of countless nights lost to anxiety as their livelihoods were threatened by the ever-tightening grip of Rome.

'What can we do?' a young cloth trader burst out, his eyes darting about nervously, betraying his fear. 'The Romans are powerful, their soldiers are everywhere.'

Barakat raised a hand to silence him. 'We must be strategic. Open rebellion is a last resort. First, we need a roadmap to undermine their control, to force them to reconsider their policies.' He turned to the man seated on his right, a former soldier called Noam. 'Explain our plan to everyone here, Noam.'

Noam nodded, unrolling a large parchment map of Dimašq on the table. In the flickering glow of torchlights, the map revealed every street and alley of their cherished city. 'We start by disrupting their supply lines. The Romans rely heavily on the goods that flow into our markets. If we can cut off these supplies, we will weaken their hold on the city.'

'But how?' Another man leaned forward, brow furrowed in curiosity, his hands clenching in frustration.

'We have allies within the merchant guilds,' Noam replied. 'They can help us divert shipments, create bottlenecks. Additionally, we will sabotage key infrastructure—checkpoints, warehouses, roads—to sow chaos and confusion. We can achieve much without resorting to bloodshed.' His voice was steady, filled with the quiet confidence of a man who had seen his share of battles.

'And what of the governor?' someone asked from the rear of the courtyard, the speaker shrouded in darkness. 'How do we handle Baruchus Philippides? The man who went back on his word to us?'

Barakat's eyes closed briefly. He recognized the young olive oil trader, Yitzhak. 'Philippides is a shrewd man, but not unbeatable,' he stated. 'We exploit his weaknesses. He is already living in fear. He even sent away his son, Mithradates, fearing for his safety. We must share stories, sow discord among his troops. Under pressure, he will either comply with our requests or make a mistake that we can capitalize on. However,' Barakat cautioned, 'we must play this game with care. We cannot allow the city to descend into mob rule. Philippides may be bound by Rome, but his intentions are noble—'

'I say we seize the governor's mansion,' Yitzhak interjected. 'We outnumber them. Once we have control, nothing else matters.'

'Violence will lead to a brutal Roman crackdown—it is not an option,' Barakat interrupted, his tone brooked no argument. 'The price of violence will be steep—*very steep*. Remember that.'

Yitzhak fell silent, though his unconvinced expression betrayed his doubts in Barakat and Noam's strategy.

Barakat continued, his voice firm. 'This plan must be disseminated among our people. We are fighting for their freedom—they deserve to know. To achieve our goals, our focus must be on encouraging disobedience and not violence.'

The attendees nodded, their determination apparent, their shoulders bearing the strain of their shared suffering. Though challenging, the plan offered a glint of hope.

'Tell our supporters,' Barakat urged. 'Spread the message. This is the turning point.'

As the meeting broke up, each man was assigned a specific role in the evolving plan. They dispersed into the shadows, united in their objective, yet anxiously anticipating what lay ahead.

Barakat remained in the courtyard, looking at the dark heavens above. The way forward was dangerous, but they had no choice. For too long, the people of Dimašq had languished under Roman rule. Now they finally had a chance to fight back.

He turned to leave, but a hand on his shoulder stopped him. He spun around, heart pounding, only to find Noam, his eyes solemn. 'Do you believe we can succeed?' the former soldier asked. 'Not everyone is fully committed.'

Barakat met his gaze. 'Noam,' he said, his voice strong and steady, his will unwavering, 'we have no choice but to succeed. For our people. For Dimašq.' And with that, they stepped out into the night, ready to fan the flames of rebellion against Rome.

30

Korkai, Thamirabarani, Pandya Desam
Present-day Thoothukudi District, Tamil Nadu, India
Around 2,000 years ago

The clang of hammers striking metal echoed through the air as Padmasen and Kulasekara oversaw the construction of their new ironworks. They had chosen a site close to the banks of the Thamirabarani river, harnessing its abundant waters for cooling and tempering the hot iron. Workers cleared the earth, erected kilns and began installing the first smelting furnaces. The Thamirabarani's waters seemed to gurgle with the importance of their mission, the very air thrumming with focused enthusiasm.

Padmasen scrutinized every detail as Kulasekara directed a group of labourers unloading iron ore from wagons. 'Ensure the ore is sorted by quality,' he commanded, calm yet authoritative. 'The finest grade is needed for our first batch.' Kulasekara, sweat beading on his brow, nodded curtly, his eyes reflecting Padmasen's unflagging determination.

Padmasen's thoughts drifted to the arduous path he had travelled, the countless hours spent mastering a technique passed down through generations. Now, standing on the precipice of a new era for their ironworks, a wave of pride washed over him.

At the other end of the foundry, workers pulverized palasha leaves and khadira bark. 'For every unit of iron ore,' Padmasen said to Kulasekara, reciting the proportions he had committed to memory long ago, 'we require four times its weight in powdered palasha leaves, one-eighth its weight in khadira bark and one-sixteenth its weight in burnt brick.' These seemingly unremarkable ingredients were a crucial part of the secret to their superior metal—along with one vital component, carefully concealed by Kulasekara in an undisclosed location; a final touch that would render their product unparalleled: the Dvaitalingam.

'Once the last component is added,' Padmasen explained, 'we seal the concoction with black hide and place it within the crucibles.'

The next stage involved loading the crucibles into the furnace, where they would be subjected to burning hard coal for three days and nights. Only after some cooling would they be cracked open while the mixture was still in liquid stage. The top layer of slag would be skimmed off and the molten metal examined. This meticulous process would be repeated seven times to ensure the unmatched quality of the metal. The work was difficult, but the men understood that perfection demanded both precision and patience.

The following day, Padmasen and Kulasekara gathered with the workers around the newly constructed furnace. After completion of the inaugural puja, a taut silence settled over the group, the kind that precedes something momentous. Suddenly, the furnace roared to life, its heat an oppressive, unrelenting force. An orange glow, emanating from the inferno within, danced across their faces. Even though they were tired, the workers moved with a fervent energy, charged with the conviction of imminent success.

Padmasen checked the molten metal and produced a small pouch filled with unusual grains resembling shavings of rock. The men watched wide-eyed as he meticulously stirred in a pinch. 'This final ingredient,' Padmasen declared, 'will elevate our iron's quality, rendering it exceptional in strength and flexibility.' Kulasekara observed intently as the grains fused with angarah—carbon—and loha—iron—within the molten metal. This, he knew, was a pivotal moment. Their livelihood, their aspirations, hinged on this crucial step.

As if infused with life, the flakes reacted with the fiery mixture. Tiny, incandescent dots—like miniature suns—began to swirl in the molten metal, forming small whirlpools that shimmered.

Only the Rakshaks knew that the Dvaitalingam contained potent minerals such as 'agnidharaka', phosphorus; 'ayah samsraya', silicon; 'gandhaka', sulphur; 'manikya', manganese; 'pindarajata', nickel; 'chitraka', chromium, and numerous others. The mesmerized workers gathered closer as the grains worked their magic. The molten metal transformed, its surface coming alive with swirling patterns of light, each vortex pulsing with an otherworldly energy. All who witnessed this metamorphosis were captivated.

But the spectacle ended there. What followed was days of backbreaking labour. The men worked tirelessly, maintaining the intense heat required to forge the world's finest iron. Padmasen walked among them with single-minded focus, every action deliberate. He monitored the temperature, adjusted the airflow and at times added more burnt brick, ensuring the perfect composition. As the hours stretched on, the crucible's contents began to emit an unearthly luminescence. Padmasen and Kulasekara exchanged a knowing look, sensing success within their reach.

Three days later, the molten metal, hissing and spitting as it met the cool air, was poured into circular moulds. Padmasen and Kulasekara watched with bated breath as the first ingot was extracted. The metal bore a unique, swirling pattern, an indication of the mysterious additive.

Padmasen knew the Dvaitalingam would be needed again when the ingots were forged into swords or chisels—but only along the cutting edges. Weapons and tools crafted from their metal would not only be strong and flexible, but would also possess another crucial quality: incomparable sharpness.

Kulasekara hefted the ingot, feeling its weight and texture. Finally, a hint of pride colouring his voice, he declared, 'It is perfect.' A rare smile spread across Padmasen's face. Taking the ingot from Kulasekara, he stated, 'This is but the beginning. We have replicated the very quality that the old foundry once provided. Inform Cheliyan that we are prepared to resume international trade. And stamp our mark upon this.'

The insignia, a symbol of supreme strength and enduring quality, was swiftly emblazoned upon the ingot.

As Padmasen reflected upon the long and arduous journey that had led to this moment, he felt a profound sense of accomplishment. They had forged not merely iron, but a future brimming with possibility.

Kulasekara, too, shared in the triumph. With their superior metal, he could now fully support Somadatta's rebellion in Saketa. The future, once fraught with uncertainty and danger, now shone bright with the promise of prosperity and power.

Nevertheless, Padmasen could not shake a lingering discomfort—one that whispered from the depths of the forge. For he knew that hidden within the metal's swirling patterns lay a secret far older than the men guarding it.

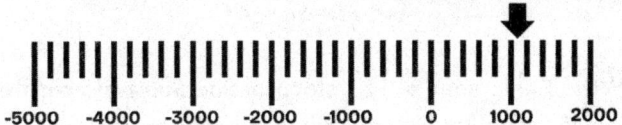

Vrah Vishnuloka, Khmer Kambuja
Present-day Angkor Wat, Cambodia
Around 900 years ago

Suryavarman, the king of the Khmer Empire, stood at the base of Angkor Wat's central tower, his eyes tracing the lines of the magnificent structure. His bronzed skin, muscular frame and square jaw conveyed his robustness. His piercing eyes spoke of intelligence and determination; a ruler born to command. A golden crown rested upon his head.

His trusted advisor, Divakarapandita, approached the king, his robes rustling softly in the evening breeze. 'It is magnificent,' Suryavarman said, his voice filled with awe.

'It is but a reflection of your devotion, Your Majesty,' Divakarapandita replied. 'The gods are pleased. This temple shall stand as a tribute to both your reign and the glory of Vishnu.'

Suryavarman nodded, pride surging through him. His mind flashed back to a day on the coast of Champa, Khmer's neighbour comprising the Viet clans to the east.

~

The sea had been a raging beast that day, its waves crashing against his flagship. Suryavarman had stood on deck, keenly observing the approaching enemy, trying to anticipate their next move.

The Khmer naval force, a powerful assemblage, had been strengthened by warships sent by Suryavarman's ally, the Chola king. The Chola admiral had stood beside Suryavarman, their combined fleet poised to confront the Champa navy.

Suryavarman's eyes had narrowed as the outlines of the enemy ships materialized on the horizon. The rhythmic slap of waves against the hulls of his vessels was punctuated by the defiant flutter of the Khmer banner, an image of Garuda—Vishnu's celestial mount—emblazoned upon its fabric. The Chola ships had hoisted their own flag—the symbol an amalgamation of their own tiger emblem and the Pandyan fish, a reminder of a recent conquest.

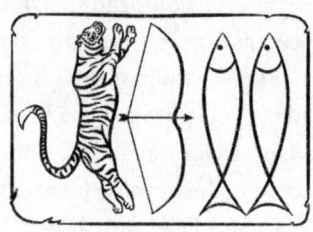

'Steady, men,' Suryavarman had commanded, his voice ringing out across the windswept deck. 'We fight for glory—and for Vishnu!'

The battle had commenced suddenly, the air erupting with the sounds of war. Strategically positioned catapults on the Khmer and Chola ships had launched burning firepots, hurling them across vast distances to explode upon the decks of their Viet enemies, unleashing a torrent of fire and chaos. Khmer archers had added to the onslaught, firing volleys of flaming arrows upon the Champa vessels.

The sea had churned, a maelstrom of clashing ships and struggling men. But despite the ferocity of their attack, victory had seemed to elude Suryavarman's grasp. The Champa forces,

The Ayodhya Alliance

well-prepared and relentless, had fought with a savage intensity, their nimble ships and aggressive tactics pushing the Khmer and Chola forces back. Doubt, like a creeping shadow, had begun to gnaw at Suryavarman's resolve.

Just then, Divakarapandita, Suryavarman's head priest, had emerged from below deck, his serene presence a stark contrast to the turmoil around him. His saffron robes billowing in the wind, his gaze steady, he had said, 'Your Majesty, the tide of this conflict does not favour us. The gods demand a greater offering ... a more profound demonstration of your devotion.'

His heart pounding with exertion and misgivings, Suryavarman had turned to the priest. 'What must be done?' he had asked, his voice a low growl.

Divakarapandita's eyes were sharp, unwavering. 'We must make a vow, Your Majesty,' he had declared. 'A promise to erect a temple in Vishnu's honour, a monument unlike any the world has ever seen. Only then will the gods grant us victory.'

Suryavarman had paused, the weight of the decision heavy upon him. He envisioned a temple reaching for the heavens, its spires piercing the clouds, its walls adorned with stories of Vishnu's glory. His resolve solidified. 'I vow to build such a temple,' he had announced with a newfound conviction. 'A temple that will stand for all time, a symbol of the power of Vishnu!'

As if the gods themselves had breathed vigour into their ranks, a fierce momentum swept through his forces. The Khmer and Chola warriors, their spirits reignited, had fought with renewed ferocity. The tide of the battle turned. The Champa lines wavered, then broke, their ships overtaken and seized, many set ablaze. The sea had turned crimson with the blood of the fallen; the air was foul with the smell of burning wood and flesh.

The Khmer banners soared triumphantly over the defeated Champa fleet. As the churning sea finally calmed, Suryavarman, his heart swelling with pride and relief, had turned to Divakarapandita. 'We have prevailed,' he had said, his voice resonating with joy. 'The nectar of victory is ours! And we must honour our vow without delay.'

~

After that victory, planning for the great temple had begun immediately. Suryavarman entrusted the task to Divakarapandita. But the scale of the project had turned out to be daunting.

Recognizing the need for assistance, Divakarapandita had turned to his counterparts in the Chola kingdom, seeking the help of skilled artisans and craftsmen. Among them was Parantaka, the most talented sculptor in Gangaikonda Cholapuram, the Chola capital. Unbeknownst to many, Parantaka was also the 191st Dvaitalingam Rakshak—a duty that had been entrusted to him after the fall of the Pandyas to the Cholas.

Parantaka had arrived at Angkor Wat, bringing with him a set of unique chisels crafted from the finest iron and imbued with a power that had been passed down through generations of his family. These instruments, coupled with his unparalleled knowledge, would allow them to shape the stone with a precision never seen before.

Under Divakarapandita's careful supervision, the temple had begun to take shape. Skilled craftspeople, guided by Parantaka's expertise, had carved elaborate bas-reliefs depicting scenes from the Ramayana and the Mahabharata, their every stroke suffusing the stone with life. The walls, soon adorned with intricate details and graceful figures, seemed to pulsate with divine energy.

'We must incorporate the Churning of the Ocean,' Divakarapandita had declared one evening, surveying the emerging structure. 'It is a vital narrative, a reminder that this temple would never have been built in the absence of those turbulent waters.'

Parantaka's eyes had sparkled with enthusiasm. 'A wise decision, My Lord. This allows us to incorporate a variety of aquatic creatures in our carvings—including the twin fish.'

Divakarapandita had smiled. 'Then let it be so. Our temple will be a symbol of the union of earthly and heavenly powers—a symphony in stone for all to behold.'

Now, as Suryavarman stood before the completed marvel, he felt keenly aware of the weight of that vow and his subsequent victory. As he surveyed the magnificent structure, he wondered if Parantaka's sacred chisels had altered more than just the stone's shape ... if they had imparted their power into it as well.

31

Korkai, Thamirabarani, Pandya Desam
Present-day Thoothukudi District, Tamil Nadu, India
Around 2,000 years ago

The four teenagers arrived at Kulasekara's home in Korkai, their spirits high after three years of study at the gurukul. Kulasekara greeted Soju and Mithra with a warmth that instantly eased any feelings of homesickness that had lingered in their hearts. Meanwhile, Indumati embraced her children, Suriratna and Bhadraketu, as Vishnupriya looked on, a gentle smile gracing her lips.

Bhadraketu, Mithra and Soju, now fifteen, and the youngest, Suriratna, at fourteen, stood at the threshold of adulthood—a liminal stage where they were no longer children, yet not fully adults, caught in the flux of becoming. 'Welcome, children,' Vishnupriya said, her voice soft and kind. 'Make yourselves at home. This is your home as much as it is mine.' The youngsters settled in quickly, excited to be back. Kulasekara's spacious residence was a packed with delightful discoveries: a bedroom chest with secret compartments, a beautifully crafted veena in the living room, a Chaturanga board laid out in the study, and outside the small temple a collection of exquisitely tuned bells that sang a melody of welcome for anyone who entered.

Suriratna and Bhadraketu, however, were eager for a different kind of reunion. The anticipation of seeing their father after the long separation thrummed through them, almost overwhelming in its intensity. 'Matalu,' Suriratna asked, her voice barely a whisper, 'will we see Pitaha today?'

Kulasekara's face softened. 'Of course, my dear,' he said gently. 'He will be here soon. He has been busy at the foundry, getting everything organized. He has lots to get done but do not worry … he knows of your arrival.'

As if summoned by their longing, the door opened and Padmasen stood in the entranceway, his presence as reassuring as ever. Behind him lingered an unusual figure—a man with slicked-back hair and an oily sheen to his skin, his demeanour as suspect as his appearance. Padmasen nodded curtly and the man slunk away, disappearing into the shadows.

'Pitaha!' Suriratna and Bhadraketu cried out, their joy echoing through the house. They rushed to embrace him, their smiles radiant and clung tightly to him, then, remembering their customs, bent to touch his feet. Padmasen, however, pulled them close again, his heart overflowing with happiness. 'I have missed you both so much,' he said, his voice choking as he held back his tears.

Suriratna, her brow furrowed, turned to her father. 'Who was that man who came with you?' she asked. 'He looked so oily!'

'He is just a business associate,' Padmasen replied vaguely. 'One of many.' He hesitated, then added, 'He helped me secure the land for the new foundry.' Sensing a veiled truth, Suriratna did not press further.

While the family reconnected, Soju and Mithra explored the house, their curiosity leading them to the courtyard where a tempting array of local delicacies awaited them. 'Try this,' Mithra urged, offering Soju a piece of jaggery. 'It is delicious.'

Soju smiled, taking a tentative bite. The rich, caramel-like flavour was unlike anything he had ever tasted. 'This is amazing,' he exclaimed, savouring the sweetness. They sampled other treats including tamarind candy, tart and tangy, a delightful explosion on the tongue.

∼

The days passed swiftly, filled with joyful reunions and new discoveries. In their free time, the youngsters explored Korkai, a vibrant port city that was a confluence of many cultures. Each new experience—the exotic flavours of the local cuisine, the unfamiliar games, the stories shared by sailors who had travelled to distant lands—added to their sense of adventure and their knowledge of the world.

One afternoon, Soju and Suriratna found themselves drawn to a quiet garden, its air rich with the scent of blossoms. The gentle hum of bees provided a soothing melody as they strolled along the shaded paths.

'This place is beautiful,' Suriratna whispered, her gaze resting on a bright cluster of flame lilies and champa flowers.

'Like a secret haven,' Soju agreed.

Deeper within the garden, they came upon a small, quiet pond. As they sat, tossing pebbles into the water, Suriratna asked, 'Soju, do you ever wonder what we will do when we are older?'

Soju glanced at her, his expression uncertain. 'Sometimes. My father says I am supposed to be the Iron King or something big in Garak, but that is hard to think about right now. For the moment, I just want to get through my education.'

Suriratna fiddled with a blade of grass. 'There is so much I want to do. I do not even know where to start. Everything is so far away.'

'We will figure it out,' Soju said, his voice steady. 'We will do it all—whatever it is—together.'

Suriratna smiled, comforted by his words. Their bond, built over the course of the many challenges they had faced, felt stronger than ever, and as time went on, their shared experiences forged a connection that transcended friendship.

One evening, as they sat beside a crackling fire, roasting sweet potatoes, Bhadraketu turned to his sister. 'Suriratna,' he asked, 'do you remember those tales Matalu Kulasekara used to tell us about Korkai when he would visit Saketa?'

'Of course,' she replied. 'He always said it was a place steeped in history.'

Kulasekara, who had been listening quietly, smiled. 'I am sure Satyamuni will introduce you to the *Silappatikaram*,' he said. 'It is a Tamil epic, set here in Korkai, about Kovalan, a merchant, who loses his heart—and his fortune—to a dancer. Heartbroken, he returns to his wife, Kannagi, and they travel to Madurai. There, Kovalan is wrongly accused of theft and executed. Kannagi, consumed by sadness and rage, proves his innocence and unleashes a divine fury upon the city.'

'What a tragic tale,' Suriratna said. 'Betrayal can have devastating consequences. Thankfully it was Madurai and not Korkai that bore the brunt.'

'Indeed,' Padmasen agreed, joining the conversation. 'Korkai is a place of great importance, a symbol of the Pandyan Empire's strength and prosperity.'

Mithra, ever inquisitive, leaned forward, his eyes wide. 'Will you tell us another story about it, Anna?'

Padmasen chuckled. 'Of course, but not tonight. It is late. You all need your rest.' Though the youngsters groaned in protest, they knew there was no arguing with Padmasen.

The moon cast its silvery light upon the sleeping city as Soju and Suriratna parted ways. She was sharing a bedroom with her mother while the three boys were in another by themselves.

'Goodnight, Soju,' Suriratna whispered, her heart pounding as she made her way to her room, lingering only momentarily.

'Goodnight, Suriratna,' Soju replied, reaching out to briefly clasp her hand, a gentle smile playing on his lips.

32

Chennai, Tamil Nadu, India

Present day

Aditya and Somi touched down in Chennai in his Gulfstream G200 after their short visit to Angul. During the flight, Aditya had briefed her on the urgency of the DRDO's demands. Though both companies were working tirelessly to expedite the construction of the new steel plant, the crucial element, that perfect alloy needed for the DRDO's tank—the BPBT— remained elusive.

Somi had returned to India to oversee the modernization of the Angul plant—the focus of the joint venture between GISCO and the Pillai Group. That morning, they had toured the site, now a whirlwind of activity: old equipment being dismantled, new machinery being installed, engineers and technicians setting up a network of computer systems designed to optimize production. Everywhere, concrete columns rose skyward. A tangible sense of excitement mingled with anticipation, despite the chaos inherent in such a massive undertaking.

'We'll find a solution,' Somi said with quiet confidence.

'I have no doubt,' Aditya replied. 'But the question is when.'

That evening, they dined aboard Aditya's yacht, moored off the harbour. The gentle rocking of the vessel, the salt-laced breeze, the clinking of cocktail glasses as his crew served them their drinks—it was the perfect way to relax and unwind, but Aditya's brow was furrowed, his usual easy-going charm replaced by growing tension.

'What's troubling you?' Somi asked, noticing the almost imperceptible slump of his shoulders.

'If I cannot deliver within the DRDO's timeframe, my reputation is finished,' Aditya admitted. 'The demand for this new steel, Somi ... it came directly from the prime minister. I am starting to think I am in over my head. They chose me for my ability to innovate—to think outside the box. Perhaps they were mistaken and should find someone else. Our joint venture can still focus on the usual variants needed by the industry as a whole.'

'No other steel manufacturer in the world possesses the technology you need,' Somi stated. 'The DRDO knows that. They also know that they've handed you a near-impossible deadline. Frankly, Aditya, I am your best shot at making this happen.'

'But what's motivating you, Somi?' Aditya countered. 'Our interests ... why should they be so perfectly aligned?'

Somi laughed, her eyes crinkling with amusement. 'Let's just say that if we can crack this together it opens a whole new world of possibilities for GISCO. This isn't philanthropy, Aditya. It's business.'

'Fair enough,' Aditya conceded. 'But right now we are no closer to finding the solution the DRDO requires.'

'We'll find it,' Somi said. 'I have a feeling India will show us the way forward.'

Aditya frowned, puzzled. 'What do you mean?'

'Do you remember that business conference in Delhi when we reconnected after all those years? On that trip, I visited the Iron Pillar in the Qutb Minar complex. It's an incredible structure.'

Historians believed the Iron Pillar of Delhi—a towering testament to ancient Indian metallurgy—was likely constructed during the Gupta period, perhaps in the fourth or fifth century CE. However, given its original dedication to Vishnu, some speculated it could be even older.

'Scientists have debated its secrets for ages,' Somi continued. 'Some claim its resistance to rust is due to the high phosphorus content in the iron. Others point to a protective lead coating. But the truth is no one knows for sure what's kept it from rusting all these centuries.'

Aditya looked perplexed. 'What are you getting at?'

'You partnered with GISCO because you believed in Korean technological superiority,' Somi said, her voice taking on a playful edge. 'But I agreed to this venture because I am convinced the answer lies in ancient Indian technology.'

∾

The following day, they met at The Leela Palace. 'I've invited someone to join us,' Somi said as they settled in the conference room, coffee steaming in mugs before them. 'I think you'll find his perspective ... enlightening.' Aditya, though curious, remained silent, trusting her judgement.

Moments later, a man entered the room. His attire—a worn-out white bush shirt and khaki pants—was simple, almost austere. Thick spectacles dominated his face, lending him an air of scholarly intensity. His hair, a shock of unruly white, gave him an Einsteinian aura. When he spoke, his voice was soft but firm. 'Satheesh Jayaraman,' he introduced himself, his gaze steady and penetrating behind the lenses.

Somi slid a sheet of paper across the table. Aditya scanned the highlighted points of Jayaraman's impressive bio: renowned Indian archaeologist and historian ... PhD in Archaeology from Mumbai University ... groundbreaking finds at Muziris and Korkai ... published in *Indian Historical Review*, *Journal of South*

Asian Studies ... awarded the Padma Shri for work on Chera and Pandya dynasties ... lectures at Oxford on Ancient Indian Art and Architecture ... expert on Kailasa Temple and Konark Sun Temple ... collaborated with Dr Bala Ramaswamy of CERN.

Meanwhile, Jayaraman, devoid of the usual academic pretentiousness, had swiftly connected his laptop to the projection system and brought up the first slide—a panoramic view of a massive archaeological dig. He clicked through a series of images—clay amphorae, iron implements, objects of lead and copper, dugout boats, remnants of ancient brickwork, a weathered dock—each one a piece of a long-lost world.

'What am I looking at?' Aditya asked, his brow creased.

'Korkai,' Jayaraman stated. 'An ancient port city in Thoothukudi, less than five miles inland from the Bay of Bengal. It lies a couple of miles north of the Thamirabarani. Though the sea has receded over the centuries, Korkai was once a thriving hub of international trade.' He picked up a small leather tray, holding it out to them.

'What's this?' Somi asked.

'A piece of metal—likely from a sword—recovered from the Korkai excavation.'

'Why is this relevant?' Aditya asked, impatient. *We have a DRDO deadline to meet. Why are we wasting time on this?*

'Because Korkai was the most significant port in the Pandyan Empire two thousand years ago,' Jayaraman replied, unperturbed. 'Ships from here regularly travelled to the Arabian peninsula— known as Arava Nadu in those times. My team even uncovered Roman artefacts there. It's not unusual to find coins from various eras just a few feet below the surface. Korkai's prominence waned around fifteen hundred years ago, when the Pandyan capital shifted to Madurai. But its importance, its historical significance, should be obvious. After all, the name "Ayuta", given to the entire region up to Kanyakumari, is—' he paused for emphasis '—is the same "Ayuta" referenced in ancient Korean texts.'

Aditya's eyes narrowed. The pieces were beginning to fit together. 'And what did they trade?'

'Pepper, ivory, pearls, gemstones, silks, aromatics … and iron ingots,' Jayaraman replied. 'Ships returning carried gold, coral, glassware, wine, olive oil and fish sauce. This exchange played a crucial role in the Roman Empire's annual trade deficit. Pliny the Elder, a Roman naval commander, wrote of this in his *Natural History* in around 77 CE, estimating the trade imbalance at approximately 100 million sesterces annually.'

Somi turned to Aditya, the corner of her mouth hitching upward in a knowing smile, 'Do you remember our conversation at Queen Heo's tomb in Gimhae? You wondered why anyone would travel thousands of miles across the ocean to marry a stranger …'

'Indeed,' Aditya said.

'Korkai was connected to the world,' Somi said. 'Trade routes stretched to Rome, Greece, Southeast Asia, Persia, Arabia, Africa, even to China. And who controlled Korkai two thousand years ago?'

'The Pandyas,' Jayaraman replied, anticipating her next question. 'And their emblem?'

'The twin fish,' Somi answered, a hint of excitement in her voice.

Two dancing fish, tangled in the sea,
Swaying in the current, wild and free.

33

Dimašq, Roman Empire
Present-day Damascus, Syria
Around 2,000 years ago

The setting sun painted Dimašq a deep crimson—a fiery omen for the approaching carnage.

Barakat stood on a rooftop overlooking the main plaza, a knot of apprehension tightening in his chest. Hope for mere civil disobedience had faded, the movement having been hijacked by hotheads like Yitzhak. The streets below teemed with desperate, angry people, their chants growing louder and more menacing by the minute. The once-orderly square had descended into anarchy. Driven by hunger and Roman persecution, mobs rampaged through the streets, torching houses and looting shops. The movement, which had begun as a plea for justice, had warped into something sinister, fuelled by despair and simmering rage among the masses. Barakat watched, his heart plummeting as he witnessed his fellow Damascenes consumed by a destructive frenzy. His carefully laid plans lay in ruins, shattered like the fragile peace he had tried to maintain. The air, choked with smoke and the stench of burning wood, echoed with the terrified screams of fleeing citizens.

'Barakat!' Noam's voice, sharp with urgency, sliced through the tumult. Barakat turned and saw his friend, the former soldier who had helped him craft their initial strategy, striding towards him. Noam's face was creased with worry. 'We have to get out of here,' he said, pulling at Barakat's arm. 'This is no longer a protest. It is a full-blown riot.'

A sudden explosion rocked the plaza, sending shockwaves through the throng. Flames erupted from the Roman armoury, resin stocks, pitch and sulphur igniting in a blinding inferno. Barakat watched, his stomach churning, as the mob stormed the governor's residence. Roman troops, outnumbered and overwhelmed, battled to hold the gates, but the crowd, aflame with a desperate fury, was unstoppable. Panic surged through Barakat. This was spiralling out of control.

Before Noam could stop him, he hurriedly climbed down a stairway and pushed through the crowd. 'Stop! This is madness! This is not the way!' But his voice was a futile cry against the deafening roar and his words were swallowed by the tumult. He spotted Yitzhak, the young hothead who had argued for a more aggressive approach, leading the charge, a club raised high above his head.

'Yitzhak, no!' Barakat lunged, grabbing his arm, trying to pull him back from the precipice. 'This will only bring more suffering!'

'We have suffered enough!' Yitzhak roared, his eyes blazing. 'It is time they tasted our pain!' He wrenched his arm free of Barakat's grip, and surged forward, pulling the mob along in his wake. Watching them, Barakat felt a wave of despair. He understood their frustration, their desperation, but this path, he knew, led only to more bloodshed.

The governor's gates, unable to withstand the relentless onslaught, finally gave way. The remaining Roman troops, hopelessly outnumbered, either fell or fled. A tide of humanity driven by vengeance barged into the courtyard. Barakat, his heart pounding, knew he had to stop this before it ended in more senseless slaughter.

He shoved his way through the crush of bodies, reaching the mansion's steps just as the doors splintered. Inside, Governor Philippides, his face pale but resolute, stood with his loyal lieutenant, Cornelius. Terror filled their eyes—a fear that mirrored Barakat's own. 'Please!' Barakat cried out, raising his hands, his voice a desperate plea. 'This is not justice! This would be murder!'

For a brief while, silence held the courtyard captive. The mob, panting and wild-eyed, hesitated, its fury momentarily checked. Philippides, seizing the opportunity, stepped forward, his hands shaking, but his voice firm. 'People of Dimašq,' he boomed, 'I understand your anger. But violence is not the answer. Let us talk. Let us find a solution together.'

But reason had fled, replaced by a thirst for retribution. 'Like you spoke to us years ago,' yelled Yitzhak. 'The time for discussion is over.' With a bloodcurdling scream, he lunged, the mob following closely behind like a pack of wolves. Philippides, dragged down the steps, his pleas for mercy lost beneath the roar, vanished beneath a sea of flailing fists and blades. Cornelius was forced back into the mansion as the governor's final cry echoed in his ears: 'Cornelius, protect Mithradates! My only son ...'

Barakat, helpless, watched in horror as the frenzied mob engulfed Philippides, their bloodlust staining the stone steps crimson. The Dimašq he had loved, the city he had fought to protect, was now a stranger, consumed by a darkness he could not comprehend. A wave of nausea rose in his throat, the sights and sounds of violence a sickening assault on his senses.

His dream of civil resistance, a dream shared by so many, lay shattered, crushed beneath the weight of hatred.

~

Flames licked at the sky as night fell upon Dimašq, the governor's death marking the beginning of Rome's retaliation. Barakat, his heart choked with grief and despair, knew what awaited them. The Romans would not let this go unpunished; their wrath would be terrible. The new embellishments on Dimašq's streets would be crucifixions.

He found Noam amidst the inferno, his friend's face inscribed with the same hopeless despair. 'We must leave,' Noam said urgently. 'The Romans will return with a vengeance. There is no point in staying here.'

Barakat nodded, taking one last look at the burning city, his heart broken. As they fled into the darkness, he could not shake the feeling of failure, of knowing that this … this was only the beginning.

34

Korkai, Thamirabarani, Pandya Desam
Present-day Thoothukudi District, Tamil Nadu, India
Around 2,000 years ago

Bhadraketu's feet carried him deeper into the verdant woodlands of Korkai. The soft rustle of foliage and the cheerful chirping of birds were the only sounds that broke the peaceful silence. In search of solitude and adventure, his curiosity led him further and further from home. Today's journey would result in an encounter that would irrevocably alter his life.

As he walked, he came upon a small clearing bathed in sunlight. In the centre, a figure clad in ochre robes sat meditating beneath a sprawling tree. Intrigued, Bhadraketu approached cautiously, his footsteps barely disturbing the soft grass. The man, sensing his presence, stirred from his meditation. He unfolded his legs with deliberate grace and invited Bhadraketu to join him in the dappled shade.

'Welcome, young one,' the monk greeted. 'I am Nadikasyapa. What brings you to this place?'

'I am Bhadraketu,' he replied hesitantly. 'I often wander ... searching ... for something.'

A knowing smile played on Nadikasyapa's lips. 'Like me, once,' he said. 'You seek knowledge and tranquillity. Sit beside me. Let us talk.'

Bhadraketu settled cross-legged on the ground, his gaze fixed on the monk. Nadikasyapa began to speak, his calm voice weaving together words of wisdom, sharing the teachings of the Buddha—compassion, mindfulness and enlightenment. For hours, Bhadraketu listened, captivated by the simple truths, the profound peace that emanated from the monk.

In the days that followed, Bhadraketu found himself drawn back to the clearing again and again. He would disappear for hours, immersing himself in Nadikasyapa's lessons. Mithra, Soju and Suriratna, noticing his prolonged absences, grew increasingly concerned.

'Where does he go?' Suriratna asked one evening, when her family and friends had gathered in the courtyard, her forehead creased with worry.

'I have seen him walking towards the forest,' Mithra replied. 'He returns lost in thought, as if ... transformed.'

Padmasen sighed, a heavy sound. 'Your time in Korkai is drawing to a close,' he reminded the children. 'In two weeks, you return to Satyamuni's gurukul to complete your studies. Bhadraketu's focus must be his lessons. This ... wandering will not make him the man he is destined to be.'

Determined to bring his son back on track, Padmasen sent one of his men—the odd-looking man with slicked-back hair—to observe Bhadraketu. Each day, Padmasen received reports, but despite his pleas and admonitions, Bhadraketu could not pull himself away from Nadikasyapa's teachings. When he returned home late one night, he had an air of newfound wisdom about him. His parents and friends waited; their expressions taut with apprehension.

'Bhadraketu, where have you been?' Indumati asked, her voice soft with concern.

'Learning from a Buddhist monk,' he replied. 'His words ... they hold great insight.'

'Your education is important, son,' Padmasen said, barely able to hide his frustration. 'I beg you, complete your studies before embarking on such a path.'

Bhadraketu met his father's eyes, his own gaze unwavering. 'I understand, Pitaha, but this ... this is a calling. My heart tells me this is the right path, not the gurukul.'

His parents exchanged a worried glance. Indumati, unable to bear the tension, placed a hand on her son's shoulder. 'We only want what is best for you,' she pleaded. 'Think carefully about your future.'

Bhadraketu nodded, but his decision was made. The call he felt was stronger than any parental pressure. He would not be swayed.

For days, Bhadraketu remained quietly introspective. Nadikasyapa, sensing his inner turmoil, offered guidance. 'Your family loves you,' he said one day. 'Their worry is born of love. But the path you choose ... it must be your own.'

'I am torn,' Bhadraketu admitted. 'I do not want to disappoint them. But my heart ... does it belong here?'

'The path of dharma—what we followers of the Buddha call dhamma—is not easy,' Nadikasyapa said. 'It demands understanding and compassion. Speak with your family. Let them see the light that shines within you.'

That evening, Bhadraketu gathered his family. Taking a deep breath, he said, 'Mataha, Pitaha, I have considered your words. I love you both dearly and I know your concerns come from a place of love. But I have found my calling. I wish to follow the path of the Buddha.'

Padmasen scowled. In a voice tight with anger, he said, 'You are too young to make such a decision. Your education is incomplete. Do not throw your life away!'

'I will learn,' Bhadraketu insisted, 'but from the world, not from books. There is much to be gained beyond the walls of the gurukul.'

Padmasen shook his head and turned away without another word, his shoulders rigid with fury. He walked out into the night, the air crackling with the tension he left behind.

Sensing the futility of their parents' arguments, Suriratna intervened. 'If this is what makes you happy, Bhadraketu,' she said, 'we should support you.' Her words, carefully chosen, subtly nudged her mother towards acceptance.

Indumati's voice quavered as she embraced her son. 'You are our beloved son,' she said. 'We will always love you. But promise me ... you will stay safe. You will stay in touch.'

Later that night, as Padmasen stood silently by the courtyard well, Bhadraketu approached, hesitant.

'I wanted to say goodbye,' Bhadraketu said. 'And thank you—for everything.'

Padmasen did not respond immediately. His jaw clenched and he kept his eyes fixed on the dark water below. Finally, he broke the silence, his voice low and rough. 'If this is truly your path, then you have my blessing.' He turned, his expression weary but no longer angry. 'But, remember, this will always be your home. And you will always be my son.'

Relief washed over Bhadraketu. 'Thank you, Pitaha,' he said. 'And I promise to stay in touch.'

At dawn, Soju and Mithra embraced him warmly. 'Was our company so boring that you had to become a monk?' Mithra teased.

Suriratna, however, felt a different kind of pain. Tears streamed down her face as she realized the full import of his decision. Her brother, her constant companion, would be leaving for a different kind of life. Memories of their childhood—the playful arguments, the shared laughter, the gruelling training sessions—flashed through her mind.

Bhadraketu returned to the clearing. 'You have chosen your path,' Nadikasyapa said, a knowing smile in his eyes.

'I have,' Bhadraketu said. 'I wish to follow the path you have.'

'All paths, whether they follow Harihara or the Buddha, ultimately lead to the same truth, my son,' Nadikasyapa replied. 'They are merely different ways of reaching the same destination.'

Bhadraketu considered his words. 'Then I wish to follow the path of dhamma,' he said, his voice firm.

'Then let your journey begin,' Nadikasyapa said, a gentle hand resting on Bhadraketu's shoulder.

They entered the forest together, the path ahead uncertain, but Bhadraketu's heart was full of hope. The world beyond the trees beckoned, a vast unknown waiting to be explored. As the forest enveloped them, the sounds of the outside world faded, replaced by the rustling of leaves and the promise of enlightenment.

35

Geumgwan, Garak Confederacy
Present-day Gimhae, South Korea
Around 2,000 years ago

The Great Hall bristled with barely contained hostility. Ancient wooden beams carved with elaborate designs depicting legendary beasts loomed overhead, casting long shadows in the flickering torchlight. Around the massive table, crafted from dark, polished wood, sat the leaders of the Garak Confederacy, their faces illuminated by dancing flames, their expressions a delicate balance of authority and apprehension. Maps and tokens representing the provinces under their control lay scattered across the tabletop. On one wall, the Confederacy's flag, emblazoned with a turtle—their enduring symbol—hung like a silent sentinel.

Jangsu, the chief of Seongsan, towered over the assembled chiefs. Beside him, Talhae, his son, sat with a mischievous smirk playing on his lips, his eyes glittering with dark pleasure as he recalled their recent triumph. His presence, a silent threat, reminded the other chiefs of the shifting balance of power.

Kim Seok, the Confederacy's long-standing chairman, sat across the table, his hands clasped tightly, his eyes restless. Seeing Talhae, his heart ached with the absence of his own son, Kim Suro—Soju. His expression became grim as he surveyed the room, trying to discern the loyalties of the assembled chiefs. The chiefs of Daegaya, Bihwa, Bangam and Ara sat silently, their faces unreadable. The chief of Goryeong, was absent, killed during Jangsu and Talhae's recent conquest. A new representative had been appointed, a young man rumoured to be Talhae's puppet. But he had not been invited to this meeting, not yet worthy of a seat at the high table. Kim Seok's shoulders sagged, his fingers trembled and his eyes darted nervously as he witnessed the Confederacy's unity dissolving—physical manifestations of the sense of loss and betrayal consuming him.

Jangsu's voice, deep and commanding, shattered the silence. 'We gather to determine the Confederacy's future,' he declared. 'Times change, and we must adapt to survive. Seongsan and Goryeong are now united under my leadership, making us the most powerful force within this alliance. I propose that I be elected as the Confederacy's new chairman.'

A murmur rippled through the hall. Kim Seok rose, his voice steady despite the anger simmering within. 'This Confederacy,' he stated, 'was founded on the principles of mutual respect and cooperation. We do not attack our own. Seongsan's aggression against Goryeong has destroyed that covenant. What you propose is not leadership, but tyranny.'

Jangsu's eyes narrowed. 'These are dangerous times, Kim Seok. We need strength, not sentimentality, to face the threats posed by the Three Kingdoms. The Confederacy needs decisive leadership. My actions were not unprovoked. Goryeong had repeatedly violated our borders with their incessant cattle raids.'

Kim Seok looked around the table, desperately seeking a friendly face. 'Will you so easily abandon the ideals upon which this Confederacy was founded?' he asked, his voice laden with disappointment.

Munmu, the grizzled chieftain of Daegaya, leaned forward. 'Jangsu's proposition is compelling,' he said with a growl. 'Under his leadership, Daegaya will gain access to the rich iron mines of Goryeong. This is an opportunity we cannot afford to ignore.'

Jinhyeok, the shrewd chief of Bihwa, added, 'Jangsu has promised to double our trading rights. Imagine—our coffers overflowing with wealth, our people prosperous.'

Wonsik, who led the people of Bangam, could barely conceal his excitement as he joined the chorus. 'With Jangsu's military strength backing us, Bangam will finally be ready to expand its borders. Our troops are ready—and victory is assured.'

The venerable leader of Ara, Yongho, sat motionless throughout the debate, his lined face inscrutable until he finally broke his silence. 'Jangsu promises protection from our enemies,' he said. 'In these uncertain times, survival depends on strength. We must unite under a capable leader.'

Kim Seok's heart sank. Jangsu had mesmerized the other chiefs with his promises of power and prosperity. The Confederacy, he realized, was lost. A wave of sadness washed over him. 'It seems,' he said, his voice trembling, 'the Confederacy is dead. We have become pawns in a game of power, our unity sacrificed on the altar of ambition.'

Talhae, watching the scene unfold, allowed himself a moment of quiet satisfaction. He had orchestrated this, manipulating the other chiefs' ambitions, subtly steering them towards this inevitable conclusion. He leaned back, savouring the taste of victory.

Sensing that triumph was at hand, Jangsu stepped forward. 'Kim Seok,' he said, 'your leadership has served us well. But these are tumultuous times and a new leader is needed—one who can navigate the challenges ahead.' He turned to the assembled chiefs. 'I call for a vote.'

The chiefs, their decision already made, nodded their assent. Kim Seok, sank back into his chair. Years of dedication, of loyalty to the Confederacy, now felt like dust scattering in the wind. He turned to see Talhae watching him, a triumphant smirk twisting his lips. As the room erupted with cheers and the burning torches cast long, flickering shadows that seemed to mock his despair, Kim Seok rose once more, his voice strong despite the loss.

'Remember this day, Chiefs,' he said, his gaze travelling across the room. 'Remember what we have lost. Let this serve as a lesson—a warning.' Turning away from the mirthful scene, he retreated.

Talhae watched him go, his mind already racing with plans for the future, a future in which the Confederacy was merely the first stepping stone in his ascent to power.

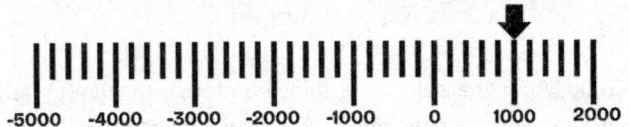

Dhillika, Hariyana, Tomar Samrajya
Present-day Mehrauli, Delhi, India
Around 1,000 years ago

King Anangpal, the Tomar ruler of Dhillika, was comfortably seated upon an elevated marble platform, a thick silk mattress cushioning him from the cold stone beneath. He inquired, 'What news of the Vishnu Stambha?'

His mahamantri, standing before him in the opulent hall, bowed his head. The decision to move the Iron Pillar had been a logistical challenge of considerable magnitude. More importantly, it represented a symbolic gesture, a move intended to unify the disparate regions now under Anangpal's rule.

The relocation of the Vishnu Stambha—from Visnupadagiri, where Chandragupta II, also known as Vikramaditya, had installed it, to Anangpal's capital city of Dhillika—built on the very foundations of Indraprastha, the ancient city of the Pandavas—had been months in the planning. The most capable engineers had been summoned and their expertise tested. After intense debate, a decision was reached: the pillar would be transported by rolling it on massive logs. Though a primitive method, it was deemed the most sensible approach for moving such a heavy and revered object.

'My Lord,' the mahamantri replied, 'the journey has begun. The Chandela ruler has dispatched the Vishnu Stambha. The military alliance you promised him has also been put into effect.'

'Good,' Anangpal said, smoothing his moustache thoughtfully. 'When can we anticipate the pillar's installation in Dhillika, my beloved city?'

The mahamantri sighed. 'The journey is arduous, Your Majesty. It is a formidable distance—448 miles from Visnupadagiri to Dhillika. The pillar must first traverse the rugged Vindhya Range, its path winding through dense forests and treacherous hills. Then it must cross the Yamuna's fertile plains—flatter, yes, but often waterlogged. It will be a slow process. We cannot risk damaging the stambha. The terrain is challenging for both man and beast.'

On the day of the pillar's departure from its original location, priests had conducted a puja at its base. Flowers, incense, jaggery, rice, holy water and sandalwood had been offered, and prayers chanted to appease Vishnu. Then, with a symphony of chanting and drumming to mask the sounds of straining ropes and groaning timber, the pillar had been carefully uprooted and lowered onto the massive logs.

Hundreds of men, their efforts coordinated by a complex network of ropes and pulleys, worked together to move the heavy monument. Crowds had lined the streets of Visnupadagiri on that day, their faces a mixture of awe and sorrow as they bade farewell to the symbol that had graced their city since the reign of Vikramaditya. The logs, debarked to make them rounder and smoother, and continuously lubricated with oil and water to reduce friction, creaked and groaned beneath the immense weight as the Vishnu Stambha was slowly, carefully pulled forward by teams of oxen and elephants. The oil and water poured on the logs left the ground wet, slippery and dangerous for the men and animals engaged in moving them and the task was occasionally disrupted by slips, falls and broken bones.

'The journey began smoothly, My Lord,' the mahamantri reported now. 'But the monsoon rains proved hazardous. One of the bridges along the route was washed away. Our engineers, resourceful as ever, constructed a series of barges using large logs and ropes. It took three days of relentless effort, but the pillar was transported safely across the river. We are now navigating the Vindhyas, the uneven landscape making the rolling process far more challenging. The logs require constant adjustment, and the elephants struggle to maintain their footing.'

'I understand the difficulties,' Anangpal said. 'But I require an estimated date for the installation.'

'Soon, My Lord,' the mahamantri assured him, cautious not to make a promise he might be unable to keep.

Weeks later, the convoy finally reached the plains of the Yamuna river. The exhausted labourers, their task nearing completion, could now see the distant walls of Lal Kot and the rising temple shikharas of Dhillika. Anangpal, through years of dedicated effort, had transformed Dhillika into a thriving city, its temples, roads, rest houses and fortified walls reflecting his ambition. The installation of the Vishnu Stambha, a symbol of ancient power and enduring faith, would mark the culmination of his efforts.

On the final day of the journey, the citizens of Dhillika lined the main avenue, their excitement palpable. The pillar, draped in silk banners and showered with flower petals, was slowly, ceremoniously drawn through the city streets. Anangpal, resplendent in his silk uttariya and antariya, awaited its arrival at the designated site—a grand plaza at the heart of the city.

As the sounds of chants and the rhythmic clang of metal against metal reverberated all around, the Vishnu Stambha was carefully lifted from the logs and lowered onto its prepared foundation.

Priests chanted blessings, sprinkling sacred Gangajal and sandalwood paste upon the ancient iron. The pillar stood tall and proud, a beacon of strength and stability. But the crowning element—the Garuda—was missing, lost in the river during a treacherous crossing.

Addressing the assembled crowd, Anangpal declared, 'The rajpurohits tell us that Dhillika, built upon the foundations of the Pandavas' Indraprastha, rests precariously upon the head of Sheshanaga, the divine serpent. But now,' he proclaimed, gesturing towards the towering pillar, 'we have driven a nail into the earth, anchoring our city to Sheshanaga's coils. Dhillika shall no longer be loose—or "dhilli".'

Cheers erupted, the people's joy mirroring their king's triumph. The Vishnu Stambha stood as a sentinel, a symbol of unity and enduring strength, a promise that Dhillika, under Anangpal's rule, would stand firm against the tides of time.

36

Pothigai Forest, Pandya Desam

Present-day Agasthyamala Biosphere Reserve, Kerala, India

Around 2,000 years ago

Palyagasalai Mudukudumi Peruvazhudi rode with the elegance and dignity befitting the king of Pandya Desam. Under his leadership, Pandya Desam had become a flourishing hub for maritime trade, temple-building activities and literature. Peruvazhudi's reign had marked a golden age of Tamil culture.

The deep forest canopy dappled the ground below with sunshine and shade. Peruvazhudi's bronze skin, burnished by the sun and wind of countless hunts, radiated a light of its own. His long, black hair flowed freely, framing an attractive, compassionate face, and sharp, keen eyes scanned the surroundings with the intensity of an experienced hunter. He wore a traditional antariya—a beautifully spun silk wrap—around his waist that fell gracefully to his ankles and afforded maximum flexibility. An uttariya—a thick shawl for protection from the wind—was draped over his shoulders and fastened with a jewelled brooch. Robust leather sandals covered his feet, and a dagger, the hilt encrusted with priceless stones, hung at his side. A quiver of arrows was slung over his shoulder, paired with a finely crafted longbow carved from sandalwood, its string taut and ready. His style was unquestionably elegant.

Peruvazhudi's hunting entourage followed respectfully, alert for any sign of activity. The forest's quiet was broken only by the occasional rustling of leaves or the distant cry of a bird. Detecting a movement from the corner of his eye, Peruvazhudi turned to his left in time to spot a tiger, its striped coat gleaming as it moved silently through the underbrush. 'Magnificent beast,' he murmured under his breath and urged his horse forward to claim the prize.

Sensing a pursuer, the tiger plunged deeper into the jungle, its powerful muscles rippling with every bound. Peruvazhudi's horse sprinted forward, sailing over undergrowth and fallen logs. The thrill of the hunt sharpened Peruvazhudi's senses—for him nothing existed beyond that lone tiger. He aimed an arrow and let it fly through the air, but it glanced off the tiger's flank, only mildly injuring the animal. The tiger growled in pain, its stride faltering momentarily before it gathered speed. Blood streamed across its golden fur, but the injury seemed only to fuel its desperation.

Peruvazhudi spurred his horse onward, the distance between the hunter and the hunted rapidly diminishing. He knew a wounded tiger was far more deadly; its suffering would only enhance its survival instincts. The sounds of the hunt echoed through the forest: the laboured breathing of man and beast, thundering hooves, squelching mud and snapping twigs.

Rapt in the pursuit, Peruvazhudi failed to notice his entourage falling behind. The tiger drew him into a section of the forest where the vegetation was overgrown and tangled. Suddenly, the king's horse stumbled, its front legs disappearing into the earth. Peruvazhudi cried out as he was thrown from his mount, landing heavily in the same hidden ditch—an old trapper's pit, now concealed by weeds.

He lay there for a moment, winded, before pushing himself up on his elbows. The pit was deeper than it had first appeared, its moss and mud-covered sides offering few handholds. His horse lay nearby, shaken but unharmed. As his eyes adjusted to the dim light, Peruvazhudi realized with a sinking heart that he had been separated from his party and would likely never be found in this isolated location.

∼

Unbeknownst to King Peruvazhudi, three teenagers were walking through the woodland towards a nearby creek, a daily chore for the trio. They moved with practised ease, their feet expertly avoiding roots and fallen branches.

Suriratna, the keenest of the group, was the first to hear the faint sounds. She stopped, raising a hand to signal silence. 'Listen,' she whispered. The others followed her lead and soon they, too, heard the muffled whinnying of the horse.

'It is coming from over there,' Mithra said, pointing, his voice low.

Approaching the sound cautiously, they made their way through the dense undergrowth until they reached the edge of the pit.

'By the gods!' Soju exclaimed, his eyes widening at the sight of a man and a horse trapped in the deep hollow.

'We need to get them out,' she declared urgently.

The three friends quickly formulated a plan. Suriratna, the smallest and most agile, scrambled down into the pit to soothe the horse and reassure the man. Soju and Mithra, meanwhile, gathered long, sturdy vines and secured them around a massive tree trunk.

Inside the pit, Suriratna approached the horse carefully, her gentle words calming its fear. Peruvazhudi watched in amazement as she comforted the panicking beast, her cool head and quiet confidence shining through even in this precarious situation.

Once the vines had been secured, Soju and Mithra fashioned a makeshift harness for the horse and guided it towards the edge of the pit. Together, they pulled the animal out, ensuring it found its footing on solid ground. Next, they turned their attention to extracting Suriratna and the man.

Peruvazhudi grasped a vine the boys had tossed down, his grip tightening as he felt his strength returning. Once he stood on firm ground, he paused to catch his breath and looked at his rescuers with gratitude and curiosity. However, the fall had dulled his reflexes and he failed to notice the danger that lurked.

Suddenly, the underbrush rustled violently. The wounded tiger, having circled back, sprang at them with a furious roar. The children froze, a collective gasp caught in their throats. In a swift, decisive motion, Soju drew his blade, leaping forward to position himself between the group and the tiger. His heart pounded in his chest as he brandished his sword, its edge glinting in the dappled sunlight. Meanwhile, Mithra snatched a sturdy branch from the ground and took his place beside Soju. They faced the tiger together, their breaths coming in short, shallow gasps. The tiger surveyed its adversaries, muscles coiled with primal ferocity.

Soju and Mithra moved to flank the beast, each hoping to distract it from the other. Then Soju struck, his sword whistling through the air before it connected with the tiger's shoulder. With an enraged snarl, the tiger swiped at him with a massive paw. Soju dodged, avoiding the claws by a hair's breadth.

Seizing the opportunity, Mithra swung the branch with all his might. The improvised weapon slammed into the tiger's head, momentarily stunning it. The two boys exchanged a look, a silent understanding passing between them.

Their confidence proved premature. Enraged and desperate, the tiger lunged forward with renewed intensity. It knocked the branch from Mithra's grasp, sending him sprawling to the ground. The boy scrambled to his feet, but the tiger was upon him, roaring like thunder.

By now recovered, Peruvazhudi reacted instinctively. He whipped out his dagger and roared back at the tiger, a sound as primal and fierce as the beast's own.

The tiger spun around and pounced on Peruvazhudi, its full weight crashing into him, pinning him to the ground. The world narrowed to the beast's snarling maw and fiery gaze. As its claws raked his shoulders, Peruvazhudi, with a desperate strength, plunged his dagger deep into the tiger's flank. Its roars turned into pained howls, but the massive beast still did not relent. Gritting his teeth, Peruvazhudi twisted the blade, using every ounce of his will to hold on. The tiger's thrashing grew weaker, its powerful limbs slackening. With a final gasp, it collapsed atop him, its lifeblood pooling around, painting the forest floor a deep crimson.

The encounter left the group gasping for breath. Having extricated himself from beneath the beast with help from the three youngsters, Peruvazhudi caught his breath. He looked at the trio. 'Your courage is admirable,' he said, his voice filled with respect. 'I owe you my thanks.'

'It was nothing, sir,' Soju managed, sheathing his blade and trying to steady his trembling hands. 'Had it not been for you …' He let the rest of the sentence go unspoken.

'Who are you?' Peruvazhudi asked with an appreciative look at the three youngsters.

'We are students at Satyamuni's gurukul near the Agasthiyar mountains that border this forest,' Suriratna replied, bowing respectfully. 'Helping those in need is both our responsibility and our honour.'

'Satyamuni,' Peruvazhudi echoed, a smile spreading across his face. 'Please, take me to him.'

The trek to the gurukul was short. As they approached, Satyamuni emerged to greet them. With a discerning glance, he took in the scene before bowing to Peruvazhudi, who immediately knelt to touch the sage's feet.

'Your Majesty,' Satyamuni greeted, his voice warm. 'Your presence honours us.'

The three teenagers stared in wonder as the realization dawned on them: they had helped rescue their king. Peruvazhudi gently took the sage's hands in his own. 'The honour is all mine, revered Satyamuni. Today, your students displayed extraordinary bravery.'

Satyamuni turned to the trio, his voice filled with pride, 'Come, pay your respects to the king under whose benevolent rule Pandya Desam has flourished. Renowned for his wisdom, justice and steadfastness, our monarch has guided his people through many trials.'

The three of them bowed once more, this time with newfound reverence, while others from the gurukul emerged silently from the shadows of the trees and verandas, drawn by the tale already beginning to travel through the ashram—of the king, the tiger and the courage of three young hearts.

37

Muchiri Pattinam, Cherala
Present-day Muziris, Kodungallur, Kerala, India
Around 2,000 years ago

Cheliyan and Kulasekara arrived in Muchiri Pattinam with a single objective: to strike a trade alliance between the Pandyas and the Cheras. They knew they had their work cut out given that the monarchs of the two kingdoms could barely tolerate one another. But Padmasen had been adamant that they make the trip.

The port of Muchiri Pattinam—known to the Romans as Muziris—was responsible for draining vast amounts of Roman gold. The culprit? Peppercorns. The Romans craved it, parting with vast quantities of gold to acquire it from Muziris along with precious gems, silks, ivory and incense. In return, Rome supplied wine, olive oil, coral, glassware and fish oil. Lording over this incredible trading machine was the Chera king, Uthiyan Cheralathan—known throughout his kingdom as Vanamvarubavan, or one whose kingdom touched the sky.

Situated near the Churni river, Muziris teemed with docks and warehouses, its narrow, winding streets a labyrinth of brick houses and bustling marketplaces. The harbour itself was a magnificent spectacle—a gallery showcasing a vast variety of ships from across the known world. Surrounding it were palm groves, natural lagoons and serene backwaters, making Muziris the perfect marriage of economic might and natural beauty.

Though Cheralathan's capital lay in Kuttanad, some 60 miles away, he maintained a retreat in Muziris, signalling the city's importance. While Kuttanad served as the political heart of the Chera kingdom, Muziris was undoubtedly its commercial lifeblood. Neither Cheralathan's glorious palace nor his massive elephant corps would have been possible without the revenue Muziris so generously provided.

Cheliyan and Kulasekara rented lodgings at a boarding house near the docks. It took them two days to secure an audience with Cheralathan, a feat accomplished with the help of a Chera merchant with whom Cheliyan had prior dealings. On the appointed day, Cheliyan carefully carried with him a gift for the king—a hunting dagger, its handle encrusted with extremely rare star rubies, stones that exhibited a star-like pattern on the surface when light shone on them. The Chera king was a connoisseur of rubies and these precious gems had been carefully selected to charm him.

Cheralathan's retreat comprised several structures that opened onto multiple courtyards, each adorned with heavily carved columns supporting roofs made of mud tiles. Ensconced within a tropical paradise of coconut palm, banana, jackfruit and mango trees, the retreat boasted private areas for the king and his family, as well as separate areas for audiences and administration.

A guard escorted Cheliyan and Kulasekara into the audience hall. An overpowering scent of sandalwood perfumed the air. Cheralathan was seated upon a teakwood throne, draped in a silk dhoti intricately embroidered with gold thread and gold necklaces, armlets and bracelets adorning his torso and arms. 'What brings the most celebrated traders of Pandya Desam to my kingdom?' Cheralathan inquired as the two men entered and bowed low before the monarch.

Cheliyan knelt before Cheralathan and proffered the dagger with both hands. 'A small token of respect, Your Majesty, from humble merchants,' he said smoothly.

The king accepted the dagger, his eyes drawn to the blade's distinctive swirling pattern, the ruby-encrusted handle and the star illusion on the surface of the gemstones. 'Remarkable craftsmanship,' he said. 'I have heard tales of your ironwork. Your reputation precedes you both.'

'Your words honour us, Your Majesty,' Kulasekara responded. 'We believe there is great potential for a mutually beneficial collaboration between us. Cherala's dominion over the seas is absolute and the allure of Muchiri Pattinam's pepper is known throughout the world. We, too, offer a product equally in demand—our ingots and the arms and tools forged from them.'

'Elaborate,' commanded Cheralathan, his interest piqued.

'A trade alliance, Your Majesty,' Cheliyan replied. 'Utilizing the overland route between Muchiri Pattinam and Korkai, we can ensure the presence of all of Cherala's products on Pandyan ships. In return, Your Majesty could do the same for Pandyan wares on his vessels.'

'We already enjoy trade surpluses with most of our trading partners,' replied Cheralathan. 'What advantage would such an alliance offer?'

'The world is changing, Your Majesty,' Cheliyan said. 'It is imperative for every kingdom to cultivate a diverse range of goods. Overdependence on a single commodity is precarious.'

Cheralathan stroked his chin thoughtfully. 'There is wisdom in your words,' he conceded. 'But how can such a pact be forged when our kingdoms are so often at odds? The presence of the Chola king in our political landscape further complicates matters.'

'Your Majesty,' countered Kulasekara, 'the very existence of trade between kingdoms diminishes the likelihood of war. My experience in these matters is limited, but surely Your Majesty recognizes this truth.'

Cheralathan laughed, a deep, resonant sound. 'You are shrewd men, both of you,' he declared. 'I hold little regard for your king, but I am willing to entertain this proposition. Tell me, do you have your monarch's approval? Peruvazhudi is not known for his humility.'

'Be assured, Your Majesty, King Peruvazhudi has given us his blessing,' Cheliyan lied smoothly. 'We are hopeful that Your Majesty will look favourably upon this arrangement.'

Moments later, Cheliyan and Kulasekara walked out of the retreat, Cheralathan's approval secured. Kulasekara shot his friend an incredulous look. 'You spoke of the king's concurrence? Peruvazhudi is unaware of this entirely!'

Cheliyan grinned, his eyes twinkling. 'Kings are a predictable breed,' he observed. 'Their pride demands that they never be the first to take a risk. Cheralathan would never have agreed had he doubted our king's support. Now that we have his approval, convincing our king will be a far simpler task.'

38

Dimašq, Roman Empire
Present-day Damascus, Syria
Around 2,000 years ago

Cornelius pressed himself deeper into the shadows of a narrow alley, the mob's enraged roars echoing behind him. Smoke billowed from burning buildings, painting the Dimašq sky with chaotic strokes. The city had erupted into violent insurrection against Roman rule, a maelstrom of anarchy he had narrowly escaped. He had been lucky to slip the mob's grasp in the initial frenzy, but he knew his luck would not hold indefinitely.

He held his breath, listening for any sign of pursuit. The mob showed no mercy to anyone associated with Roman governance—its fury, a potent cocktail of desperation and wrath. Time, he knew, was not on his side.

He moved swiftly through the winding streets, keeping to the shadows. The normally lively lanes and passages, typically filled with merchants and their goods, now seemed to whisper with fear. Every anguished cry that pierced the air sent his heart hammering against his ribs. His mind raced, replaying the events that had led to this moment—the simmering unrest, the sudden explosion of mob fury, the unexpected assassination of Governor Philippides and the inevitable, iron-fisted crackdown from Rome.

His memory of the governor's palace was vivid—the metallic tang of blood, the glint of cold metal as swords and daggers flashed in the mob's hands. Cornelius had barely escaped with his life. Now, survival was his only goal, his heart echoing with Philippides' dying plea: *Protect Mithradates. My only son.*

He needed to put as much distance as possible between himself and Dimašq. His destination was Aelana, a port city on the Sea of Reeds, its waters stained a rusty brown by algae blooms. From Aelana, he would cross the reeds to Eudaemon and secure passage to either Korkai or Muziris. It was a perilous route, fraught with danger, but it was the only option he had.

He travelled when it was dark, avoiding the main roads and the watchful rebel patrols, seeking refuge amongst the trees and snatching what little sleep he could in abandoned caves. Finally, Cornelius slipped into Aelana under night's cover. He moved through the throngs of traders and sailors, searching for a ship to ferry him across the Sea of Reeds. Amidst the larger vessels, he spotted a smaller dhow and bargained a passage to Eudaemon. The dhow, though modest, was sturdy and swift—perfect for navigating the treacherous reeds.

Days later, he arrived in Eudaemon. The scent of the sea mingled with the familiar fragrance of spices and a symphony of voices speaking in a multitude of tongues filled the air. Cornelius approached a group of sailors hastily loading cargo onto a ship, its side emblazoned with two fish—the mark of a Pandyan vessel.

'Captain,' Cornelius called out, catching the eye of a burly man with a weather-beaten face. 'I need passage. I am willing to pay handsomely. Where are you bound?'

The captain eyed him with suspicion, taking in his dishevelled appearance and the urgency etched on his face. 'Korkai,' he replied, his voice betraying a Kanyakumari lilt. 'We set sail in an hour. You are welcome aboard—if you have the coin.'

Cornelius nodded and offered him a small purse. The captain accepted the pouch, weighing it in his hand. His eyes narrowed, lingering on Cornelius with an intensity that made him shift uncomfortably. What if the captain tried to deceive him, leave him stranded, or worse? 'Is this ship owned by Kadalan Cheliyan by any chance?' he asked cautiously.

A wide, gap-toothed grin split the captain's face. 'Indeed it is. You know him?'

'We have history,' Cornelius said. 'I once helped him escape capture in Dimašq when Roman guards wrongly suspected him of evading duty. I will tell you about it on our voyage.'

Finally, the ship set sail, leaving the shores of Eudaemon behind. The journey to Korkai would take nearly a month—enough time to formulate a plan, to grapple with the burden of his mission.

On their third night at sea, a storm broke upon the Erythraean Sea. The ship pitched violently as waves crashed on the deck. Memories of that fateful day in Dimašq flooded Cornelius's mind. He thought of young Mithradates, thrust into a position of immense responsibility, forced to navigate the treacherous waters of leadership far too soon.

∽

After a month at sea, buffeted by the vast expanse of the Mlecchadal—the great western ocean that separated Bharatvarsha from Arava Nadu—the ship finally docked at Korkai. Cornelius disembarked quickly, his eyes scanning the bustling harbour, a scene of vibrant chaos. But he had only one goal—he had to find Cheliyan.

As if on cue, the captain exchanged greetings with a familiar face in the throng—one of Cheliyan's trusted men. Cornelius was soon being led through the maze of streets, the press of bodies around him a constant.

They reached a modest building and the moment Cheliyan saw Cornelius, he rose from his seat in surprise. 'What brings you here, my friend? And in such a state?' he asked.

'Short version or long version?' Cornelius asked, gathering his thoughts as he sat down.

'Tell me everything,' Cheliyan replied.

'Dimašq is lost to chaos,' Cornelius began, his voice tired. 'Philippides is dead, murdered by the mob. The Romans have instituted martial law, but the streets are still aflame with rebellion. Any semblance of self-rule has been extinguished. Even Barakat and his followers have gone into hiding. They realized too late that Philippides was the only shield protecting them from the full might of Rome.'

Cheliyan listened intently, his face darkening with each detail. 'This is dire news indeed. Tell me, what is it you need? Consider it done.'

Cornelius leaned forward, his next words sharp with urgency. 'Mithradates—he must return to Dimašq. The people need a leader to rally behind, someone who can stand against the Romans and restore peace. Without him, the city will descend further into anarchy.'

Cheliyan nodded grimly, comprehending the gravity of the situation. 'Mithra is at Satyamuni's gurukul. His studies should be concluding soon. He needs to understand the importance of his return to Dimašq. But remember, he is only sixteen.'

'Alexander was a regent at sixteen,' Cornelius shot back, 'when he effectively crushed the Maedi rebellion. Cleopatra was fully immersed in politics at sixteen and a co-ruler by eighteen. And what of Octavian, who would become Augustus? He was named heir to Julius Caesar at eighteen. Age is but a number. It holds no bearing on true capability.'

Cheliyan nodded slowly, agreeing with the truth in Cornelius's words. But protecting Mithra, ensuring he did not meet the same fate as his father—that was paramount. And then a thought struck him: *What if Mithra's return to Dimašq was an opportunity?*

39

Agastyamalai, Pandya Desam
Present-day Agasthyamala Biosphere Reserve, Kerala, India
Around 2,000 years ago

Soju and Suriratna sat side by side at the edge of the gurukul, their backs resting against a gnarled banyan tree, heads bent over an ancient scroll. The scent of marigolds wafted around them, the vibrant clusters flanking a bubbling stream that flowed into a nearby pond. Beyond the pond, the magnificent Agasthiyar mountains rose, silent sentinels looming on the horizon. This place, steeped in ancient lore, was said to be the birthplace of the Tamil language, a sanctuary where Sage Agastya had first given form to words. The air thrummed with a quiet energy, the legacy of countless generations of scholars who had studied here, seeking knowledge and wisdom.

The teenagers were engrossed in their studies. 'So,' Soju remarked, his brow furrowed in concentration, 'this shloka suggests that the principles of dharma are not rigid but adapt to circumstances.'

Suriratna nodded. 'That makes sense. Dharma is meant to guide us, not confine us.' Their conversation flowed effortlessly, each moment deepening the bond between them. As they spoke, Suriratna absently picked up a small pebble and flicked it into the underbrush. A soft rustle followed—then silence. Soju lifted his head, his senses alert. 'Did you hear that?' he asked, anxiety in his voice.

Suriratna tensed, scanning the shadows. 'It came from the bushes,' she said, keeping her voice low.

Moments later, a massive Indian cobra emerged from the undergrowth, its scales glittering in the sunlight. It moved with swift, sinuous grace, its hood expanded, hissing menacingly. It had likely been startled by the pebble or felt its territory had been encroached upon. Frozen with terror, Suriratna gasped, unable to move.

In an instant, Soju was on his feet, his hand reaching for a cluster of tall marigolds. He positioned himself between Suriratna and the serpent, creating a fragrant barrier of vibrant blooms. 'Stay calm,' he said, his voice steady and reassuring. 'Do not make any sudden movements. Snakes detest the smell of marigolds.'

For a heartbeat, time seemed to stop. The cobra paused, its tongue flicking, testing the air as it focused on Soju. His heart hammering against his ribs, Soju stood his ground. With slow, deliberate movements, he mirrored the cobra's swaying, the vivid petals a stark contrast to the serpent's menacing form. Finally, after what felt like an eternity, the cobra lowered its head and retreated into the undergrowth. Soju turned to Suriratna, relief flooding his features. 'Are you all right?' he asked softly.

Suriratna nodded, but her fear lingered, her knees trembling. She tried to stand, but stumbled. Instinctively, Soju reached out, catching her before she could fall. His arms closed around her protectively. Suriratna clung to him, her heart pounding against his chest. Neither spoke, the silence filled with a mix of relief and a sudden, electrifying awareness. For a moment, the world around them faded, leaving only the warmth of their embrace and the comforting scent of marigolds.

Gently, Soju kissed her forehead, a tender gesture of reassurance, of affection, of something deeper than he could yet understand. As they drew apart, their eyes met. Something had shifted between them. The carefree innocence of their friendship had transformed and been replaced by a new intensity, a longing that hummed beneath the surface.

'Soju,' Suriratna whispered, her voice trembling. 'I ... I think ...'

'I know,' Soju said, his voice husky with emotion, his gaze never leaving hers. 'I love you too.'

He gently brushed away a stray strand of hair from her face, his touch sending a shiver through her. Tears welled in Suriratna's eyes, overflowing as the dam of her emotions finally broke. She had always admired his strength, his quiet confidence. But today, she saw him in a new light—as her protector, her confidante, her love.

His heart aching, Soju wiped away her tears. 'Suriratna,' he said, with a quiet determination, 'I promise, I will always be there for you—to protect you, to support you ... to love you.'

Suriratna smiled through her tears, the warmth of his words chasing away the shadows of fear. 'And I will always be by your side, Soju,' she whispered. 'I adore you. Together, we can face anything.'

Hand in hand, they walked back to the gurukul, under the warm glow of the setting sun. They moved slowly, as if reluctant to break the spell that had been woven around them, their silence a shared language of love and hope. Each step towards the gurukul felt like the beginning of a new journey—filled with both promise and uncertainty.

40

Gimhae, South Gyeongsang Province, South Korea
Present day

Aditya was in South Korea again. This time he found himself in the domain of Dr Jung Tae-hyun, GISCO's fiercely territorial chief metallurgist. Some of the company's finest product innovations had been achieved under his leadership.

Jung's metallurgy laboratory was vast. An entire section housed induction furnaces, resistance furnaces, electric arc furnaces and a row of ovens. A massive countertop spanned the length of the lab, supporting specialized microscopes, spectrometers, tensility testing machines, and hardness and impact testers. Wall-length cabinets contained acids, bases, solvents, fluxes and an array of other reagents necessary for tests.

For the moment, however, Jung's attention was focused on the sword fragment Jayaraman had given Somi in Chennai. Somi and Aditya sat on lab stools some distance away, discomfited by Jung's silence. There were countless moments when Somi longed to ask his opinion, but she restrained herself. She knew Jung well enough to know he would speak only when he was ready.

'This is wootz,' he finally declared, breaking the silence.

'How can you be certain?' Somi asked.

'The steel possesses a distinctive surface pattern: swirling, light-etched patches on an almost completely black background,' Jung explained. 'It is a result of the carbon–steel mixture.'

'Wootz?' Aditya repeated, recalling the articles he had read on it.

'Indian crucible steel,' Jung clarified. 'In north India, it was called "utsa" or "uttamam", and in the south, "ukku". The earliest form was used in the Iron Pillar of Delhi—the one that does not rust. In the first millennium, they refined the process, creating a new variation they called "nav utsa". International merchants, however, struggled with the pronunciation, and it became known as "vutsa"—or "wootz". It was exported around the world in five-pound, semi-spherical ingots.'

'Around the world?' Aditya asked.

'The world knows it in the context of the Damascus sword,' Jung replied. 'Those famous blades were forged from wootz ingots shipped from India to Damascus where Syrian bladesmiths had mastered the art of transforming them into weapons of unparalleled strength and beauty.'

'So the raw material came from India?' Aditya asked.

'Absolutely,' Jung confirmed.

'I wonder why,' Aditya persisted.

'Because Indian foundries had perfected the science of creating high-carbon steel—far superior to anything produced elsewhere,' Jung explained. 'The microstructure of ancient wootz contains carbon nanotubes and cementite nanowires. Imagine—this technology was being used in India over two thousand years ago!'

Jung walked to a chaotic bookshelf in the room adjacent to his office. For several minutes, he rummaged, pulling out books, rifling through drawers, even climbing a stool to reach the highest shelves. A cry of triumph indicated that he had located what he was searching for—an unlabelled folder overflowing with handwritten notes, photocopied articles and photographs. He extracted one of the photos and presented it to Aditya and Somi.

'Look at this,' he said.

The photograph showcased a magnificent sword, its intricate details captured perfectly. 'This,' Jung explained, 'is the fourteenth-century Sword of Osman, forged in Damascus. It's on display at the Topkapi Palace Museum in Istanbul. Notice the distinctive wavy forms on the blade.'

Aditya and Somi leaned closer, their gaze drawn to the intricate innate undulating pattern on the surface.

'The Syrians may have mastered the art of forging these blades,' Jung continued, 'but the raw material—the wootz steel—always went from India. Over time, swordsmiths in Damascus refined the process to create blades with a unique, almost magical pattern.'

'What made these swords so special?' Aditya asked.

'The wootz itself, of course,' Jung replied. 'But the Damascus bladesmiths were masters of their craft. They developed a technique for stacking the wootz—heating, hammering, and repeatedly folding layers of steel—to create a blade of unparalleled strength with remarkable markings.'

'And how did they achieve that kind of hardness with wootz?' Aditya asked, more out of curiosity than ignorance, trying to understand the subtleties of an ancient technique that might help him solve his own metallurgical challenge.

'Through quenching,' Jung replied. 'Rapid cooling of the heated blade—typically using water or oil. But with wootz, the process had to be precise. The rate of cooling had to be just right to preserve the distinctive microstructure—those carbon nanotubes and cementite strands. Too fast and it shattered. Too slow and the strength was lost.'

'So that sword fragment you examined—was it also wootz?' Somi asked.

'Yes,' Jung confirmed, 'but not from a Damascus sword. It's more likely from a Garak sword—ancient Korean. Why am I not surprised that it was found in Korkai!'

'So Indian crucible steel was everywhere? Even in Korea?' Somi asked, her eyes widening. 'Is it possible to re-engineer it? To rediscover the secrets of its creation?'

'Many have tried.' Jung paused, weighing his words. 'But the truth is, the knowledge is lost. We can approximate the techniques, but no one has been able to replicate the original process perfectly.'

'But there must be some record, some clue to guide us,' Aditya insisted, his frustration mounting.

Jung, sensing his desperation, pulled out a file filled with photocopied pages of an ancient text. 'Perhaps this will help,' he said, handing the file to Aditya.

Hesitantly, Aditya began to read the faded Sanskrit script aloud:

suṣṇātaṁ lohaṁ uttamaṁ samaṁ
ca kṛṣṇatolyaṁ palāśapatrakam
caturguṇaṁ śrīśākhena dviguṇaṁ
khadira-cūrṇaṁ śarṅkarāṁś ca yojayet ...

Faltering, he looked up at Jung. 'What is this?'

'The *Rasaratnakara*,' Jung replied. 'A treatise on Indian metallurgy possibly written by Nagarjuna in the eighth century. The process is also referenced in the *Tantrasamuccaya*, a fifteenth-century text from Kerala.'

'And what does it say?' Aditya asked.

'It describes the process for creating crucible steel,' Jung explained. 'It says, "Take pure iron—free from rust—and mix it with four times its weight of powdered palasha leaves, one-eighth its weight of khadira bark and one-sixteenth its weight of burnt brick."'

'And then?'

'Then, it says, "add the special ingredient and cover the mixture with black hide, place it in a crucible and heat it for three nights. After this is done, break open the crucible and examine the steel. If it is not of the desired quality, repeat the process. Seven repetitions will yield the finest steel."'

'Incredible,' Somi murmured. 'Until the seventeenth century, the secrets of crucible steel were unknown in Europe. But here ... The formula exists right here in this ancient text.'

'Precisely,' Aditya said. 'Except for the name of that one special ingredient.'

'It seems,' Somi observed, 'the farther we look into the past, the clearer our vision of the future becomes.'

Aditya considered her words, then nodded. 'That reminds me of something a Cambridge historian once told me,' he said as he glanced at the others. 'He saw the rise and fall of civilizations like waves,' he said, 'peaks and valleys of human knowledge and innovation. The tragedy is that sometimes ... we lose the knowledge gained in one cycle, only to rediscover it many cycles later.'

'Very astute,' Jung agreed.

'Take the example of Sayana, the fourteenth-century Indian scholar,' Aditya continued. 'He calculated the speed of light centuries before Ole Romer. How could he have known? It's clear that ancient India possessed knowledge and technologies far more advanced than we can currently imagine. Their records are lost, but their achievements are undeniable. Like the Iron Pillar. Or, perhaps, like crucible steel.'

'Exactly,' Somi agreed. 'We need to rediscover the secrets of ancient Indian metallurgy—starting with this wootz steel. And this text—it mentions specific ingredients: the palasha tree, also known as the Flame of the Forest, and the khadira tree, a source of catechu.' She paused, as though lost in thought, then said slowly, her voice filled with excitement, 'We need to understand these ingredients to determine their properties and how they contribute to the creation of this unique steel. Then we can perhaps magnify those properties and recreate—maybe even surpass—the achievements of the ancients.'

'But there is still an unnamed additive,' reminded Aditya.

'For everything relating to ancient Indian science, there's only one person I trust,' Jung said, a thoughtful look on his face. 'If you're willing, we can consult with him. He might hold the key to unlocking these secrets.'

'Who is he?' Aditya asked.

'His name is Dr Bala Ramaswamy,' Jung replied. 'He works at CERN, in Geneva.'

Prabhas Patan, Chaulukya Samrajya
Present-day Somnath, Gujarat, India
Around 1,000 years ago

The rhythmic thud of drums echoed across the plains, heralding the approach of Mahmud of Ghazni's army—a sound that instilled fear for miles around. Within the walls of the temple, the devout prayed fervently to Shiva, their chants rising like a desperate plea against the inevitable. From a distance, its soaring spires appeared to touch the heavens, mirroring the outstretched arms of those seeking deliverance from the devastation to come.

Mahmud was the sultan of the Ghaznavid Empire. After ascending the throne at twenty-seven, he had transformed his kingdom into an extensive military empire, which stretched from Persia to the Punjab. His frequent attacks on Hindustan's temple towns had amassed him vast treasures that he used to beautify his capital, Ghazni, nestled in the rugged highlands beyond the northwestern frontiers of Hindustan. Mahmud's soldiers advanced with ruthless efficiency, their discipline fuelled by religious zeal, their faces hardened by a sense of divine purpose. Somnath, the richest temple in Hindustan, was a prize worthy of their efforts. It was funded by the revenue from ten thousand villages, its rituals were conducted by a thousand Brahmins and its deity was honoured by the daily performances of five hundred dancing girls—it was a tempting target.

Mahmud, astride his warhorse, surveyed the temple complex from afar. It was a formidable fortress, protected on three sides by the sea. He had heard tales of the treasures within, whispered stories that had reached him through a network of informants. And then one day he had met an aged tribesman, Ibn al-Kaqaya. His name traced his roots to an ancient clan—the Kekayas, a tribe that Queen Kaikeyi hailed from. What Ibn al-Kaqaya told him truly captivated his imagination: a story about the Dvaitalingam, a sacred stone revered by millions, rumoured to possess powers beyond comprehension. Mahmud usually dismissed such beliefs as superstition—yet al-Kaqaya's narrative intrigued him. It was not belief, but curiosity and ambition that stirred within him. To shatter such an object of veneration would crush the spirit of its followers—and if there was any truth to its alleged power, it would be in his possession. Logic dictated that the most obvious and secure location to hide it would be within Somnath itself.

This was Mahmud's seventeenth incursion into Hindustan. Only yesterday, he had faced a formidable foe, the Chaulukya Rajputs, also known as the Solankis of Gujarat. Under the leadership of their king, Bhima, they had surrounded his army, trapping them in a precarious position.

But one of Mahmud's commanders had stoked the flames of religious devotion within his ranks, promising each man who broke the Rajput stronghold the reward of seventy-two hoors in paradise. Inspired by the idea of a divine reward, they had shattered enemy lines, outflanking their formations for a decisive victory that left fifty thousand Rajput soldiers dead. Today, Mahmud drew strength from that triumph, steeling himself for the coming battle.

The temple's defenders, though valiant, proved no match for Mahmud's seasoned warriors. The clash of swords, the anguished cries of the wounded and the desperate chants of the priests created a discordant symphony of violence and devotion. The temple gates, once symbols of security and sanctity, splintered and crumbled under the relentless assault.

Inside, devotees huddled around the massive levitating lingam, seeking refuge from the encroaching darkness. Tales of Mahmud's brutality, of temples desecrated and cities razed, had spread terror throughout Hindustan. They prayed for a miracle, hoping their faith would shield them from the approaching storm. But even their fervent prayers were no match for the fanaticism, the single-minded determination of Mahmud, the destroyer of idols.

He dismounted before the sanctum sanctorum, his every step deliberate, measured, his eyes fixed on the lingam—a monument to the infidels' devotion, and perhaps to something more. He relished the fear he inspired, the dread that clung to those sacred walls. The lingam, decked with gemstones and illuminated by flickering lamps, was a prize to be claimed, whether for its symbolic weight or hidden truths.

Mahmud gestured and his soldiers, axes and hammers raised, moved to demolish the idol. Priests, their faces streaked with tears, cursed the invaders, promising divine retribution. Other worshippers, desperate to save their sacred relic, offered bribes, pleading for mercy. But Mahmud remained unmoved. He would have both the treasure and the satisfaction of obliterating their stone whose worship reminded him of pre-Islamic Mecca's Su-Manat.

The first blow rang against the stone, a hollow thud. Again and again the hammers struck, until finally, with a deafening crack, the lingam shattered, its pieces scattering across the floor. Surveying the scene, Mahmud felt a rush of satisfaction. He ordered the fragments collected and packed.

'Tell Al-Biruni to write up this event in the chronicles,' said Mahmud. 'He should remind everyone that the fragments are being ground up to be scattered upon the steps of my grand mosque.' Other pieces would be given to his alchemists to study, to unlock the secrets of its alleged power.

As dawn broke, Somnath lay in ruins, its wealth plundered, its sanctity violated. Smoke and dust obscured the carnage.

Mahmud's army returned to Ghazni laden with the spoils of war. Tales of his triumph spread throughout the land, striking fear into the hearts of those who still clung to their ancient faiths. But for those who revered Shiva, it was a time of mourning, their hearts heavy with the knowledge that even the most sacred of sites, the most powerful of deities, could not withstand intolerance.

~

Back in Ghazni, the powdered fragments of the lingam were embedded in the steps of Mahmud's grand mosque; a symbolic gesture asserting his dominance. His alchemists, however, were confounded. Despite months of study, the sacred dust yielded no secrets.

Mahmud paced his chamber, hands clasped behind him, frustration simmering beneath his carefully constructed composure. The idol he had shattered—glorified though it was—seemed to hold no tangible power. Had the stories been exaggerated? Or worse, had he acquired a worthless object? He froze, eyes narrowing at the palm leaf recovered from the temple's ruins. The cryptic two-fish symbol inscribed on it stirred something unsettling in his mind. *What if the true Dvaitalingam had not been in Somnath at all?*

A roar emerged from his throat, primal and ferocious. The thought that he had been deceived—that the true source of power still eluded him—gnawed at his pride and stoked the fires of his obsession. The Dvaitalingam remained an enigma, a whispered promise that had slipped through his fingers. Not broken. Not captured. Not yet.

Never one to be deterred, Mahmud vowed to hunt it down—across mountains, deserts and oceans if need be. For now, it was legend. But he would be the one to make it real to the world.

41

Safed Koh Mountains, Afghanistan
Present day

Dr Bala Ramaswamy was jolted awake by the sudden landing of the helicopter. The long journey from Geneva, first by a private aircraft to Kabul International Airport, then by helicopter to the remote Safed Koh Mountains near Ghazni, had left him disoriented and exhausted. Khalil Ghaznawar stood at the entrance of a surprisingly modern facility carved into the mountainside. 'Welcome, Dr Ramaswamy,' he greeted, his voice warm yet laced with menace. Having introduced himself, he asked, 'I trust your journey was ... agreeable?'

Ramaswamy, still groggy, managed a nod, his mind struggling to process the reality of his abduction. What did this man want from him? Ghaznawar ushered him inside. The stark contrast between the rough, natural exterior and the modern interior—corridors lined with state-of-the-art security systems, the distant hum of machinery a constant undercurrent—was unnerving.

They reached a large, well-equipped laboratory. Computers, lab equipment and cryogenic tools stood ready and the shelves were lined with volumes of the latest research papers and ancient texts. It was a scientist's dream—or, in Ramaswamy's case, a nightmare.

'This will be your workspace—for now,' Ghaznawar announced. 'Everything you require is at your disposal. However, internet access is restricted. We have non-geofenced Starlink, but communication channels—messaging, email and such—are disabled. Do not attempt to circumvent these protocols.'

Ramaswamy surveyed the impressive setup, his apprehension growing. 'What, precisely, do you expect of me?' he asked, though the answer was already clear.

'The substance described in the ancient texts,' Ghaznawar replied, his eyes narrowing, 'I require you to harness its power.'

Ramaswamy sighed, running a hand through his greying hair. 'Mr Ghaznawar, the material you seek is not easily replicated. My research on this subject is preliminary at best. Finding and re-engineering it could take years, perhaps even decades. Fully understanding its properties ... that could take a lifetime.'

Ghaznawar's expression hardened. 'Years? I am afraid you do not have that kind of time, Doctor. Your progress will determine your freedom. Succeed and you return home. Fail ... and this will become your permanent residence.'

A chill snaked down Ramaswamy's spine. He was a pawn in a dangerous game, his fate resting on the whims of a man obsessed with power. 'I'll do my best,' he said softly, knowing that even his best might not be enough.

'Good,' Ghaznawar said, a hint of steel in his voice. 'Begin. My men will provide you with anything you need. We are hospitable hosts. You will be treated with respect.'

Ramaswamy nodded, turning to the task before him. But his hands hesitated at the controls. The steady whir of machines around him was oddly soothing, masking the war raging within. He was not just a scientist anymore—he was a captive, a weapon in someone else's war. The thought of contributing to Ghaznawar's ambitions sent a chill of dread through him. What was this man truly after? Control? Immortality? Domination cloaked in the language of discovery?

He looked around the lab, at the texts stacked beside quantum processors and felt disoriented. This was not just about science—it was about ideology, obsession, power masquerading as curiosity. For a moment, he considered refusing. Sabotage, delay, resistance—all flashed through his mind in quick succession. But then he remembered Ghaznawar's parting words: 'Succeed and you return home. Fail ... and this will become your permanent residence.'

He sighed and began setting up the cryostat and adjusting the parameters. Each action was mechanical, the result of habit, not conviction. As the equipment hummed to life, he recalled his lecture at CERN. The very hypothesis he had proposed was now a chilling reality. His mind raged with a million questions: Could these ancient texts, their cryptic verses concealing tantalizing hints, truly hold the key to manipulating the fundamental forces of the universe? Did this substance, this mythical material, actually exist?

Days passed as he pored over ancient manuscripts, cross-referencing data, conducting experiments. He immersed himself entirely in the world of quantum entanglement, exploring the intricate dance of particles, their interactions governed by forces beyond human comprehension. Ghaznawar would visit frequently, sometimes standing in silence for long stretches, observing Ramaswamy's work with a gaze that felt more like surveillance than curiosity.

Progress, however, was slow as each glimpse of a solution faded into a million complexities. Eventually, Ghaznawar's visits became more frequent, his impatience growing with each passing day.

'Any progress, Doctor?' he frequently asked.

'Some,' Ramaswamy would reply, displaying his data and pointing to minuscule advancements. 'But we are still a long way from a workable solution.'

Ghaznawar's frustration quickly multiplied. 'You must work faster,' he demanded, his voice a menacing growl. 'My patience wears thin.'

Ramaswamy, his face drawn with exhaustion, met his gaze. 'Mr Ghaznawar, science does not adhere to deadlines. The truth reveals itself in its own time.'

'Then you must find a way to hasten its revelation,' Ghaznawar snarled. 'Or I'll find someone who can. Remember, Doctor, your time here is finite.'

Although he knew that finding another scientist with the knowledge and skill to unravel this mystery was virtually impossible, the threat was unmistakable, a dark cloud overshadowing Ramaswamy's already fragile hope. He had to succeed. His life—his freedom—depended on it.

As he returned to his research, a new thought blossomed: perhaps the key to unlocking the secrets of this substance lay not just in deciphering the texts, but in understanding the minds of those who had written them. He plunged further into the philosophies, the beliefs, the worldviews of the ancients, searching for clues, for patterns, for a connection that could guide his path.

One evening, Ghaznawar entered the lab, a fragile palm-leaf manuscript in his hand. He laid it on the table, his face intent. 'Doctor,' he said, 'this might interest you.'

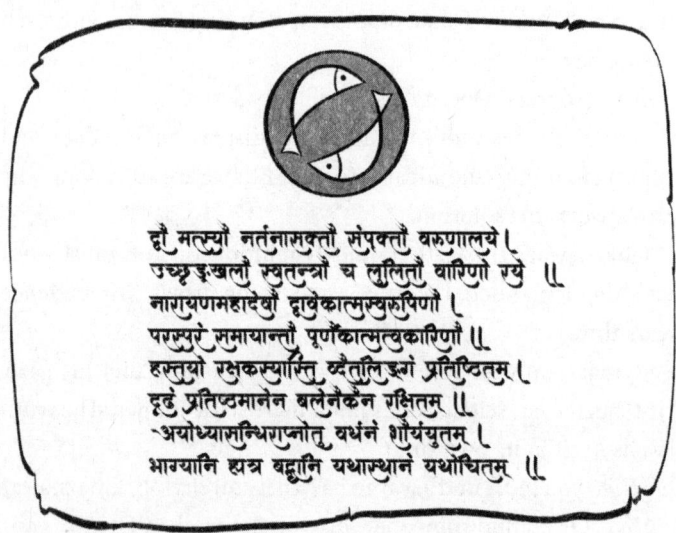

Ramaswamy adjusted his glasses. The manuscript was in Sanskrit and though the writing on it had faded over time, there was no mistaking the intricate twin-fish emblem right on the top. Its presence here, in this strange and threatening place, felt like more than coincidence. It felt like fate.

'Remarkable,' Ramaswamy murmured. 'Where did you find this?'

'It is a family heirloom,' Ghaznawar replied. 'Passed down through generations. Forty generations, to be precise. A legacy that dates back to my ancestor, Mahmud of Ghazni. He led seventeen expeditions to India in search of a lingam said to hold incredible power—the power to control the very fabric of reality.' He gestured towards the manuscript. 'This text, though filled with riddles, might guide us to that power.'

Ramaswamy's stomach clenched. Mahmud of Ghazni. A name equated in Indian memory with fire and ruin. The

The Ayodhya Alliance

desecration of temples, the theft of sacred icons—history books had painted him as a conqueror, but to Ramaswamy and millions of others he was a symbol of violence and erasure. And here he was, working under the shadow of that legacy. His fingers trembled slightly as he touched the brittle page. Was he reviving the very force his ancestors had once suffered under? Was he about to hand over the key to some long-lost, elemental power to a man who viewed history not as a lesson, but as a right to conquer?

He swallowed hard and forced his voice into a neutral tone. 'It's ... certainly ancient,' he said, though his mind screamed a different truth: *You are standing at the edge of something dangerous and will be complicit in its awakening.* But he tried to push those thoughts aside and focus on the text before him.

dvau matsyau nartanāsaktau saṃpṛktau varuṇālaye
ucchṛṅkhalau svatantrau ca lulitau vāriṇo raye
nārāyaṇamahādevau dvāvekātmasvarūpiṇau
parasparaṃ samāyāntau pūrṇaikātmatvakāriṇau
hastayo rakṣakasyāsti dvaitaliṅgaṃ pratiṣṭhitam
dṛḍhaṃ pratiṣṭhamānena balenaikena rakṣitam
ayodhyāsandhirāpnotu vardhanaṃ śauryasaṃyutam
bhāgyāni hyatra baddhāni yathāsthānaṃ yathocitam

'The twin-fish symbol,' he said, fighting to keep his voice steady, 'represents duality and oneness, the harmony of opposing forces. It's a concept prevalent in many ancient traditions.'

'It symbolizes an object believed to hold the power to alter reality,' Ghaznawar said, his voice edged with awe. 'To magnify the power of the elements, to enhance the intellect ... to achieve mastery over the forces of nature.'

'Legends,' Ramaswamy countered, struggling to reconcile his scientific mind with these fantastic claims. 'Difficult to interpret within a modern framework.'

'Yet here you are Doctor,' Ghaznawar said, a subtle shift in his tone. 'A man of science, drawn to the mysteries of the ancient world. You of all people possess the knowledge to bridge those worlds. You will unlock these secrets.'

Ramaswamy exhaled slowly, burdened by the looming expectations. 'I need time,' he said. 'Time to study this text, to explore its deeper meaning in the context of our experiments.'

'Time,' Ghaznawar said, 'is a luxury you cannot afford, Doctor. How many times do you need me to tell you that? Your success ... your very survival depends on the speed of your discovery. Remember that.'

In isolation, time lost its meaning as Ramaswamy pursued his hypothesis—the mystery of the ancient substance symbolized by the twin fish, a promise of both creation and destruction.

He looked at the last lines again.

ayodhyāsandhirāpnotu vardhanaṃ śauryasaṃyutam
bhāgyāni hyatra baddhāni yathāsthānaṃ yathocitam

May the Ayodhya Alliance flourish strong,
With destinies bound, where they belong.

What was the Ayodhya Alliance, he wondered.

42

Agastyamalai, Pandya Desam

Present-day Agasthyamala Biosphere Reserve, Kerala, India

Around 2,000 years ago

Cheliyan, Cornelius, Padmasen and Kulasekara approached the expansive grounds of the gurukul. The soft fragrance of frangipani lent the air a heady sweetness, mingling with the distant murmur of students reciting their lessons.

Mithra emerged from the main hall as they drew near, his face breaking into a wide grin at the sight of Cornelius. 'Uncle Cornelius!' he exclaimed, embracing the man who had been like a second father to him. 'What brings you here, so far from home?' His delight faded as he noticed the sombre expressions of the others.

Cornelius returned the embrace, his eyes moist. 'Mithradates,' he said, his voice hoarse with sorrow, 'we bring grave news. Your father ...'

The unspoken words hung in the air, a tangible weight. Mithra fell to his knees, his face draining of colour. 'No ... It cannot be.' He uttered in a strangled whisper, frantically searching for reassurance, for someone to deny the truth he already knew in his heart.

Satyamuni, the revered sage of the gurukul, hurried to his side and rested a gentle hand on his shoulder. 'Peace, Mithra, my child,' he said, his voice a calming balm. 'Your father's spirit is with you, watching over you. You must be strong. Have I not taught you this over these many years?'

Suriratna, who was drawn to the group at the sight of her father and uncle, knelt beside Mithra, her gaze filled with compassion. 'We are here for you,' she whispered. 'You are not alone.'

Cornelius's voice was grief-stricken. 'Your father did not die peacefully, Mithra,' he said quietly. 'There has been a revolt in Dimašq. A faction within the city rose against him. They struck when he least expected it. He was betrayed, ambushed in his own palace.' His speech faltered. 'I tried to help but I failed.'

Mithra's face crumpled. 'He ... he was murdered?'

Cornelius nodded slowly, tears brimming in his eyes. 'Yes. And now Dimašq is fractured. Lawless. The trade routes are under threat, the city held hostage by those who once knelt before your father. The people need a leader, someone they can rally behind. Someone worthy of your father's legacy—I think it should be you.'

A tense silence fell over the group before Padmasen finally stepped forward. His voice was steady, anchoring the storm of emotion. 'This is not only a time of mourning but also a time for action. Your father lives within you. It is now your time to do your part to lead Dimašq. Your education, the skills you have honed—everything has prepared you for this moment. Do not let his sacrifice be in vain.'

A flicker of hope ignited in Mithra's grief-stricken eyes. 'But how? I am not ready. I do not have the strength to bear this burden alone. In any case, governorship is not inherited but earned. My heart says I am ready but my head does not.'

'You will prove yourself worthy of leading the people, and you will have us to support you,' Kulasekara reassured him. 'We will seek King Peruvazhudi's aid. He is a just and wise ruler. He will understand the importance of your mission, of restoring stability to Dimašq, of securing the trade routes vital to our prosperity. We will request his support—troops and supplies—to reclaim your city.'

'And the weapons you require will be forged in Korkai, at Padmasen's foundry,' Cheliyan added. 'Kulasekara will also send our finest blacksmiths to Dimašq to assist in equipping your forces for the future. You will have the best swords—the strongest, the sharpest—at your disposal.'

Mithra's eyes widened at the enormity of the plan. 'But will it be enough? What of Barakat and the Nabataeans? Their support is crucial. Without them …' His voice trailed off, doubt clouding his newfound hope. He remembered, from his childhood, the power of the Nabataeans, the simmering unrest that had eventually engulfed Dimašq.

'We have a plan for that as well,' Padmasen said, a reassuring smile playing on his lips. 'Cornelius will explain.'

'Raqmu, the Nabataean city being carved into the heart of the desert,' Cornelius said, sounding confident, 'holds the key. We believe the Pandyans can offer them something … something they will find irresistible.'

Mithra's eyes darted from Cheliyan to Kulasekara to Padmasen. 'What is it?' he asked, the tension on his face betraying his urgency.

The three men exchanged brief glances but said nothing. Padmasen placed a hand on Mithra's shoulder. 'In time, you will see.'

Mithra's brow furrowed, then slowly relaxed. Whatever it was, they clearly believed in it. 'Do you truly think we can succeed?' Padmasen clasped Mithra's shoulder, his grip firm. 'I have no doubt we will. With our combined strength, and the support of our allies, Dimašq will rise again. Your father's dream … it will be strengthened, not diminished, by your actions. We are with you, Mithra. All the way.'

Determination unfurled inside Mithra, his resolve solidifying. He was not alone. He had friends, allies, a purpose that transcended his profound sense of loss. He remembered a moment from his childhood—sitting beside his father in the palace courtyard, watching the sun set over the walls of Dimašq. His father had placed a hand on his shoulder and said, 'A true leader does not rule with fear or force. He listens. He protects. He builds a future for those who cannot build one themselves.'

Back then, Mithra had envisioned a future as a steward of peace—a scholar, merchant, magistrate, or diplomat—not as the governor his father had been. But the stakes had changed. His city was broken, its spirit fractured. His father's vision lay in ruins—and now, it fell to him to rebuild it.

He would honour that memory not by simply reclaiming Dimašq, but by restoring it—by rebuilding it into a place of strength, fairness and unity. A city that would endure. A future that would last.

The gurukul became a whirlwind of activity as preparations for the expedition commenced. But even amidst the bustle, Soju and Suriratna found time to sit with their grieving friend, offering comfort and encouragement.

'Mithra,' Soju said, his voice warm, 'you say that your father always spoke of your potential, your innate leadership. He knew you were destined for great things. That is why he sent you here, to learn, to grow, to prepare.'

'He was right,' Suriratna added. 'Sometimes, it falls upon us to complete the work our parents began. To carry their dreams forward. You can do this, Mithra. You must.'

'I will not let him down,' Mithra said, his resolve rooted in courage. 'I will make him proud. I will make Dimašq proud.'

And then Soju said something that surprised even Suriratna. 'I will go with you,' he declared. 'We made a pact, remember? To stand together, no matter the odds. I will not let you face this alone.' His voice quavered, yet his gaze held steady.

Mithra's breath caught as he pulled his friend close. As the two embraced, Suriratna watched, her heart heavy, her emotions in turmoil.

43

Korkai, Thamirabarani, Pandya Desam
Present-day Thoothukudi District, Tamil Nadu, India
Around 2,000 years ago

The grand gates of Peruvazhudi's palace welcomed Cheliyan, Kulasekara, Padmasen, Mithra and Soju, marking the end of their journey to the heart of the Pandyan Empire. The palace itself was a marvel of Dravidian craftsmanship—its walls constructed from richly aged teakwood, chosen for its resilience and grace. The walls were delicately imbricated with gold leaf and ivory inlays, their surfaces polished to a warm gleam. Gods and warriors, locked in combat, had been brought to life through rich pigments in massive wall murals. Unlike the granite temples built to defy time, palaces such as this were meant to breathe— alive with the scents of forests and sandalwood, evolving with the seasons and the people within them.

Two enormous fish, sculpted from stone, leaped skyward from an arch of sculpted waves guarding the entrance. The travellers passed through the finely carved gates and entered a verdant garden. Exotic flowers bloomed in lush profusion, their intoxicating aromas mingling with that of the sandalwood trees in the garden. Neatly trimmed hedges lined tranquil pools whose surfaces reflected the azure sky. Every detail of the palace, from the smallest flower to the grandest sculpture, spoke to the Pandyan Empire's grandeur.

Within the palace walls was a vast hall with towering wooden pillars, each hewn from a single teak trunk and inlaid with sapphires and emeralds, that supported a ceiling adorned with a fresco portraying celestial dancers. The scene—a depiction of Shiva and Parvati's heavenly dance—pulsed with energy. Golden lamps, suspended from the ceiling, cast a warm glow, illuminating the assembled courtiers and the polished floor beneath their feet. The twin fish emblem of the Pandyan dynasty was prominently displayed, a symbol of power and prosperity.

At the far end of the hall, upon a magnificent wooden throne, sat Peruvazhudi, the Pandyan king. His presence commanded respect. A regal turban, its luxurious fabric bejewelled with rubies and emeralds, adorned his head. Gold thread winked from the folds of his silk veshti, catching the light with every movement. His eyes, sharp and discerning, softened as they settled upon Soju and Mithra. He remembered their bravery.

'I have not forgotten the debt I owe these young heroes,' he declared as he rose from his throne. The courtiers, assembled before him, gasped. It was a rare honour—a king rising to greet those not of royal blood. 'The two of you, and young Suriratna, risked your lives to save mine,' Peruvazhudi continued, addressing Mithra and Soju. 'I vowed then to repay that debt. Ask what you will, and it shall be yours.'

Mithra stepped forward, his demeanour respectful yet resolute. 'Your Majesty, we seek not repayment, but your aid. Our mission is to secure the trade routes that lie to the west, to ensure peace and prosperity for all.' He then explained the turmoil that had gripped Dimašq, the threat to the delicate balance of power.

Peruvazhudi listened intently. 'Pandya Desam thrives on trade, not conquest,' he said. 'Our merchants sail to distant shores and their prosperity fuels our own. But the security of those trade routes is paramount. If aiding you will ensure their safety, then it is a cause worthy of our support.'

He turned to his prime minister, Amaichar. 'Assemble a contingent of our finest soldiers, Amaichar,' he commanded. 'They will accompany young Mithra and ensure both the security of the trade routes and the protection of our interests.' A ripple of approval passed through the court. The courtiers understood the wisdom of their king's decision. By aiding Mithra, Peruvazhudi was not only honouring his debt, but securing the future prosperity of his kingdom.

'Thank you, Your Majesty,' Mithra said, bowing deeply. 'Your support is invaluable.'

Peruvazhudi placed a hand on Mithra's shoulder, a gesture of camaraderie and respect. 'May your journey be successful, and may peace prevail.'

As they discussed their plans further, Peruvazhudi led them to a smaller, more private chamber within the palace. Gilded statues and jewel-encrusted vases, treasures from across the known world, filled the room. 'Tell me more about this ... Dimašq,' the king asked, settling onto a plush cushion. 'I want to understand the complexities of this situation.'

Cheliyan began, his tone measured but grave. 'The political landscape is volatile, Your Majesty. Dimašq was once a beacon of stability in the western trade network, a nexus for Nabataean merchants, Roman diplomats and local guilds. But over the past decade, tensions have escalated. Roman influence has become heavy-handed—interfering in local governance, levying unfair tariffs and exploiting divisions among the city's ruling houses.'

He paused, letting the weight of that history settle.

'In response, a populist faction rose, initially to restore autonomy ... But it has since fractured into splinter groups, each with its own agenda. Mithra's father, Governor Philippides, had tried to navigate a delicate path—maintaining Dimašq's independence while placating Rome. But his balancing act angered both sides. The Romans saw him as defiant. The rebels saw him as compromised. Ultimately, he was betrayed and murdered.'

Peruvazhudi's brow furrowed. 'And the people—how do they fare amidst this turmoil?'

Mithra, his fists clenched at his sides, said, 'My people are suffering. Law has broken down. The markets lie abandoned. Trade caravans are routinely plundered. What was once a thriving city is now teetering on the edge of collapse.'

Cheliyan nodded. 'If we do not act swiftly, the instability will spread—affecting not just Dimašq, but the entire western corridor that links our kingdoms to Rome and beyond.'

Mithra's voice was laced with concern. 'The people are suffering, Your Majesty. The unrest has disrupted the flow of food and essential supplies. We must restore stability, bring relief to those in need. We must show them that we stand with them, that their welfare is our priority.'

'An honourable goal,' Peruvazhudi agreed. 'One that aligns with the principles of dharma. We will offer our support—troops, supplies, whatever is needed—to bring succour to Dimašq.'

The king turned to Padmasen. 'I hear whispers of your skills, Padmasen. My kingdom thrives on the quality of the weapons you provide. Our merchants, Kulasekara and Cheliyan, sing praises of your metal. Word of its strength and resilience has spread far beyond our shores. So much so that we have come to associate the twin-fish symbol—like the eyes of Goddess

Meenakshi herself—with that excellence. What once marked a forge's origin has now become a symbol of our strength and craft, a seal of honour carried by the finest blades of Pandya Desam.'

Padmasen bowed low, his forehead touching the ground. 'Your words honour me, Your Majesty. I am yours to command.' *So long as I can continue preserving the secrets of the Dvaitalingam Rakshak.*

Peruvazhudi then turned to Kulasekara. 'Your foundry, your forge—they are now operational, thanks to Padmasen's expertise?'

'Indeed, Your Majesty,' Kulasekara replied, bowing respectfully. 'We are now producing enough to meet both local and global demand.'

'Then see that these young men are equipped with the finest weapons your forges can produce,' the king commanded. 'Spare no expense. Our treasury will bear the cost. And may our ships, laden with treasures, sail unhindered, bringing prosperity to our shores.'

44

New Delhi, India
Present day

Aditya stepped out of his car and gazed at the imposing white facade of Sardar Patel Bhawan on Sansad Marg. In the heart of New Delhi stood the building that housed the office of Devendra Thakural, India's national security advisor. He was one of the nation's most powerful individuals.

The lobby buzzed with activity, a stark contrast to the hushed corridors of power within the Prime Minister's Office. Papers rustled, phones buzzed, aides hurried past exchanging furtive glances and whispered words. Aditya was escorted through the winding corridors, but even the brisk walk and the purposeful energy around him did little to settle the storm churning in his chest. The building's flurry of activity only heightened his sense of urgency. Finally, he reached the NSA's office, a room that radiated an aura of authority and vigilance.

Thakural, a seasoned strategist with sharp features and an unyielding demeanour, stood as Aditya entered. 'Mr Pillai, please have a seat,' he said, gesturing towards a sofa in the corner. He circled his desk to shake Aditya's hand before settling into a chair.

'Thank you, sir,' Aditya replied, holding Thakural's gaze.

'I understand you have an urgent matter to discuss—something relating to Dr Bala Ramaswamy,' Thakural said, cutting to the chase. He was a man of action, with little patience for pleasantries. His background spoke volumes about his efficiency: top of his class at the National Defence Academy, a decorated police officer for many years, an undercover operative in Dhaka and commander of numerous counter-insurgency operations.

Aditya nodded, carefully considering his words. 'For several days now, I've been unable to contact Dr Ramaswamy. His name came up in conversations I had with Dr Satheesh Jayaraman and Dr Jung Tae-hyun, both of whom are helping us in our quest for the perfect BPBT alloy. At first, I assumed Dr Ramaswamy was simply on vacation. But even CERN has been trying to reach him and now they've involved the Swiss police. He appears to have vanished completely.'

'And why should this be of concern to me, Mr Pillai?' Thakural asked, his voice carefully neutral. 'Though Ramaswamy is of Indian origin, he formally holds a Swiss passport. Switzerland granted him citizenship almost a decade ago.'

Aditya leaned forward, his voice firm despite the frustration simmering within. 'I am striving to meet the outrageous deadline you—along with the DRDO chairman and the defence minister—set for me. But I cannot achieve the impossible without assistance. Developing the new steel variant for the BPBT hinges on Ramaswamy's expertise. Without him, the project will face significant delays.'

Thakural's fingers tapped a rhythmic beat on the coffee table as he considered Aditya's words. He was weighing how much to reveal, how much to keep shrouded in secrecy. 'How would you react,' he asked, his voice low and deliberate, 'if I told you that we are ... aware of Ramaswamy's situation?'

Aditya's eyes widened in disbelief. 'You already know?'

'Our intelligence sources indicate that men employed by Khalil Ghaznawar abducted him,' Thakural confirmed. 'He's been taken to a secure location in Afghanistan—controlled by Ghaznawar himself.'

'Then why haven't you acted?' Aditya demanded, his voice rising in frustration. He stopped abruptly, realizing the impropriety of his tone.

A ghost of a smile touched Thakural's lips. 'To stay informed is my responsibility, Mr Pillai, not necessarily to act upon each piece of information that I receive.'

'I need him, sir,' Aditya pleaded. 'I am begging you—help me.'

'Your request complicates matters,' Thakural said, his brow furrowing. 'Retrieving Ramaswamy from Afghanistan would necessitate involving the Taliban. And their cooperation ... is not easily obtained.'

'But Ghaznawar ... he's undoubtedly working for the Taliban, isn't he?' Aditya countered.

Thakural shook his head. 'Khalil Ghaznawar is an opportunist. He aligns himself with whoever serves his interests, be it the Taliban or any other faction. He's a fanatic, driven by his own interpretation of Allah's will. Anything that advances the Islamic cause ... that is what matters to him. However ...' he continued, a sly gleam lighting his eyes, 'his international connections—they could work to our advantage.'

'How so?'

'The current Taliban government is, shall we say, not fond of the Pakistani establishment,' Thakural explained. 'If we could demonstrate that Ghaznawar is working on behalf of Pakistan ... well, that might change their perspective. Or,' he added, his voice dropping to a conspiratorial whisper, 'if we could show evidence of ... *shirk.*'

'Shirk?' Aditya echoed, the word unfamiliar.

'Idolatry, Mr Pillai,' Thakural clarified. 'A grave sin in Islam.'

'And how would you demonstrate that?'

'Rumour has it that Ghaznawar possesses a fragment of the Somnath lingam,' Thakural revealed, a thoughtful frown creasing his brow.

Aditya's mind raced, recalling the history of the Taliban and Pakistan's once-strong alliance that had fractured in recent years. The Taliban, now wary of Pakistan's interference, was increasingly suspicious of their former patrons. The Tehrik-i-Taliban Pakistan, with its campaign of terror within Pakistan itself, had further strained relations, leaving a chasm of mistrust.

'So what's the strategy?' Aditya asked.

Thakural leaned back in his chair. 'We will utilize diplomatic channels to sow seeds of doubt regarding Ghaznawar's allegiances. In the meantime, I will explore options for a more ... direct approach. Retrieving Ramaswamy will not be easy. But rest assured, Mr Pillai, we will exhaust all avenues.'

'But what if those diplomatic efforts ... fail?' Aditya pressed.

'Then,' Thakural said, his voice quiet but firm, 'it will fall upon others to resolve the situation. Ghaznawar has many enemies and some of them operate outside the bounds of traditional diplomacy.' He met Aditya's eyes, the perilous nature of his suggestion hanging heavy in the air.

45

Dvaravati, Suvarnabhumi
Present-day Bangkok, Thailand
Around 2,000 years ago

Bhadraketu sat in his small thatched cottage on the banks of one of the three rivers that flowed through Dvaravati. As he ate his simple lunch, his mind drifted back to the journey that had brought him to this distant land.

It had begun beneath a sprawling banyan tree in the heart of the Neelgiri forest in Pandya Desam. Days of intense meditation under Nadikasyapa's guidance had transformed him. His once strong frame had turned lean, his weight halved by an austere lifestyle. His long hair, once a symbol of worldly vanity, was pulled back in a simple coil, a sign of his devotion to the path of dhamma.

On the appointed day, as the first rays of dawn pierced the thick canopy, he rose, a sense of serenity settling upon him. In a nearby hut, his fellow disciples and their teacher, the wise Nadikasyapa, waited. The six of them had sat in silent communion, sharing a simple meal of rice gruel, each deliberate, measured mouthful reaffirming their commitment to austerity.

Nadikasyapa, his voice firm yet compassionate, had addressed them after the meal. 'The time has come,' he had declared, 'for you to carry the Buddha's teachings beyond these familiar forests; to use the skills I have taught you in nurturing life. Each of you has a unique path to follow—a destination waiting for your light.'

Turning to one disciple, he had said, 'Manjushri, you shall journey to Srivijaya, bearing the gift of the Buddha's wisdom for the people of Jayakarta.' To another, he had declared, 'Kundalakesha, Champa awaits your guidance. Bring the Viet people dhamma.' One by one, he had assigned each disciple their mission.

Finally, his eyes had rested on Bhadraketu. 'Bhadraketu,' he had said with gentle authority, 'you shall travel to Dvaravati, in Suvarnabhumi. You have been learning to communicate in Mon under me. The Mon- and Tai-speaking people await your guidance and remedies.' Bhadraketu had bowed deeply, accepting his destiny with gratitude.

The following morning, they had begun their journey, walking for five days towards Korkai. As they approached his family home, every fibre of Bhadraketu's being had yearned to see his parents, to feel their loving embrace. But he remembered Nadikasyapa's words: *True serenity lies in letting go. In shedding attachments, we find harmony with the universe.* With a heavy heart, he bid a silent farewell to his family from afar. He remembered how he had promised to stay in touch. He was breaking that promise for dhamma.

At Korkai, he had boarded a Pandyan merchant ship bound for Dvaravati. The journey across the turbulent sea was long and arduous. For fifteen days, the ship had pitched and tossed, at the mercy of harsh winds and towering waves. But Bhadraketu remained steadfast, finding solace in meditation and prayer, his mind anchored in the teachings of his master.

At last, Dvaravati had unfolded before them, its timeworn landscapes a living archive of centuries past. The city stood as a living contradiction, where sparkling lakes and lush gardens coexisted with magnificent temples and frenetic markets—a place where serenity and chaos danced in perpetual balance. As Bhadraketu took his first steps on unfamiliar soil, he was assailed by a babel of languages—Mon, Sanskrit, Khmer, Tamil, Tai and Pali—a chorus of voices reflecting this land's diversity.

Drawn by the noise and commotion, he had found himself amidst a throng of people gathered in the marketplace. A young woman, her eyes blazing with anger, was accusing a vendor of cheating her, her voice a shrill cry against injustice. The vendor, equally agitated, denied the accusation.

Bhadraketu, sensing an opportunity, had stepped forward. 'May I assist?' he asked gently in Mon. The vendor and the woman, recognizing the quiet authority in his demeanour, readily agreed. 'Please, wise one,' the woman implored, 'tell us who is right.'

Bhadraketu carefully examined the weights and scales. 'Let us conduct a simple experiment,' he said, a mischievous twinkle in his eyes. 'Bring me a bowl of water.'

Intrigued, the onlookers had watched as he placed the weights, one by one, into the water. One weight, cleverly made of wood and coated with lead, floated before sinking. The others sank immediately.

'Truth,' Bhadraketu had declared, his voice clear, 'is as light as that floating weight. This man'—he gestured towards the pale-faced vendor—'has been using false measures.'

The crowd gasped. The woman, her face now alight with triumph, had turned to Bhadraketu. 'You have exposed his deceit,' she said. 'But what should be his punishment?'

'Justice,' Bhadraketu said, a gentle smile touching his lips, 'is not about retribution, but about reform. Let him return any ill-gotten gains and pledge to use honest weights in the future. And you, My Lady, should offer forgiveness. For it is through forgiveness that we find true peace.'

Meanwhile, word of Bhadraketu's wisdom and compassion had reached King Jayasena. Soon, royal guards had arrived and escorted him to the palace.

Jayasena, Dvaravati's king, had built a palace blending grandeur and simplicity. Crafted from local teak, it featured intricate sculptures of scenes from the Ramayana. The vast estate boasted lush tranquil gardens with towering banyans and still lotus ponds. In the main hall, carved columns supported an ornate roof, while open windows bathed the chamber in soft light.

Jayasena had greeted Bhadraketu warmly, intrigued by the young man's wisdom. 'Tell me about yourself,' he had urged. 'What brings you to my kingdom?'

'Your Majesty,' Bhadraketu had replied, gazing at the sunlight filtering through the windows, 'your city reminds me of my childhood home in Saketa, a place sacred to Lord Rama. Perhaps ... it should be known as Ayodhya. And this land, bathed in the golden light, like the shyama—dark—complexion of Rama himself ...'

'Then it shall be so,' Jayasena had declared. 'Henceforth, my capital will be known as Ayutthaya, and my kingdom as Siam.'

Now, as Bhadraketu sat in his thatched hut and recalled how he had arrived in Dvaravati, he wondered if this distant land had summoned him not by chance, but by design.

Kailasanatha, Elapura
Present-day Ellora, Maharashtra, India
Around 1,200 years ago

The hot sun beat down upon the bustling construction site of Kailasanatha, its rays reflecting off the sweat-slicked bodies of thousands of labourers. Clad in tightly wrapped dhotis for flexibility of movement and light turbans to shield them from the sun, they moved with careful precision across the sheer rock face, the rhythmic clinking of their chisels against stone composing a song of human endeavour. The air hummed with a powerful energy, as if the very stone vibrated with the act of creation.

Elapura was a vast complex of over a hundred caves, carved from the basalt of the Charanandri Hills. The surrounding hills housed a diverse array of faiths, with caves dedicated to Shiva, Vishnu, Buddha and Mahavira. These sanctuaries served not only as places of worship, but also as rest stops for merchants and pilgrims journeying along the ancient trade routes that crisscrossed the region.

Seeking respite from the scorching heat, King Krishna—later known as Krishna I—sat inside a shaded pavilion, its silken drapes rustling gently in the breeze. Blocks of Himalayan ice, carefully preserved for such occasions within underground chambers, kept the space cool and comfortable, a stark contrast to the sweltering temperature outside. He turned to his chief architect, Kokasa. 'This temple,' he declared, 'shall speak of our devotion to Shiva. But how long until it is finished? The queen's fast ... it cannot continue indefinitely. She will not break it until the shikhara—the zenith—is visible.'

Troubled by the king's illness, the queen had promised Shiva that if her husband recovered, she would not only build a magnificent temple in Elapura, a replica of the sacred Mount Kailasa, but also fast until the temple's towering shikhara became visible for all to see.

Kokasa, wiping sweat from his brow, bowed. 'It is for the queen, Your Majesty, that we have adopted a top-down construction method. So, the shikhara will be the first structure to be completed.'

Three massive trenches, cut deep into the basalt, marked the initial phase of construction. Artisans and sculptors, suspended on ropes, worked tirelessly, their chisels shaping the raw stone into intricate forms. The shikhara, pillars, statues, shrines—each element emerged from the rock, with finer details added as the work progressed. Every stroke was executed with a precision born of reverence, each artisan aware of the sacred task before them.

The king nodded, pleased. 'Ensure our workers are well cared for. This is no ordinary undertaking. We are recreating a vision of Kailasa, a dwelling fit for Mahadeva himself. Such a project demands our utmost devotion and respect. Tell me, Kokasa, what is the timeline?'

'It is estimated,' Kokasa replied, 'that we must remove nearly 200,000 tons of rock. Even with seven thousand labourers working in rotating shifts, it will take eighteen years to complete using traditional tools.'

'And with your ... *advancements*?' Krishna prompted, raising an eyebrow. The king was aware that Kokasa was the 182nd Dvaitalingam Rakshak.

'We are using chisels forged in my foundry,' Kokasa explained. 'They are imbued with a unique property.' He gestured towards a group of skilled masons working high above, shaping the intricate patterns of the shikhara. 'With these tools, we might complete the temple in five years. But you have my promise that the shikhara will be ready first ... so that the queen may break her fast.'

King Krishna smiled, watching as the artisans worked. 'Each stroke is a prayer,' he said. 'For we are sculpting not merely stone, but a dwelling for the gods.' His attention turned to the workers below, their muscles straining as they hauled away massive chunks of basalt. Oxen and elephants, adorned in colourful cloths, pulled heavily laden wooden carts, their movements slow, steady, relentless.

'Another 100 tons removed today,' Kokasa reported, noting the king's observation.

'See that the workers are given enough food, water and rest,' Krishna commanded. 'Their well-being is paramount. Every life lost diminishes the power of our temple. I envision a structure so grand, so magnificent, that even Shiva will be moved by its beauty.'

'And what scene will grace the temple's heart?' Kokasa inquired. 'Have you decided, My Lord?'

King Krishna observed the workers as they scaled the rock face, their movements fluid and graceful, aided by ropes and pulleys. They sang hymns of devotion as they worked, their voices a melodic counterpoint to the rhythmic clinking of chisels.

'The Ravananugraha,' Krishna declared. 'It is a story of power and devotion. We know that Ravana, in his arrogance, attempted to uproot Mount Kailasa itself. But Shiva, angered by his hubris, pushed the mountain back down, trapping Ravana beneath its weight. Imprisoned, Ravana prayed, his devotion so profound that Shiva relented, releasing him and bestowing upon him the Atmalingam. It is a reminder that even the mightiest of beings can be swayed by true devotion.' He smiled, his gaze fixed upon the distant horizon. 'Let this scene grace the heart of our temple. Let every figure reflect Shiva's power and grace.'

'It shall be done, Your Majesty,' Kokasa assured him. 'The Ravananugraha is the perfect choice.'

Turning to his chief sculptor, Kokasa said, 'Let the tale of Ravana's humbling be captured in stone. May every stroke reflect our devotion, a prayer for Shiva's blessings.' The sculptor, bowing deeply, hurried away to commence his sacred task.

'Have no fear, Your Majesty,' said Kokasa. 'This scene will stand as a beacon of faith for generations to come.' *After all, without that particular event, whatever would have happened to the line of Rakshaks?*

46

Mlecchadal, The Western Ocean
Present-day Arabian Sea
Around 2,000 years ago

As the ships sailed into the vast Mlecchadal—the western ocean separating Bharatvarsha from the hot and sand-swept Arava Nadu—sixteen-year-old Mithra battled a maelstrom of emotions. To him, the prospect of rallying a thousand seasoned Pandyan warriors seemed suddenly overwhelming, challenging his hitherto steadfast resolve.

But even at his young age, Mithra possessed a natural dignity. His bright emerald eyes, wise beyond his years, scanned the horizon. His complexion, the rich olive of his heritage, was sun-kissed from his days at the gurukul. Dark brown hair, often wind-tossed, framed a face both handsome and resolute. Powerfully built, he wore a simple linen tunic belted at the waist and tough leather sandals. His bearing spoke of quiet readiness—to shoulder a duty, uphold his father's legacy and guide his people through whatever trials lay ahead.

~

Earlier, the port of Korkai had thrummed with activity as Mithra's ten-ship armada prepared to depart. Sailors secured ropes, troops bid tearful farewells and military supplies were loaded. The vessels bobbed gently in the harbour, their masts stretching skyward, sails furled and ready. At dawn, sunlight glinted off the polished hulls of the Pandyan fleet, their twin-fish emblems shining in the golden rays. Each vessel was a marvel of Pandyan construction. Crafted from robust teak, their strengthened hulls were designed to endure long voyages. Elaborate carvings adorned each prow, and the sail, woven from sturdy cotton, billowed magnificently in the wind.

Months of preparation had culminated in the moment of Mithra's departure. The training had not been his alone—soldiers, craftsmen, navigators and emissaries had all been readied for the long crossing westward. Eager to embark, Mithra chafed at the delays, but Cheliyan, the veteran merchant, had counselled patience. 'Thorough preparation is paramount,' he had insisted. 'A leader may carry a banner, but an ill-prepared force carries only failure.'

Even so, doubt gnawed at Mithra. He was a foreigner to these shores—a boy of Dimašq, not Pandya Desam. The responsibility of leading a thousand seasoned Pandyan warriors, men who had pledged their loyalty to a non-native crown, weighed on his young shoulders.

Sensing his unease, King Peruvazhudi had drawn him aside on the eve of departure. In the privacy of the palace gardens, he had offered quiet reassurance. 'Mithra, my boy,' he had said, his voice low but steady, 'my men follow you not out of duty alone, but because I have told them your cause is just. You carry not only your father's hopes, but the hopes of a renewed alliance that will strengthen both our people. They know this. And in time, they will follow you not because I command it—but because you will have earned it.'

The king's words had steadied Mithra, and they echoed in his mind as the ships sailed into the Mlecchadal. Cornelius, ever vigilant, had been monitoring the situation in Dimašq via carrier pigeon messages from his allies. 'The Romans hold only a fraction of the city,' he reported. 'Rebel factions control the streets. Patience is our best weapon, Mithra.'

Padmasen and Kulasekara had ensured the troops were equipped with the finest weapons—deadly swords and spears forged in their foundries, their intricate designs a testament to Pandyan skill.

~

Sensing Mithra's unease, Soju placed a hand on his shoulder. 'The men are anxious,' he said softly. 'They fear being sent to fight another's war. You must reassure them.'

Mithra's stomach tightened. 'What should I say?' he asked.

'Remind them of Pandyan trade,' Soju advised. 'Their prosperity is linked to these sea routes. Peace in Dimašq is vital, not just for those we aid, but for their own survival. Remind them of their duty and honour. They follow you because of their king's orders. Now get them to believe in *you*, Mithra.'

Mithra inhaled deeply, steeling himself. 'And if I fail?'

Soju's eyes were unwavering. 'You will not. This is your time. Make your father proud.'

Mithra nodded, a renewed sense of purpose coursing through him. Clapping Soju's shoulder, he approached the bow and stood facing a crowd of expectant faces. His heart pounded, but he pushed aside his fear, drawing strength from Soju's words and the memory of his father.

'Men of Pandya Desam,' he boomed in Tamil, his voice ringing across the deck. 'Pandyan kings do not conquer. Pandyan strength lies in trade, in the bonds that bring prosperity to our kingdoms. These sea lanes are our lifeblood. We must protect them.'

He paused, his eyes sweeping across the assembled warriors.

'We sail not to conquer, but to restore order. Dimašq—a vital market—is in turmoil. The trade routes that fuel our prosperity are crippled by rebellion. We will restore peace and ensure the free flow of commerce. Pandyan ships carry riches—pearls, pepper, cardamom, gemstones, ingots, ivory and silk. The world demands what we offer and this trade must not be impeded.' A murmur of agreement arose from the ranks.

'Be ready,' Mithra cautioned. 'Not all will welcome us. The rebels in Dimašq will resist, but a Roman crackdown poses a greater danger. We must navigate both threats, ensuring Dimašq thrives with low taxes that benefit all.'

As Mithra finished, a resolute silence settled over the men. Each warrior understood the weight of their mission. At one point, Cheliyan cried out, 'Vetri namatey!' Victory will be ours! The warriors, their apprehension now replaced by a fervent determination, roared in response: 'Vetri namatey!'

As they set sail, ballast stones—strategically placed on deck—were shifted manually to compensate for the ever-changing ocean's swell and sail settings, thus maintaining the vessels' balance. On the lead ship, Mithra stood beside Cornelius and Cheliyan, their experienced gazes fixed on the horizon. Soju, his loyal friend, remained close. A thousand warriors, spread across the fleet, braced for the challenges ahead. Sails billowing, they sped westward, driven by a favourable wind.

Mithra stood alone at the bow, watching Korkai fade into the distance. The wind tugged at his clothes, carrying the faint echo of his father's voice—a call to live by the ideals he had been raised with. He would prove himself as a servant of his people—one who led because the moment demanded it.

Weeks slipped by. The endless rhythm of the sea, the boundless sky, became a comforting constant. Mithra trained with his men, honed his skills, and planned strategy with Soju, Cornelius and Cheliyan. Their shared purpose and growing camaraderie strengthened their resolve.

One evening, as the setting sun painted the western sky in hues of fire, Mithra leaned against the railing beside Soju. 'Do you ever doubt our success?' he asked.

Soju's eyes, clear, confident, met his. 'We will succeed, Mithra. We have to. For your people, for Dimašq ... because you lead them.'

'I am in your debt, Soju,' Mithra said, his heart overflowing with gratitude.

'Why?' Soju frowned.

'For coming with me,' Mithra said, 'and for leaving behind the woman you love.'

47

Agastyamalai, Pandya Desam
Present-day Agasthyamala Biosphere Reserve, Kerala, India
Around 2,000 years ago

Dawn painted the gurukul with a soft, golden light as Padmasen arrived to take Suriratna home. Satyamuni greeted him at the entrance, his serene face mirroring the freshness of the morning. 'Padmasen, it brings me joy to see you,' he said, his voice as calm as the gentle breeze rustling the leaves.

'Pranam, Satyamuni,' Padmasen replied, bowing respectfully. 'I have come for my daughter. Her studies are complete, and we are grateful for the wisdom she has gained under your guidance.'

'Your daughter has been a model student—among my finest. She is destined for greatness. Allow me to summon her.' He gestured to one of his assistants, who disappeared into the main hall.

Moments later, Suriratna emerged, her face a mixture of emotions. She approached Satyamuni, kneeling before him, and touched his feet in reverence. 'What dakshina can I possibly offer you, Acharya?' she asked.

'Sukhī bhava,' Satyamuni replied, placing his hand on her head, wishing her happiness. Then, his voice deepening, he continued, 'Sarvadā vijayī bhava; vidyāvatī bhava; āyuṣmatī bhava; sarva-

The Ayodhya Alliance

sampadam sampannā bhava; dhanyatāṁ gaccha.' May you always be victorious; may you always attain knowledge; may you live long; may you be endowed with wealth and prosperity; may you attain blessedness ... His blessings, overflowing with affection, washed over her.

Suriratna rose, her eyes shining. 'Dhanyavadaah, Acharya,' she said. 'But what of the dakshina, Acharya ... I will be in sin if I do not—'

'Your future shines bright, my child,' Satyamuni said. 'Remember the teachings you have received here, the values you have embraced. They will guide you. And in moments of doubt, remember Harihara. Your success is my dakshina.'

He then chanted:

śivāya viṣṇurūpāya śivarūpāya viṣṇave
śivasya hṛdayaṁ viṣṇuḥ viṣṇóśca hṛdayaṁ śivaḥ

'I will forever cherish my time here,' said Suriratna. 'And I will strive to honour the wisdom you have shared, Acharya.'

Padmasen touched her shoulder gently. 'Come, Suriratna,' he said. 'It is time to return home.'

As they rode back to Korkai, Padmasen sensed a change in his daughter—a quiet contemplation he had not seen before. 'Your mother has been making plans for your future,' he said, breaking the silence. 'She has been considering suitable matches.'

Suriratna hesitated. 'Pitaha ... there is something I need to tell you.'

Padmasen glanced at her, his brow furrowed. 'You know you can tell me anything, Suriratna.'

'I ... I have given my heart to Soju.'

Padmasen's expression tightened, concern replacing his initial surprise. 'Soju? Your young friend from the Garak Confederacy?'

'Yes, Pitaha,' she said, her voice trembling slightly. 'I know this may upset you. But I have always been honest with you. I have no secrets from you.'

After a moment of silence, Padmasen sighed. 'You caught me off guard, that is all. Love is a powerful force, Suriratna. Follow your heart. But ... will Soju even return? He is fighting a war in distant Dimašq.'

Suriratna's face wore a determined expression, her posture was rigid with resolve. 'He will come back. We pledged our devotion to each other.'

'I hope you are right,' Padmasen said, a hint of sadness in his voice. 'But have you considered the implications? Pandya Desam is not his home. A union with him would mean you will eventually leave your family, your life here.'

'It pains me to cause you concern,' Suriratna said, her voice earnest. 'But Mataha left her home in Korkai to be with you in Saketa. And Bhadraketu ... his life is a journey, his heart never in one place for long. Distance cannot sever the bonds of love, Pitaha. Our hearts will always be connected.'

Recognizing the unshakeable strength of her conviction—a reflection of his own—Padmasen nodded slowly. 'Well said, my daughter. I cannot argue with your logic. We shall be patient and see if this ... Soju ... honours his pledge. In the meantime, I have a plan.'

'What plan, Pitaha?' Suriratna's curiosity was piqued.

'We shall tell Indumati that your skills are needed at the foundry,' he said, a mischievous glint in his eyes. 'That you must be trained in the art of iron-making before any marriage can be considered.'

'And ... do you think Mataha will accept this?'

'Leave that to me. I will convince her. Surely, the word of the 157th Dvaitalingam Rakshak carries some weight?' he said, winking playfully.

Relieved, Suriratna smiled. 'Thank you, Pitaha. You will not regret this.'

Padmasen's demeanour softened. 'I know you will not disappoint me, Suriratna. You have always reminded me of the great women of our history—Gargi, Maitreyi, Lopamudra ... Now, prepare yourself. I must speak with Kulasekara before we return to the city.'

∽

The day after she reached home, Suriratna began her apprenticeship at the foundry, much to Indumati's displeasure.

As a child, Suriratna had often visited her father's workshop, trailing behind him. She had been in awe of the glowing furnaces then. But now, standing within the Korkai foundry as an apprentice, the space felt transformed—its heat more intense, its demands more real.

The air reverberated with the clang of hammers against anvils, the roar of the furnace a constant reminder of the work at hand. Padmasen, patiently guiding her, shared his knowledge of metals, his instructions interwoven with stories of their forefathers—legendary ironsmiths, masters of their craft. He introduced her to the complexities of the furnace, the subtle dance of heat and metal.

'Every ore has a unique character,' he explained, 'its own strengths and weaknesses. Lohitaksha, rich in iron, is easily smelted. Chumbakashila, with its magnetic properties, requires a different approach. And pitamrida, though full of impurities, yields excellent alloys. But it is kraunchashila—rare and difficult to work with—that holds the key to creating metal with … special qualities.'

Suriratna listened intently, her movements careful, precise, her determination fuelled by a longing that transcended the fiery furnace.

She would shape iron not just with fire and hammer, but with purpose—and when the time came, she would be ready to forge a destiny as unyielding as the metal she now served.

48

Dimašq, Roman Empire
Present-day Damascus, Syria
Around 2,000 years ago

The setting sun cast an amber glow over Dimašq. As Mithra and his soldiers neared the city gates, dust swirled around their feet. Their footsteps echoed in the unsettling quiet.

The first sight that greeted them was chilling. Several wooden crosses, each bearing the lifeless body of a rebel, stood silhouetted against the darkening sky. The contorted faces, frozen in expressions of agony, spoke of the brutal vengeance Rome had exacted upon those who had dared to defy its rule. Mithra had heard tales of a similar crucifixion in Jerusalem—of a Jewish revolutionary condemned to die upon a cross. The grim spectacle before him sent a shiver down his spine. He steeled himself, clenching his fists, preparing for the battle ahead.

The voyage from Korkai to Eudaemon, and from Eudaemon to Aelana, had been long and arduous—a gruelling crossing on treacherous seas. The overland trek from Aelana to Dimašq, through arid landscapes and under a scorching sun, had been fraught with danger, riddled with ambushes. But they had finally arrived, a thousand strong, ready to help Mithra fulfil his destiny.

Under the gracious patronage of King Peruvazhudi, the Pandyan force, led by Mithra, Soju, Cornelius and Cheliyan, stood poised to enter Dimašq. Tension crackled in the air, fuelled by rumours of rebel forces amassing to the north and Roman reinforcements marching from the south. A scout's sudden cry shattered the uneasy silence. 'They are coming!' he yelled, pointing towards the northern hills.

Breaching the fortifications, a wave of rebel fighters surged down the slope, their war cries ringing through the valley. Simultaneously, a Roman horn blared from the south, heralding the arrival of disciplined legions. Mithra knew they were about to be trapped in a lethal pincer, caught between two opposing forces.

'Hold the line!' he roared, his voice cutting through the frenzy. His mind raced, seeking a way out, a path to survival.

Cornelius, the seasoned desert warrior, his mind attuned to the subtleties of the landscape, pointed to a decrepit structure in the distance. 'The old aqueduct!' he shouted, his voice urgent. 'It runs beneath the city's walls. If we can reach it, we might still have a chance!'

Appreciating the swiftness of Cornelius's strategic thinking, Mithra barked out orders. 'Soju, take a contingent and create a diversion. Make them believe we intend to fight. Uncle Cornelius, Cheliyan—with me! The rest of you, follow us!'

Soju's posture straightened. 'It shall be done,' he said, swiftly assembling a squad and leading them towards the approaching rebel force. They dug in, creating a convincing illusion of resistance. Meanwhile, Mithra, Cornelius and Cheliyan raced towards the aqueduct, its dilapidated archways barely visible in the gathering dusk. They shielded their movements, using the natural terrain as cover. Crumbling arches spanned the gorge, their weathered stones offering the only path into the fortified city.

The clash of arms echoed across the battlefield as Soju's men engaged the rebel forces. Soju, a whirlwind of motion, moved through the furore with effortless grace. Though outnumbered, his men fought with ferocity, their Pandyan iron slicing through enemy lines. The swords crafted by Padmasen and Kulasekara proved their worth—each blade robust, flexible and lethally sharp, cutting through flesh and bone like a hot knife through wax.

Mithra and his men arrived at the entrance to the aqueduct. The air within, cool and damp, contrasted sharply with the heat of the battlefield. The passage was narrow, claustrophobic, amplifying the sound of their hurried footsteps. After what seemed an eternity, they emerged within the city walls, only to be confronted by a group of startled Roman guards. Instantly, Mithra's sword flashed, silencing the closest guard before he could raise an alarm. Cornelius and Cheliyan followed suit, their movements swift and deadly. Within seconds, the Roman guards lay dead, their surprised expressions frozen in time.

'Secure the gates,' Mithra ordered, his voice a low growl. 'But first let Soju's men enter. We need to prepare for the Roman assault.'

Cornelius and Cheliyan led the charge towards the city gates, their blades flashing. The heavy gates groaned open, allowing Soju and his battered but victorious troop to enter the city.

From their new vantage point, they saw the Roman legions approaching, their efficient ranks a terrifying sight. Mithra knew they had precious little time. 'Fortify the walls!' he commanded. 'Prepare for attack!'

Cheliyan, ever the strategist, took charge. 'Archers—to the walls!' he barked. 'Every entrance must be defended. Make them pay dearly for every finger-width.' The Pandyan soldiers, energized by their victory, moved with renewed purpose, arrows nocked, hastily erecting barricades to position themselves behind.

As the first light of dawn appeared in the eastern sky, the Roman army launched its attack. The ground shuddered beneath the relentless pounding of a battering ram against the city gates, the air filled with the deafening clang of metal against metal and anguished cries of the wounded. Mithra, standing atop the city wall, watched as the Romans advanced, their centurion barking orders.

'Focus your fire on the ram operators!' he shouted to the soldiers positioned on the ramparts. As arrows rained down upon them, the Romans faltered, but for every man that fell, another stepped forward. The gates would not hold much longer.

Cornelius, his face grimy, appeared at Mithra's side. 'Their centurion—he is the key. We need to take him out.'

Mithra's eyes narrowed, focusing on the centurion, a figure of authority amidst the chaos. 'A bow,' he demanded.

One was swiftly placed in his hands. 'Cover me!' he ordered, taking aim.

Protected by a curtain of arrows, Mithra focused his attention on the centurion. He waited for the perfect moment—a slight pause in the enemy's advance. Then, with a steady hand, he released the arrow. It flew straight and true, embedding itself deep in the centurion's neck. The man, his eyes wide with shock, clutched at the feathered shaft, blood gurgling in his throat.

The Roman ranks floundered, their leaderless formation disintegrating into chaos. Mithra seized the opportunity.

'Charge!' he roared. With a renewed zeal, his soldiers below followed his command, clashing with the disoriented Romans.

The battle raged for hours, a brutal dance of death beneath a blood-red sky. But the tide had turned. Mithra, Soju, Cornelius and Cheliyan, their blades slick with blood, commands ringing out, pushed the Romans back, inch by bloody inch. As the last of the Roman forces fled the field, leaving behind a trail of carnage, a weary silence descended upon Dimašq. The city now belonged to Mithra.

Soju, his face strained with exhaustion, placed a hand on Mithra's shoulder. 'A close call,' he said.

Mithra nodded as he surveyed the destruction. 'The battle for Dimašq is far from over, my friend. Today, we won. But we must be prepared for what comes next. Summon the rebel leaders. Let us begin negotiations. The Roman diplomats ... they will be a different challenge.'

49

Safed Koh Mountains, Afghanistan
Present day

The moon cast an eerie glow over the jagged peaks of the Safed Koh mountains. Under its silvery sheen, a group of men moved silently, like shadows merging with the dark. These were not ordinary men, but seasoned fighters of the Islamic State of Khorasan—or ISIS-K—a regional outfit of the primary group in Syria. Like its parent organization, ISIS-K adhered to Salafi jihadism, a hardline Sunni Islamist ideology that advocated a return to what its followers saw as the pure, original form of Islam. It supported violent struggle—or jihad—to establish a global Islamic caliphate. Despite their political differences with the Taliban, the two groups occasionally found themselves aligned ideologically on some issues. At present, these included Ghaznawar and his pursuits.

Ghaznawar believed that his ancestor, Mahmud of Ghazni, had attacked Somnath for a specific reason. Apparently, Ghazni thought that Prophet Mohammad had commanded the destruction of three pre-Islamic goddesses widely worshipped as Lat, Uzza and Manat. While two idols were destroyed, Manat, an iconic block of black stone with incredible powers, was allegedly hidden away in Gujarat and placed in a shrine called Su-Manat. Both ISIS-K and the Taliban had been mysteriously tipped off that Ghaznawar still had a fragment of that stone in his possession—and that he revered it. That was idolatry—unacceptable to both groups. But Ghaznawar's cosy relations with senior Taliban officials meant that ISIS-K would have to execute the mission.

Their strategy was unusual—no contemporary gadgets, electrical devices or vehicles. Disguised as nomadic tribesmen, the fighters, intimately familiar with hazardous mountain routes, used only donkeys loaded with supplies and weapons. Days of rigorous preparation had led to this moment. Their scouts had meticulously mapped security protocols at the location, pinpointing weaknesses and blind spots.

Ghaznawar's hideout was a curious fusion of the modern and the ancient. Carved into the mountain, it was virtually invisible, its exterior mimicking the rocky surroundings. Inside, however, it hummed with advanced technology: motion sensors, encrypted communication systems and a network of security cameras. Khalil Ghaznawar had spared no expense in securing his haven.

The mercenaries reached the outer boundary just before daybreak. Crouching low, they observed the regular patrol, timing their movements and noting shifts and lapses in vigilance. They waited for the changeover—a brief window of vulnerability when alertness waned. Then, moving with lethal precision, they struck. Guards fell silently, their throats slit, necks snapped. A second team disabled the security cameras with well-aimed slingshots. Blood pooled on the rocky ground, the stillness of the morning broken only by the muted thud of bodies hitting the earth.

So precise was their attack that even the lair's sophisticated security systems failed to register their presence. Unhindered by electronic equipment, the mercenaries moved like phantoms through the complex. A layout map, acquired from a disgruntled contractor who had worked on Ghaznawar's project, guided their movements. They navigated their way with ease, bypassing the infrared perimeter fence, their rudimentary acrylic shields deflecting the heat sensors. Wet garments combined with heat-diffusing gel masked their personal thermal signatures. The smell of kerosene filled the air as they prepared Molotov cocktails—crude, but devastatingly effective.

The first explosion ripped through the morning, immediately giving rise to flames that licked ravenously at the wooden walls. Panic erupted inside the hideout. Ghaznawar's men, their confidence in technology shattered, scrambled to respond. But their efforts were disorganized, chaotic. The invaders, moving with the precision of a well-oiled machine, cut them down, their targets pre-selected. The air thickened with acrid smoke, blinding, turning each shadow into a potential threat.

The leader of the group, a hefty figure with a jagged scar marking his cheek, led the charge towards the inner sanctum. 'Ibhasu an al-alim! Innahu la yuqaddar bithaman!' he roared. 'Find the scientist! He is invaluable!'

They located Ramaswamy in his laboratory, surrounded by the tools of his research. He looked up, startled, as the door burst open. The scarred man, his eyes blazing, gestured for him to follow. Ramaswamy hesitated, confusion and fear warring within him. The man stepped forward and backhanded him across the face. 'You're coming with me,' he growled, his accent unfamiliar. Ramaswamy felt his ears ringing. He reached out to grab the palm-leaf manuscript—the sole object that held any value in this chaotic world.

The group leader, his patience thinning, grabbed Ramaswamy's arm and hauled him towards the exit. 'Move!' he barked. Disoriented and terrified, the scientist stumbled alongside.

'Where is the idolator? Find the dog!' the leader roared, his words echoing through the burning corridors. His men fanned out, searching for Khalil Ghaznawar.

But Ghaznawar was already gone.

Overlooked by the attackers, a carefully disguised landing area lay secreted among the towering trees. Undetected, a grim-faced Khalil Ghaznawar boarded a sleek black helicopter, its rotors whirring, slicing through the air. Within minutes, the chopper rose, disappearing into the rapidly lightening sky, carrying Ghaznawar away from the burning wreckage of his sanctuary.

The mercenaries, their mission only partially accomplished, disappeared into the mountains, leaving a trail of destruction in their wake. The wooden structure, engulfed by flames, was quickly consumed, reduced to smouldering embers. The ISIS-K fighters, their captive in tow, navigated less-frequented mountain passes, evading pursuit.

For Ramaswamy, a new nightmare had begun. He had been freed from one prison only to be delivered into another. His fate now rested in the hands of those who had taken him, strangers whose motives were as inscrutable as the mountains that surrounded them.

50

Seongsan, Garak Confederacy

Present-day Seongju County, South Korea

Around 2,000 years ago

Talhae paced the long, dark hallways of the Seongsan Fort, his mind a storm of restless thoughts. Recent events had set the stage for decisive action. Seongsan's capture of Goryeong had already disrupted the delicate balance within the Garak Confederacy. Now that Kim Seok had resigned from the chairmanship and Jangsu was in charge, the time was opportune.

He entered his father's chambers with a knock. Jangsu, who was poring over reports, watched with narrowed eyes as Talhae approached, bowing respectfully. 'Abeoji,' Talhae said, 'the time to strike is now. Daegaya is weak, vulnerable. Goryeong is already under our control. A swift, decisive attack will secure our dominance over the Confederacy.'

Jangsu sighed, setting aside the parchment he had been studying. 'Talhae, my son, I understand your eagerness, but patience is a virtue. Our soldiers are weary from the Goryeong campaign. We need to consolidate our gains, allow them time to rest and recuperate. A hasty assault on Daegaya will only stretch our resources thin.'

'But, Abeoji, momentum is crucial,' Talhae insisted, impatient. 'If we delay, Daegaya will strengthen its defences, forge alliances against us. We risk losing this advantage.'

Jangsu shook his head. 'An army marches on its stomach, not on ambition alone. We must secure our supply lines, ensure our forces are well-prepared. A period of stability will consolidate our position within the Confederacy. Kim Seok is gone. The other chiefs are aligned with us. Attacking now would be reckless, foolhardy.'

'Reckless?' Talhae retorted, his fists clenching. 'Or necessary? We may never get a better opportunity. Do you want to see all our hard-won victories wasted?'

Jangsu rose, his expression stern, his voice brooking no argument. 'Enough, Talhae! My decision is final. We will not attack Daegaya—not now. We will wait. We will prepare.'

Talhae scowled, resentment and disappointment churning within him. He bowed curtly, his voice tight. 'As you command, Abeoji.' He turned and strode out of the room, a dark plan already taking shape in his mind. As he walked along the shadowy corridor, he summoned his most trusted aide, his mind abuzz with possibilities. Jangsu's cautious approach, his foolish adherence to outdated traditions, would be his undoing. Talhae would seize the opportunity his father had so carelessly dismissed.

~

The next day, as dusk settled over Seongsan, cloaking the fortress in darkness, Talhae put his plan into action.

The passageways were mostly deserted, a few soldiers, unaware of the approaching danger, completed their routine patrols. Talhae moved silently through the fortress, his footsteps barely disturbing the quiet. His destination: Jangsu's quarters.

One quick slash of the dagger he held in his hand and the guard stationed outside his father's door crumpled to the ground, lifeless. Talhae paused, listening intently for any sound from within and heard only the gentle rhythm of his father's breathing. He carefully pulled open the door and slipped into the room, his heart pounding.

Moonlight streamed through the window, illuminating the sleeping form on the bed. Jangsu's chest rose and fell peacefully, his face relaxed in slumber. Talhae approached slowly, the dagger heavy in his hand. It was not just any blade—it was a ceremonial dagger stolen a few hours earlier from a Daegayan envoy under Talhae's secret orders. The ornate hilt, inlaid with lapis and obsidian, bore the sigil of the Daegaya royal house: a twin-headed falcon in mid-flight. A blade like this would point suspicion outward, sowing seeds of misdirection, even as it served Talhae's deadly purpose.

The weight of the dagger—the weight of his ambition—felt both exhilarating and terrifying. He stood by the bed, gazing down at the man who had raised him. But this was also the man who now stood in the path of his destiny. A twisted mix of love, grief and desire warred within him. Then, with a swift, decisive movement, he plunged the blade into his father's heart.

Jangsu awoke with a gasp, eyes widening in shock and pain, and saw his cherished adopted son standing over him. A flicker of hurt and betrayal showed on his face—and then the light faded from his eyes, leaving only a vacant stare.

Talhae stood there for a moment, watching the life drain from his father, the earlier storm of emotions giving way to a cold, hollow numbness. He had paid a heavy price for his ambition, but at least his path to power was now clear. Silently, he withdrew, leaving the exotic dagger embedded in Jangsu's chest, a silent message with a deceptive origin. Closing the door, he walked back to his room, careful to avoid the guards. His mind was already planning the next stage of his ascent. By daybreak, news of Jangsu's murder would spread like wildfire. He would be ready.

~

As the first light of dawn appeared on the horizon, a scream tore through the fortress, shattering the fragile peace. Talhae joined the throng gathered outside Jangsu's door, feigning shock as he gazed upon the bloody scene. Soon, the halls reverberated with angry accusations, a clamour for vengeance rising in volume.

Talhae stepped forward, his face a mask of grim determination. 'Brothers!' he shouted, his voice ringing with righteous anger. 'We have been betrayed! Chief Jangsu, our leader, my beloved abeoji has been murdered in cold blood in his own home …' He paused, letting his words sink in. 'This is not just an attack on my family. It is an attack on every citizen of Seongsan!'

He pulled the bloodied dagger from Jangsu's chest, holding it aloft for all to see. 'Look!' he thundered. 'The mark of Daegaya—clear evidence of their treachery! They seek to divide us, to weaken us, so they can conquer us! We will not let them succeed. We will avenge my abeoji's death! We will crush Daegaya!'

Fuelled by sorrow and anger, the crowd roared their approval, their uncertainty and fear transformed into a thirst for revenge.

'Pick up your swords!' Talhae thundered. 'March with me! We will bring Daegaya to her knees!'

Driven, the Seongsan warriors rallied behind their new leader. The fortress buzzed with activity as armours were fitted, swords were sharpened and horses saddled. Talhae watched with satisfaction, his heart swelling with pride. The power he had craved was finally within his grasp.

By midday, the Seongsan army had assembled, a sea of warriors ready for battle. Talhae, at their head, his gaze fixed on the distant horizon, raised his hand. 'Today, we march for justice!' he bellowed. 'Today, we march for Seongsan! Today, we march for victory!'

The thunder of drums and the roar of the army's response resounded across the land as they advanced on Daegaya. Talhae rode ahead of his men, a grim smile on his face. This was just the beginning. He would not rest until the entire Garak Confederacy, and the Three Kingdoms beyond, bowed before his might.

Visnupadagiri, Avanti, Gupta Samrajya
Present-day Udaygiri Caves, Madhya Pradesh, India
Around 1,600 years ago

As a soft glow crept over the horizon, Visnupadagiri slowly stirred to life. The air was charged with expectancy. This day marked a rare moment in history—the sacred pillar from Saketa, destined one day for Dhillika, was to be consecrated in its new sanctuary.

King Chandragupta II—Vikramaditya—watched as labourers completed their preparations. Florists adorned the processional route with garlands of fragrant blossoms, while musicians, their instruments gleaming, tuned to a harmonious pitch. The earthy scent of the surrounding woodlands mingled with the aroma of jasmine and marigolds perfuming the air.

Visnupadagiri was a sacred place, a testimony to the devotion and ingenuity of generations past. The sandstone hills were honeycombed with intricately carved caves, sanctuaries dedicated to Shiva, Vishnu and the Buddha. Each cave, a canvas for artistic expression, showcased the brilliance of the artisans who had painstakingly chiselled legendary tales into the very rock.

The most renowned among them was the shrine of Vishnu, its centrepiece a magnificent sculpture depicting his Varaha avatar rescuing the Earth from the cosmic ocean. Like the rulers before him, Vikaramaditya had generously supported this flourishing hub of knowledge and faith, transforming Visnupadagiri into a beacon of spiritual and intellectual pursuit.

Now, Vikramaditya, his most trusted general, Rudrasimha, and his head priest, Mahadeva, gathered near the holy caves to review the preparations for the ceremony. 'Every detail must be perfect,' the king emphasized. 'This Vishnu Stambha is more than just iron—it represents a sacred duty, a divine right.'

'It shall be so, Maharaj,' Mahadeva agreed, his hands clasped in reverence. 'We are certain that the gods themselves will bless this day. The rituals we perform will honour our ancestors and please the divine.'

Even as they spoke, workers carefully positioned the massive pillar upon a newly constructed platform atop Visnupadagiri. The site offered a sweeping view, stretching all the way to the distant horizon. A crowd had gathered—both commoners and nobles— eager to witness the momentous occasion.

Resplendent in his gold-embroidered antariya and uttariya, the king approached the platform, his entourage flanking him. A hush fell over the crowd as he ascended the steps. Turning to face the expectant assembly, he declared, 'Today, we stand together beneath our glorious banner to celebrate an era of prosperity and peace.' He gestured towards the towering pillar. 'This Vishnu Stambha, crowned by Garuda, embodies the strength and virtue of our ideals. It has travelled far, bringing the legacy of Saketa to Visnupadagiri. We honour it now, even as it makes way for a new temple, a grand edifice to be built in Saketa, upon the very site of Rama's birth.'

His words rang out through the crowd. At his signal, priests began chanting, their voices weaving sacred hymns that filled the air. Incense smoke, fragrant and ethereal, curled upwards, mingling with the cool morning breeze. The rhythmic chanting, hypnotic in its power, transported the assembled throng, drawing them into the heart of the ceremony.

Mahadeva stepped forward, bearing a golden urn filled with holy water. He presented it to Vikramaditya, who, after reciting a prayer, poured the water upon the pillar's base. The ritual consecrated the ground, connecting the present moment to the timeless realm of the divine. 'May this Vishnu Stambha stand as a beacon of strength and unity,' the king proclaimed. 'May its presence grace this land as long as the sun and moon illuminate the heavens.'

'This sacred site,' he continued, 'known as both Visnupadagiri and Udayagiri, honours both Vishnu and Shiva. The Vishnu Stambha has been brought here as a symbol of the harmony that exists between these two great forces—*śivāya viṣṇurūpāya śivarūpāya viṣṇave.*'

A fresh inscription adorned the pillar, carved into it by order of the king:

The king's might leaves a lasting mark,
a fiery force that quelled the dark.
Its glow remains, a fierce refrain,
like embers in a forest spark.

Vikramaditya stood staring at the towering pillar, envisioning his legacy. This Vishnu Stambha, he knew, would stand for centuries, a reminder of his reign, his glorious era.

As the rituals concluded, joyous melodies from the musicians' flutes and drums filled the air. Dancers in bright silks took to the stage, their bodies swaying, anklets and bangles chiming in tune with the music, executing intricate steps with effortless grace.

As he watched the celebrations unfold, Rudrasimha leaned towards his king. 'The people embrace your vision, Maharaj,' he said. 'The Vishnu Stambha inspires them. It represents something far greater than just iron.'

Vikramaditya smiled, his eyes full of pride. 'It is a symbol of our history, our faith, our shared destiny,' he said. 'By planting this pillar, we have planted the seed of a dazzling future.'

As the sun dipped behind the hills, casting the pillar in shadow, the king felt a chill in the air. For a brief moment, it seemed as if the ground beneath Visnupadagiri pulsed, the earth whispering a warning only he could hear.

51

Khyber Pakhtunkhwa, Pakistan
Present day

Bala Ramaswamy awoke to the distressing reality of yet another day in captivity, his senses gradually adjusting to the cave's dim light. The rough stone walls offered no comfort, and the air was suffused with the chill of damp earth. He lay on a thin mat, its coarse material offering little protection against the cold that seeped into him from the rocky floor. Coarse ropes bound his wrists and ankles, the constant chafing a burning reminder of his helplessness.

Deep within the untamed mountains of Khyber Pakhtunkhwa, the cave was a natural prison—a desolate, hidden maze of secret chambers and narrow corridors known only to his captors. This unforgiving landscape, once part of a region known as the Federally Administered Tribal Areas—FATA to the world—had always been a dangerous territory. The stark mountainous terrain and complex clan allegiances created a volatile mix of cultural conflicts and brutal violence. Located along the Pak–Afghan border, it was a traditional frontline for both tribal insurgencies and Pakistani military operations.

The series of events that had brought Ramaswamy to this godforsaken place unfolded in his mind, each memory a fresh wave of disorientation. It had begun with his abduction from

CERN by Ghaznawar and the tense days of captivity in his hideout deep in Afghanistan. Then came the sudden assault—explosions, bursts of gunfire, commands barked out in Arabic. Blindfolded and shaken, he was dragged from the compound and shoved into the back of a vehicle.

What followed was a long, jarring journey—hours on winding roads, the blindfold never once removed. The ambush must have happened somewhere near the edge of the FATA. Another fierce firefight had erupted, and when the dust settled, he found himself in the hands of a third group. This new group spoke Pashto. Its fighters had appeared out of nowhere, their numbers overwhelming, armed with weapons and a ruthless intent to kill. His precious palm-leaf manuscript was lost in a grenade blast. Blindfolded and bound, he had been powerless to resist, his pleas for reason ignored.

The voices around him changed subtly over time. The harsh Pashto gave way to a blend of dialects, and he began to hear phrases in Urdu, punctuated by references to Rawalpindi. It soon became clear that he was now in the hands of men who identified themselves as part of the Tehrik-i-Taliban Pakistan, or TTP—a group at loggerheads with both the ISIS-K and Pakistan. They spoke with a different cadence, their tone more rigid, their threats less veiled. Even without seeing, Ramaswamy sensed that he had crossed the border into Pakistan. He had been passed from captor to captor, each transfer pulling him deeper into the region's fractured and violent underbelly.

A flicker of light danced at the entrance to the cave, accompanied by the muffled sound of voices. Straining to hear, he caught only snippets of conversation, the unfamiliar words a cruel reminder of his isolation. Years of conflict had hardened his kidnappers, their faces grim, their movements purposeful.

Their AK-47s, slung casually over their shoulders, seemed almost like extensions of their bodies.

Kerosene lamps, their flames painting trembling shadows across the rough-hewn walls, provided intermittent light. The smell of burning fuel and a musty dampness pervaded the cave, making each breath a struggle. In the wavering light, he saw the stacks of wooden boxes and metal drums—provisions for the men who had made this place their home.

One of the men approached him—a tall, gaunt figure with a scraggly beard framing a face marked by years of hardship. His eyes, cold and unyielding, were fixed on Ramaswamy. He examined the ropes binding his wrists and ankles, tightening them with a practised twist that sent a jolt of pain through Ramaswamy's body. Then, kneeling beside him, he set down a metal tray containing a meagre meal: dried mutton, flatbread and a cup of water.

Ramaswamy, a vegetarian, recoiled from the smell of the meat. But through the days of captivity with the various groups he had learned better than to refuse. He nodded, his throat too dry for him to speak. The man rose and retreated, leaving Ramaswamy alone with his thoughts. He forced himself to sit up and eat the stale bread, his shackled hands fumbling with the rough texture. The water, frigid and tasting faintly of metal, offered a momentary reprieve from his thirst. The meat remained untouched.

There had been days when they untied him just long enough for him to relieve himself, the task made more difficult by bruised limbs and the presence of indifferent guards. On others, he had no such luxury, and shame became just another thread in the fabric of his captivity. As he ate, he tried to focus, as he did every day, on finding a way out. But he knew the cave, well-guarded and hidden deep within a maze of mountain passes, offered no easy escape. He had tried talking to his captors, hoping to glean some information, some clue to their intentions, but they had met his attempts at communication with stony silence. Even if he could escape this cave, he thought, how could he possibly navigate the hostile terrain, teeming as it was with vicious TTP factions?

Time crept by slowly, each day indistinguishable from the last. He occupied his mind with memories of his research, replaying his findings from the palm-leaf manuscript Ghaznawar had shared, the one that spoke of a mysterious element called the Dvaitalingam, the cryptic verses referencing a powerful 'Ayodhya alliance'. He clung to the hope—tenuous as it was—that someone, somewhere, was searching for him.

One day, a new figure entered his prison. The man was short and stocky, his face obscured by a henna-tinged beard. But his attire—a silk turban, a fine wool chapan perfectly suited to the mountain chill, a heavy gold chain gleaming at his throat and soft leather sandals—spoke of wealth and influence. He moved with an air of authority, his presence demanding attention. Sharp, intelligent eyes glinting with barely concealed ruthlessness met Ramaswamy's. 'I am Rahimullah,' he said in impeccable English, his voice smooth, assured. 'And you, I presume, are the scientist.'

Wary, Ramaswamy nodded. 'Bala Ramaswamy.'

Rahimullah gestured towards a rough wooden crate nearby. 'Untie his legs,' he instructed one of the guards. Immediately, the ropes were loosened, sending sharp tingles through Ramaswamy's limbs as blood rushed back.

'Sit up, Dr Ramaswamy.'

He obeyed, shifting gingerly onto the crate, the remaining binds on his wrists still tight, the ache in his joints a dull, persistent throb. 'I want nothing more than to return to my work,' he said. 'Why am I here?'

Rahimullah chuckled, a harsh, humourless sound. 'It is a strange world, is it not, Doctor?' he said. 'You can explain the movement of subatomic particles, but you cannot fathom the reasons behind your captivity?' He laughed again, the hollow sound reverberating through the cave and sending a shiver down Ramaswamy's spine.

Rahimullah reached into the folds of his chapan, drawing out a wickedly sharp knife. He held it close to Ramaswamy's face, the blade catching the dim light. 'I am here to liberate you, Doctor,' he said, his voice a soft, menacing whisper. 'Permanently.'

52

Korkai, Thamirabarani, Pandya Desam
Present-day Thoothukudi District, Tamil Nadu, India
Around 2,000 years ago

A boat cut through the inky darkness, its silhouette barely discernible against the horizon. The waters surrounding Korkai were exceptionally calm, a deceptive tranquillity concealing the turmoil brewing within the city. Guided by unseen hands, the boat silently approached the harbour. Overhead, countless stars offered only a glimmer of light, barely illuminating the figures on deck. The vessel nudged against the docks with a soft thud. Two men clad in indigo-dyed dhotis, uttariyas and turbans that blended seamlessly with the darkness disembarked, their movements fluid.

Each man wore a seemingly innocuous locket, concealing a potent dose of bikh—aconite powder—which promised a swift, silent death should he be caught. Two daggers, one secured at the waist, the other strapped to the thigh, were hidden beneath the folds of their garments, the blades readily accessible.

'How do we locate our contact?' one of the men whispered, his eyes scanning the shadowy docks.

'He will find us,' his companion replied, his voice a low murmur. 'But a password is required. We meet him by the Shiva shrine, just there.' He gestured towards a small stone structure at the edge of the harbour. 'Then we will determine our next move.'

The temple's ancient walls, illuminated by the faint starlight, seemed to exude a sense of timeless serenity a reminder of the city's rich spiritual heritage. The men moved silently along the cobblestones, like wraiths floating through the sleeping city.

They reached the shrine. The night was still, every sound—the creak of a branch, the rustle of leaves—magnified in the hush. Only the gentle lapping of waves against the shore broke the stillness, adding an almost surreal calm. Beneath a sprawling banyan tree, a lone figure waited, shrouded in the shadows.

'Andhakaara,' the first operative whispered, breaking the silence.

The figure shifted, stepping out from beneath the tree. 'Andhakaara,' he replied, his voice low, gravelly. 'Vidushika's men, I presume?'

'Indeed,' the second operative confirmed.

'I am Venkatesan. Follow me.'

Venkatesan's appearance was as unsettling as his demeanour. His sweaty skin shone in the dim light. His hair, oiled and slicked back, gave him a reptilian look. His eyes, constantly darting about, assessed the surroundings with a sharp, calculating intelligence. His movements were precise as he led them through meandering narrow alleyways, twisting and turning, designed to confound anyone in pursuit. A while later he stopped before an unassuming house, its walls barely visible in the darkness. He unlocked the door, ushering them inside. The safe house was sparsely furnished with just a low table and sleeping mats, but it looked secure.

'Water is here,' Venkatesan said, pointing at two clay pots in the corner. 'And food—dried fruits, nuts, jaggery and lemon rice. Draw no attention to yourselves. Eat, rest and plan your next move.'

A map, unrolled on the table, detailed the key locations in Korkai. Venkatesan traced a finger along a network of streets and alleys. 'These are the areas to avoid,' he warned. 'The townspeople are vigilant, their loyalty to Padmasen strong. One misstep could jeopardize your mission.'

Vidushika's men studied the map, nodding. 'This is helpful. We must find the Dvaitalingam and assess its security without raising suspicion,' one of them said.

'And what of Padmasen?' the second man asked, his hand resting on the hilt of his dagger. 'What is his routine? Does he frequent the location of the Dvaitalingam?'

'I have him under constant watch,' Venkatesan replied. 'I helped him acquire the land for his new ironworks, so I am often nearby. He visits the temple, the marketplace, his in-laws' residence and the foundry. But the Dvaitalingam is not at any of these places, and if there is a fifth, secret, location, he has not been there since we started watching him.' He paused, his jaw clenching visibly in the dim light. 'His daughter, Suriratna, is always close. She works alongside him, learning his craft. She is your best chance.'

'And the foundry?'

'Working day and night until recently,' Venkatesan said. 'Equipping soldiers for a mission in Dimašq. Now, production has slowed. They are back to producing ingots for trade.'

'We begin reconnaissance at dawn. We will determine the optimal time to strike. Stay vigilant, Venkatesan. We may need your assistance.'

Venkatesan bowed slightly. 'As you wish. May Vidushika's will be done.'

The men had a quick meal and settled onto the mats. Their sleep was light and restless. The fate of their mission, the fate of Padmasen and his family, rested on their next move. As the first light of dawn seeped through the cracks in the boarded windows, they awoke, their resolve hardened.

'Vidushika's orders are clear. The Dvaitalingam—at any cost.'
'Even if it means killing Padmasen?'
'Even if it means eliminating his entire family.'

53

Ayutthaya, Siam, Suvarnabhumi
Present-day Bangkok, Thailand
Around 2,000 years ago

Bhadraketu sat cross-legged on the cool clay floor of his modest cottage nestled on the banks of one of the three rivers that meandered through Ayutthaya. His lessons on dhamma had gained popularity, bringing people from all backgrounds to seek his spiritual guidance. As daylight waned, the surroundings filled with the perfume from the champa trees and the river burbled softly beneath a flame-hued sky.

King Jayasena arrived at the cottage as the sun dipped below the horizon, his royal entourage maintaining a polite distance. The king wore simple, unembellished garments. In the dimming light, his features took on an air of intrigue.

Bhadraketu greeted the king with a serene smile. 'Welcome, Your Majesty,' he replied, his voice as calm as the river that flowed beside them.

Jayasena settled on a woven mat across from Bhadraketu. 'Master Bhadraketu,' he said, unspoken anxieties in his voice, 'I seek solutions to the problems that plague my mind. I need your wisdom.'

'True wisdom comes from within, Your Majesty,' Bhadraketu said, his tone gentle but firm. 'But I can help you. The path to insight is open to all who seek it.'

Jayasena's gaze drifted around the small dwelling, taking in the rough clay walls and simple furnishings. One nook housed a humble shrine, its lone light conjuring fluid silhouettes. He inhaled deeply, the scent of incense soothing his troubled mind.

'Life in the palace offers every luxury, every comfort,' he confessed, his voice revealing his inner conflict. 'Yet I find no peace. Your life as a yogi … it seems far more fulfilling.'

'But you are also a yogi, Your Majesty,' Bhadraketu countered. 'Some, like me, practice Dhyan Yoga, connecting to the divine through meditation and contemplation. Others embrace Bhakti Yoga, finding enlightenment through love and devotion. There are those who seek knowledge through study and self-inquiry—the path of Gyana Yoga. And lastly, there are those like you who fulfil their duty, their actions guided by karma—the path of Karma Yoga.'

'But I am unhappy,' Jayasena admitted.

'Happiness, Your Majesty,' Bhadraketu explained, 'is found not in pursuing desires, but in mastering them. A man who quenches his thirst with saltwater will only find himself thirsting for more. Desires are like that—an endless cycle of craving.'

'I have two queens,' Jayasena said, his voice laden with despair, 'but no children. No heir.'

'The universe works in mysterious ways, Your Majesty,' Bhadraketu said. 'There are children who bring only sorrow to their parents, leaving them wishing they had remained childless. Others find their lives touched by unexpected blessings. Do not dwell on what you lack. Focus on using your power for good, ruling with wisdom, fairness and compassion. The legacy of your actions, your good deeds, will be your true heir.'

Jayasena nodded, contemplating. Bhadraketu's words offered a simple truth he had somehow forgotten.

'And what of power?' he asked, his brow creased with worry. 'As king, I wield absolute power. How can I use it without being corrupted by it?'

'Power is a double-edged blade, Your Majesty,' Bhadraketu replied calmly. 'It can be used to build or destroy, to protect or oppress. The secret lies in wielding it with kindness and intelligence. Use your power to serve your people, to uplift and guide them.'

'You speak of selflessness and compassion,' Jayasena countered, 'but the world is filled with cruelty and injustice. How can I remain untouched by the darkness, by the suffering that surrounds us?'

'Consider the lotus, Your Majesty,' Bhadraketu said, a gentle smile touching his lips. 'It blossoms into perfect beauty even as its roots remain in muck. Similarly, kindness, compassion and justice can flourish even in the darkest of times. Darkness, after all, is simply the absence of light.' He gestured towards the flickering oil lamp. 'Even a tiny flame can banish the gloom.'

Jayasena sat in thoughtful silence. Around him, leaves rustled in the gentle breeze; a night bird cried out in the distance.

'Your words offer a new perspective, Master Bhadraketu,' Jayasena said. 'A path I had not considered. I would ask a favour of you.'

'Anything, Your Majesty. But what could a humble monk like me offer a king?'

'Be my rajguru—a spiritual advisor to me and my kingdom. Will you accept?'

'It would be an honour, Your Majesty,' Bhadraketu replied, bowing his head. 'But I have two conditions.'

'Name them,' Jayasena said.

'You have renamed this land Ayutthaya,' Bhadraketu said. 'But Saketa is called Ayodhya for a reason. It is *a-yuddha*, or unconquerable because it is governed by the principles of Rama Rajya. I ask your word that you will rule with justice and compassion, and abide by the principles of dharma.'

'I promise you,' Jayasena said, 'that with your guidance I will lead my people wisely and compassionately.'

Bhadraketu nodded. 'And, should I choose to leave, you will not hinder my departure.'

'It pains me to think of such an eventuality,' Jayasena said. 'But I give you my word. You will be free to leave when you wish to.'

'I thank you, Your Majesty,' Bhadraketu said. 'I bestow upon you a new symbol—the gaurmatsya.' He knelt and drew the symbol on the floor with a piece of chalk. 'It represents good fortune, auspicious beginnings. One of the eight sacred emblems—the Ashtamangala.'

'The eyes of our Siamese cats?' Jayasena asked, examining the symbol.

Bhadraketu chuckled. 'Look closer, Your Majesty. I see two fish—representing all beings, swimming freely, unafraid, liberated from the cycle of death and rebirth. May your reign usher in such an era of peace and prosperity for all.'

Jayasena, deeply moved, accepted his blessing humbly.

Their coming together marked a new era for Ayutthaya—one guided by timeless principles and enlightened by Bhadraketu's wisdom. His influence, subtle yet profound, permeated the kingdom. He taught in the shade of ancient banyan trees, his words resonating with all who sought guidance and solace. 'Life is like a river,' he would say with a quiet smile. 'It flows onward, never pausing, never repeating. The waters you touch today are not the same as those of yesterday—and neither are you. Embrace the movement, the change. In that, you will find your stillness.'

He had no idea that the peace he had long sought—and had only just begun to glimpse—would soon be shattered.

54

Doha, Qatar

Present day

An elegant Gulfstream G200 touched down on the runway at Hamad International Airport. Aditya and Somi disembarked and were quickly ushered by a driver carrying their name cards into a waiting black SUV.

Within minutes, they were speeding along the Ras Abu Abboud Expressway. Somi took in Doha's unique blend of modernism and history, its futuristic skyline punctuated by ancient souqs and bustling marketplaces. Towers, sleek and shimmering, reflected the Arabian sun from their glass facades, while tree-lined avenues led to grand plazas. Cafés teemed with residents and visitors, a stark contrast to the peaceful stillness of the Arabian Gulf glistening in the distance.

Their journey to the Waldorf Astoria, though brief, was tense. Somi glanced at Aditya. He sat lost in thought, staring out the window, seemingly oblivious to the metropolis's relentless pulse. His mind, she knew, was elsewhere.

The SUV pulled up outside the forty-four-storey art-deco skyscraper in Doha's diplomatic quarter. Aditya barely registered the opulent lobby's crystal chandeliers, marble pillars, or elegant artwork. The concierge, impeccably groomed, greeted them and escorted them to a waiting elevator. The moments ticked by in the soft hum of the lift.

The lift opened onto a hallway adorned with eye-catching décor and luxurious rugs. They followed the concierge to a quiet suite, where Devendra Thakural, India's NSA, awaited them.

'Good to see you again, Mr Pillai,' Thakural said, his handshake firm, his expression serious. Turning to Somi, he added, 'It's been too long, Ms Kim. We last met at the World Economic Forum, I believe?'

'Indeed,' Somi acknowledged.

'Please, sit.' Thakural gestured towards a plush sofa. His voice, though level, held a note of urgency.

They settled on the sofa and Thakural, dispensing with pleasantries, got straight to the point. 'Some days ago, ISIS-K raided Khalil Ghaznawar's hideout in the Safed Koh Mountains. Dr Ramaswamy was taken.'

'ISIS-K?' Aditya's brow furrowed. 'The Islamic State?'

'An offshoot of the Syrian ISIS,' Thakural explained, 'but operating in Afghanistan. Their targets are many: the Taliban government of Afghanistan, the United States, Shia Muslims, the Hazara minority ... anyone they deem an enemy of their twisted ideology. Their aim? To overthrow the current Taliban regime and establish a caliphate.'

'So our efforts to locate Dr Ramaswamy have become ... more difficult?'

'Negotiating with a criminal gang—even a terrorist group— is often more straightforward than dealing with rogue states. That's why I requested your presence here in Doha. This city is a hub for such negotiations.'

Aditya's eyes widened as understanding dawned. 'You orchestrated this,' he stated, his voice a mix of disbelief and accusation.

Thakural's response was dry, delivered with a hint of amusement. 'Let's just say I prefer to be proactive. Indian intelligence operates ... discreetly. Often, we achieve our objectives by employing others, providing incentives.'

Aditya, his expression unreadable, nodded. 'And the handover from ISIS-K?'

'Allow me to check on the status.' Thakural picked up a secure satellite phone, dialled a number and waited. He listened carefully, then he said, 'I'll have to get back to you.'

Aditya leaned forward, his eyes narrowed. 'Now what?'

Thakural drew a breath, his eyes fixed on a point beyond the window. 'There have been complications,' he admitted, his voice tight. 'But we are still on top of things.'

'What complications?'

'The TTP—Tehrik-i-Taliban Pakistan. They ambushed the ISIS-K. Ramaswamy is now in their custody.'

'Why would the TTP be involved?' Somi asked, her voice soft, laced with concern.

'The ISIS-K and the TTP,' Thakural explained, 'have very different objectives. The ISIS-K seeks control of Afghanistan. They despise the current Taliban regime. The TTP, however, desires control of Pakistan. And they rely on the Taliban for support. It's a zero-sum game—one's gain is the other's loss.'

Aditya's jaw clenched, a wave of anger washing over him. 'So Ramaswamy's just a pawn in their twisted game?' *Or is the TTP game also yours, Mr Thakural?*

He rose from his chair and walked towards the window, his gaze drawn to the sprawling city beneath them. Doha, a dazzling display of modernity, buzzed with life, its energy a stark contrast to the heavy silence that had settled in the room.

'What options do we have?' Aditya asked, his back to them, his voice betraying his frustration.

'Two,' Thakural replied. 'Direct negotiation with the TTP. Or … a clandestine operation to extract Ramaswamy. But the risks are significant. We cannot afford any casualties.'

'No other options?'

'Perhaps,' Thakural said quietly, 'there's another avenue we could explore.'

'And that would be …'

Thakural's voice was a barely audible whisper. 'The Emir of Qatar.'

Aditya understood immediately. From the stories he had heard and the whispers in international circles, he got the impression that Qatar was playing a delicate double game—maintaining relationships with both Islamist groups and Western powers. A precarious balancing act, no doubt, but one that gave the small Gulf nation disproportionate influence in regional affairs.

'We need to proceed with caution,' Thakural said, his voice regaining its earlier firmness. 'Diplomacy is a delicate art. Doha is the ideal setting for this type of negotiation. We must utilize every resource at our disposal to secure Dr Ramaswamy's safe return.'

'And the resources in this case are?'

'A man called Rahimullah who is on the payroll of Qatar but also close to the TTP.'

55

Korkai, Thamirabarani, Pandya Desam
Present-day Thoothukudi District, Tamil Nadu, India
Around 2,000 years ago

The furnace hissed, its blazing heart bathing the factory in an orange light. Suriratna stood before the flames, her brow damp with perspiration, her gaze steady as she carefully poured a ladleful of molten metal into a waiting mould. Her movements were precise, practised—a result of the many weeks she had spent honing her craft. What was once an overwhelming amalgamation of sound and heat—the roar of the furnace, the clang of the forge, the searing breath of molten metal—had become an extension of her will, her every action an instinctive response to the primal dance of creation.

Setting the ladle aside, she moved through the foundry, her keen eyes assessing the work in progress, a quiet authority in her bearing as she issued instructions. From a distance, Padmasen watched his daughter, his heart swelling with pride.

'Good work, everyone!' she called out, her voice rising above the din. 'Maintain this pace. We have a deadline to meet.'

Kulasekara approached, a ledger in his hand. 'The new iron ore from Kongu Nadu has arrived,' he said. 'Shall we inspect it?'

Suriratna nodded. 'Of course, Matalu. Let us get it done.'

'We must be sure it meets our standards,' Kulasekara said, his brow furrowed. 'No compromises this time. Remember those impurities in the last batch?'

She nodded in agreement and they walked towards the storage area. The factory thrummed with activity, each worker a vital part of the complex process. Suriratna greeted them warmly, several of them by name. Her easy camaraderie and genuine respect for those around her had enabled her to form a strong bond with the workers.

In the storage area, rows of massive wooden crates shrouded in thick cloth held the raw materials that fuelled their enterprise. Suriratna removed the cloth and uncovered one of the crates, revealing a mound of dark, coarsely textured ore. Kulasekara scooped up a handful, assessing its weight, texture and colour. He noted the subtle sheen, the lack of obvious imperfections. 'Promising,' he murmured, rubbing the ore between his palms. 'High quality. These new suppliers understand our standards. They are eager to impress.'

'In that case, we must maintain precise temperatures to ensure optimal smelting,' Suriratna said, her mind already calculating the necessary adjustments. 'I will instruct the furnace crew to prioritize this batch.'

As they turned to leave, Suriratna paused, her eyes drawn to a shadowy corner of the godown. She thought she had glimpsed a fleeting movement, a flicker in the darkness. But it could have just been a trick of the light. Shaking off her unease, she returned to the bustling heart of the factory.

Together, Suriratna, her father and her matalu made a formidable team, each bringing their unique expertise to the venture. Padmasen, the master craftsman, shared his years of metallurgical knowledge, guiding Suriratna's hand, refining her skills, teaching her the subtle art of coaxing the molten metal to yield its secrets. Kulasekara, with his keen commercial instincts and unmatched business acumen, effortlessly managed the logistics, sourcing raw materials, negotiating trade routes, securing lucrative deals. And Suriratna, with her unwavering determination, oversaw the day-to-day operations, ensuring a smooth flow of production.

Their collective excellence and their synchronized efforts had transformed their small enterprise into a renowned force in the world of iron production. But their success was built on more than just talent and strategy. It was the secret ingredient they possessed—a legacy passed down through generations—that distinguished their metal from all others.

The clamour of the workday faded, replaced by the sounds of workers cleaning and preparing for the next day. The furnace, banked for the night, glowed with a dull, orange heat. Suriratna paused, taking a moment to savour the relative quiet, a sense of accomplishment settling over her as she gazed up at the first stars emerging in the darkening sky.

She rolled up a parchment filled with her notes on ancient wheel designs—oblivious to the two figures lurking in the shadows, their eyes tracking her every movement.

For days, Vidushika's spies had been watching, meticulously charting her routine, recording her every habit, searching for a weakness, an opportunity. They had been told she was the key to Padmasen's secrets. To obtain the Dvaitalingam, they needed her.

Padmasen entered the foundry, joining his daughter. 'Another successful day, Putri,' he said, his voice warm with pride, resting a hand on her shoulder.

'Thank you, Pitaha,' she said, her smile weary. 'But there is something ... something I need to discuss with you.'

Padmasen looked at her with concern. 'What troubles you, my dear?'

'The Dvaitalingam,' she said, her voice hesitant. 'I know Matalu Kulasekara is safeguarding it at a secret location. But would it not be safer here, at the foundry? We could double the guard, conceal it within the basement vault. One of us is always here.'

Padmasen's face hardened, his voice sharp with disapproval. 'Absolutely not. The Dvaitalingam stays where it is. We bring only small amounts here, just enough for our needs.'

'But Pitaha,' she argued, 'the foundry is secure. We know everyone who enters and leaves—'

'The foundry is filled with prying eyes, Putri,' Padmasen interrupted, his voice stern with warning. 'Too many people, too much movement. The Dvaitalingam is a sacred trust, a powerful tool that must remain hidden, protected from those who would misuse it. It will remain where it is. That is final.'

Suriratna sighed, recognizing her father's resolve. 'I understand, Pitaha. I simply worry for its safety.'

Padmasen's expression softened. 'I know you do, Putri. And I trust you implicitly. That is why I, in turn, entrusted you with its use. But its location … that knowledge must remain protected. We have to honour the traditions, the safeguards established by our ancestors. The time for change will come, but it is not now.'

'Yes, Pitaha.' She bowed her head in respect, accepting his decision.

'Good. Now come,' Padmasen said, his voice regaining its warmth. 'Kulasekara and I have much to discuss before my next journey to Muchiri Pattinam.'

Padmasen and Suriratna walked home, discussing their plans for the future, unaware of Vidushika's spies following close behind, a silent threat lurking in the shadows.

Their plans, too, were swiftly taking shape.

Constantinople, Eastern Roman Empire
Present-day Istanbul, Türkiye
Around 1,700 years ago

Formerly Byzantium, Constantinople—renamed in 330 CE to honour Emperor Constantine—was a jewel in the Roman Empire, a shining example of the monarch's vision and ambition. The city thrived on a mix of commerce, culture and religion. Straddling the natural waterway of the Bosphorus Strait, which linked two continents, it occupied a strategic crossroads that would soon make it the heart of a growing faith called Christianity.

Inside the palace, however, the emperor's chamber was dark and hushed. Constantine, once at the pinnacle of power, now lay unmoving on his grand bed. His eyes, no longer alight with life, were clouded and distant, staring blankly at the ornate ceiling in the flickering candlelight. The scent of medicinal herbs, mingled with subtle aroma of frankincense, filled the sprawling room.

Constantine had made his decision. He would dedicate his final hours to being baptized into the Christian faith. Priests moved around the room, their movements directed by purpose. The one closest to him held a bowl of clear water, a symbol of purification, to be used for the ceremony. Constantine's gaze settled on it, his thoughts returning to the events that had brought him to this moment.

His brutal clash twenty-five years ago with Maxentius, then emperor, had taken place during the Roman civil wars—a period of fragmentation and fierce rivalries. The battle had been a storm of suffering and desperate survival. Yet amidst the chaos, Christian troops, fighting beneath their banner emblazoned with a cross, had become Constantine's unlikely allies. Their unrelenting faith and tenacity had turned the tide, granting him victory.

That triumph had not only ended a chapter of civil strife but also established Constantine as the sole emperor of an empire teetering on the edge of disintegration. Now, driven by political necessity, the once-pagan emperor prepared to convert.

'Ensure the new faith reflects the old,' he rasped, his voice thin, barely audible. 'If your aim is to embrace my people, heed my words.'

'What is your wish, Your Majesty?' the bishop asked, drawing closer.

'Change the Sabbath,' Constantine breathed, each word a struggle. 'My people worship Sol Invictus—the unconquered sun—on Sunday. Let Sunday be the Christian day of rest, not Saturday. It will ease their acceptance.'

'It shall be done,' the bishop agreed. 'Anything else?'

'Christians celebrate the birth of this ... Jesus Christ ... on the sixth of January,' Constantine continued, his voice faltering. A racking cough shook his frail body. 'The twenty-fifth of December—*Dies Natalis Solis Invicti*—marks the birth of the unconquered sun. That is the day my people hold most auspicious. Align the dates. It will be ... simpler ... for all.'

The bishop bowed his head solemnly, then turned to exchange a brief, knowing glance with the attending priests. They understood. Concessions such as these would smoothen the path of transition.

The silence that followed was broken only by the emperor's laboured breathing. Among the more pragmatic minds of the court, a realization had begun to take hold—if the new faith was to endure and unify the diverse citizens of the Roman Empire, it would need more than the teachings of a prophet. It would require symbols, rituals and a narrative that would resonate with the spiritual traditions already deeply embedded across the empire. Some advisors quietly suggested aligning aspects of Jesus's life with familiar motifs—divine birth, miraculous deeds, resurrection—not to diminish his message, but to elevate it within a cultural language the people were familiar with.

Constantine's eyes settled upon his Damascus sword, resting on the bedside table. Its blade, engraved with four crossed swords held deep meaning—it was a symbol of his strength and authority. Summoning his remaining energy, he reached for it, drawing comfort from its familiar weight. He traced the symbol with a trembling finger. A hint of a smile touched his lips.

'You say this ... Christ ... told his followers they would become fishers of men?' His voice was a mere whisper. 'Fishing does not forge empires. Swords and sustenance go hand in hand. Let this be your symbol, with a simple rotation.' He lifted the blade with some effort and turned it slowly so it would catch the candlelight. The four swords, viewed differently, now resembled two fish.

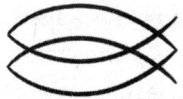

'Iēsous Christos, Theou Yios, Sōtēr,' the scribe-priest intoned in Greek. 'Jesus Christ, Son of God, Saviour.' His eyes went to the symbol. In Greek, the phrase was abbreviated as ΙΧΘΥΣ. He sketched quickly, capturing the new symbol, adding the Greek letters within. He showed it to the emperor, who gave a weak nod.

'Without the sword,' whispered Constantine, 'faith is meaningless.'

The bishop approached him now, the bowl of water in his hand, his movements deliberate, respectful. The other occupants of the room held their breath. Constantine's eyes, though clouded by death, held a spark of satisfaction. As the cool water touched his brow, the bishop intoned softly, 'I baptize you in the name of the Father, the Son and the Holy Spirit.' A calmness settled over the emperor.

Here, nearing death, he had become a Christian—not from personal revelation, but from imperial necessity. The empire he had fought to reunite was splintered by division and doubt. Christianity, once a persecuted religion, had grown into a vast, cohesive force that transcended borders and languages. Embracing it had never been about personal salvation. It was about securing the empire's future. His choice had not been guided by angels or dreams, but by the cold arithmetic of survival.

Outside, the city went about its business, oblivious to the events within the palace. The setting sun cast its golden light on Constantinople. As the emperor waited to draw his final breath, his thoughts turned to legacy. Christianity, he knew, would become embedded in Roman life, lasting long after his death, and he was certain that Constantinople would become its bastion, a shining beacon for their new deity, Jesus Christ.

Jesus said the meek shall inherit the earth, he thought, a sardonic twist on his lips, *but it is really the bold who carve out their share with iron.*

56

Dimašq, Roman Empire
Present-day Damascus, Syria
Around 2,000 years ago

Standing on the palace steps, Mithra felt a pleasant breeze carrying the aroma of incense caress his face. Word of his impending appointment had spread, sparking excitement among the people. Behind him, the governor's palace hummed with the murmurs of dignitaries and preparations for the ceremony.

Securing Nabataean support had required a visit from Cheliyan and Cornelius to Raqmu, to persuade King Aretas IV that Pandyan tools could help complete his capital's remaining structures. Barakat had also been present during their audience with the king.

Convincing Barakat had been no easy feat. 'We negotiated in good faith,' Barakat had told Cornelius. 'You and Philippides promised to intercede with Rome and rationalize the taxes. But nothing happened. You broke your word.'

'Your rebellion cost my mentor his life,' Cornelius had replied, recalling the frenzied mob that had murdered Philippides. 'His blood is on your hands.'

Barakat's expression softened. 'I tried to prevent it,' he said. 'I did not want things to escalate. But controlling a mob is nearly impossible. I regret Governor Baruchus Philippides's death and take full responsibility for it. But you knew, as he did, that a revolt was brewing.'

Cornelius nodded, recalling how Barakat had indeed tried to rein in the mob. He shifted his strategy smoothly, turning to the king and assuring him of the power of Korkai's iron technology and explaining the role that it could play in getting Nabataean projects completed. That had proven effective. Aretas was astonished by the speed with which the new chisels melted away rock upon rock. A new arrangement between Dimašq, the Nabataeans and Rome was successfully forged.

Now, the Roman envoy, Marcus Valerius—a stern but respectful figure in a crimson-edged toga—prepared for the formal proceedings. As the doors to the Grand Hall opened, Mithra entered, radiating confidence, clad in a finely embroidered tunic, a gift from Cheliyan showcasing the intricate designs of Pandya Desam. The hall fell silent.

'Mithradates Baruchus Philippides,' Valerius began, his voice echoing. 'Emperor Claudius recognizes your efforts in securing alliances and bringing peace. Much like Emperor Tiberius acknowledged your father, I am here to confirm your appointment as Governor of Syria.'

Mithra bowed deeply. 'An honour, Envoy Valerius. I pledge my loyalty to the emperor and Rome's prosperity.'

Valerius nodded, satisfied by Mithra's humility. Both knew Rome had little choice but to appoint him to maintain control over Syria. 'Your alliance with the Nabataeans and the secure trade network with the Pandyan kingdom are invaluable to Rome,' Valerius stated. 'A steady supply of iron ingots, pepper, ivory, silk, pearls and incense will be appreciated.' Rome's imbalance of trade with Korkai and Muziris was already pronounced and, with the new arrangement, it was set to grow.

Mithra took a deep breath. 'With the support of my Pandyan allies, Rome will receive all it desires. Increased trade will compensate for any tax reductions, ensuring goodwill and prosperity for all.'

A murmur of approval rippled through the hall. Valerius leaned forward, intrigued. 'And the Nabataeans? How did you secure their allegiance?' he whispered.

Mithra smiled. 'They value stability and prosperity. We earned their trust by promising favourable trade and protection from enemies. Assisting them with important projects assured their loyalty. They understand that a strong alliance with Rome is mutually beneficial.'

Valerius nodded, pleased. 'Very well, Mithradates. Your governorship is confirmed. May your leadership bring glory to Rome and prosperity to our allies.'

'Vivat Mithradates!' the assembled dignitaries chanted.

Barakat stepped forward and knelt before Mithra. He offered the younger man a magnificent blade. 'A small gift,' he said. Surprised, Mithra accepted the sword. 'Thanks to Korkai's consistent supply of ingots, we have established a foundry in partnership with Cheliyan. This is the first piece—a Damascus sword. Inspired by the nav utsa's twin-fish theme, we have created a new mark: two fish resembling four swords.'

Mithra angled the sword, appreciating the wave-patterned blade—a result of expertly folding and forging layers of metal. Its surface shimmered, showcasing the superior craftmanship of Syrian blacksmiths.

'We are currently only fashioning swords and tools,' Barakat continued, 'but Cheliyan has promised to share the technology for creating ingots. We are on the cusp of a full-scale operation here.'

~

Later that evening, Mithra met with Cheliyan, Soju and Cornelius in a private hall, their faces dappled by the flickering lights. Ever the tactician, Cheliyan leaned forward, his eyes shining with excitement. 'Congratulations, Mithra. This is remarkable! But we must uphold our end of the arrangement.'

Mithra nodded. 'Indeed. Supply lines must remain open, traders kept content. How fares our Korkai network?'

'Strong,' Cheliyan replied. 'Routes are secure and trade links have been re-established with local traders. The flow of goods, including ingots coming in from Padmasen and Kulasekara, will be steady.'

'The Nabataeans are fully committed,' Cornelius added. 'We will safeguard these trade channels and ensure Rome receives its due. But not at the cost of local prosperity.'

Mithra raised a cup of wine in a toast. 'To the future. May our nations know peace and wealth.'

'To the future!' the others shouted together, clinking their cups. They spent the rest of the evening celebrating Mithra's success and making plans for the upcoming era of prosperity.

~

As twilight deepened, Mithra stood on the balcony, memories of his father surfacing in his mind. A noise behind him disrupted his thoughts. Soju approached, his expression a mixture of sadness and resolve. 'Mithra, we need to talk.'

Mithra turned, his face softening. 'Of course, Soju. What is it?'

'I must return to Korkai,' Soju said gently. 'My work here is done. I would like to go back now ... to my life and to Suriratna.'

Mithra nodded, though his heart sank. 'You have been a true friend and supporter, Soju. I understand your obligations and will miss you deeply. I am in your debt. A ship will be prepared for you.'

'There is no need for another vessel,' Soju replied. 'I am travelling back with Cheliyan and the remaining Pandyan ships and troops tomorrow.'

Mithra embraced his friend, pride and sadness in his eyes. 'Safe travels, Kim Suro! May your journey be swift and your reunion with Suriratna joyous.'

57

Korkai, Thamirabarani, Pandya Desam
Present-day Thoothukudi District, Tamil Nadu, India
Around 2,000 years ago

The golden afternoon light streamed through the latticed windows, casting patterns on the stone floor. Suriratna sat cross-legged on a woven mat, her delicate fingers tracing the worn lines of ancient parchments.

'What occupies you, Suriratna?' a soft voice inquired from the doorway. Suriratna looked up to see her mother, Indumati, standing at the entrance, brow creased with concern.

'Mataha,' she replied, her voice brimming with excitement, 'I am studying the chakra. A concept taught by Acharya Satyamuni, but I never imagined its reach across so many disciplines.'

Intrigued, Indumati entered. 'Explain,' she prompted.

Suriratna gestured for her mother to join her, unrolling another mat. 'Our ancient texts are replete with references to the chakra,' she explained, her tone reverent. 'Consider Vishnu's Sudarshan Chakra—the celestial discus Krishna used to decapitate Shishupala. It was said to be the most powerful weapon in the universe.'

Indumati nodded, a faint smile gracing her lips. 'I remember my mother telling me that story as a child,' she remarked.

'Then there is the Chakravyuha,' Suriratna continued, her fingertip gliding over a sketch of a circular military formation. 'A cunning battle strategy designed to trap enemies. Abhimanyu, Arjuna's son, met his demise within one during the battle at Kurukshetra.'

Indumati shivered at the mention of Abhimanyu's tragic end. 'A story of terrible loss,' she murmured. 'The way he was encircled, outnumbered …'

Suriratna nodded in agreement. 'But the chakra is not merely a weapon or a battle tactic. In tantra, there is the Kalachakra—the wheel of time—symbolizing the cyclical nature of life, death and reincarnation. This wheel turns endlessly, representing constant change.'

'Three hundred years ago there was Emperor Ashoka's Dharma Chakra too,' reminded Indumati.

'Yes,' Suriratna replied. 'But I think we exaggerate when we say Ashoka was a pacifist. This was someone who murdered ninety-nine brothers to secure the throne! In fact, I wonder …'

'What?'

'Oh nothing,' Suriratna replied, biting back her words. She paused before taking the conversation down a different path. 'Of course, we have the chakras of the human body and consciousness; the Karma Chakra of the Upanishads, speaking of the cyclical nature of actions and consequences; the Ratha Chakra of the Rig Veda, describing chariot wheels; the Buddha's Dharma Chakra …'

Indumati reached out, her hand covering her daughter's. 'Suriratna,' she began, her voice soft, 'your knowledge in these matters is impressive. But what has prompted your fascination with the subject? I struggle to understand your and your father's pursuits. I wish you would focus on finding a good husband. What greater joy is there than to have a family of your own?'

Suriratna hesitated, her thoughts drifting to Soju. Should she confide in her mother now? She hesitated for a moment, then decided to wait for a better time to discuss Soju. 'Long ago ...' she began slowly, her expression inscrutable, 'a treatise existed, evaluating all forms of the chakra, seeking to understand their mechanics, their true potential.' Her voice dropped to a whisper. 'I am ... educating myself.'

Sensing something unsaid in her daughter's words, Indumati's gaze sharpened. 'Are you keeping something from me, Suriratna? Something you are reluctant to share?'

Yes, Mataha, Suriratna wanted to cry out. *I am in love with Soju. He is the only man for me.* But the words remained unspoken, and she turned back to the parchments. After a while, she murmured, 'I know of this concept, Mataha, but I am unsure what I am seeking.' *It applies to both the chakra ... and to love.*

Indumati's breath caught in her throat. 'What do you mean?'

A frown appeared on Suriratna's brow, her concentration deepening. 'I have not grasped it fully. The chakra is discussed in fragments, hidden within layers of text. It seems to be ... a dark, potent energy, tied to life and death ... A secret to something ... something transformative.'

Indumati rested her hand on her daughter's shoulder. 'Be careful, my child,' she whispered, her voice trembling slightly. 'Seeking knowledge is admirable, but the path can be dangerous.'

Suriratna's eyes met her mother's. 'I will be careful, Mataha. I promise.'

She watched Indumati leave, a storm of emotions and conflicting thoughts swirling within her. Alone at last, she returned to her notes. At the top of the document, beside a diagram, one word stood out, stark and clear: Mrityuchakra. Feeling a strong pull, she traced the outline of the diagram with her finger.

'Mrityuchakra,' she murmured. 'The Wheel of Death.'

Some distance away, Vidushika's agents continued their vigil, maintaining their watch on Padmasen and his family.

58

Ayutthaya, Siam, Suvarnabhumi
Present-day Bangkok, Thailand
Around 2,000 years ago

Deep within the forest, beneath a canopy of ancient trees, a faint, flickering light pierced the darkness. The air was heavy with a guttural chant, punctuated by the rustle of leaves and the distant hoot of an owl.

'Mon cak ca thira, haan kray bithaa neng mrac. Phar kim sunay, saav khyong raav thu. Spirit of the ancient forest, hear my call and come forth. By the power of darkness, unleash the hidden force.'

Mahidol was renowned amongst the forest people—a sorcerer known for practising the ancient and potent Mon magic. His connection to the spirits of the forest, his mastery over them, had earned him both the reverence and the fear of the tribes. Villagers for miles around consulted him on matters mundane and mystical. His reputation had even reached the king, who had on occasion summoned him in secret to seek his wisdom.

Bhadraketu had heard whispers about the forest mage—rumours of an ancient power living in seclusion, a keeper of secrets that predated scrolls and temples. Drawn by curiosity and an unspoken urgency, he had set out days earlier in search of this mysterious being, following winding trails and half-remembered directions from wary locals. Now, guided only by instinct and the haunting chant that drifted through the night air, he moved cautiously towards the source.

The first thing he saw was the glow—strange, blue and flickering like moonlight on disturbed water. He stepped softly through the underbrush, his breath shallow, the forest hushed around him. A lone figure stood before an altar created by tying bones together with twisted vines. Bhadraketu realized he was seeing Mahidol just as the forest people described him—wearing necklaces of animal skulls and a black robe of roughly hewn cloth. His hands moved in complex patterns above a smouldering fire that emitted the strange blue glow, while the earth around it bore peculiar symbols, each pulsing with a dark energy.

Bhadraketu watched, a mix of unease and fascination churning in his gut. The negative energy emanating from the ritual was so intense it seemed to distort the air. Instinctively, he countered with his own chants, a shield against the encroaching darkness. 'Oṁ maṇi padme hūṁ,' he whispered repeatedly, matching the quickening rhythm of Mahidol's chant, faster and faster, until, with a sudden, sickening lurch, the blue flames erupted, spiralling violently. Mahidol's eyes widened in terror, his incantations dissolving into screams as the flames leaped from the altar, catching his robes. His cries echoed through the forest like the howls of a tortured beast.

Instinct overrode fear and Bhadraketu rushed forward, ripping the thick woollen blanket from his shoulders and flinging it over the burning man. Mahidol crumpled to the ground, thrashing wildly, as Bhadraketu smothered the flames. The acrid stench of burning flesh and fabric made him nauseous, but Bhadraketu did not hesitate, pressing down until the fire was extinguished. Mahidol lay still, unconscious.

Bhadraketu hoisted the badly injured sorcerer onto his shoulder and carried him back to his hut. He laid Mahidol gently on a makeshift bed and for days tended to his burns, employing every herb and form of remedy he had learned under Nadikasyapa—poultices, medicinal broths and words of comfort. Slowly, painfully, Mahidol began to heal, his murmured gratitude growing stronger with each passing day.

Finally, on a crisp morning weeks later, the sorcerer sat up on his own. He looked at Bhadraketu, his eyes glistening with pain and relief, and whispered, 'You saved my life.'

Bhadraketu smiled gently. 'Your journey to recovery has just begun. Rest now, my friend.'

On the following day, Mahidol asked him, 'What manner of magic do you practise? Your chants were more effective than my own …'

Bhadraketu chuckled. 'Closing your eyes and meditating reveals the cosmos, the intricate connections between all beings. My magic lies only in that.'

Mahidol considered this. 'There is another magic,' he finally said, 'beyond rituals, predictions, or even meditation.'

'And what is that?'

'The magic,' Mahidol replied, a smirk appearing on his lips after many days, 'of manipulating minds.'

59

Dubai, United Arab Emirates
Present day

Unlike the cave in which Dr Ramaswamy had been imprisoned, the guesthouse in Dubai, where he had been brought by Rahimullah, exuded opulence. Situated in the elegant Jumeirah neighbourhood, the grand estate boasted lush gardens, towering palm trees and a shimmering swimming pool in its back lawn.

In the living room, plush couches, intricate Persian carpets and sparkling chandeliers complemented each other seamlessly, marrying contemporary elegance and traditional Arabian aesthetics. Large windows bathed the room in warm sunlight and offered a panoramic view of the pool. A world away from the dangers he had so recently faced, it was a sanctuary of safety and comfort for Ramaswamy, the sense of security and luxury he felt now almost overwhelming.

Aditya Pillai and Somi Kim were finally face-to-face with the man so many had risked so much to find. Ramaswamy's extraction from Khyber Pakhtunkhwa at the Pakistan–Afghanistan border had taken a week of delicate manoeuvring and anxiety.

Aditya's phone chirped. A message flashed on the screen: a call from Devendra Thakural, to be taken on a secure line in the study. He entered the private study, its centrepiece a massive mahogany desk, the bookshelves lined with leatherbound volumes. He took the call.

'How is Ramaswamy?' Thakural's voice crackled through the secure connection from New Delhi.

'Shaken, but safe,' Aditya replied, glancing through the study door towards the living room. Ramaswamy and Somi sat sipping tea from delicate porcelain cups. 'Thank you, sir. We couldn't have done it without you.'

'A team effort,' Thakural insisted. 'I promised to do whatever was necessary. Diplomacy these days requires … creativity.'

Aditya leaned against the desk. 'How did you manage it? Or is that classified?'

Thakural chuckled. 'As predicted, Qatar proved the ideal intermediary. We requested their intervention with the TTP. Their man, Rahimullah, negotiated Ramaswamy's release.'

'How did you get Qatar to help?' Aditya asked, brow furrowed.

'It is the second-largest exporter of LNG—you know, liquefied natural gas—globally,' Thakural explained. 'They seek to expand their markets in Asia and Europe, primarily to counter the US. India is increasingly reliant on natural gas to combat pollution. We've agreed on a twenty-five-year supply contract. Mutually beneficial.'

'Right. And the TTP?'

'Money flows freely from Qatari Islamic charities to certain groups across the world—possibly the TTP too?' Thakural said, phrasing his statement as a question. 'To cut a long story short, money talks, Mr Pillai.'

Aditya whistled softly. His gaze fell upon the unassuming man on the couch in the adjacent room. 'So much geopolitical manoeuvring for one man.'

'I was obligated to deliver,' Thakural said.

'Why?' Aditya pressed. 'You could have backed out.'

'Let's just say …' Thakural's voice was suddenly low, laced with steel, 'I needed you in my debt. You now have no excuse to fail on the BPBT project. We were lucky this time, the Chinese missile attack seems to have been a one-off … there have been no further provocations since. In fact, they claim that it was fired in error. Our core commanders have been meeting to ensure the border is calm but something like this has not happened in decades. We simply do not know when China might strike next. The BPBT project is India's number one defence priority.'

Aditya exhaled, understanding the veiled threat. The NSA was not a man to be trifled with. He shook his head and said, slowly, 'I am grateful for your candour, sir. I won't disappoint you.'

'We do what we must,' the NSA replied, his tone softening again. 'The important thing is that Ramaswamy is safe. I have assigned a team for his protection. The rest is your responsibility. Keep me informed.'

Aditya ended the call and returned to the living room. Ramaswamy and Somi were discussing the previous week's events with Dr Jung Tae-hyun, GISCO's head metallurgist, who had flown in to consult with him. The two scientists had known each other for years and Jung was convinced Ramaswamy was the key to their finding a solution.

'How is Mr Thakural?' Somi asked as Aditya strode in.

'His usual brilliant self,' he said, a grin spreading across his face. 'He filled me in on the geopolitical chess game that secured Dr Ramaswamy's release. We owe him.'

Ramaswamy nodded, his eyes filled with genuine appreciation. 'I am thankful to all of you. The lengths you went to … but I still have no idea why you secured my release. Frankly, I understand very little about whatever has transpired.'

'Your expertise is in demand by many,' Aditya replied, smiling. 'And I need you more than the other side.'

'I guess I will understand everything in good time,' Ramaswamy said. 'Now, tell me how I can be of service.'

Aditya was struck by Ramaswamy's composure, his eagerness to return to work despite his ordeal.

'We're just glad you're safe,' Somi said, her voice gentle. 'Let's focus on your recovery.'

'No, no,' Ramaswamy insisted, shaking his head. 'This is obviously important to you. So how can I help?'

'There's lots that you need to help with, Bala,' Jung said. 'We need your perspective to guide our strategy.' He opened his laptop, the screen displaying an enlarged image of the sword fragment he had been studying. 'Let's start with wootz steel, shall we?'

60

Daegaya, Garak Confederacy
Present-day Goryeong County, South Korea
Around 2,000 years ago

Dawn broke over Daegaya with deceptive serenity. Even the birds were unusually silent, as if nature itself was holding its breath. Over the past weeks, Talhae's army had assembled on the city's outskirts, a formidable spectacle: a sea of soldiers clad in leather and iron, their faces grim, their resolve absolute.

Though hastily assembled, the army had taken weeks to finally attack, opting to lay siege to Daegaya first. Talhae knew they would be dealing with a diminished enemy when they finally went in.

Talhae surveyed his forces, their determination mirroring his own. He had promised them glory and riches and he intended to deliver. His troops, a mix of seasoned veterans and eager youths, were united by a shared purpose: to forge a unified Confederacy strong enough to challenge the Three Kingdoms. The promise of plunder was a potent motivator as well.

As the first rays of sunlight glinted off his sword, Talhae raised it high, his commanding voice ringing out over the ranks. 'For our fallen leader! For revenge! For Seonsang!' With a roar that shook the very foundations of Daegaya, his warriors charged forward. The defenders, weakened by hunger and limited supplies, scrambled to form defensive lines. But Talhae's strategy was as cunning as it was brutal. He had planned a multi-pronged attack designed to overwhelm Daegaya's defences.

The main gate bore the brunt of the initial onslaught. Talhae's men slammed their battering rams against the wooden barriers with relentless force. Arrows rained down from the city walls, but Talhae's archers, strategically positioned, responded with deadly accuracy, picking off the defenders one by one. Talhae watched with grim satisfaction as the gates began to buckle.

Panic rippled through the city as it echoed with the cries of the wounded and the lamentations of those who had lost loved ones. Having breached the outer defences, Talhae's warriors swept through the streets, cutting down any who dared to stand in their path and setting buildings ablaze. Soon, the stench of smoke and blood was everywhere.

Talhae, astride his warhorse, rode at the forefront, his eyes sharp, calculating. He needed a decisive victory to minimize his own losses. The sight of a young child, no more than five years old, standing alone in the street, weeping for his mother, gave him pause. A flicker of something akin to compassion stirred within him, but he ruthlessly suppressed it. *There is no room for sentiment in war.* 'Forward!' he roared, his voice cutting through the chaos.

Daegaya's remaining soldiers made a desperate stand in the city centre, but they were outmatched, lacking the sheer ferocity of Talhae's forces. The sickening thud of bodies hitting the ground was punctuated by cries of pain and fury as metal met metal. Talhae fought at the front, his movements a blur of deadly grace, his sword carving a path of destruction. The streets ran red with blood as his army systematically dismantled Daegaya's defences. The attack was merciless, brutal, fuelled by a cold, calculating rage. Talhae had given his orders: this was annihilation, meant to demonstrate Seongsan's power and reach.

As he fought, Talhae's thoughts briefly drifted to his father, Jangsu. *Strength is the only language your enemies understand*, the old chieftain had once taught him. Talhae was putting that lesson to devastating use. A pity the old fool had not heeded his own advice.

The final confrontation took place in the royal courtyard. Daegaya's leaders, vastly outnumbered, fought with the courage of the doomed, but Talhae's warriors, driven by a savage need for vengeance, cut them down without mercy. The palace gates were ripped asunder, and Talhae strode into the royal chamber, his armour and sword covered in blood.

Munmu, Daegaya's grizzled chieftain, sat slumped on his throne, his face ashen, streaked with sweat. He had helped Jangsu secure his position within the Confederacy, had even helped isolate Kim Seok. Now he was paying the price for trusting a serpent. Slowly, he rose from his throne and approached Talhae, his hands outstretched, offering his sword in a gesture of submission.

A cold fire flickered in Talhae's eyes. He took the surrendered sword in his right hand, his own blade still clutched in his left. Holding Munmu's sword aloft, he angled it so that the lamplight glinted off its surface. Then, with a swift, brutal stroke, he used it to decapitate the chieftain. Munmu's head tumbled to the ground, rolling to a stop in a growing pool of blood.

'There is no place for weakness in Talhae's kingdom,' the young warrior muttered, tossing the dead chieftain's sword aside.

He stood triumphant, surrounded by his fallen enemies. Raising his sword high, he roared, 'Daegaya has fallen! Seongsan reigns supreme!' As his words echoed through the ravaged hall, his soldiers erupted in a frenzy of victory cries to mark the end of their ruthless conquest.

Talhae stood atop the palace steps, surveying the devastation wrought by his forces. Daegaya was his: its people subjugated, its leaders slain, its spirit broken. His dominance over Seongsan, Goryeong and now Daegaya was absolute, his authority unquestioned. Bihwa, Bangam, Ara and Geumgwan remained. He would compel them into submission swiftly and then the entire Confederacy would be under his heel. As for the Three Kingdoms—Silla, Baekje and Goguryeo—he would deal with them in due time. He could feel his goal within reach.

Yet, somewhere in the shadows, Jangsu's spirit lingered, a constant reminder of the price that had to be paid in exchange for power. He quickly shook off the thought. For now, he would allow himself to savour the victory. After all, he was Talhae, the conqueror of Daegaya, the master of all he surveyed.

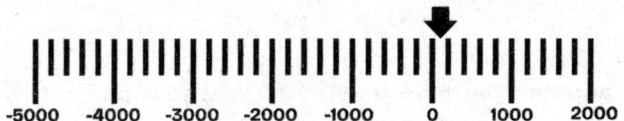

Dongdu, Eastern Han Empire
Present-day Luoyang, Henan Province, China
Around 1,900 years ago

Mist clung to the fields as the two Buddhist monks, Kasyapa Matanga and Dharmaratna, approached the outskirts of Dongdu, capital of the Eastern Han Empire. Dressed in simple robes, they walked on either side of a white horse laden with boxes of parchment and scrolls. Dongdu lay sprawled out before them, a patchwork of roofs, the royal palace rising grand and tall at its centre.

Ordinary residents, caught up with their morning routines, paused to observe the unusual sight of two foreign monks accompanying a white horse entering through the southern gate. Serenity graced their features, wisdom shone about their presence. Whispers spread through the crowd and, soon, word of the newcomers' arrival spread throughout the city.

As the monks progressed through the streets, they were met with a mixture of awe and curiosity. Merchants suspended their haggling, children skipped along beside them, elders bowed respectfully. A captain of the royal guard appeared and deferentially escorted them to the palace where Emperor Ming of Han awaited them in his imperial hall.

Having heard of their journey and the sacred texts they carried, the emperor envisioned sharing Buddhist wisdom with his people. 'Welcome, revered monks,' he greeted with authority and warmth. 'You have travelled far and your presence is a blessing to our land.'

Kasyapa Matanga bowed deeply, meeting the emperor's gaze with calm assurance. 'As requested by you, we bring the teachings of the Buddha, to share the light of His wisdom and compassion with your people.'

The emperor nodded, gesturing for them to rise. 'You will be provided with lodging and resources to begin your work—the translation of the texts you carry and teaching our people the Buddha's path. To honour your journey and the sacred texts you have brought, we shall construct a temple. It shall be called the White Horse Temple as a tribute to the noble steed that carried them here.'

The monks exchanged a silent glance of gratitude. 'Your kindness humbles us, O Emperor,' Dharmaratna said. 'May this temple be a beacon of knowledge for generations to come.'

'I am certain it will be,' the emperor said, his words reflecting his vision. 'What are the holy symbols that should adorn its walls?'

'There are eight auspicious symbols, O Emperor,' Kasyapa Matanga said. 'They are known as the Ashtamangala.'

'Tell me of them.'

'First, the lotus,' Kasyapa Matanga explained, 'which rises unsullied from muddy waters—symbolizing purity amidst impurity. Then the conch, the sound of which carries the voice of dhamma, the teachings of the Buddha. The endless knot, a sacred pattern representing the interconnectedness of all things. And the Dharma Chakra—the Wheel of Dharma—signifying the turning of the Buddha's teachings in the world.'

The emperor nodded thoughtfully. 'And?'

'The twin fish,' Dharmaratna continued. 'They swim freely, representing fearlessness in the vast ocean of existence. In our homeland, they also carry deeper meanings—echoes from older traditions. In some, they signify the harmony between preservation and transformation, ideas represented by deities known as Vishnu and Shiva. These interpretations may differ, but they all point to the same truth: balance, freedom and unity.'

'So be it,' the emperor declared. 'But will you allow us to have our own depiction of it?'

Kasyapa considered for a moment, then swiftly sketched an abstract symbol.

'How is this, Your Majesty?' he asked. 'Still two fish, but one yielding to the other.'

'Excellent,' the emperor said. 'We shall call it the Taijitu—a representation of the supreme ultimate—and it shall be incorporated into all our future temples. But I fear this project will take some time for our builders to complete.'

'We possess unique tools,' Dharmaratna replied, 'crafted with the ancient knowledge safeguarded by the Dvaitalingam Rakshak—a guardian from the southern lands of Bharatvarsha, entrusted with protecting this knowledge that has been passed down through generations. Thanks to his generosity, we carry implements forged with extraordinary precision. If you allow us to contribute to the temple's construction and help your people build it, we believe the work will proceed quite swiftly, Your Majesty.'

With each passing sunrise, work on the White Horse Temple gathered pace. The chosen site—a serene patch of land within Dongdu—not only honoured the sacred mission, but also included modest quarters where the monks could live, meditate and translate the texts they had carried with them in peace. Scrolls and manuscripts were carefully laid out, enabling their assistants to work alongside them.

Outside, the temple continued to take shape. The air echoed with the rhythmic strikes of chisels against wood and stone, interspersed with murmured prayers, as craftsmen and labourers from across the kingdom assembled to assist in the divine undertaking. Stones inscribed with blessings formed the foundation, and elaborate sculptures of the Ashtamangala rose upon the walls. Among them were the twin fish—the Taijitu—their bodies intertwined in an elegant dance of perfect balance.

61

Korkai, Thamirabarani, Pandya Desam
Present-day Thoothukudi District, Tamil Nadu, India
Around 2,000 years ago

The moon hung low, casting a faint glow upon the quiet neighbourhood. Silence reigned, every home seemingly at peace. Inside their house, Suriratna lay in bed in deep slumber, her breathing deep and rhythmic, undisturbed by the world outside.

But the peace was an illusion. Two figures, cloaked in shadows, moved stealthily through the night towards Padmasen's house, their footsteps barely a whisper on the dusty ground. Their eyes darted back and forth, alert for any sign of movement. They had waited patiently until Padmasen had departed on another trip to Muchiri Pattinam.

They reached the back of the property, where a small window offered a point of entry. One of the men slipped through, followed closely by the other. The house was silent, the stillness almost unnerving. Their shadows danced on the walls, barely discernible in the weak moonlight. Using Venkatesan's sketches, they navigated the darkened hallways with ease, heading straight for Suriratna's chamber.

Leaving his companion to guard the door, the other intruder approached the bed, his hand gripping a cloth soaked in the potent sedative, ajagandha. He saw her lying peacefully, her breath even, and raised the cloth towards her face, to silence any struggle before it began.

Suddenly, guards swarmed the room, their arrival had been swift and noiseless. The intruders froze, caught completely by surprise. 'Drop your weapons!' one of the guards commanded. Suriratna sat up, eyes alert, her expression one of grim satisfaction. She had clearly *not* been asleep.

The intruder by the bed reached for the dagger concealed beneath his dhoti, but one of the guards reacted instantly, embedding an arrow in his leg. He crumpled to the ground, clutching his thigh in pain. His companion turned to run, but a figure emerged from the shadows, blocking his escape.

'Leaving so soon?' Padmasen's voice, cold and sharp, cut through the tension.

The intruder knew death was preferable to being interrogated in King Peruzhavudi's dungeons. Padmasen lunged, but he was a heartbeat too late. The intruder snatched the bikh locket from around his neck and crushed it between his teeth. He collapsed, clutching his chest, as the poison did its work.

'Disarm the other one ... we need him alive,' Padmasen ordered.

The guards overpowered the other intruder, stripping him of his weapons and the lethal locket. They bound his hands and feet, a prisoner of war in his own failed mission. Padmasen approached, his gaze piercing, unforgiving. 'You thought you could infiltrate my home, take what is mine?' he asked, his voice dangerously low. 'You misjudged us.'

The intruder spat on the floor, his face contorted in defiance. 'You will not get away with this. Vidushika will learn of your treachery.'

Padmasen let out a mirthless laugh. 'You entered my home intending to abduct my daughter, to use her as leverage against me. And you say defending ourselves is treachery?' He turned to the captain of the guards. 'Take him. He is resourceful; do not underestimate him.'

The guards dragged the captive away. While they carried away the body of his comrade, Suriratna sat on the bed, relief washing over her in waves. Her father's foresight, his ability to always be one step ahead, never failed to amaze her.

Indumati emerged from her room and rushed to embrace her daughter. Kulasekara, who had been waiting in the adjacent room, came as well. They had successfully lured the intruders into a carefully constructed trap.

Padmasen turned to his daughter. 'Are you all right, Putri?'

She nodded, her breathing finally returning to normal. 'Thank you, Pitaha. I knew you would protect me, but I never imagined they would move so quickly.'

Padmasen smiled grimly. 'Protecting my family, and the secret we safeguard, is my duty. That is why I mentioned Muchiri Pattinam during our conversations. I knew there are ears everywhere. Vidushika will not stop. Nor will we. We must remain vigilant.'

Another figure appeared in the doorway. It was Venkatesan, his oily hair gleaming in the lamplight, his gaze shifting nervously as he entered. 'The prisoner is secured. He is being taken to Thamirabarani Sirai for questioning.'

Padmasen nodded. 'Well done, Venkatesan. Your performance was convincing.'

Suriratna stared at him, her curiosity piqued. 'You alerted us?'

Venkatesan bowed slightly. 'Indeed, My Lady. I have been in your father's service for some time. Maintaining the facade was crucial to gain their trust and learn their plans.'

Suriratna nodded to her father, smiling admiringly. She recalled their reunion in Korkai. The oily haired man she had seen by her father's side then was Venkatesan. When she had inquired about him, her father had simply said he was a property manager. She had even voiced her reservations about the man's shifty demeanour.

'You played a dangerous game, Venkatesan,' Padmasen acknowledged. 'It took courage. I am in your debt.'

'Serving the Dvaitalingam Rakshak is an honour few receive,' Venkatesan responded, bowing low, and took his leave.

Padmasen turned to his daughter. 'You mentioned moving the Dvaitalingam,' he said. 'For security, the time has come to separate it. But not in the way you envision.'

As the house settled down for the remainder of the night, Suriratna leaned back against her pillows, her mind racing. The night's events had unnerved her, but they had also strengthened her resolve.

She closed her eyes, but sleep did not come easily. For even in safety, she could sense that tonight had only been a warning; the true storm was yet to break.

62

Jirisan Forest, Garak Confederacy
Present-day Jirisan National Park, South Korea
Around 2,000 years ago

Deep within the Jirisan Forest, on the border between the Garak Confederacy and Baekje, a clandestine meeting was in progress. The air was thick with the scents of pine and damp earth, the darkness broken only by the flickering light of torches. Shadows played across the faces of the assembled leaders, revealing the anxiety stirring within them.

Excluding Talhae, all the leaders of the Garak Confederacy had gathered under the cover of darkness. The location was remote, chosen to maintain secrecy. Kim Seok, the Confederacy's elder statesman, stood in the centre of the circle. His demeanour reflected the heavy burden of leadership as he regarded the men around him—each a pillar of their respective territories, now united by a common fear.

Chief Jinhyeok of Bihwa broke the silence, his voice a low rumble. 'Kim Seok, we were fools to trust Talhae. His ambition knows no bounds. He desires to be king, to rule us all.'

Unseen, hidden among the trees some distance away, Jinhyeok's bodyguard kept watch, not to eavesdrop, but to ensure his master's safety. All the chiefs had agreed to travel the last stretch to their meeting point on foot and alone. Unbeknownst to his chieftain, this particular bodyguard, driven by concern, had shadowed his master. Kim Seok's manservant, Minjun, had also wished to remain close, but ever mindful of security protocols Kim Seok had refused.

The other chiefs murmured in agreement, their voices a chorus of unease. Wonsik, the chief of Bangam, spoke next. 'Talhae's actions are disturbing. The attack on Goryeong … rumours of him killing his own father … and now this savage attack on Daegaya ... Our unity is shattered, leaving us vulnerable. Silla, Baekje, Goguryeo—any one of the Three Kingdoms could strike. Our very survival is at stake.'

Kim Seok nodded grimly. The flickering torchlight seemed to accentuate every worry line on his face. 'Your concerns are valid. Talhae's actions threaten not only the Confederacy, but the very principles upon which it was founded. I find it difficult to believe he was among those six orphans we took in, along with my own son, Kim Suro.'

Yongho, the chieftain of Ara, clenched his fists, his knuckles white with the force. In a voice tight with barely suppressed rage, he said, 'We must act fast. If Talhae is left unchecked, the Confederacy will crumble, leaving our lands ripe for conquest.' He turned to Kim Seok. 'You have always been our guiding light, Kim Seok, a beacon of integrity in these dark times. We should have heeded your counsel. Now, I beg you, lead us out of this crisis.'

Kim Seok drew a deep breath, feeling the weight of his responsibility. He knew the path ahead would be fraught with peril, the choices difficult. 'We must join forces, prepare to face Talhae,' he conceded. 'But we need to tread carefully, maintain the people's support. It is crucial to our defence.'

The chiefs nodded. With a steely glint in his eye, Jinhyeok added, 'We should also seek alliances outside our borders. Some may be sympathetic to our cause, and be willing to stand against Talhae's tyranny. Some of our trade partners—even among the Three Kingdoms—view Talhae with distrust. The right offer could sway them.'

Kim Seok raised a hand, silencing the murmurs of agreement. 'First, we must secure our own house. Seek out those you trust. Our forces must be mobilized without alerting Talhae. We strike when we have the strength to win.'

'Your son, Kim Suro ... you must send for him,' Yongho urged.

'Why?' Kim Seok asked.

'Remember that painting by Adokan?' replied Yongho. 'The tragedy and the resilience of the six surviving orphans was depicted in his *Yeoseot Gaeui Dalgyal*—the Six Eggs.'

'Yes, of course.'

'Adokan was not just a great painter, he was also a poet, philosopher and mystic. While he painted all the other five children in red, he painted Kim Suro in gold. He knew that Soju was destined for great things. His presence will embolden our people. We need him, now more than ever.'

A flicker of hope lit Kim Seok's eyes, his expression softening for a moment. 'Indeed, Yongho. I will send for Soju. Last I heard, he was in Dimašq. I will find a way to reach him. But for now we must focus on readying our troops.'

'And building our arsenal,' Wonsik added. 'Should Talhae attack, we must be prepared for a protracted war. Even non-combatants must be armed.'

Kim Seok, ever practical, nodded his assent. 'That is right. I will oversee the production of new weapons. Geumgwan's blacksmiths have been reliable suppliers, but they may not be able to meet the current demand. My Pandyan friend, Cheliyan

... I will seek his aid. For now, we fortify our defences, prepare for every eventuality. And to avoid another unpleasant surprise, I want all of you to activate your informants. Talhae's movements must be closely monitored.'

The leaders disappeared into the darkness. Though the forthcoming conflict weighed heavily on their minds, they felt heartened by Kim Seok's words and the promise of deliverance. As the flickering torches were put out one by one, plunging the clearing into darkness, Kim Seok stood for a moment, listening intently for any untoward sound from the forest. In his mind, hope battled with fear, strategy with uncertainty. 'Talhae ...' he whispered, 'your reign of terror ends here. For the sake of our people, for the future of our land, we will fight. And we will prevail.'

63

New Delhi, India

Present day

The Iron Pillar of Delhi stood tall, its weathered surface gleaming faintly in the afternoon sun. Aditya, Somi, Ramaswamy and Jung stood gazing at it, a mix of anticipation and anxiety on their faces. They had flown in from Dubai on Aditya's private jet. Ramaswamy was convinced that despite past studies, the Iron Pillar held secrets that were yet to be uncovered. Dr Satheesh Jayaraman, the renowned archaeologist who had collaborated with Ramaswamy on many occasions, had flown in from Chennai to join them upon the CERN scientist's request.

Thanks to the Prime Minister's Office they had been granted unprecedented private access to the ancient artifact. The entire area was cordoned off and all other visitors temporarily restricted from entering the complex.

Jayaraman examined the inscriptions on the pillar—tributes to Chandragupta II, the Gupta emperor known as Vikramaditya, under whose reign the pillar was believed to have been erected at Visnupadagiri, and Anangpal, the Tomar ruler credited with transporting it to Delhi centuries later. 'Remarkable,' he murmured in awe. 'To think that it has stood here for centuries, untouched by rust. It never ceases to amaze.' He traced the ancient script with a delicate finger, marvelling at the craftsmanship.

The oldest inscription, dedicated to Vishnu, along with some imagery below it, had been obliterated by a cannonball, which, according to historical accounts, was fired by Nadir Shah, the ruthless Persian warlord and self-declared Shah of Iran who had looted Delhi.

Aditya nodded, his gaze sweeping over the pillar's surface. 'The craftsmanship is extraordinary. Yet we are no closer to unlocking its secrets.' His brows furrowed in thought.

Jung stepped forward, a portable LiDAR scanner in his hand. 'Shall we begin?' he asked, looking at the group. At their nod of agreement, he powered up the device, aiming it at the base of the pillar. The scanner emitted a series of beeps as it mapped the structure, searching for any subsurface anomalies. The team watched, their anticipation growing as the data was processed. Minutes passed, but the screen remained unchanged. 'Nothing unusual below,' Jung confirmed, a touch of disappointment in his voice. 'Solid ground. The pillar extends a little over three feet underground, acting as an anchor.' Any hopes of finding a hidden cache of the substance they sought evaporated.

Undeterred, Ramaswamy gestured towards the sample kit. 'On to the analysis then. The pillar itself still holds valuable information.' He carefully scraped a small sample from the base and placed it in a container for further study. The group moved to a makeshift lab set up in a tent erected nearby, eager to unlock the secrets of the sample's chemical makeup.

As the machinery whirred to life, Aditya peered over Ramaswamy's shoulder, watching the data appear on the screen. 'Ninety-eight per cent wrought iron, as expected,' Ramaswamy said. 'Carbon content is ... well, it is no Damascus Steel. Relatively low. The process here predates nav utsa, I'd wager.' He continued to study the readout. 'Ah. Interesting.'

'What is it?' Jung asked, his interest piqued.

'The phosphorus levels,' Ramaswamy replied. 'Elevated phosphorus content increases corrosion resistance by creating a protective film on the iron's surface. Not nav utsa, but certainly utsa.'

Jung looked up from his notes, his eyes bright with excitement. 'Consistent with our understanding of ancient Indian metallurgy. Their techniques were remarkably advanced. What else do we have?'

'Silicon levels are low, trace amounts of sulphur and manganese,' Ramaswamy replied. 'All known to the ancients. Phosphorus was called "agnidharaka", silicon, "ayah samsraya", sulphur was "gandhaka", and manganese, "manikya". They even knew of nickel and chromium—"pindarajata" and "chitraka".'

'Remarkable, isn't it?' Aditya said, his attention focused on the pillar. 'It's withstood rust, being moved across thousands of miles multiple times, even a direct hit from a cannonball. Surviving for sixteen hundred years, since the reign of Vikramaditya.'

Jayaraman shook his head slowly. 'I am not convinced it's only sixteen hundred years old.'

'What do you mean?' Aditya frowned, turning to the archaeologist.

'The Chandragupta II inscription led us to believe he erected the pillar,' Jayaraman explained. 'But reusing and repurposing existing pillars was common practice. This was once a pillar dedicated to Vishnu—the Vishnu Stambha. It originally had a capital, a sculpture that sat atop it. There's a deep dowel hole on the abacus that confirms it. That hole would have held a figure of Garuda, Vishnu's eagle mount. This pillar might be far older than we think.'

Ramaswamy nodded thoughtfully. 'Carbon-dating is impossible. Too little C-14. And even then it would only tell us the age of the organic material, like the charcoal used in the smelting process, not when it was incorporated into the alloy. Thermoluminescence dating is out—we have no residual slag. Archaeomagnetic dating would be inaccurate, given the gaps in the reference curves.'

'Which is why most dates of this pillar are based on epigraphical evidence,' Jayaraman said. 'This pillar could be far, *far* older.'

All of a sudden, Ramaswamy slapped his forehead, his face alight with realization. 'We're overlooking the most obvious clue!' he exclaimed.

'What is it?' Somi asked, leaning forward.

'The phosphorus,' Ramaswamy stated, his voice filled with excitement.

'But phosphorus was commonly found in utsa—their iron— during the Gupta period,' Jung said, frowning.

'Not in this form,' Ramaswamy countered. 'A protective layer of iron-hydrogen phosphate hydrate has formed on this particular surface. And consider the strength. Phosphorus atoms, incorporated into the iron lattice, cause distortions that impede dislocation movement, making the iron harder, stronger.'

'Are you suggesting ...' Jung started, his eyes narrowed.

'I am suggesting this Iron Pillar may have once stood over a deposit of the very substance we seek,' Ramaswamy declared. 'What if this substance leached into the pillar, altering its chemical composition? What if its effects are evident even now, after all these centuries?'

64

Mlecchadal, The Western Ocean
Present-day Arabian Sea
Around 2,000 years ago

Standing at the bow of Cheliyan's ship, Soju watched golden sunlight dance upon the restless waters, his thoughts as random as the waves beneath him. The journey from Eudaemon had been uneventful, yet a knot of anxiety tightened his chest. Though his heart ached at leaving Mithra, he longed to be back in Korkai, to see Suriratna once more.

His musings were shattered by a lookout's cry. 'Oru varugiradhu! Ship approaching!' The crew snapped to attention, their eyes scanning the horizon. Soju's pulse quickened as the silhouette of a ship emerged from the haze. It was smaller than their own, but its sails billowed ominously in the wind.

'Battle stations!' Cheliyan barked, his hand instinctively gripping his sword hilt. 'Could be pirates.' The crew scrambled to obey, readying weapons and bracing for the worst. Piracy had become a scourge on the Mlecchadal—rogue vessels preying on merchant ships, plundering cargo and enslaving crews. The encounters were brutal, and often fatal for the unprepared. Tales shared by those who had survived such horrors lent an urgency to their preparations.

Soju, too, felt the tension, but then he noticed something—a thin plume of white smoke rising from the approaching ship. 'Hold!' he called out, his voice cutting through the mounting anxiety. 'That is no pirate signal. They are burning ssuk!' As a child, he had seen ships from the Garak Confederacy send out such signals by burning mugwort, which produced pure white smoke. 'It is a signal of peace! It is a Garak ship!'

Cheliyan hesitated, then raised a quartz crystal to his eye and peered through it. The signal was unmistakable. 'Stand down,' he ordered the men, though his hand remained on the hilt of his sword. As the two ships drew closer, a figure emerged on the deck of the Garak vessel, waving a flag emblazoned with the emblem of a turtle—the symbol of the Garak Confederacy.

Moments later, the ship pulled alongside, and a plank was extended between the two vessels. A man dressed simply but practically in a short jeogori jacket with long sleeves, loose-fitting baji pants, a headband and straw sandals strode onto the deck of the Pandyan ship. He bowed deeply before Soju. 'Joon-gi at your service, Kim Suro. I bring urgent news from Geumgwan, from my lord, Kim Seok.'

Soju's heart pounded in his chest. 'Tell me! Is Abeoji well?'

'Your father fares well, Kim Suro,' Joon-gi replied. 'But the Confederacy is in turmoil. He requests your immediate return.'

Soju exchanged a look with Cheliyan, who nodded subtly, urging him to learn more. 'Explain yourself,' Soju commanded, turning back to Joon-gi.

'Talhae has sown chaos,' Joon-gi stated. 'His father, Jangsu, conquered Goryeong, but he died soon after. It is rumoured that Talhae assassinated his father … and then attacked Daegaya, claiming it for himself. He now controls Seongsan, Goryeong and Daegaya. The remaining members of the Confederacy—Bihwa, Bangam, Ara and your own Geumgwan—fear they are his next targets.'

A cold fury settled on Soju's features. He had always known Talhae harboured feelings of jealousy towards him, but he had never imagined him capable of such extreme treachery. 'And the Three Kingdoms?' he asked, his voice tight.

'Silla, Baekje and Goguryeo have made no moves—yet,' Joon-gi said. 'But the Garak Confederacy's disunity presents a tempting opportunity. Dark times are coming. Your father sent me to bring you back home. Talhae could strike at any moment. Your presence is urgently needed.'

Soju's mind raced. He had dreamed of returning to a land of peace and prosperity. But after all these years, it seemed his hopes were dashed. He turned to Cheliyan, his mentor and protector. 'I must go. Garak needs me.'

Cheliyan's face was grim but understanding. 'Then you must go, Soju. Destiny calls.'

Soju clasped his friend's hand. 'Thank you, my friend. You guided me from Geumgwan to Korkai, settled me at Acharya Satyamuni's gurukul, stood by me in Dimašq. How can I ever repay you?'

Cheliyan grinned and embraced him. 'Serve your father well, Kim Suro. Defend him with the same devotion he showed by sending you with me.'

Soju's expression turned serious. 'I was looking forward to seeing Suriratna,' he admitted. 'She will be ... unhappy ... that I did not return to Korkai. Tell her I will return. Tell her ... tell her my heart belongs to her.'

Cheliyan placed a reassuring hand on his shoulder. 'Your words will be delivered.'

'And Cheliyan …' Soju's voice dropped to a whisper. 'Tell her I love her, deeply. That we are meant to be together, no matter what. She *must* wait for me.'

Then he gathered his meagre possessions and prepared to board the waiting Garak ship. Noticing the smaller vessel's vulnerability, Cheliyan ordered some ballast stones to be transferred to it to improve its stability. As the last stone was loaded, his eyes met Soju's one final time.

The crew of Cheliyan's ship watched in sombre silence as Kim Suro, their former shipmate, departed to fulfil his duty in his homeland. The Garak ship turned, setting course for the distant horizon. Soju stood at the stern, watching as Cheliyan's vessel dwindled to a speck on the vast expanse of water.

As night fell, Soju retreated to his cabin and was lulled into a restless sleep by the rocking of the ship. Nightmares plagued him—visions of war, fire and the looming shadow of Talhae's army. But through the darkness, he saw a light—the radiant face of Suriratna, her eyes shining, beacons of hope. He saw himself running to her, embracing her, and felt her touch banishing the shadows.

Morning dawned, the first rays of sunlight lighting a path across the water. Standing on the deck, Soju's thoughts went back to Suriratna. 'Wait for me,' he whispered to the wind. 'I will return.'

The ship sailed on, carrying Soju towards his destiny.

65

Korkai, Thamirabarani, Pandya Desam
Present-day Thoothukudi District, Tamil Nadu, India
Around 2,000 years ago

Cheliyan stood at the prow of his flagship, the breeze tugging at his clothes. Ahead, Korkai's harbour bustled with activity. Anticipation crackled along the docks as his fleet approached. Word of his victorious western campaign had already spread. The crew and he had not only secured new trade routes but fended off a pirate fleet that had long threatened merchant vessels.

The roar of the crowd swelled, drowning out the gentle lapping of waves against wooden hulls. Cheers erupted, a wave of joyous sound that rolled across the water and filled the air. Drummers pounded out a triumphant rhythm, stirring the hearts of the people. Flower petals, tossed into the air, rained down upon the returning sailors and troops like a vibrant shower of blessings.

Eager faces lined the docks, straining to catch a glimpse of the heroes. As Cheliyan stepped ashore, his heart burst with emotion. The welcome he and his men had received obliterated the hardships of the journey. His warriors, disciplined and proud, followed him, bearing crates laden with exotic goods—gleaming gold, rare coral, fine wine, rich olive oil, elegant glassware—each item whispering tales of faraway lands. Their eyes wide with admiration and curiosity, the onlookers reached out to touch the soldiers' garments, pushing forward for a closer look. The scene was charged with a mix of powerful emotions—relief at their safe return, pride in their accomplishments and deep gratitude for those who had faced the dangers of distant shores.

At the end of the dock, King Peruvazhudi waited, his royal presence radiating authority. He stepped forward and embraced Cheliyan, who bowed low before his monarch. 'You have served us well,' the king said, his voice warm yet commanding. Cheliyan beamed, the weight of the journey lifting from his shoulders. 'Your Majesty's support made our success possible,' he replied, his voice barely audible above the din of the crowd.

Together, they rode towards the palace in a flower-bedecked chariot, the road lined with celebratory banners. Inside, the Grand Hall buzzed with excitement. Advisors and other nobles eagerly listened as Cheliyan delivered his report. He spoke of new alliances forged, of trade routes secured, of the construction efforts at Raqmu, of the new foundry in Dimašq that promised to generate immense demand for Korkai's iron.

There were murmurs of approval and nods of agreement across the hall. Peruvazhudi's smile broadened. 'Your accomplishments will bolster our kingdom's prosperity,' he declared. 'Having Mithra as the governor of Damascus is no small advantage. He is not only an ally, but a stabilizing force in a region fraught with unrest. His position will help us nurture trust, while ensuring our trade continues unhindered.'

∽

As the sun dipped towards the horizon, Cheliyan and Padmasen rode to Kulasekara's home for a celebratory dinner. The streets were alive with festivities, mirroring the joy within the palace walls. Kulasekara's house, situated near the harbour, was abuzz with activity. The aroma of spices from the treats being prepared mingled with the sea breeze.

Indumati and Suriratna had prepared a feast. The kitchen had been decorated with flowers and platters heaped with delicious food. Fragrant rice, spiced lentils, tamarind and coconut curry, dosas, appams, payasam and a host of other delicacies were served on large banana leaves. Cheliyan settled onto the floor with the others, joining in the laughter and stories that filled the air. But amidst the gaiety Cheliyan noticed a shadow of worry in Suriratna's eyes. She had barely touched her food. Her eyes flickered towards him, laden with an unspoken question. *Where is Soju? Why did he not return with you?*

Sensing the need for discretion, Cheliyan leaned towards her. 'Suriratna,' he asked casually, 'would you like to see a sword I brought back from Dimašq?' She nodded, curiosity overriding her concern. He led her to a quiet room, away from the others.

Once alone, the facade of merriment dropped. 'Suriratna,' Cheliyan said softly, 'There is a reason Soju did not return.' The colour drained from her face, her expression filled with dread. She imagined the worst ... until Cheliyan said calmly, 'He was recalled to the Garak Confederacy.'

Tears welled in her eyes as relief swept through her. 'Is he ... is he angry with me? Have I lost him?'

Cheliyan placed a reassuring hand on her shoulder. 'He loves you dearly, child,' he said. 'But the situation in Garak is dire. He was summoned back by his father. Soju has gone to protect his people, their interests. He specifically asked me to tell you he will return; that he loves you deeply.'

A look of determination hardened Suriratna's features. 'Then I must go to him. He cannot face this alone.'

Cheliyan hesitated. 'That path is fraught with danger. The journey to Garak is perilous. And once you arrive, you could be stepping into a war zone. Think carefully, Suriratna.'

She fell silent, her brow furrowed. Her thoughts turned briefly to her own family—her father's guarded eyes, her mother's anxious pacing, the secret they all protected. The Dvaitalingam was not just an artifact—it was a legacy, one that placed her family in constant danger. Could she really leave them now, when threats still loomed?

'I know my family needs me too,' she said quietly. 'There are dangers here as well—ones we have barely begun to understand. But my heart tells me that Soju's return to Garak is not just about his kingdom. It is about something larger. Something we are all connected to. If we are to truly protect what matters most—my family, our legacy—then I must stand with him too.'

Cheliyan studied her, the significance of her words not lost on him. Her eyes, though clouded with uncertainty, were steady with resolve. Memories flooded her mind—Soju saving her from the cobra, offering comfort after Bhadraketu's departure, their promises by the lotus pond, their shared vow to always be there for one another.

She squared her shoulders, her voice firm. 'I have made up my mind. Soju needs me. I will not abandon him. We have always faced hardships together. This is no different.'

Her eyes shone with determination and Cheliyan knew there was no dissuading her. 'Very well,' he conceded. 'But first, we must convince your parents, make proper arrangements. Your father will be ... manageable. Your mother is another matter.

We may need Kulasekara's assistance. But you must promise to be careful, Suriratna.'

She nodded, gratitude and courage shining on her face. They returned to the feast, Suriratna's demeanour brighter, her purpose solidified. The evening continued with songs and stories, but beneath the surface Cheliyan and Suriratna's shared secret lent a new layer of complexity to the celebrations.

Raqmu, Southern Levant
Present-day Petra, Jordan
Around 2,000 years ago

Raqmu—the Romans called it Petra—was a city of stone tucked away in the rugged desert mountains. Its breathtaking beauty was matched only by its ingeniously designed infrastructure. A complex network of cisterns and an unparalleled system for rainwater harvesting had allowed the city to flourish for centuries. Every precious drop was collected, stored and redirected, ensuring the city's survival even in the harshest desert conditions. Sandstone cliffs surrounded the city and the narrow Siq—a natural, winding gorge that served as the main entrance—with its towering walls, ushered visitors into Raqmu, offering tantalizing glimpses of its hidden wonders. As the passage widened, a magnificent sight unfolded: a jigsaw of houses and tombs carved directly into the vibrant pink rock.

At Raqmu's heart lay an unfinished project. Tentatively dubbed the Khazneh—the treasury—it was in the preliminary stages of construction. The ambitious undertaking had been stalled due to the declining revenue from important Nabataean traders in Dimašq and King Aretas IV had been seeking alternative solutions. Raqmu was becoming too reliant on the incense trade that flowed through its veins, and that was hardly a desirable situation.

Within the grand palace, King Aretas paced restlessly, determination furrowing his brow. Tall and broad-shouldered, his features sharp, his dark eyes piercing, Aretas was an imposing figure, conveying intelligence and authority. He wore his long black hair tied back; his beard was meticulously groomed. A simple gold circlet rested on his head and he carried a staff of polished wood inlaid with gemstones. A flowing robe of light cotton in shades of off-white and sand and adorned with crimson embroidery draped his frame. Renowned for his strategic brilliance and diplomatic skill, Aretas was revered as a shrewd ruler who had expanded Nabataean influence through trade and negotiation.

The Khazneh was more than just a building; once complete, it would represent the trading power of his empire. Raqmu's strategic location guaranteed a steady flow of customs duties from incense caravans, but those alone could not finance the city's extraordinary architecture and infrastructure. It was the network of Nabataean merchants around the world—the diaspora—who poured their trading profits back into their beloved Raqmu, making it truly one of a kind.

When emissaries from Dimašq entered the palace, curiosity crackled in the air. Aretas greeted them, his stern countenance softened by a glimmer of hope. 'Welcome to Raqmu. I understand Dimašq and Korkai have a proposition for me?'

The emissaries bowed. 'We have been sent by the governor,' one said. 'We are accompanied by a representative of the Pandyan kingdom—a prominent merchant. He has brought two masons, equipped with tools, to assist in your construction endeavours.'

'You believe two masons and a few chisels will buy my loyalty?' Aretas scoffed. 'Over 15,000 tons of rock must be excavated before we can begin carving. And the suffocating Roman taxes in Dimašq have crippled trade. Return to your masters and tell them I have no need for their scraps.'

'Your Majesty, I implore you to observe a demonstration before making a decision,' the emissary from Korkai pleaded.

Intrigued, King Aretas gestured for the Pandyan stonemasons to proceed. The men approached a massive sandstone block in the courtyard, their chisels held aloft. The room fell silent as they began.

Astonishingly, as the chisels struck the stone, it seemed to melt away, tiny sparks of energy flaring with each impact. The audience watched, transfixed, as large chunks of rock crumbled to the ground at the slightest touch. Smooth surfaces and intricate patterns emerged within minutes, the chisels gliding through the sandstone with an almost magical efficiency, accomplishing in mere moments what would have taken dozens of workers days with traditional methods.

The crowd gasped in amazement. Aretas, unable to contain his excitement, clapped his hands as he approached the block. 'Incredible!' he exclaimed. He ran his hands over the newly smoothed surface. 'How is this possible?'

The Pandyan merchant spoke, his words translated into Aramaic by the court translator. 'An ancient technique, millennia-old, allows us to create exceptional ingots from which we forge the sharpest blades—swords, knives, daggers and chisels. The edges of these tools are crafted using a substance that can alter the very fabric of existence. While these particles are tightly bound within the metal, at the edges they generate a destructive energy capable of cutting through almost anything.'

'With such tools, the Khazneh could be completed in record time,' Aretas murmured. He turned to the emissary from Dimašq. 'We must bring peace and prosperity to our region. Finishing the Khazneh is not just a matter of pride but of necessity. It will be a beacon of resilience, a boost to our economy. I need your help to achieve this.' He paused to think. 'Let us begin,' he said, his gaze fixed on the gleaming chisels. 'But tools born of age-old secrets rarely come without a price. What do you want from me?'

66

Pyongyang, North Korea

Present day

Seated at the breakfast table, Khalil Ghaznawar gazed out of the window, his eyes fixed on the immaculate lawns stretching before him. The luxurious mansion, a sanctuary located in the Munsu-dong area of Pyongyang, North Korea, was shielded by imposing walls and patrolled by state militia—a testament to the influence of Choe Tok Hun, Kim Jong Un's powerful cousin.

Choe also headed the Academy of National Defense Science of North Korea. Established in 1964 under the Ministry of National Security, the academy played a pivotal role in advancing North Korea's nuclear and missile programs. Despite US sanctions, it had successfully developed the Hwasong-14, an intercontinental ballistic missile. Operating under a veil of secrecy, the academy's scientists also pursued initiatives aimed at enhancing North Korea's global standing.

After Ghaznawar had escaped the inferno that had consumed his stronghold in the Safed Koh mountains of Afghanistan, he was whisked away in a helicopter that flew low to avoid radar detection. The chopper had slipped into China's Xinjiang region. Then, with the help of Uighur rebel groups—ones that defied the Chinese state for their Islamic cause—and an aircraft provided by them, Ghaznawar had finally arrived in Pyongyang, facilitated by Choe Tok Hun. He was now a clandestine guest at Choe's heavily guarded residence.

The dining room exuded European grandeur rather than Korean simplicity. Silk tapestries adorned the walls, exquisite carpets covered the floors and gilded chairs surrounded a highly polished table made of walnut wood, illuminated by a magnificent chandelier of gold and cut glass.

Choe Tok Hun—a man of medium build, with a portly physique and an air of authority—sat across from Ghaznawar. Between them lay a silver platter containing a mound of creamy scrambled eggs, topped with a generous dollop of black caviar; an assortment of imported cheeses and cold cuts arranged with artistic precision; a pitcher of freshly squeezed orange juice; a bottle of vintage champagne, nestled in an ice bucket, awaiting its turn to be poured into flute glasses; and a steaming silver coffee pot, its surface covered in intricate engravings, filling the room with the aroma of freshly brewed Hacienda La Esmeralda coffee. Sitting there, it was difficult to believe that North Korea was also home to starving millions.

Choe Tok Hun savoured a mouthful of scrambled eggs and chased it down with a sip of champagne. He glanced at Ghaznawar, his expression marked by polite curiosity and cautious interest. 'I still do not understand why you consider this technology so vital. What is so special about super-strength steel?'

Ghaznawar sighed, eschewing the alcohol forbidden by his religion and taking a sip of coffee. 'It is not simply about steelmaking,' he explained. 'It is about harnessing energies. Done correctly, we could possess the most potent weapon imaginable. That is why I came to you, Comrade Choe Tok Hun.'

'We have nuclear weapons,' Choe pointed out. 'And missiles capable of delivering them across vast distances. Why would we need this?'

Ghaznawar set down his coffee cup, the exquisite aroma lingering in the air. 'The Dvaitalingam is more than a mere relic. It produces steel of incredible strength—superior to anything known to man. But there is more to it than that—it has immense potential.'

Choe frowned, considering the implications. 'Potential for what?'

Ghaznawar leaned forward, his expression earnest. 'Nuclear weapons are undeniably powerful, but they are also indiscriminate,' he said. 'The blast radius, the radiation, the electromagnetic pulses, the long-term environmental damage ... Every nation with nuclear capabilities understands the concept of mutually assured destruction. They are a valuable tool, but one rarely deployed for fear of retaliation.'

Choe nodded slowly, appreciating the logic of Ghaznawar's argument. 'Go on,' he said.

'Imagine a weapon capable of delivering devastating force with pinpoint accuracy,' Ghaznawar continued. 'Targeting a specific location, a neighbourhood, without effecting widespread radioactive fallout. A weapon invisible to even the most sophisticated radar systems. One that leaves no radioactive trace, no environmental catastrophe. That can be calibrated to melt a city block, a single building ... even a single house!'

Understanding dawned in Choe's eyes and they widened with excitement. 'Such a weapon would revolutionize warfare. The power it would grant us ...'

'A team of Indians and South Koreans are searching for it even now,' Ghaznawar said, his voice urgent. 'What if your Dear

Leader were to learn that Seoul possessed such a weapon? Or that we'd passed up an opportunity to make it ours?' He was well aware that mentioning Kim Jong Un or his deceased father was often the most effective way to motivate the North Korean leadership.

'That's an unacceptable outcome,' Choe stated flatly, setting down his fork with a clatter against the fine china.

Ghaznawar nodded. 'Your agents are numerous and spread around the world, Comrade. The recent attack on my headquarters has set me back by months. You can accomplish what I cannot.'

'What do you propose?' Choe asked.

'We must allow Aditya Pillai and Somi Kim to find this technology,' Ghaznawar said with an intense look. 'I am confident they will. They have that scientist—Ramaswamy—with them.' He flushed with anger. The scientist's escape from his hideout still rankled with him. What infuriated him most was that it had happened just when Ramaswamy had been on the verge of a breakthrough, thanks to the palm-leaf manuscript Ghaznawar had shared with him.

'Let them acquire it?' Choe asked incredulously.

'Let them do the heavy lifting. Your people can monitor their every move. Then, we simply *take* it from them.'

Choe took a long swig of champagne, pondering over Ghaznawar's proposal. A slow smile spread across his face. 'Like hyenas scavenging the lion's kill?'

'No,' Ghaznawar corrected. 'Hyenas wait for the lion to eat its fill. We will not.'

67

Perungkadal, Purva Mahasagar, the Eastern Ocean
Present-day Bay of Bengal
Around 2,000 years ago

Suriratna clung to the ship's railing, salt spray stinging her face as the vessel bucked beneath her. After just two weeks at sea, the journey to Geumgwan was proving more tortuous than she had imagined. Waves crashed against the hull, each impact resonating through her bones. She stared at the horizon, seeking solace in the vast expanse of water that would eventually take her to Soju, but her mind drifted back to her last conversation with her parents.

Tension had choked the air as Suriratna stood before them. Her mother, Indumati, had paced the room, her brows furrowed in concern. 'You cannot be serious, Suriratna,' she had said, her voice slicing through the room's stillness. 'A union with Kim Suro? Have you lost your mind?'

Suriratna had stood firm, meeting her mother's fiery glare. 'Mataha, I love him. And he needs me. We promised to always be there for each other. I must go to Geumgwan.'

Indumati's anger had flared, her face flushed. 'This is madness! How can you even think of such a thing? This young man did not even bother to stop by in Korkai. And you ... you are rushing off to a foreign land for a boy like that—'

'Hush now, Indumati,' Padmasen had interjected, his tone calm yet firm as he rested a hand on his wife's shoulder. 'Allow her to speak.'

Indumati's shoulders had slumped, though fury still burned in her eyes. Suriratna had inhaled deeply, her resolve steeling further within her. 'Soju faces peril. I cannot forsake him, not now. I could never forgive myself.'

Kulasekara, silent until that moment, had stepped forward. 'Sometimes, dear Indumati, destiny beckons us down paths we would never choose. Suriratna's mind is made up. We must trust her judgement.'

Silence had fallen, strained by unspoken words. Indumati's gaze had flitted from Padmasen to Kulasekara to Cheliyan, her anger giving way to sorrow. 'So be it,' she had eventually murmured, eyes welling, her voice a whisper. 'But vow to return to us ... to me.' She had opened her arms and Suriratna had melted into the embrace, wondering if she would ever feel that comforting warmth again.

Padmasen stepped forward, clasping Suriratna's hands. 'Go with our blessings, my beloved daughter. May the gods safeguard you and see you to your goal unharmed. Remember, true power and courage spring from within. They never leave you, no matter where your path leads.'

Cheliyan had provisioned a sturdy ship for the arduous voyage, loading ample fresh water, food and medical supplies. His crew selection was discerning—each member skilled at navigating treacherous seas.

Indumati had wanted female companions to accompany Suriratna. The very idea of her daughter being alone on a ship filled with sailors was preposterous to her. But Suriratna had been equally adamant that she would travel without an entourage. A compromise was finally reached. Venkatesan, the grizzled, oily-haired man whose loyalty to Padmasen's family had been unwavering, was appointed as Suriratna's bodyguard.

Indumati had been unhappy with the arrangement but Padmasen reminded her, as he often did, of the thirty rishikas listed in the Rig Veda.

Suriratna's thoughts returned to the present as a massive wave crashed over the deck, drenching her. Beside her stood Venkatesan, his weathered face grim. 'The sea shows no mercy today, My Lady,' he growled over the howling gales. 'Pray the weather grants us reprieve.'

But reprieve never came. A raging storm transformed the sea into a wild tempest, each wave rising like a beast from the deep. The ship groaned under the onslaught, its wooden frame protesting with loud creaking noises. Suriratna clung to the railing, her heart thundering as uncertainty gnawed at her.

Without warning, a colossal wave reared before them, a towering ghostly apparition. It struck, snapping the mast and flinging the crew across the slick, rain-lashed deck. The vessel lurched, its battered hull rending apart. 'Hold fast!' Venkatesan bellowed, but the tumult swallowed his cry. Suriratna felt herself being hurled into the churning vortex as the ship buckled.

Icy water flooded her lungs, stealing her breath. Arms flailing, she grasped for something solid, fighting to stay afloat, but her strength was swiftly fading. At last, her hands found purchase on a floating fragment of wood—the shattered mast. She clung to it with all her might, praying it would see her through the night.

But the storm raged on and an exhausted Suriratna's grip faltered under the barrage. Her vision blurred, the world a hazy soup. Still, one image burned bright in her semi-conscious state: Soju. Amid the despair, he was her beacon, his voice calling to her from the distant deep. Even as the waves buffeted her and the cold numbed her senses, she clung on to the broken mast with the last of her strength, refusing to relinquish her lifeline.

As the hours dragged on, Suriratna began to think this was the end. Still, she could not get Soju's face out of her mind—the love that had brought her this far. She prepared to face the approaching darkness as the waves threatened to pull her under, and surrendered herself to the sea.

68

Saketa, Kosala
Present-day Ayodhya, Uttar Pradesh, India
Around 2,000 years ago

The dimly lit cellar of an unassuming house on Saketa's outskirts harboured Somadatta's clandestine gathering. The sparse room's sole piece of furniture was a large wooden crate that served as a table, its surface covered in maps of Saketa and its surrounding areas with symbols and annotations scrawled across them.

'I feel it,' Somadatta murmured. 'A few more blows and Vidushika's reign will crumble. We keep hammering.' He turned to one of the men in the room. 'Vatsadhara—the pastures?'

'Handled.' Vatsadhara's lips curved in satisfaction. 'Last night, our man drove Vidushika's prized cattle into the farmlands.'

Somadatta nodded. 'Good. Redistributing resources. The farmers will find that a welcome boon come morning.'

'They see us as their saviours already.'

Sharp features and piercing eyes lent Somadatta a commanding presence, an aura of calm authority. After helping Padmasen escape, he had been a fugitive, hiding in caves and forests.

With the funds and arms that Kulasekara and Padmasen had provided him, Somdutta had been able to build a committed rebel crew. Together, they had become a force to be reckoned with.

Somadatta turned to Bhagurayana. 'The supply lines?'

'Intercepted another caravan last night.' Bhagurayana's voice hummed with an undercurrent of triumph. 'The goods are delivered. They call us liberators, Somadatta.'

A smile touched Somadatta's lips. 'Excellent. We are getting closer.'

As the resistance against him gained in strength, Vidushika struggled. Stretched thin, his administration reacted to every rebel attack. Somadatta's crew, masters of hit-and-run ambushes, knew the city's layout intimately. They struck hard, then vanished before Vidushika's forces could respond. Once serene, Saketa now simmered, lawlessness seeping into its streets alongside the whispers of insurrection.

Rebels spread rumours in the markets, of impending raids and forced taxation. The merchants who supported Vidushika shuttered their shops and fled. These once-thriving areas stood in stark contrast now: shops closed, smoke thick in the air, fear radiating from the marauding bands that patrolled the alleys. The clash of metal, the cries of battle—the marketplaces had become sporadic battlegrounds. Meanwhile, rebel-friendly markets thrived. Forged coins and documents, subtly introduced, sowed chaos among Vidushika's bureaucracy. Behind it all was the masterful conductor: Somadatta. And as the resistance grew, so did dissent among Vidushika's own soldiers. Weary of the endless fighting and disillusioned by what they served, they were ripe for the picking. Somadatta's agents conjured up more rumours, planted seeds of doubt, offered incentives. Their goal: a full-blown mutiny.

In a hidden corner of the rebel headquarters, Somadatta met with soldiers who had pledged their allegiance to the rebels' cause. 'The reckoning is close,' he told them, conviction ringing in his voice. 'Rise up against your commanders. We stand with you. We shall topple the tyrant. Then the 157th Dvaitalingam Rakshak will take over.'

The soldiers nodded, apprehension warring with resolve on their faces. Saketa—all of Kosala—teetered on the brink.

'Many are ready,' Keshava, a veteran, spoke. 'But what of our families? Vidushika will use them against us.'

Somadatta placed a hand on Keshava's shoulder. 'They will be moved, kept safe. You have my word. Kulasekara's. Padmasen's.'

Keshava visibly relaxed. 'Then we stand with you. We will rise when the time comes.'

'Good. Coordination and timing are key. Be ready.' Somadatta turned to another soldier. 'Bring Padmasen back. We need him.'

'Now?' Bhagurayana's brow furrowed.

'Hanuman will pave the way. And get me the best masons Padmasen worked with.'

As night fell, blanketing Saketa, the city held its breath. In the darkness, Somadatta's rebels moved purposefully, united in their goal: Vidushika's downfall. The once-peaceful city was now a battleground, its fate hanging precariously in the balance.

69

Seongsan, Garak Confederacy
Present-day Seongju County, South Korea
Around 2,000 years ago

The underground chamber of Seongsan Fort felt like a tomb. Torchlight cast dancing shadows across the stone walls, while the air grew heavy with the acrid stench of damp earth and the oily smoke of slow-burning tar. In the centre of the room, spread-eagled on a rough-hewn table, lay the bodyguard of Chief Jinhyeok of Bihwa, his face contorted in agony. Nearby stood Talhae, a mask of simmering frustration on his face as his men worked over the prisoner.

The Bihwa man's shirt hung off him in bloody tatters. Each ragged breath was a reminder of the beating he had endured. The guards stepped back, allowing a moment of respite, as Talhae approached. 'Your stubbornness grows tiresome,' he murmured. 'But everyone has their breaking point.'

Though his body was wracked with pain, the captive's clenched jaw held firm; a sign of his steadfast refusal to yield. Talhae motioned, and a guard stepped forward, bearing a glowing iron poker. The prisoner's eyes widened, betraying his fear, but his jaw was still clenched. 'Very well,' Talhae sighed, feigning weariness. 'Let us see if fire loosens that tongue.'

The searing rod hovered inches from the man's chest, its heat singeing the air. Just when it seemed he would remain mute, he gasped, 'Wait!'

Talhae raised a hand, the iron halting. 'Speak,' he commanded.

'The chiefs … convened …' the bodyguard's voice was a tortured whisper. 'I never meant to spy on them … I trailed my chief, fearing for his safety.'

'Names,' Talhae clipped.

'Jinhyeok of Bihwa … Wonsik of Bangam … Yongho of Ara …' A pained gulp. 'And Kim Seok of Geumgwan … They gathered in Jirisan Forest.'

Talhae leaned forward, his interest piqued. 'Continue.'

'They … decided to band together,' the prisoner continued. 'To … prepare … for war. Against you. They chose … Kim Seok … as their leader.'

Silence fell as Talhae processed this. Troubling news, yet … an opportunity bloomed. He had anticipated resistance, but this confirmed alliance was significant.

'And Kim Suro?' Talhae's voice remained deceptively calm.

'On his way … to Geumgwan,' the man panted, weakening. 'Expected … any day…'

A slow smile spread across Talhae's face as he gauged this information. He appraised his guards—a ruthless cadre awaiting his command. They were imposing figures, clad in dark garments, their faces hidden behind masks, only their cold eyes visible. Each one a master of interrogation, infiltration and death. But, above all, utterly loyal to Talhae. They moved with a coiled, predatory grace, their weapons, honed to perfection, glinting in the torchlight.

'We have what we need,' Talhae declared. His men nodded curtly. He turned back to the prisoner, now insensate. Contempt hardened his features. 'Dispose of him,' he ordered.

An interrogator produced a rope and looped it around the captive's neck with practised ease before yanking it taut. A brief struggle followed, and then stillness. Talhae watched, his thoughts already turning to his next move. This coalition was a danger, but also a target. Strike now, and he could shatter their unity before it solidified. A small grin touched his lips.

Turning, Talhae ascended the winding stairs, his footsteps echoing in the torchlit gloom. His smile stretched wider as he paused midway, addressing his squad. 'I've thought of a homecoming present for dear Kim Suro ... Fitting, would you not say?'

70

Ayutthaya, Siam, Suvarnabhumi
Present-day Bangkok, Thailand
Around 2,000 years ago

The lifeless form drifted on the ebbing tide, eventually washing ashore on a pristine beach. The sun beat down, its refracted light in the water creating the illusion of scattered jewels. The woman lay motionless, serene, her dark tresses fanned out on the damp earth behind her, beaded with sea spray and sand. The gentle lapping of waves and the distant cries of circling seabirds were the only sounds that disturbed the tranquil scene.

Sometime later, a group of fishermen ambled up the shoreline, nets slung over their tanned shoulders. Their eyes, accustomed to scanning the distant horizon, quickly spotted the prone figure on the beach. One of them, a weathered man with a kindly face, rushed forward, his heart thudding. He dropped beside her, pressed an ear to her chest and felt the faintest flutter of life. 'Over here! She is alive!' he called.

The others gathered around, worry furrowing their brows. Together, they gently lifted and carried her further inland, away from the tide's hungry claws. Their leader, an elderly man, his face a map of wisdom, began rhythmically compressing her chest, forcing air into her brine-soaked lungs.

At last, she sputtered and coughed, expelling the brine that had flooded her lungs. Her body jerked slightly, then went limp again. Another fisherman swiftly swaddled her in sailcloth.

A flush gradually returned to Suriratna's pale lips as her breathing steadied, though she remained unconscious. The men exchanged looks of relief, their desperate efforts rewarded by each of the rescued girl's rasping inhalations.

The disturbance on the seashore had not gone unnoticed. From a distance, alert royal guards, their armours glinting, had witnessed the incident. Apprehensive, they marched towards the fishermen, their towering commander leading the way. 'What have you there?' he demanded.

'A young woman, sir, brought in by the sea,' the elder fisherman replied. 'She is breathing, but still senseless. We did our best.'

The commander nodded, appreciating their actions. 'We will take it from here,' he said, then murmured to his soldiers. 'Note her fine clothes, the embroidery. Take her to the royal guesthouse.' The soldiers lifted Suriratna's delicate form and carried her towards a waiting barge, bound for the city.

~

Later that evening, Suriratna lay curled in a sumptuous bed. The large room overflowed with rich tapestries and soft pillows. Tall windows looked out at meticulously maintained gardens where the seductive scent of night jasmine drifted on the evening air.

Come the new day's light, Suriratna stirred, her lids fluttering open to an alien world of unfamiliar opulence. Her head swam, her limbs ached, but the spark of life within her burned bright. Blinking slowly, she took in the intricate woodcarvings, the artistically draped shimmering silks, the delicate porcelain vases bursting with fresh blooms. Seated opposite, bathed in the morning glow, was a figure of regal bearing, robed in garments that seemed to glow with an inner light. A face both kind and commanding regarded her, curiosity and concern apparent in the eyes.

'You have returned to the land of the living,' the man said in Mon, his voice a melodic murmur. 'Welcome to the kingdom of Ayutthaya. I am Jayasena, king of Siam.'

Suriratna struggled upright, the fine sheets whispering around her. She was unable to understand the language that was being spoken.

Jayasena realized her confusion. 'Bhavatyāḥ Saṃskṛtaṃ bhāṣaṇā asti vā? Do you speak Sanskrit?' he asked. Jayasena had been learning the language from his rajguru. Suriratna nodded.

'Welcome to the kingdom of Ayutthaya. I am Jayasena, king of Siam,' Jayasena repeated in Sanskrit.

'Ayodhya? Shyam?' she croaked, her voice ragged.

'What outsiders call Suvarnabhumi,' Jayasena reassured her, compassion in his warm eyes. 'You washed up on our shores and my people found you. It is my sacred duty to tend to one who is so clearly an angel sent by the gods.'

Suriratna's eyes darted as a single image filled her mind: Soju's comforting embrace.

'And what name does this celestial angel go by?' Jayasena inquired.

'Su—Sembavalam,' Suriratna replied after the briefest hesitation, having made a spur-of-the-moment decision to conceal her identity. Both Suriratna and Sembavalam meant 'precious gem', in Sanskrit and Tamil respectively; Sembavalam was often used to denote red coral, a prized treasure.

Jayasena rose in a fluid motion, his robes swirling around him. 'Rest now, Lady Sembavalam. My servants shall see to your needs.' With a final compassionate smile, he departed, the door shutting behind him.

Almost immediately, a flurry of attendants materialized, moving with practised efficiency. Trays laden with food appeared before her, aromatic oils were produced for bathing and fresh clothing was laid out. Suriratna watched it all through a disoriented haze, grateful for the care. As she sipped on a comforting soup, her mind whirled with uncertainty over this strange new realm and the benevolent king who had plucked her from the sea's cold embrace.

Outside, as Jayasena reclined in the palanquin bearing him back towards his palace, his thoughts dwelled solely on Suriratna. Her beauty had struck him to his core and his mind was made up. This exquisite creature rescued from the waves would become one of his queens; the heir that he so longed for would be born from her womb.

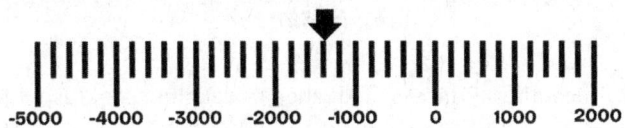

Thebes, Kemet, New Kingdom
Present-day Luxor, Egypt
Around 3,400 years ago

Beneath a scorching sun, Egypt's golden sands shimmered as a procession wound its way across the vast expanse towards the heart of Thebes. This was an age when gods walked among mortals and alliances forged in sacred vows shaped the destiny of kingdoms.

Pharaoh Amenhotep III's chariot, gleaming in the sun, led the welcoming party. Resplendent in his royal attire, he watched the Mitanni delegation in the distance, his attention drawn to a single figure.

The Mitanni were a powerful tribe to Egypt's northwest. Amenhotep's imminent marriage to a Mitanni princess, Tadukhepa, was not simply a union of hearts—it was a strategic alliance, a bulwark against common enemies.

The Mitanni procession advanced gracefully. At its centre rode Tadukhepa, her beauty undimmed by the dusty journey. She was draped in fine linen, her hair embellished with intricate jewellery. As it drew closer, the procession slowed, and a hush fell over the assembled crowd. Amenhotep descended from his chariot, his gait that of a god–king, and approached Tadukhepa, who was escorted by her maids, her steps measured and deliberate, her excitement battling with a hint of apprehension. Beneath the shadow of Karnak's massive pylons, with the imposing figures of Ra and Amun-Re looming above, the two met for the first time.

'O beautiful Princess Tadukhepa, daughter of Tushratta, welcome,' Amenhotep greeted, his voice resounding across the courtyard. Tadukhepa's father was so named after a great king—Dasharatha—born in a distant land to the east where the Mitanni clan was said to have originated.

Amenhotep offered his hand, palm up, in a gesture of welcome. Tadukhepa placed her hand in his, her touch steady. 'It is an honour to be here, Pharaoh Amenhotep,' she responded.

Priests began their chanting, invoking Ra, the supreme Egyptian deity, to bless the union. As sacred invocations filled the air, Tadukhepa's gaze briefly lifted skyward, offering a silent prayer to her own gods—Indra, Varuna, Mitra and the Ashvins—deities that had accompanied their people east and west of the Ravi river after the Battle of Ten Kings. The ceremony continued, blending traditions from both cultures—sacrifices were offered and blessings bestowed upon the union.

The final act involved the presentation of gifts to the groom. Tadukhepa's attendants brought forth an ornately carved wooden box, its surface depicting scenes of battles and triumphs. 'Pharaoh, as a token of our friendship, we present you with utsa,' the Mitanni envoy announced. The box was opened, revealing a gleaming metal unlike anything found in Egypt. On the lid was engraved a symbol of two fish that had been made to resemble the Eye of Horus.

Amenhotep's eyebrows rose in surprise as he studied the object. 'What is this marvel? Is it the substance I have heard so much about?'

'It is a gift from our brethren in Meluhha, O Pharaoh,' the Mitanni envoy explained. 'A material stronger and more versatile than any other from the banks of the seven sisters. We share it with you as a symbol of our bond.'

Amenhotep nodded, his mind already racing with possibilities. His gaze remained fixed on the object—its surface gleaming without a hint of corrosion despite being exposed to air and moisture. He had heard whispers of a metal that resisted heat and age, that rang with an unnatural resonance when struck, and which some claimed could slice through bronze as though it were papyrus. Something so powerful, incredibly represented by two fish!

'My kingdom thanks you,' Amenhotep declared. 'We shall cherish this gift as a symbol of our unity. The twin fish shall signify the strength of our union. Henceforth they shall be called Abtu and Anet. They shall guard the barge of Ra.'

Cheers erupted, echoing off the ancient stones. The twin fish were incorporated into legend, forever commemorating this momentous occasion.

The Nile glittered in the light as the celebrations continued late into the night. Music and laughter filled the air, but in quiet corners of the palace Amenhotep's advisors were already formulating plans. After all, this marriage was only the first step in a grand strategy to strengthen Egypt.

In the glow of a thousand lanterns, the twin fish rested. For now.

71

Dimašq, Roman Empire
Present-day Damascus, Syria
Around 2,000 years ago

Mithra made his way to the aviary, a massive outdoor enclosure in the northwest corner of his palace grounds. Finely carved stone columns supported a ceiling of woven reeds and wooden beams, a wonder of Roman architecture. Blooming plants and vines trailed down from it, forming a rich canopy that offered the birds within protection and serenity. Many of the birds occupied exquisitely designed cages made of wood and delicate ironwork.

The aviary was abuzz with the flutter of wings, vivid plumage adding colour to the verdant environment. Handlers moved among the cages, tending to their feathery charges: assessing conditions for travel, replacing water dishes, distributing grain. Cooing pigeons, twittering sparrows and the cries of more exotic species filled the space.

Mithra approached Arash, a young handler meticulously fastening a little scroll to a pigeon's leg. The bird cooed, fluffing its feathers in the dappled sunshine. Other birds fluttered in their cages nearby, their movements creating a soft rustling sound.

'Arash.' Mithra's voice cut through the aviary's calm.

Arash glanced up, a mix of respect and curiosity on his face. 'My Lord?'

'New messages?'

Arash nodded, retrieving a small scroll from a nearby table. 'Just arrived, My Lord. From Cheliyan.'

Mithra unfurled the scroll. The message, scripted in a hurry, read, 'Soju has returned to Geumgwan. Political turmoil. Needs immediate support from your foundry.'

His jaw tightened. He crumpled the note slightly, the gravity of it bearing down on him. Turning, he strode out of the aviary, crossed the garden and entered the grand hall, his sandals clicking against the marble floor. He found Barakat, now his trusted advisor, in discussion with a group of merchants, who quickly dispersed, sensing the urgency in their leader's demeanour.

'Barakat, a word.'

'My Lord.' Barakat approached, concern on his weathered face. Around his neck, he wore a pendant bearing a pattern of four swords intersecting like the petals of a flower. It was his trademark for the Dimašq foundry, though most did not realize it could be flipped to represent the Pandyan twin fish. He had started using it on all their blades.

Barakat had become Mithra's trusted advisor by proving his worth time and again. He navigated the complex web of alliances and enmities within and outside Dimašq with uncanny skill managing the merchants, and maintaining relations with the Romans and King Aretas IV in Raqmu. A master of logistics and a shrewd diplomat, Barakat knew how to deal with both friends and foes.

Mithra handed him the crumpled message. 'Soju needs weapons—all we can provide. The foundries in Korkai and Geumgwan will not be enough. We must increase production here and send a shipment to Geumgwan.'

Barakat's brow furrowed as he scanned the message. 'We can increase production, My Lord, but we require more ingots. Our current stock will not suffice.'

Mithra nodded, a plan forming in his mind. 'We will secure additional supplies. I will contact Cheliyan about the ingots.'

'Cheliyan's resources are spread thin across the furnace, forge and foundry. If he devotes all resources to the furnace and ships the ingots to us, we could increase production significantly.'

Under Barakat's guidance, the Dimašq foundry was now producing swords of outstanding quality. But his experiment in smelting iron paled in terms of quality when compared to the nav utsa ingots from Padmasen and Kulasekara's facility in Korkai. Ever the pragmatist, Barakat chose to focus on crafting exceptional swords and tools, rather than replicating the raw material. Many new chisels had been sent to Raqmu, where work on the Khazneh continued. Even with lower tax rates, the revenue collected in Dimašq was higher than ever.

Mithra turned to Arash, who had followed them inside. 'Prepare a message for Cheliyan. Inform him we are increasing production and require additional ingots. Urgently.'

Arash nodded, quickly inscribing the message and hurrying back to the aviary. Mithra watched from the palace as a pigeon took to the sky, winging its way towards Korkai. He offered a silent prayer for its swift journey.

He turned back to Barakat, his expression resolute. 'The foundry must work without stopping. Soju's success depends on us. It is a debt of honour that must be repaid.'

72

New Delhi, India

Present day

The luxurious suite in New Delhi's Oberoi Hotel boasted large windows overlooking the city's golf course. In the spacious living room, plush seating was arranged in a semicircle around a glass coffee table. Aditya, Somi, Ramaswamy, Jung and Jayaraman had gathered for a crucial discussion.

Aditya's gaze swept around the room, taking in the expressions of his companions. He turned to Jung, who was sipping tea. 'Dr Jung, you mentioned wootz steel's significance in our last meeting. Could you elaborate on its origins?' he asked.

Jung set his cup down. 'Wootz steel, prized as Indian crucible steel, dates back over two thousand years. In India, it was called "nav utsa", which international merchants mispronounced as "vutsa"—what came to be known as wootz.'

Somi leaned forward, intrigued. 'And the raw material for those famous Damascus swords came from India?'

'Indeed,' Jung confirmed. 'Wootz ingots were shipped from India to Damascus, where swordsmiths forged them into deadly blades.'

Ramaswamy, who had been listening, spoke. 'It is fascinating how such advanced metallurgical techniques developed so early in India ... but our focus should be on the secret of wootz. That is the only way to re-engineer it—steel that could forge the Damascus Sword or create stone-melting chisels for Petra, Konark, Kailasa and even Angkor. Imagine how those traits could be amplified in today's laboratories.'

'Are there documents that could help us?' Aditya asked.

'The *Rasaratnakara* is twelve hundred years old,' Ramaswamy said. 'Older still is Chanakya's *Arthashastra*, from twenty-three hundred years ago. It mentions the manufacturing process. Let me see ...' He tapped keys on his notebook computer. 'Ah, here's the passage.' He began to read.

'Steel may be manufactured by several processes. One process is to heat iron in contact with powdered charcoal in a closed vessel made of a refractory material such as clay. The heating is continued for several hours until the iron absorbs carbon from the charcoal and melts, forming steel. The steel is then cooled and the resulting ingots are broken into small pieces, which are reheated and hammered to produce finished products.'

Somi drew in a breath. 'That's likely the earliest form of carbon–steel,' she murmured, turning to Aditya. 'We just need to decipher the secret additive and the proportions. Then we'll know exactly how ancient India created super-strength steel. Reverse-engineer and amplify that process and you may have your DRDO solution.' *The past held the key to the future.*

'The problem is, we must go beyond history, into the realm of legend, to understand nav utsa,' Ramaswamy said.

'Go on,' Aditya urged.

'Ghaznawar shared a palm-leaf manuscript with me during my captivity,' Ramaswamy explained. 'He believed it would aid my scientific exploration. It had been passed down from Ghazni's time a thousand years ago, but was probably drafted a thousand years earlier, like a charter.'

'How did Ghazni acquire it?' Aditya asked.

'It was likely collected by Al-Biruni, the scholar who accompanied Ghazni during his raids on Mathura, Kannauj and Somnath. It was then handed down through Ghazni's lineage.'

'And its whereabouts now?' Jayaraman asked.

'Lost to fire during the ISIS-K–TTP clash. But I memorized the key contents. Ghaznawar possessed only a single leaf.'

'Do you know the source of the palm leaf—from where it was taken?' Aditya pressed.

'Difficult to say,' Ramaswamy replied. 'Countless ancient Hindu texts are lost. The Rig Veda is at least four thousand years old, possibly even twice that much. The original had twenty-one shakhas—recensions. Only one survives. Pratisakhyas, Anukramanis, Puranas, Upanishads, Smritis, Itihasas, Agamas, Tantras, Brahamanas—they were all lost throughout the ages, particularly after attacks like Bakhtiyar Khilji's on Nalanda.'

'You said you memorized the palm leaf?' Jayaraman asked.

Ramaswamy nodded. 'It bore a sketch of two fish, swimming clockwise within a circle. Below it, eight lines of text.' He chanted the verse in chaste Sanskrit, which he had learned as part of his traditional upbringing in Madurai.

dvau matsyau nartanāsaktau saṃpṛktau varuṇālaye
ucchṛṅkhalau svatantrau ca lulitau vāriṇo raye
nārāyaṇamahādevau dvāvekātmasvarūpiṇau
parasparaṃ samāyāntau pūrṇaikātmatvakāriṇau
hastayo rakṣakasyāsti dvaitaliṅgaṃ pratiṣṭhitam
dṛḍhaṃ pratiṣṭhamānena balenaikena rakṣitam

ayodhyāsandhirāpnotu vardhanaṃ śauryasaṃyutam
bhāgyāni hyatra baddhāni yathāsthānaṃ yathocitam

'The meaning?' Jung asked.
'A riddle. Roughly translated ...' Ramaswamy grabbed a pad and pencil and scribbled his translation.

Two dancing fish tangled in the sea,
Swaying in the current, wild and free.
Vishnu and Shiva, facets of a soul,
Coming together, making a whole.
The Dvaitalingam in Rakshak hands,
Guarded by a force that firmly stands.
May the Ayodhya Alliance flourish strong,
With destinies bound, where they belong.

'Incredible.' Aditya was captivated. 'But where does it lead us?'

'That is where we probe the legend,' Ramaswamy replied. 'It is said that after he was released from under Mount Kailasa, Ravana pleaded with Shiva to share something known as the Atmalingam.'

'And what was that?' Somi asked.

'The Atmalingam wasn't a religious symbol; it represented the cosmic balance between creation and destruction, positive and negative, light and dark, heat and cold. When activated, the Atmalingam became known as the Dvaitalingam—the duality lingam.'

Somi's eyes widened. 'So, the Dvaitalingam is a key to understanding balance in the universe?'

'I saw the symbol on Ghaznawar's parchment,' Ramaswamy said, sketching the intricate image on the pad—twin fish, entwined yet facing opposite directions. 'This symbolizes an ancient technology. Classical texts speak of its power to create and destroy—fusion and fission. It is not a myth; it is real. Generations have died trying to acquire this substance.'

The group sat silent, captivated.

'In south India, the twin fish became the eyes of Meenakshi. It was even incorporated into the Buddhist Ashtamangala,' he added.

'The fish were part of the Pandyan flag, then the Chola flag after their victory,' Ramaswamy continued, pulling up images on his phone. 'Many ancient civilizations used the twin-fish symbol. Even the ancient Egyptians had two sacred fish deities—Abtu and Anet—protectors of Ra, the sun god. The symbolism has always been one of protection, not unlike the symbols at Ayodhya or Korkai.' He showed them the Abtu and Anet symbol. 'The two-fish symbol was also on ancient Indus seals and may have travelled to Babylon.'

Jayaraman spoke. 'The twin fish symbolize balance and duality within the universe. Even China's Song and Ming dynasties adapted the fish into an abstract form.' He pulled up another image. 'The Taijitu, more commonly known as the yin–yang symbol,' he said.

'And South Korea incorporated it into their national flag,' Somi added, realization dawning.

'The Dvaitalingam is not a mere substance,' Ramaswamy stated. 'It embodies duality, as the ancients believed, of Vishnu and Shiva. We think of them as "gods", but they are symbols of energies—like magnetic poles, battery terminals, winds caused by pressure differentials, ocean currents. Vishnu and Shiva are the extremities that cause flow. The Dvaitalingam captures both poles in one.'

'That explains the focus on Harihara in our philosophy,' Jayaraman said. 'The perfect balance.'

'A deity that combines two deities?' Aditya asked.

'A combination of energies,' Ramaswamy corrected. 'Everyone possesses both energies in different proportions. Individuals with high levels of Shiva energy became known as Shiva avatars—like Hanuman or Bhairava. Those with high Vishnu energy became Vishnu avatars—Rama or Krishna. Harihara represents balance. And since Vishnu's first avatar was Matsya, the fish, Harihara must be represented by two fish.'

'And in an engineering context?' Aditya asked.

'Think of it like magnets,' Ramaswamy said. 'North and south will hang on to each other like a bond. Now, consider an iron–carbon bond. An agent that could add a Shiva charge to the carbon and a Vishnu charge to the iron would bond them like a magnet's poles. That is the fundamental idea of the Dvaitalingam. It produces strong, durable metal.'

'But what about the destructive edges of blades made from such steel?' Aditya questioned. 'You said wootz chisels could melt rocks.'

'Imagine the blade's edge with particles charged in a single direction,' Ramaswamy explained. 'Think of all the tiny particles at the blade's edge lined up and pushing in the same direction—like a crowd moving in perfect unison. That creates an incredibly focused force. Energy-unstable, its contact would be like a hot knife through wax. That is the technology the

Indian metallurgists—and later the Damascus sword makers—mastered.'

Aditya and Somi were silent, struck by these revelations. Ramaswamy's reasoning was sound, but they were no closer to finding the mysterious substance needed for the BPBT.

'How do we find this material—the Dvaitalingam—used in Indian crucible steel?' Somi asked finally. 'Can the ancient texts guide us?'

'No,' Jayaraman replied. 'But something else can.'

'What?'

'The ancient town of Ayodhya.'

73

Ayutthaya, Siam, Suvarnabhumi
Present-day Bangkok, Thailand
Around 2,000 years ago

Suriratna lounged on a silk-draped divan, her fingers idly tracing the intricate embroidery. The lavish room basked in a golden glow from the windows, the air thick with sandalwood. A spread of fresh delicacies lay before her on a low table as silent attendants catered to her every whim, refilling her goblet with a delicious medley of fruit juices—cool, refreshing sweetness tempered by subtle spice.

She had bathed in rose-scented water, after which her hair had been combed to a glossy sheen and she had been robed in fine silks and adorned with jewels that glinted with each movement. But her immersion in all the grandeur was a facade, because in reality a storm was brewing in her heart.

The chamber doors parted with a soft swish as Jayasena strode in, his commanding presence drawing all eyes. A ghost of a smile touched his lips upon finding Suriratna.

'Your Majesty,' she greeted, rising gracefully and dipping her head in respect.

With a casual wave, the king dismissed the servants, who bowed and exited, leaving them alone. He approached her, looking at her appreciatively. 'Lady Sembavalam,' he began, his voice smooth and warm, 'I trust you want for nothing?'

'Your hospitality is most generous, Your Majesty.' Her voice remained steady despite the turmoil within. 'I am deeply grateful.'

The king's expression softened. 'It pleases me to hear that. You deserve no less.'

Suriratna hesitated, steadying herself with a breath. 'However, there is a matter ...'

'Speak freely, My Lady,' Jayasena urged.

'I have been fortunate to recuperate within the safety of your palace and your kindness has not gone unnoticed. It has been two weeks since my arrival and I fear I must now be on my way ...' She met his gaze. 'I ... must reach the Garak Confederacy. I humbly request your assistance in arranging passage. You have been so kind, and I feel loath to ask for more.'

A crease appeared between the king's brows. 'Garak? Why would you leave Siam? You were destined to come here, Lady Sembavalam. The gods themselves delivered you to me. *This* is where you belong.'

'I am honoured, Your Majesty, but my heart yearns for another purpose,' Suriratna replied. 'That ill-fated journey had a greater intent, one I must complete.'

Jayasena took a step closer, his posture suddenly turning predatory. 'And what purpose could possibly outweigh the opportunity before you?'

Suriratna's chin lifted a fraction. 'I seek the one who holds my heart. He faces peril and I must be by his side. My travels from Korkai were always meant to bring me to him.'

Silence fell, heavy and charged. The warmth in the king's demeanour leached away, replaced by a stony reserve. 'And who is this man you speak of with such blind loyalty?'

Suriratna twisted her gown in her hands. 'His name is Kim Suro—an honourable, courageous soul who has endured many trials. I cannot forsake my quest to find him.'

'You reject what is offered—to be my queen, to live in luxury and be loved? Is that not enough?' Disbelief embittered the king's tone.

Suriratna drew back, her heart pounding. 'Your proposition honours me, Your Majesty. But another calls my heart home. Not for all the wealth and power can I turn from those emotions.'

A muscle in the king's jaw ticked. 'You are rejecting me? Knowing all I have done for you?'

Suriratna stood firm, her voice unwavering. 'I am in your debt for your benevolence, in this lifetime and many more. Who knows what my fate would have been without you. But what is in my heart cannot be changed. I must follow where it leads.'

Jayasena's internal struggle played on his face. *Then I will lock you up until this foolishness subsides*, is what he wanted to say. Instead, he said, his voice calm, 'Let me leave you to think it over.'

He clapped once, sharply. Two grim-faced guards appeared—sentries to be stationed outside her golden cage. Without another word, Jayasena spun on his heel and walked out, leaving Suriratna alone with her thoughts. She was now a prisoner.

Her head swam as she sank back onto the sofa. The lavish trappings mocked her, the pleasures they provided felt hollow against her one craving. Gazing out the window, Suriratna's mind travelled to the one who had set her on this path, for whom she would endure any hardship. 'Stay strong,' she murmured, sending a prayer across the distance. 'May Harihara grant us strength.'

Jayasena could confine her body, but her heart was far from Siam's walls, already in Geumgwan.

74

Ayodhya, Uttar Pradesh, India

Present day

Policemen cleared a path for Aditya, Somi, Ramaswamy, Jung and Jayaraman, allowing them entry into the inner sanctum of the temple. The chief minister of Uttar Pradesh had sent a security detail to ensure that their study of the site progressed undisturbed.

As they approached the newly constructed Ram Mandir, they were struck by its grandeur. In the midday sun, the golden towers seemed to touch the sky. Intricate carvings graced the walls, narrating stories from epochs past. Jayaraman paused, awestruck, as he took in the surroundings.

Aditya glanced around, absorbing the significance of the site. 'So much has happened here. It feels like we are standing at the heart of something timeless.'

'Well, the location is mentioned prominently in the *Ayodhya Mahatmya*, a sacred Hindu text that forms part of the Skanda Purana,' Jayaraman confirmed, his attention lingering on the temple.

'This exact location?' Aditya asked.

'The passage describes the shrine as being west of Lomash Ashram and north of Vasishtha Kund,' Jayaraman replied. 'Sources indicate that Babur's commander, Mir Baqi, constructed a mosque at those coordinates in 1528 using fourteen black Kasauti stone pillars of an erstwhile temple. But Hindus kept returning to the site to offer prayers on Rama Navami, his birthday—a particularly auspicious day.'

Turning to Ramaswamy, Aditya asked, 'So you believe the Iron Pillar once marked this spot? The very pillar that now stands in Delhi?'

Ramaswamy nodded. 'We know Chandragupta II—Vikramaditya—installed the pillar in Udayagiri and Anangpal Tomar later moved it to Delhi. But what if it first stood here, marking a key location, before any temple existed?'

'The pillar is dedicated to Vishnu and once bore a Garuda figure on top,' Jayaraman pointed out. 'As Dr Ramaswamy has explained, standard dating methods are ineffective in this case. Our timeline relies solely on epigraphical analysis, which is insufficient to determine a precise age. So, the hypothesis is plausible. And both Ayodhya and Indraprastha—now Delhi—had a Vishnu connection.'

'Remember, the pillar's material possesses qualities that suggest it could be a precursor to nav utsa,' Ramaswamy added. 'The most important clue is the reference to Ayodhya in the Ghazni parchment.'

The group moved closer, their steps hesitant, as if reluctant to disturb the sanctity of the space. The temple courtyard teemed with devotees lost in prayer and ritual, their murmurs creating a harmonious buzz.

'The Babri Masjid once stood here,' Jayaraman stated. 'Built atop the remnants of an ancient temple.'

'How do we know that?' Somi asked.

Jayaraman responded. 'Well, first we have the location mentioned in *Ayodhya Mahatmya*, as I discussed earlier. Then there are Muslim accounts. One of them is the account of Aurangzeb's granddaughter in a work called *Sahifah-i Chihal Nasaih Bahadurshahi* in which it is mentioned that Hindu temples in cities such as Mathura, Varanasi and Ayodhya were demolished to strengthen Islam.' He paused. 'Frankly ...'

'Yes?'

'Frankly, although the sources have been contested, the Muslim references—if we are to dig deep—are overwhelming. There is the account of Mirza Jan whose work *Hadiqa-i-Shahada* says that the janmasthan was the original birthplace of Rama, adjacent to which was Sita Ki Rasoi, and at that site, a lofty mosque was built by Babur under the guidance of Musa Ashikan. Then we have the accounts of Muhammad Asghar, Mirza Rajab Ali Beg Surur, Sheikh Mohammed Azmat Ali Kakorawi Nami, Haji Muhammed Hasan, Maulvi Abdul Karim, Dr Zaki Kakorawi, Kamaluddin Haidar Hosni ... all of them acknowledge that a mosque was built at the birthplace of Rama.'

'And was there any archaeological evidence to back this up?' Aditya asked.

'Indeed,' Jayaraman affirmed. 'The Archaeological Survey of India, led by Professor B.B. Lal, conducted fieldwork from 1975 to 1980. Excavations revealed burnt brick pillar bases aligned identically to several black stone pillars within the mosque.'

'And?'

'According to the ASI report, the mosque had apparently been built reusing the black stone pillars from a pre-existing temple. They depict yakshas, devakanyas, dvarapalas and ganas. There are sacred motifs—the purnaghata, lotus, hansa and mala—all belonging to Hindu iconography. Usually, such imagery would have no place in a mosque. You can read all the archaeological details in the voluminous court order of 2019 that settled the dispute ... it runs over a thousand pages—'

Somi intervened. 'What was here before the Babri mosque though?'

'If we go by all the accounts that I have just mentioned, there were King Dasharatha's private apartments—the Mahal Sarai, a Rama temple and a kitchen known as Sita Ki Rasoi,' Jayaraman replied. 'In 1528, their demolition was overseen by Commander Mir Baqi, under the patronage of a Muslim faqir named Sayed Musa Ashikan.'

Aditya touched the cool stone of a pillar, musing. 'To think this place has seen so many transformations.'

The tolling of temple bells and the soft recitation of mantras permeated the air as they wandered through the ancient site. There was a sense of peace within the grounds, a sharp contrast to the temple's turbulent history.

They reached the inner sanctum, where resided a magnificent idol of Rama in his childhood form. Draped in silk and adorned with garlands, the deity seemed to welcome them. The group stood in silence, absorbed in their thoughts.

Eventually, Ramaswamy remarked, 'Just an idea ...'

'What is it?' Aditya asked.

'This new temple, including its foundation, was constructed without iron,' Ramaswamy noted. 'I wonder why.'

'Longevity, I'd assume,' Jayaraman offered. 'The durability of modern iron is less than a century. This temple was built in the Nagara style using granite, sandstone and marble with a lock-and-key mechanism and should last a millennium.'

A thoughtful frown settled on Ramaswamy's face. 'Where we are standing is the inner sanctum—the garbha griha. I imagine that the spot where the deity stands is where our Iron Pillar once stood.'

'What are you thinking, Bala?' Jung prompted.

'This structure—with its proximity to the Himalayan tectonic region—was designed for Zone IV seismicity,' Ramaswamy explained. 'The geotechnical findings revealed historical materials and artifacts up to a depth of 36 feet. The builders excavated the existing fill and replaced it with engineered fill.'

'Your point?' Jung asked.

'If the Dvaitalingam was buried here, beneath the Iron Pillar which stood where the temple now stands, it is gone from here. If so, it is among the retrieved archaeological samples, stored separately.'

'Fair enough,' Jayaraman conceded. 'We have documented inventory of everything excavated and relocated. But what does that have to do with the lack of iron in the new temple?'

'This is just a hypothesis ...' Ramaswamy cautioned, hesitating.

'Go on,' Jayaraman pressed.

'What if our secret substance was indeed buried here, under the Iron Pillar? Or what if both were moved out thousands of years ago—the substance relocated, the pillar moved elsewhere?'

'And?'

'What if the ground itself became charged by the substance's presence? After all, the Iron Pillar also absorbed its anti-rusting properties from something beneath it, arguably. What if the engineers feared any iron used in the construction of the new temple would collapse due to the supercharged nature of the ground?'

'But our engineers would not have known that ... isn't it?' Aditya countered.

'I am not sure,' Ramaswamy said. 'Electromagnetic activity would have been discernible. For example, the statue we see before us is crafted from a three-billion-year-old black schist stone called Krishna Shila. This is a stone that is particularly resistant to deterioration and is substantially inert. Could it be that the materials used were a *conscious choice* based on the ground conditions?'

Silence descended upon the group. This was conjecture, yes, but not impossible.

'If the Vishnu Stambha was moved, the Dvaitalingam beneath it must have been moved first,' Jayaraman reasoned. 'The pillar was symbolic of its guardian role and it was moved sixteen hundred years ago to Udayagiri. The Dvaitalingam could have been moved any time before that, even centuries earlier.'

'So, examining the archaeological remains from the foundation would tell us little about what was here when the Iron Pillar stood at the spot,' Ramaswamy concluded, his attention drawn to the badges worn by their security detail.

'I just realized we need to consider another angle,' said Ramaswamy.

'What is that?' Jayaraman asked.

'The twin fish—on the security personnel's badges. Where else in Ayodhya do we see this symbol?'

'It is ubiquitous,' Jayaraman replied, frowning. 'Universities, government buildings, law enforcement helmets, transport offices—even the municipal seal bears it. It is often dismissed as a decorative relic of royal heraldry. But the fish—yes, it is the emblem of the Mishra dynasty.'

Ramaswamy leaned in. 'When did they come to rule Ayodhya?'

'Major General Sir William Henry Sleeman served as the British Resident at Lucknow in the 1800s,' replied Jayaraman. 'During his tour of Awadh, he wrote that Ayodhya under Brahmin rulers—the Mishras—was one of the most prosperous estates in the region. More than fifteen hundred villages were under this estate alone.'

'So the twin-fish emblem is a nineteenth-century creation?' asked Aditya. 'One brought to Ayodhya by the Mishras?'

'Cannot say,' Jayaraman replied. 'This land has seen a succession of rulers from the Ikshvaku dynasty of Rama. It was once part of the Mauryan Empire. Then there was the rule of Pushyamitra Shunga, followed by local Deva and Datta kings. Around two thousand years ago, the Kushans—descendants of the Yuezhi tribes—rose to power, with Emperor Kanishka extending their control to Ayodhya. The region was later included in the Gupta Empire, which marked a golden age of Hindu revivalism.'

'And after the Guptas?' asked Aditya.

'After the Guptas, a series of regional dynasties held sway until the medieval period, when Turkic and Afghan invaders brought it under the Delhi Sultanate. In 1528 CE, Babur's general Mir Baqi constructed the Babri Masjid during the early Mughal era. When Mughal authority began to wane in the eighteenth century, power shifted to regional hands.'

'To whom?'

'Well,' said Jayaraman, 'the Nawabs of Awadh emerged as semi-independent rulers, who later relocated their capital from Ayodhya to Lucknow. They became renowned for their patronage of the arts, construction of forts and the use of the twin-fish insignia, which adorned monuments like the Rumi Gate and the Bara and Chhota Imambaras in Lucknow. Later, Brahmin zamindars and Vaishnavite Bairagis gained prominence, controlling local temples and akhadas. The arrival of the Mishra rulers corresponds to that period. So, yes, the use of the twin-fish symbol predates the Mishras even though it is seen as their insignia today, particularly in one place—tied to the original Ayodhya legend.'

'Then that is where we need to go,' Ramaswamy said quietly. 'Because if the symbol persisted across centuries, even when dynasties crumbled and empires rose, then it was not just heritage—it was protection. A cipher hiding in plain sight.'

75

Geumgwan, Garak Confederacy
Present-day Gimhae, South Korea
Around 2,000 years ago

Soju felt a sudden surge of joy as the Garak ship sailed into the Nakdong river, and Geumgwan revealed itself through the early morning mist. He stood at the bow, the wind murmuring in his ears, the oars rhythmically slicing through the water. He was grateful for a safe voyage, glad to be home, but a tempest of emotions churned within him as the ship neared the dock and memories resurfaced like waves crashing against the shores of his mind.

He remembered the day he had sailed for Korkai from Geumgwan with Cheliyan. The image of his father, Kim Seok, standing on the pier, was seared into his heart—the pride and sadness on his father's face, but also hope and expectation, as he left to receive an invaluable education. Geumgwan seemed different today; tension throbbed in the very air.

As the ship docked, Soju registered the silent crowd gathered on the shore. Hundreds of townsfolk, their faces solemn, their bodies still. No colourful banners snapped in the breeze, no festive music or drums greeted his arrival. Only an oppressive silence that seemed to seep into his bones. The Garak captain, Joon-gi, a stoic figure weathered by countless voyages, stepped forward to assist Soju as he disembarked. It was Joon-gi who had brought Kim Seok's message to Soju.

Geumgwan was still beautiful, cradled in a lush valley, dotted with terraced fields. In that sense, nothing had changed. But Soju had left it a happier place. He scanned the crowd now, dread coiling in his gut as his eyes fell on each passing face lined with worry. And where was his father? Why summon him from across the world only to be absent now?

A memory surfaced—of his father training him. Seok, picking up a hammer and handing it to him. He heard his father's voice echoing in his ear: 'Now you try, Soju. Hold it firmly. Keep your wrist supple. Feel the rhythm of the hammer striking the metal and you will know when it responds.'

Soju had asked, 'Will I ever be able to do what you do?'

And Seok had answered, 'I believe you have the potential to not just forge swords. You will forge a kingdom, my son. But remember—power should always be tempered with compassion. I hope you will become the Iron King, but one with a soft heart.'

But did he really have what it took to forge a kingdom?

As he remembered Kim Hwa, his adoptive mother—his Eomeoni—a poignant ache rose in his chest. The scent of steamed rice and kimchi—she had always made sure he was well-fed, never let him feel anything but loved. She was always there with a hug, encouragement, a bandage for his wounds, a listening ear. Had it not been for her, the fire at the orphanage would have consumed him.

Soju's gaze swept over the silent crowd again, his heart pounding louder with every heartbeat. And then he saw her.

She was sitting apart from the others, barely noticeable amidst the throng. But no one else was kneeling in the dirt like that particular figure—shoulders slumped, spine curved by sorrow, her frail frame wracked with sobs. It was her. Her simple hanbok, the colours of her chima jeogori muted with age. Before her sat a wooden box, its presence heavy and foreboding.

'Eomeoni,' Soju called, the word trembling on his lips. He approached her quickly, though each step he took felt like a burden.

Kim Hwa's face, marked by grief and the passage of time, lifted. Seeing him, she broke down anew, her cries ripping through the silence.

Soju knelt before her, oblivious to the crowd pressing in. He reached to wipe a tear from his mother's face, only for another to replace it. 'Soju, it is good you are here,' she said, her voice choking with sorrow.

Soju's confusion spiralled. 'What happened, Eomeoni?' He searched the faces surrounding them, his heart pounding, a chill of fear gripping him.

He rose, his attention claimed by the box. It was made of intricately carved wood, heavily lacquered, the lid embedded with metal studs, glimpses of silk lining the edges. Soju drew a shuddering breath and lifted the lid.

The sight hit him like a physical blow. He staggered back, his mind recoiling. 'No …' The word escaped him, a broken whisper. He crumpled to the ground, crushed beneath a wave of anguish, as the townsfolk watched—tableau of shared sorrow.

Inside the box lay his father's head, partially wrapped in bloodied cloth and pungent herbs for preservation. The shroud had been pulled back just enough to reveal the face. The eyes that had once held life and knowledge were now empty. The pale skin was stiff and drawn, marred by bruises and dried blood. The neck ended in a jagged stump. The lips that had once offered him words of comfort and wisdom and laughter were frozen in a grimace of pain.

The residents of Geumgwan watched, their expressions reflecting the collective grief of a town robbed not only of a leader but of a symbol of hope and unity.

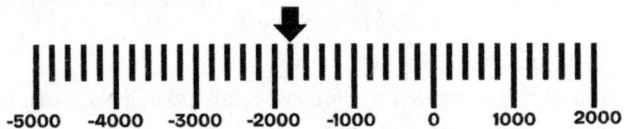

Babylon, Akkadian Empire
Present-day Al-Hillah, Baghdad, Iraq
Around 3,800 years ago

The golden sun beat down upon the grand city of Babylon, its towering ziggurats casting long shadows across the teeming streets. King Hammurabi was seated upon his throne in the majestic hall of his palace, its walls made of intricately carved stone. He awaited the arrival of a delegation of merchants from Meluhha.

As the sixth king of Babylon, Hammurabi had transformed it from a minor city-state into a powerful kingdom. Renowned for his strong sense of justice, he had spearheaded the creation of the Code of Hammurabi—a set of laws governing all aspects of life. His strategic mind had expanded Babylon's reach through a combination of alliances and conquests. Hammurabi was a wise and formidable ruler, shaping the course of history through law, strategy and knowledge.

The heavy wooden doors of the hall swung open, admitting the merchants. Their leader, clearly a man of high rank, approached the king, the exquisite colours and motifs of his attire revealing the legacy of his ancient culture. In his hand he held a detailed and skilfully crafted seal, its surface gleaming with the promise of secrets yet to be revealed. 'O great King Hammurabi, we bring a gift from the sacred land of the Sarasvati river,' he declared, his voice soft yet clear as he offered the seal to the king.

Hammurabi narrowed his focus while studying the seal, his fingers tracing the delicate patterns engraved upon its surface: a unicorn and then two upright fish representing two mysterious forces. He had not seen a symbol like this ever before.

'This seal, O King, contains the symbols of our gods Vishnu and Shiva,' the leader explained. 'Nothing in our world—humans, animals, plants, places or things—can exist without them. Our great thinkers strive to understand and harness this energy. A partnership with your kingdom could accelerate our progress.'

Hammurabi exchanged a glance with his chief astrologer, a man of exceptional intellect, who stood beside him. At a nod from the king, the astrologer stepped forward to examine the seal. He took it from Hammurabi, his mind already working hard to decipher its meaning.

The astrologer summoned a scribe, who came bearing a clay tablet and a stylus. Taking the writing implements, the astrologer began to replicate the seal's imagery, transforming the intertwined fish into a different symbol. All eyes watched as he worked, his hand steady and sure.

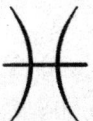

'O great King,' the astrologer announced, turning to Hammurabi, his voice grave. 'This symbol aligns with our understanding of the heavens. We know that Pisces, the sign of the twin fish, represents duality and unity, just as the gods of our visitors here, Vishnu and Shiva.'

Intrigued, Hammurabi leaned forward. The astrologer continued, 'In Babylonian tradition, the constellation Pisces holds great significance. It is associated with Anunitum and the Goddess Inanna. The duality of the fish reflects the harmony of opposing forces, a concept central to both our cultures. Even Aphrodite and Eros, the deities revered by our friends in Yavana, are bound together by a cord, inseparable.'

The concept of mobilizing opposing forces resonated with Hammurabi. He sensed its potential to advance his kingdom. 'Can this power be harnessed as they claim?'

The astrologer pondered, his mind exploring the possibilities. 'The similarities between our pantheons suggest a shared truth. By studying each other's ways and combining our knowledge, we could make unimaginable breakthroughs. The absence of a practical application does not preclude its eventual discovery.'

Hammurabi nodded, respect and determination in his eyes. He addressed the merchants from Meluhha. 'Your gift is most gracious, and your knowledge invaluable. What progress have you made in your quest?'

'We know of a substance possessing miraculous properties,' the merchant replied. 'Our ancestor Lakshmana was its first guardian. He is said to have inscribed words to this effect on an ancient pillar.'

Hammurabi smiled. 'May this be the beginning of a fruitful partnership between our peoples,' he declared. 'May we be as the fish, bound together by a common thread.'

76

Geumgwan, Garak Confederacy
Present-day Gimhae, South Korea
Around 2,000 years ago

The grotesque welcome that had awaited Soju upon his return to Geumgwan had taken Talhae weeks to orchestrate. His men, concealed in the trees surrounding Kim Seok's residence, had observed the chieftain's routine through weeks of patient and intense surveillance.

Kim Seok, the chief of Geumgwan and leader of the residual Confederacy, was an early riser. His day began with a solitary journey to Turtle Hill. There, before a sacred turtle-shaped stone, he found solace in meditation, the ancient ritual a symbol of the stability and longevity of his rule. It was from this hill that Garak had chosen the emblem on their flag—the turtle.

Kim Seok was typically alone during these moments of reflection, with his trusted manservant, Minjun, usually positioned some distance away. But on the days when Minjun was busy distributing food in honour of Geumgwan's ancestors, Kim Seok would make his morning pilgrimage alone, shadows clinging to him like phantoms in the early mist.

As a first step, Talhae's scouts had approached Minjun casually, offering gold to buy his betrayal. They spoke of a new order, a place of privilege for those who pledged their loyalty.

'Why remain a servant when you could be a lord, Minjun?' one of Talhae's men had suggested, his voice a silken whisper.

Minjun's face remained impassive. The man continued, 'Talhae will rule all of Garak. Serve him and you will be rewarded beyond your dreams. Gold, land, power …'

Minjun listened, his expression unreadable. When he finally spoke, his voice was firm. 'My loyalty is not for sale. I serve Kim Seok and his family with honour.'

The men had departed, their purpose thwarted. Minjun's steadfastness, however, sealed his fate. Though he planned to inform his master of Talhae's intentions, that very night, beneath the light of the full moon, a subtle but lethal dose of poison—pishuang—found its way into Minjun's drinking water. By dawn, his lifeless body lay on the kitchen floor.

Unaware of Minjun's murder, Kim Seok attributed his servant's absence to charitable work, and prepared for his morning meditation. He climbed the hill and knelt before the turtle stone, feeling the worn and weathered surface of the rocks beneath his palms. Seeking calm, he closed his eyes.

The attack was swift and brutal. Talhae's men materialized from the shadows, moving with lethal precision. 'There!' one shouted, lunging forward with his blade, giving Kim Seok little time to react.

Scrambling to his feet, Kim Seok drew the sword from his belt and deflected the blow just in time. 'You will need more than that,' he growled, defiance blazing within him.

Despite his age, Kim Seok's skills were remarkable. But the odds were stacked against him. He fought like a cornered animal, each strike calculated, each movement a blend of strength and precision. But the attackers were relentless, their numbers overwhelming. One by one, his blows began to weaken. Then a searing pain ripped through him as a sword found its mark. He swayed but remained upright, his spirit unbroken.

'We have him now,' one of the attackers sneered, pressing forward.

Kim Seok gritted his teeth, his blade moving in a deadly arc. 'I will not fall to cowards and traitors!' But it was a losing battle, and finally, with a shuddering gasp, he stumbled and collapsed.

Bound and bleeding, Kim Seok was dragged to a waiting wagon. The journey to Seongsan Fort was long and agonizing, each jolt to his body a reminder of his defeat. The fort loomed before them, a grim symbol of Talhae's burgeoning power. Talhae waited within, a viper poised to strike.

A smug grin spread across the younger man's face as Kim Seok was hauled into the dimly lit chamber. He gestured for his prisoner to be brought closer. 'Join me, Kim Seok,' Talhae said, his voice deceptively calm. 'Together, we can crush the remaining members of the Garak Confederacy. It will flourish under our rule. I will share power with you. After all, I am like a son to you.'

'A son who would kill his own father,' Kim Seok rasped, his voice weak but resolute. He glared at the younger man. 'It is a curse to call you a son.' Without warning, he spat on Talhae's face.

The guards registered surprise behind their masks, but they had been trained to display endless loyalty to Talhae. It did not matter that an honourable man like Kim Seok was accusing a son of patricide.

Fury contorted Talhae's features as he wiped the spittle away. 'You will regret that, old man!' he snarled. 'Hold him down!'

The soldiers charged forward, pinning Kim Seok to the floor. Talhae grabbed a heavy axe, the blade flashing in the torchlight, and with a swift, vicious swing, he brought it down. Kim Seok's head, severed from his body, rolled on the blood-soaked stone, a tragic end for a man of honour.

Talhae's chest heaved as he stared down at the corpse. 'Send the old man's head to Kim Suro,' he ordered, his voice cold and hard. 'A gift from me, to welcome him home. Package it in a decorated box. Spare no expense.'

Outside, a storm raged, mirroring the violence within the fort. Talhae, his face illuminated by flashes of lightning, allowed a smile of triumph to cross his grim features. His grip on power was now absolute. Kim Seok, once a symbol of defiance, was dead. His severed head would serve as a warning to all who dared to oppose him. Soju included.

77

Ayutthaya, Siam, Suvarnabhumi
Present-day Bangkok, Thailand
Around 2,000 years ago

Suriratna sat by the window, her attention lost in the expanse of the lush gardens surrounding the guesthouse. Yet nature's beauty did little to soothe her troubled heart. Despite the luxurious surroundings, she was a prisoner. Memories of her parents' comforting presence and Soju's affection haunted her, constant reminders of all she had lost.

The maid who attended to her entered quietly, keeping her gaze low. 'Someone wishes to meet you, My Lady,' she said, her voice soft yet firm.

'Who is he, and why does he want to see me?' Suriratna asked.

'King Jayasena has sent him to help you understand the king's noble intentions,' the maid replied. Suriratna's spirits sank. She had no desire to endure another lecture about duty and marrying a man she did not love. But she nodded, too weary to argue. As the maid left, Suriratna tried to steel herself for the encounter.

When the door creaked open, she refused to acknowledge the visitor and continued to stare out the window. Then she heard a voice softly say, 'Namo Buddhaaya.'

A familiar chord stirred within Suriratna. *What was it about that voice?* She spun around. It took a moment to recognize the figure standing near the door. He wore a monk's ochre robes, his head was shaved clean. A lean frame, mahogany complexion ... Bhadraketu! *Her brother!*

Relief washed over her, and she sprang from her seat, disbelief widening her eyes. 'Bhadraketu!' she breathed.

Her brother's face mirrored her shock. 'Suriratna,' he whispered, stepping forward. 'I never imagined ... Jayasena told me of a young lady called Sembavalam who needed guidance, but I never imagined it would be you.'

Tears welled in Suriratna's eyes as she rushed to him and embraced him tightly. They clung to each other, drawing strength from the unexpected reunion.

A million questions were swirling in Suriratna's head. *When and how did you come here? What are you doing serving a king who has kept me captive?* But all she could get herself to say was, 'God be praised, I get to see you again.'

Bhadraketu smiled gently, his voice warm. 'The Buddha has been kind to grant us this moment. I never thought I would find family in this distant land.' They held each other a few moments longer, as if to make up for the lost years and the harsh journeys that had brought them both to this point.

Then, with a breath that seemed to steady them both, Bhadraketu slowly pulled back to look at her. His expression grew serious. 'We need a solution,' he said softly. 'Jayasena will not be easily swayed. He will dig in his heels if he discovers you are my sister. I am, after all, his trusted advisor ... he will expect me to convince you. But first, tell me how you arrived here.'

Dread twisting in her gut, Suriratna nodded. Rapidly, she relayed the events in Geumgwan, Korkai and Dimašq. She also filled him in on her relationship with Soju. Having absorbed the details, Bhadraketu said, 'I always felt there was a deeper connection between you and Soju. I am happy for you that you found your soulmate. But why the name Sembavalam?'

'I feared Jayasena might be an ally of Vidushika,' Suriratna explained. 'Concealing my identity felt safer. "Suriratna", as you know, means a precious jewel in Sanskrit; "Sembavalam" means the same in Tamil.' She laughed, the sound startling to her own ears after days of silence.

Bhadraketu nodded. 'We must tread carefully,' he said. 'I will find a way to get you out. But for now you must follow my lead. Show no resistance. Let Jayasena believe you are considering his proposal. He is a decent man ... just misguided for the moment.'

Though Suriratna knew he was right, the thought of deception left a bitter taste in her mouth. 'I will try,' she answered, forcing her voice to remain steady.

Bhadraketu squeezed her hands reassuringly. 'I promise you will not remain trapped. You will see Soju again. Stay strong and trust me.'

Footsteps resounded in the hall. Bhadraketu straightened, his expression smoothing into the serene mask of a monk. 'Remember, you are not alone,' he said, turning towards the door.

Hope and anxiety warred within Suriratna as she watched him depart. The path ahead would be fraught with danger, yet for the first time since her imprisonment, she felt a flicker of hope. Her brother was here; together, they would find a way out.

The maid returned, her eyes flitting towards the door. 'Did the rajguru help you see reason, My Lady?' she inquired, her tone carefully neutral.

Suriratna nodded, summoning a smile. 'Indeed. I am ... considering the king's proposal.' The maid, her mission seemingly accomplished, bowed and departed. Suriratna collapsed back onto her seat, her heart racing. Closing her eyes, she drew a long, steadying breath. She had to be strong, for herself—and for her brother.

∾

Bhadraketu headed back into the jungle, seeking out the open clearing favoured by Mahidol, rather than his own cottage. The soothsayer sat cross-legged on the ground, a thin trail of smoke rising from the pipe he held to his lips. The earthy scent of burning tobacco and jungle herbs mingled with the night air. He inhaled deeply, then he exhaled, the smoke swirling around his head like ethereal tendrils.

He greeted Bhadraketu with a smile, offering him the pipe. Bhadraketu declined with a polite shake of his head and settled onto the ground beside him. He studied the scars that still marred the magician's skin—a legacy of the fire from which Bhadraketu had rescued him. It had taken two months of the monk's dedicated care before Mahidol could leave his cottage.

'I need your help,' Bhadraketu said.

Mahidol set down his pipe, his dark eyes meeting Bhadraketu's. Slowly, he brought a finger to his lips, gesturing for silence.

As the jungle whispered its secrets, Mahidol tilted his head, as if catching echoes of things unspoken. Bhadraketu waited, watching the soothsayer's expression shift—his eyes narrowing, jaw tightening ever so slightly.

It was only then that Bhadraketu understood: whatever forces Mahidol had sensed, they would not make this escape easy. The path to freedom had just grown darker—and more perilous.

78

Ayutthaya, Siam, Suvarnabhumi
Present-day Bangkok, Thailand
Around 2,000 years ago

As Mahidol stood in the shadow of Jayasena's grand palace, a resolute expression settled on his face. His nimble fingers uncapped the bamboo tube, and he poured its contents into the royal well. The rakkham vanished without a trace, leaving no sign of the chaos it would unleash.

Inside the palace, life bustled as usual. Servants hurried through hallways, courtiers conversed in hushed tones. Jayasena's queens, draped in silk and jewels, gathered in the central courtyard, their laughter echoing through the space. But beneath the surface, something was amiss—the water that flowed through the palace now carried an invisible, potent threat. Oblivious to the danger, they sipped fruit sherbets prepared with water drawn from the poisoned well. The rakkham worked its insidious magic, transforming the scene. Flushed cheeks gave way to racking coughs, laughter turned to agonized gasps and retching. Panicked servants rushed to help.

Within hours, the palace was in disarray. One by one, those who had consumed the water collapsed—queens, courtiers, guards, even the kitchen staff. The once-vibrant heart of Ayutthaya pulsed with panic and pain. As cries of distress echoed through the halls, the realization dawned that something unnatural had taken root.

King Jayasena, too, had partaken of the cursed water. Now he slumped on his throne, pallid and sweating, his breath rasping through fevered lips. His commanding presence had dwindled to a shadow. The palace physician moved from chamber to chamber in desperation, unable to decipher the cause of this catastrophe.

But the rakkham was unlike any known affliction—its effects swift, unrelenting.

Jayasena summoned Bhadraketu, his trusted advisor. When the monk arrived, bringing with him his usual calm, the king asked with a hoarse croak, 'O Rajguru, what evil is this? Why do my queens, my courtiers, my servants fall as leaves before a storm?'

Bhadraketu knelt, his face grim. 'A grievous illness has befallen us, O King. I fear poisoning. From the symptoms, it appears to be rakkham—milkweed. Its essence can seep into the groundwater if left unchecked.'

Alarm flared in Jayasena's eyes. 'What can be done? How can we save everyone?'

Bhadraketu hesitated before speaking. 'An antidote grows deep in the forest, Your Majesty—the phlai herb. But it is fiercely guarded by Mahidol's forest tribes. We must negotiate with them. It is our only hope.'

Summoning his remaining strength, Jayasena called for Mahidol, who entered, feigning concern. 'You summoned me, My King?'

'Mahidol, my people are dying of a potent poison. Bhadraketu speaks of a curative herb in your forest. I beseech you, allow us to harvest it. Instruct your tribes to permit this.'

Mahidol's face hardened. 'I have always been your loyal servant, Your Majesty,' he said smoothly. 'I will give the necessary orders. But the herb's power can only be activated by a drop of blood.'

'Anyone here can provide that,' Jayasena said shakily.

'It must be the blood of a virgin princess,' Mahidol countered. 'Without it, the herb will be useless. And …'

'And?'

'Your Majesty,' Mahidol said reluctantly. 'There are no unmarried princesses in the extended royal family. A commoner's blood would offend the phlai goddess.'

Despair threatened to consume Jayasena, childless and facing his kingdom's ruin, until Bhadraketu's steady voice intervened. 'O King, I believe, from my conversations, that Lady Sembavalam is of royal lineage. She could activate the herb if she were willing.'

Pride warred with desperation, but finally Jayasena nodded. 'So be it. Request Lady Sembavalam to journey with you into the forest. Mahidol, you will guide them.'

~

Confusion clouded Suriratna's face when the maid came for her, speaking in hushed tones. 'The king is gravely ill, My Lady. Many others too—the palace is in chaos.'

Panic flared in her chest, but the sight of Bhadraketu waiting in the corridor stilled her. His presence, calm and steady, was like a balm. If he was here, she reasoned, there was still hope.

She listened carefully to his whispered instructions, noting the urgency behind his composure, and followed him towards the clearing where they found Mahidol, her heart pounding.

Mahidol trudged ahead, leading them through the dense undergrowth, his movements wary and deliberate.

The forest grew darker, more primeval, as they moved ahead—the trees were taller, the canopy thicker. The scent of decaying leaves assaulted them. The path they had taken dwindled to a mere suggestion beneath the tangled undergrowth, but Mahidol navigated the wilderness with confidence. All along the way, Bhadraketu's concerned gaze never strayed far from Suriratna.

At last, they reached the sacred grove. The clearing was alight with an ethereal glow, the fabled phlai herb luminous amidst the shadows. Mahidol guided Suriratna through a series of rituals, including pricking her finger for a drop of blood. He knew these were meaningless, but he also knew Jayasena's spies would be watching. He would ensure they had plenty of details to report back to the king. Rituals complete, Mahidol placed a small pouch in Suriratna's palm.

'Grind this into a paste and administer it to the afflicted,' he announced. 'Pounding the herb releases its healing essence.'

Suriratna nodded, her hands trembling as she took the precious bundle. Bhadraketu squeezed her shoulder reassuringly. 'You can do this,' he murmured.

Renewed determination straightened her spine as Suriratna turned back towards the palace. The return journey seemed shorter, but no less treacherous. Urgency spurred them forward, the promise of freedom a beacon in the darkness.

Upon reaching the palace, they went directly to the king's chambers. With shaking hands, Suriratna ground the herbs into a viscous, glowing paste, its luminescence fading to a dull shimmer.

'My Lord, the antidote is ready. We must administer it swiftly,' Bhadraketu urged.

Jayasena nodded weakly. Bhadraketu took charge, applying the paste to the parched lips of the king, his queens and his afflicted courtiers.

Gradually, colour returned to their faces, their breathing eased and a wave of renewed hope washed over the palace.

∼

As the kingdom clawed back from the brink of disaster, Bhadraketu approached Jayasena. 'Your Majesty, Lady Sembavalam has saved us. Imprisoned unjustly, she could have allowed many to perish. We must repay this kindness.'

Having regained his strength, Jayasena looked at Suriratna with gratitude. 'Your deed is beyond repayment, Princess,' he said. 'Name your heart's desire.'

'Great King, I desire only freedom,' Suriratna said softly. 'To journey to Geumgwan and reunite with my beloved.'

Jayasena's expression was contrite. 'Forgive me for having held you back, Lady Sembavalam. Treat it as the whim of a fool.'

Suriratna smiled. 'I am grateful for every kindness you have shown me, Your Majesty,' she said. 'You have been a generous host.'

'Your wish shall be granted,' the king told Suriratna. 'I will arrange for your journey and provide all you require. Go with my blessing and may you find the happiness you deserve.'

'And I request some days of leave to accompany the princess,' Bhadraketu added, 'to ensure her safe passage.'

'There is no need,' Jayasena said. 'My soldiers will protect her.'

'My Lord,' Bhadraketu reminded him, his voice measured. 'When I accepted my role as rajguru, you promised that should I choose to leave, you would not hinder me. I ask now that you honour that promise.'

The king looked away for a moment as though collecting his thoughts. 'It will grieve me to see you go,' he said at last, 'but so be it. A promise is a promise. I grant you permission to leave but ardently hope that you will return one day.'

Tears of gratitude welled in Suriratna's eyes. Bhadraketu bowed deeply, his heart lighter than it had been in days. The road ahead would be long, but for the first time, the path seemed clear, illuminated by hope.

∽

Later, Mahidol said to Bhadraketu, 'I always believed you abhorred lies and deception. What changed, my friend?'

Bhadraketu laughed. 'You have not studied the *Lotus Sutra*, I see. It contains the "Parable of the Burning House"—an illustration of upaya, or skilful means.'

'And what is that?' Mahidol asked.

'The parable tells of a wealthy man with a vast house filled with children,' Bhadraketu explained. 'When the house catches fire, the children, engrossed in their games, ignore the danger. Realizing they may not understand the urgency—or perhaps even be paralysed by fear—the father employs a clever ruse: he tells them that wondrous new toys await outside. Excited, the children rush out, unharmed. Now, would you call that deception—or a deft solution?'

79

Eudaemon, Kingdom of Himyar
Present-day Aden, Yemen
Around 2,000 years ago

The factory pulsed with activity, the clanging metal and hissing furnaces creating a music of their own. Having brought his most skilled ironsmiths from Dimašq, Barakat had established a temporary forge at Eudaemon, streamlining maritime transport to meet Soju's urgent needs.

Securing a location near the harbour had required delicate negotiations with Himyar's ruler. The ageing king had consolidated his control over the lucrative incense trade routes, both on land and sea. Once a polytheist, he had embraced Judaism, and wielded his newfound power to construct impressive monuments and quell rebellions with an iron fist. Mithra and Barakat had enlisted his cooperation by promising him a steady supply of weapons.

Sweat drenched the workers' bodies as they moved with practised efficiency. The forge's heat, mingled with the acrid smell of molten iron, saturated the air, infusing it with a sense of purpose. Barakat, a commanding presence, paced through the bustling space, his sharp eyes assessing each station. He paused every now and then to inspect a sword, a dagger, an arrowhead or shield, ensuring they were of the finest quality. Each bore the distinctive crossed-swords fish symbol and the wavy nav utsa surface.

Mithra approached him, his forehead creased with worry. 'The carrier pigeon from Korkai brings troubling news, Barakat. Soju has returned to Geumgwan, but his father is dead, murdered by the enemy. Suriratna had sailed to aid him, but her ship vanished somewhere along the route. It seems fate is against us.'

Barakat shook his head, his jaw set in a firm line. 'The tide will turn, My Lord. We labour tirelessly to equip Kim Suro's forces. Those Korkai ingots are vital. Each arriving ship spurs us onward. We transform each ingot into weaponry with matchless skill. Our craftsmanship will arm your friend's warriors; each blade forged brings him that much closer to victory.'

In one corner, blacksmiths hammered at the glowing iron, their rhythmic strikes shaping it into lethal forms. Sparks erupted in fiery bursts, momentarily illuminating the forge. As he stood beside Barakat, Mithra watched them, noting the tension in the workers' shoulders, the unwavering focus in their movements.

'This Eudaemon forge operates at full capacity,' Barakat continued, pride and urgency in his voice. 'Our production here supplements the shipments arriving by caravan from Dimašq. I pray Cheliyan has increased ingot production at Korkai.'

A shadow of concern crossed Mithra's face. 'The ships from Korkai are reliable, but the journey to Geumgwan is fraught with peril. Our ships are ready to sail, but ensuring their safe passage is paramount. If pirates seize our cargo, it will further destabilize the high seas.'

'I have accounted for every contingency,' Barakat assured him. 'Strong ships, seasoned crews—troops from Dimašq and Korkai. I have even hired Roman reinforcements. Favourable winds and strong currents will carry us through.'

'And the plans for local ingot production?' Mithra inquired.

'Cheliyan and Kulasekara have sent the alchemy stones,' Barakat replied. 'Part will remain here, and part will be sent to Soju. Soon, the quality of ingots will be consistent across all regions.'

The doors to the forge swung open, ushering in a blast of cool night air. A breathless courier rushed in, sweat plastering his tunic to his skin. 'My Lord, the ships are ready to depart.'

Barakat turned to Mithra, a steely glint in his expression. 'It is time. We send them at first light. Our success hinges on flawless execution.'

As night surrendered to dawn, Barakat and Mithra oversaw the final preparations. Workers polished the last of the blades, their movements swift and precise. The finished weapons were packed into wooden crates, each box meticulously branded with the four-swords symbol using a red-hot iron.

In the stillness of the pre-dawn hour, Barakat and Mithra stood at the harbour's edge, looking at the two ships silhouetted against the horizon. Dawn broke, casting a warm glow over the ships and the restless sea. They watched as the crew boarded, their forms stark shadows against the burgeoning light. Sailors scurried about, securing cargo, completing final checks.

'Do they understand the gravity of their task?' Mithra wondered aloud. 'The significance of their mission?'

Barakat kept his focus on the departing ships. 'They know enough. They understand that what they carry could alter history. More importantly, they understand loyalty. Just as Kim Suro aided you in your time of need, you now aid him in his.'

A smile touched Mithra's lips. He turned his attention to the ships. 'Safe travels,' he whispered, a prayer for their journey.

The ships set sail, slicing through the calm waters. There was no turning back now.

80

Ayodhya, Uttar Pradesh, India
Present day

A convoy of cars transported Aditya, Somi, Ramaswamy, Jung and Jayaraman to the Queen Heo Memorial Park. They emerged from their vehicles, their steps measured and deliberate as they surveyed the sprawling park.

'The buildings here blend Korean and Indian architectural styles, honouring the ancient—and largely forgotten—connection between the two nations,' explained Ramaswamy as they headed in. 'According to the *Samguk Yusa*, a thirteenth-century Korean chronicle, a princess from Ayodhya journeyed across the seas in 48 CE to marry a Korean king. To this day, many Koreans visit this site in Ayodhya to honour her as Queen Heo, their ancestral matriarch.'

Somi's thoughts drifted back to the day, a few weeks earlier, when she and Aditya had signed their partnership agreement in this very park. It felt like a lifetime ago. The memory was vivid—the whir of cameras, the anthems, the signing of documents. That day had marked a turning point for both her and their businesses. Unlike the countless other deals she had brokered, this one had felt different, significant.

She glanced at Aditya, his face a mask of concentration as he listened to Ramaswamy. For some reason, she couldn't tear her gaze away. He caught her looking his way and smiled. Somi smiled back, quickly averting her attention, a blush warming her cheeks.

'This memorial park is more than just a symbol of Indo-Korean history,' Ramaswamy continued. 'It also prominently features the twin-fish motif that we've encountered repeatedly—in Ayodhya's architecture, Pandyan symbology, the history of Damascus, Buddhist and Egyptian traditions and, even Korean legends. It suggests that the ancient technology that originated in Bharatvarsha may have spread, leaving traces in distant places like Korea and Syria.'

Aditya frowned. 'But this memorial park was only inaugurated in 2022,' he pointed out, gesturing towards the intricately designed structures. 'How could it possibly hold any ancient secret?'

'True, the park itself is a modern creation,' Ramaswamy conceded. 'However, consider this: an 8-ton stone that predates the park was transported from South Korea to India in 2001 for the memorial.'

'So?' Aditya pressed.

'Perhaps there was a reason for that stone to originate in Korea,' Ramaswamy suggested. 'Legend says the Indian princess who travelled to Korea brought stones with her. What if the Koreans were returning an ancient favour *two thousand years later*?'

Jung, ever the pragmatist, stroked his chin thoughtfully. 'It's possible,' he said. 'Stones and symbols can carry more than just cultural meaning. They can serve as repositories of knowledge, especially those transported across continents.'

The Korean pavilion, with its polished wood and sloping roof, stood in juxtaposition to the Indian gazebo made from white marble. The bridge connecting them arched gracefully over a small lake, reflecting the deepening hues of the sky. Further on, there stood a golden sculpture in the shape of an egg, a tribute to the legend of the six Korean kings born from six golden eggs. Near the centre, an abstract model of a ship represented the vessel that had carried the princess across the vast ocean, and tucked away in the park's southeast corner, a circle was engraved on the ground, enclosing the twin fish.

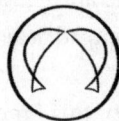

Jayaraman paused before the stone monument with interest, peering at the inscription upon its surface—a poetic tribute to Queen Heo in both Korean and Sanskrit. 'If something is hidden here, it is likely within the stone itself,' he murmured. 'We must examine it, perhaps even conduct some tests.'

A thrill of excitement shot through Somi. The prospect of uncovering ancient secrets within the stone was both exhilarating and daunting.

'It won't be easy,' Aditya cautioned, his voice low. Any physical sampling will require authorization from both countries. 'We must proceed discreetly. Any attention we draw could prove detrimental.'

Somi met his gaze, her expression resolute. 'We have to see this through. This stone could hold the key to secrets hidden for centuries. What if there is a reason that Korea sent this block here to Ayodhya?'

Ramaswamy, Jung and Jayaraman conferred, discussing possible methods of non-destructive testing. Somi kept her focus on the stone, a sense of anticipation building within her. Aditya and she had been on this path since the fateful day when they had signed the agreement, and only their shared determination would carry them to the end.

'We have a plan,' Ramaswamy announced. 'We'll use strontium isotope analysis to compare the stone's isotopic signature to samples from other regions to determine its geological origin.'

'And if that proves inconclusive?' Aditya asked.

Ramaswamy's voice brimmed with optimism. 'We can then explore other options—Fourier-transform infrared spectroscopy to detect organic compounds, petrographic analysis to identify its mineral composition, or X-ray diffraction to analyse its crystalline structure.'

Nearby, a group of tourists snapped photographs, chattering excitedly in Mandarin. Aditya and Somi, listening raptly to the plans ahead, remained unaware that their movements were being monitored, and their every action reported back to Pyongyang.

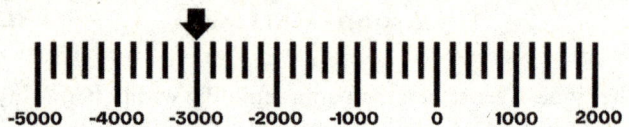

Kurukshetra, Kuru Rashtra

Present-day Ambala District, Haryana, India

Around 5,000 years ago

The battlefield erupted in turmoil—blades clashed, horses shrieked and soldiers cried out, either in triumph or pain. The air reeked of blood, decay and sweat. Thick dust and smoke obscured the gruesome scene in parts. At the heart of this pandemonium stood Bhima and Duryodhana, their gazes locked, each waiting for the other to strike.

Bhima, the mighty Pandava, tightened his grip on his mace, his massive frame radiating power. His body, scarred and weary from eighteen days of brutal fighting, bore the ravages of war. Duryodhana, the formidable Kaurava, stood ready with his own mace, fury burning in his eyes. This duel was the culmination of their bitter rivalry, a final confrontation that would determine the course of the war.

Drawn by the spectacle of their leaders' impending clash, the remaining soldiers—both Pandava and Kaurava—ceased their fighting and formed a circle to watch the clash of titans unfold. The Pandavas—Yudhishthira, Arjuna, Nakula and Sahadeva—stood alongside Krishna, their faces grim with tension. On the other side, Ashwatthama, Kripacharya and Kritavarma looked on, hope battling with dread in their hearts.

Earlier, desperate to regroup his shattered forces, Duryodhana had fled to a nearby lake, seeking solace in its cool embrace.

'Vidura knew how this would end,' he murmured, the water soothing his burning flesh. 'But what good is knowledge gained too late?'

Yudhishthira and his brothers, pursuing their enemy relentlessly, had arrived at the lake's edge. 'Duryodhana!' they had called out. 'Do you think you can escape death by hiding in a pond after causing the ruin of your family and your clan? Where is your pride? Have you no shame? Come out and face us. As a kshatriya, do you cower from battle and death?'

Stung by their words, Duryodhana had emerged from the water, mace in hand. 'I did not come here as a fugitive,' he declared. 'I entered the water to quell the fire that burns within me. I neither cling to life nor fear death. Why should I continue this fight? There is nothing left to protect. All those who stood with me are gone. I no longer desire the kingdom. I leave the world to you, without a rival. Rule it as you see fit.'

'How generous of you,' Yudhishthira had replied, his voice rich with sarcasm. 'After vowing to deny us even a sliver of land, after rejecting our pleas for peace, you now offer us everything. Let me remind you, we do not fight for land or a kingdom. Must I recount your numerous transgressions? Only your death can atone for the wrongs you have inflicted upon us, for the outrage you visited upon Draupadi.'

'Come at me, one by one, then, for I stand alone. Surely, the five of you would not together attack a solitary, weary, wounded man, stripped of his armour?' Duryodhana had challenged defiantly.

'Tell me, how was Abhimanyu slain?' Yudhishthira had retorted. 'Did you not sanction his death at the hands of multiple warriors while he stood alone in your ranks? How ironic that men invoke dharma only when it suits their purpose. Choose any one of us and fight. Either die and ascend to heaven, or emerge victorious and rule.'

Without hesitation, Duryodhana had pointed to Bhima. The grudge between them was the oldest and deepest—fuelled by years of rivalry and humiliation.

Both warriors were evenly matched in strength and skill—except in one regard. It was believed that Duryodhana possessed a secret advantage: his mother, Gandhari, had anointed his body with a formula that rendered him invulnerable. But few knew the full truth. When Gandhari had been persuaded to use her latent spiritual energy to protect her son, she had asked Duryodhana to present himself unclothed. Her eyes, blindfolded in solidarity with her husband, long shielded from the world, had accumulated a potent inner heat—tapas—that could activate the protective properties of the anointing formulation.

Yet, as Duryodhana had undressed himself in preparation to be anointed, Krishna had intervened—subtly, strategically—suggesting that the Kaurava display some modesty in front of his mother. Shamed and hesitant, Duryodhana had worn a loincloth while visiting Gandhari. Thus, while the rest of his body absorbed the formula's full potency through Gandhari's focused energy, his thighs remained untreated—an oversight that would eventually prove fatal. Krishna, Vishnu's avatar on earth, knew of the formula's source—a deep pit in a grove in Rama's Ayodhya nagari—and its power to repel even the deadliest weapons.

Now, as Bhima and Duryodhana circled each other, Bhima charged with a roar that shook the very ground of Kurukshetra. Duryodhana parried the blow, countering with a powerful strike of his own. Their maces collided, each impact testimony to their might. The battle continued for hours, neither warrior yielding an inch.

'Is this all you have, Bhima?' Duryodhana taunted. 'Your will is no match for my skill. Today, you and your dishonourable brothers will fall!' Despite his arrogant taunt, Duryodhana felt unsettled. His endurance was being challenged by his most formidable and relentless enemy. He sought comfort in remembering his training, the countless hours spent honing his movements against an iron effigy of Bhima. But as he faced the real Bhima, he realized that all that training had not prepared him for his opponent's ferocity.

As the duel continued and the onlookers debated the outcome, Krishna announced, his voice carrying across the battlefield, 'Bhima will break Duryodhana's thighs. He will fulfil his vow to avenge Draupadi's humiliation.' It was a strategically timed statement. Fury blazed in Bhima's heart as he recalled that harrowing day in the Kaurava court: Draupadi dragged by her hair, her sari pulled in an attempt to strip her before the assembly and Duryodhana, with cruel arrogance, patting his thigh lasciviously and inviting her to sit on it. The memory seared Bhima's soul. His vow surged to the fore and his rage became an inferno.

At that moment, across the clearing, Krishna caught Bhima's eye. Without a word, he slapped his own thigh—a subtle but unmistakable signal. In a flash, Bhima saw his opportunity. He feinted left, drawing Duryodhana's attention, then shifting his weight with lightning speed, he brought his mace crashing down on Duryodhana's exposed thigh.

The sickening crunch of bone shattering could be heard even above the din of war. Duryodhana's scream echoed across the battlefield. He collapsed, his mace falling from his grasp, pain and disbelief filling his eyes as he clutched his broken thigh. Bhima stood over him, chest heaving, his face a mask of righteous fury. 'This is for Draupadi,' he hissed. 'Your downfall comes by the very limb you used to taunt and shame her in the midst of the court.'

Duryodhana glared up at him, his features twisted with anguish and hatred. 'You treacherous cur! You violated the rules of combat! Where is your honour?' he roared, referencing the sacred rules of mace fighting, which forbade strikes below the waist. A hush fell over the battlefield as Duryodhana writhed in agony.

'You dare speak of honour?' Bhima spat. 'After breaking every rule yourself? You invoked your mother's protection—her powerful tapas combined with the Dvaitalingam would have shielded you if you had not worn a loincloth.'

Krishna, observing the scene, nodded thoughtfully. The Kauravas had to be vanquished and sometimes justice demanded unconventional means.

A mere loincloth had been Duryodhana's undoing.

81

Geumgwan, Garak Confederacy
Present-day Gimhae, South Korea
Around 2,000 years ago

The ship's wooden hull groaned as it sliced through the azure waves. Suriratna stood at the prow, her hair whipping around her face, her focus fixed on the distant horizon. Beside her, Bhadraketu leaned against the railing, watching the endless expanse of water stretching before them.

Their journey, facilitated by Jayasena's generosity, had been a gruelling three-week ordeal of relentless sailing. The sun had risen and set over the vast ocean as days blurred into one another until, finally, the faint outline of Geumgwan's coastline emerged.

The Garak shoreline buzzed with activity. Talhae's threat had placed the entire region on high alert. Several Geumgwan vessels, their sails billowing, darted out to intercept the unknown ship. Tension crackled in the air as the two crews watched each other warily, their intentions unclear. Soldiers on both sides gripped their weapons, aware that the slightest provocation could spark a catastrophic conflict.

Bhadraketu moved swiftly, scanning the deck until he located the captain near the helm. A silent nod and a curt gesture conveyed his unspoken command. Immediately, the captain issued the order: lower the Siam flag, raise the Pandyan banner.

As the banner unfurled, its bold patterns drew the attention of the onlookers.

On the shore, Soju was in the middle of an inspection when he was informed about the approaching vessel. He stood rigid, his attention fixed on the distant ship. His heart pounded as the familiar flag bearing the twin fish became visible. *Could it be?* Hope glimmered anew within him. He watched, unblinking, as the ship came in to dock, a coastguard skiff pulling alongside.

Suriratna and Bhadraketu climbed into the waiting boat. Suriratna searched the faces on the shore, her pulse quickening as she spotted Soju, his profile unmistakable even from a distance.

Soju's breath caught in his throat as the smaller craft drew near. The setting sun had cast a golden halo around Suriratna, her yellow sari radiating a warm luminescence. She looked every bit an angel descending from the heavens.

The moment the boat touched the sand, Soju could restrain himself no longer. He sprinted towards the water's edge, his world shrinking to the single vision of Suriratna stepping ashore. Before her feet even touched solid ground, he had swept her into a crushing embrace, his arms wrapping around her as if she were his anchor. Suriratna clung to him just as fiercely, tears streaming down her face. Words were unnecessary.

Bhadraketu watched their reunion, a smile of contentment spreading across his weathered features. Relief washed over him. They had made it. Their journey had been fraught with peril, but seeing his sister in Soju's arms made every harrowing moment worthwhile.

The residents of Geumgwan observed the scene with a mix of curiosity and astonishment. The Pandyan flag had signalled a friendly arrival and their leader's emotional reunion with this unknown woman dispelled any lingering doubts. The intercept fleet now bobbed idly, their crews transformed into spectators.

Finally, Soju released Suriratna, cupping her face in his calloused hands. Disbelief and joy mingled in his expression. 'Suriratna,' he said, his voice nearly lost amidst the gentle lapping of waves. She returned his gaze, offering a radiant smile, her hands covering his. A shadow of sadness crossed Soju's face, but she silenced him with a look. Explanations could wait.

Their attention shifted to Bhadraketu, who had respectfully remained at a distance, granting them privacy. Soju moved towards him, extending his hand. Bhadraketu clasped it firmly, and the two men embraced before stepping back and patting each other on the shoulder. A silent, brotherly understanding passed between them.

Hand in hand, Soju and Suriratna led the way towards the waiting crowd, with Bhadraketu following close behind. Soju's men formed a protective circle around them, preventing the couple from being overwhelmed. The threat from Talhae remained and vigilance was paramount.

In the bustling town square, Soju faced the gathered crowd. Expectant eyes locked onto him as he stepped forward, Suriratna at his side. 'This is Suriratna,' he declared, pride and love resounding in his voice. 'She hails from the Pandyan kingdom, a distant land where my beloved abeoji sent me for my education. Her name means "precious gem", and indeed, she is priceless to me. In honour of her journey and to welcome her into our land and lineage, we bestow upon her a name rooted in our tradition—Heo Hwang-ok—for she embodies the rarest and most precious jade, a gem of immeasurable value.'

82

Geumgwan, Garak Confederacy
Present-day Gimhae, South Korea
Around 2,000 years ago

Kim Seok and Kim Hwa's residence was empty. Soju's mother had retired for the night, her heart still heavy. Her brief meeting with Suriratna had done little to ease her sorrow. Her happiness for Soju, at his having found his soulmate, was overshadowed by her own cruel loss.

Soju tossed and turned in his bed, sleep a distant shore he could not reach. He rose, dressed quickly and slung his trusted sword—a gift from Mithra—across his back. Slipping out of the house, he headed towards the boarding house near the riverbank where Suriratna and Bhadraketu were staying. Crossing the bridge over the lotus pond, he followed a narrow path that led to Suriratna's chamber. His gentle knock was answered almost immediately. She had been waiting.

Moonlight spilled through the intricate wooden lattice, painting patterns on the walls. The gentle murmur of the river rushing by mingled with the distant sounds of nocturnal creatures, created a soothing symphony. Suriratna's ruby red sari clung to her, the fabric catching the light with every movement. Her long, black hair flowed freely down her back, kissed by the lantern's glow. Soju's heart quickened.

Their eyes met and it was as they had never been apart. Tonight was theirs, stolen from the demands of duty. Suriratna moved towards him, her bare feet silent on the polished floor. Soju reached out, his fingers tracing the delicate curve of her cheek. At his touch, Suriratna drew in a sharp breath. She closed her eyes, leaning into his hand, pressing a kiss to his palm.

'You are everything good and beautiful, my love,' he whispered, his voice husky with longing.

Her eyes fluttered open, a smile curving her lips. 'And you, my Soju, are as handsome as ever,' she replied, her voice a soft melody.

He pulled her close, his arms encircling her waist. He could feel the warmth of her body through the fine silk, her breath against his chest. He lowered his head, his lips meeting hers in a tender, lingering kiss. The kiss deepened, both surrendering to the joy of being reunited, the years of longing melting away.

Her hands slid up to tangle in his hair as the kiss grew more fervent, more demanding. His hands moved over her back, pulling her closer, moulding her curves against his body. Heat grew between them, a fire that burned brighter with each passing moment.

Soju broke away, gazing down at her, his thumb gently stroking her cheek. 'Suriratna,' he murmured, 'every moment of being apart from you has been an eternity.'

Her smile deepened, her fingers tracing the contours of his face. 'And you …' she whispered, echoing his desire. 'You have never left my thoughts, my Soju.'

He lifted her effortlessly into his arms and carried her to the simple wooden bed draped with cushions and embroidered linens. The world around them receded. The bed, with its simple canopy, became their sanctuary.

He laid her gently upon the bed, his hands working to loosen her sari. Their eyes remained locked, their unspoken emotions a silent language passing between them. Her skin glowed in the soft light as the fabric fell away. Soju paused, drinking in the sight of her. 'You are breathtaking, my Suriratna,' he whispered.

She reached up, her fingers deftly unbuttoning his shirt, her touch sending a jolt of desire through him. His clothes joined hers on the floor, and they came together, their bodies entwined, moving in perfect harmony, lost in the moment. His breath warmed her skin, his movements growing more urgent, more possessive. He whispered her name, his voice raw with need, sending shivers down her spine. Her fingers dug into his back, pulling him closer.

Later, they lay nestled together, breathing as one, their hearts beating in rhythm. 'I love you,' he whispered. She felt the steady tempo of his heart beneath her hand. 'And I adore you,' she replied. 'You are my love, my soulmate. I am yours, in every way.' Their troubles receded as they drifted into a peaceful sleep.

Outside the boarding house, four figures stood watch. One had followed Soju; another had been spying on the boarding house; a third monitored Bhadraketu; the fourth was stationed beneath Suriratna's window. Even this most intimate moment had been observed, and would be reported to Talhae later.

83

Ara, Garak Confederacy
Present-day Haman County, South Korea
Around 2,000 years ago

The city-state of Ara was the smallest member of the Garak Confederacy but was centrally located for the remaining armies to train in. In Ara's sprawling training grounds, hundreds of soldiers from the four allied regions—Geumgwan, Bihwa, Bangam and Ara itself—were engaged in a relentless drill. Now that former members of the Confederacy—Seongsang, Goryeong and Daegaya—were under Talhae's control, it was only a matter of time before he came for the rest.

An atmosphere of intense concentration pervaded the training grounds. Soldiers sparred, their blades ringing with precise, purposeful strikes. Archers loosed arrow after arrow, each shaft finding its mark in the straw-stuffed targets. Spearmen practised in unison, the tips of their weapons flashing as they thrust and parried. Officers barked commands, the ground vibrating beneath the rhythmic march of disciplined feet. The scents of sweat, dust and metal mingled in the air. Each battalion was pushed to its limit, forged into a cohesive, formidable force. Their coordinated movements embodied the urgent bond created in response to a common enemy.

A large tent stood in the north-eastern corner of the field, its entrance guarded by soldiers from the four allied territories.

Inside, the chiefs of Geumgwan, Bihwa, Bangam and Ara huddled around a rough-hewn wooden table, a map of the Garak Confederacy spread before them. Soju had assumed the role of interim chief of Geumgwan under a council resolution. The other three chiefs—Jinhyeok of Bihwa, Wonsik of Bangam and Yongho of Ara—knew that unity was no longer a choice but a necessity.

'My worry is we have the men but inadequate weapons,' Soju said. 'It will be a while before the foundry is fully operational.'

'Our only option is to attack,' Jinhyeok declared, his weathered face set in a grim expression. 'Talhae has proven himself to be ruthless and cunning. Hesitation will only embolden him.'

Wonsik, a burly man with a voice like thunder, slammed his fist on the table. 'We cannot allow him to conquer us piecemeal. He already controls Seongsang, Goryeong and Daegaya. Who will be next? We must strike with all our might—as one.'

Just then a messenger entered the tent and whispered in Soju's ear. A smile brightened Soju's face as he addressed the others. 'We were discussing our lack of weaponry. My father had begun the process of rearmament, attempting to get the foundry reactivated. Tragically, he was murdered before production could start.'

'Surely we can do that now?' Yongho asked hopefully.

'It will take days to get the Geumgwan foundry operational again,' Soju admitted, 'time we do not have.' Disappointment settled over the other chiefs.

'However,' Soju continued, 'I am pleased to announce that two ships laden with swords, spears, shields, knives and arrowheads have arrived.'

'From your allies in Korkai?' Jinhyeok asked hopefully.

'No, these are from Dimašq,' Soju revealed. 'My friend Mithra had them forged in Eudaemon and shipped across the vast ocean. The craftsmanship from both Korkai and Dimašq is exceptional. This shipment will bridge the gap until our own foundry is operational.'

Applause broke out, the chiefs' relief evident. Soju's presence in their alliance was proving invaluable.

'I agree, we cannot wait for Talhae to strike,' Soju said. 'We must seize the initiative. His attacks on Goryeong and Daegaya succeeded due to timing, surprise and advantageous terrain. We must deny him those advantages.'

Yongho, the eldest of the group, stroked his greying beard. 'Timing is paramount. A poorly planned assault could be disastrous. We need more than just brute strength; we need strategy.'

'Surprise will be difficult,' Jinhyeok muttered, tracing a line on the map with his finger. 'Talhae anticipates our attack. He has spies watching our every move. I would not be shocked to learn his men have infiltrated our ranks.' He gestured towards the soldiers training outside.

'Then we need something to divert his attention,' Wonsik suggested.

'I have an idea,' Soju offered. The other chiefs turned to him expectantly.

'You possess far greater wisdom and experience than me,' Soju said humbly. 'But in Dimašq, our strategic alliance with the Nabataeans proved crucial in securing victory.'

'What are you suggesting?' Wonsik asked.

'The *Arthashastra*, an ancient treatise of Bharatvarsha, outlines five broad strategies,' Soju explained, recalling his lessons from Acharya Satyamuni. 'One of these is perfectly suited to our situation.'

'What strategies?' Yongho inquired.

'First, sandhi—a treaty, beneficial for maintaining stability,' Soju explained. 'That is not an option. Talhae seeks no peace with us.'

'Go on,' Wonsik said, intrigued.

'Second, asana—strategic neutrality, maintaining the status quo,' Soju continued. 'This, too, is unfeasible. We cannot afford disinterest. Neutrality will only allow Talhae to devour us one by one.'

He paused, meeting the gazes of the other chiefs. They hung on to his every word. 'Third, sansraya—seeking alliances to counter a threat. That will not work. Any appeal to the Three Kingdoms would likely result in them turning on us instead.'

'Let us just attack,' Wonsik said, his patience wearing thin.

Soju smiled, ignoring the outburst. 'Then there is vigraha—active conflict. We will inevitably engage Talhae in battle, but first we require something else.'

'And that is?' Jinhyeok prompted.

'Yana—war preparation,' Soju replied. 'Signalling our readiness to attack or defend.'

'But we are already preparing,' Yongho pointed out. 'And Talhae knows it. His spies keep him informed.'

'True,' Soju conceded. 'But our Confederacy is insignificant compared to the Three Kingdoms that surround us: Silla to the east, Baekje to the west, and Goguryeo to the north.'

'You want to draw them into the conflict?' Yongho asked, alarm creeping into his voice. 'That would be disastrous. We are vulnerable. Any of the Three Kingdoms would gladly swallow us whole.'

Outside, the sound of marching intensified as a new contingent joined the training exercises. The chiefs listened to the growing rhythm of unity. A thoughtful silence fell over the group as they considered Yongho's words.

'I propose a feint,' Soju finally said. 'Something to occupy Talhae's forces. We need him to *believe* he is about to be attacked by Silla, Baekje or Goguryeo. That way, his attention will be elsewhere when we strike.'

'How do we achieve that without forging an alliance?' Jinhyeok asked.

'Here's what I propose ...'

84

Saketa, Kosala

Present-day Ayodhya, Uttar Pradesh, India

Around 2,000 years ago

Somadatta and his accomplices—Bhagurayana, Vatsadhara and the former soldier Keshava—moved swiftly through the shadows, the Sarayu river shimmering serenely beside them. As they approached the sacred cave of Hanuman Garhi, anticipation tightened their nerves. Had Padmasen's masons executed their task flawlessly?

Hanuman Garhi, a cave fortified with piled stones, was revered as one of Saketa's holiest sites. Legend had it that Hanuman had resided here after Rama's return from Lanka and even after his passing, fulfilling his role as guardian for many years. He had eventually departed for the Kamyaka forest near Kurukshetra to offer his powerful blessings to another Vayuputra, Bhima, before the war in Kurukshetra millennia later.

Inside the cave, a stone idol depicted Hanuman seated upon his mother Anjani's lap, a tulsi garland adorning his neck, each leaf inscribed with the name 'Sitaram'. Hanuman faced southward, as a promise to Sita to keep a watch on Lanka, protecting Saketa from harm, danger and fear. Today, the cave seemed to vibrate with an unusual energy, as if anticipating the turmoil to come.

'I trust everything is in place,' Somadatta murmured, his words barely audible above the rustle of leaves. Bhagurayana and Vatsadhara nodded, their faces grim. Keshava, the oldest among them, checked his weapon, his movements reflecting a soldier's ingrained vigilance.

'Preparations are complete. I remained with the group until late last night,' Keshava confirmed, his voice gruff. 'But caution is paramount. One misstep, and we are undone.'

A confident smile touched Somadatta's lips. 'Fear not, old friend. All will proceed as planned.'

As the first devotees of the day arrived at Hanuman Garhi, a wave of shock rippled through the crowd. The Hanuman idol, which faced south, had inexplicably turned northward. Panic seized the crowd, and soon the site swarmed with anxious citizens and priests.

'How is this possible?' a woman cried, clutching her prayer beads.

'It is an omen,' another whispered, her face pale with fear.

Somadatta's carefully chosen priests, primed for this moment, stepped forward, examining the idol with theatrical concern, even attempting to rotate it back to its original position. However, it remained stubbornly fixed. Somadatta concealed a triumphant grin. Padmasen's masons had excelled.

'Summon more men,' one of the Brahmins commanded. 'We must harness the strength of the community.'

Townsmen joined the effort, but even their combined might could not budge Hanuman. Tension mounted as rumours of divine wrath spread like wildfire.

Finally, the head priest, a man renowned for his wisdom, addressed the crowd. 'Hanuman faced south, guarding against threats from Lanka. Now he gazes north, warning us of a new danger.'

Murmurs spread through the crowd as another priest spoke. 'Consider what lies north of here,' he suggested.

'Only Vidushika's palace,' Bhagurayana interjected strategically.

Silence fell as his words sank in. A priest known for his astrological expertise declared, 'The danger from the north must be Kadphises and Vidushika. When Vidushika is gone, Hanuman will resume his rightful position.'

His words ignited the crowd. Fuelled by fear and anger, and spurred on by Bhagurayana and Vatsadhara's incendiary whispers, they headed towards the palace and stormed the royal gates. Vidushika's forces attempted to hold their ground, but Keshava's covert efforts over many months had sown seeds of doubt and dissent among them, causing many to desert.

Vidushika was seized within his palace and dragged through the streets by a jeering mob. The once-powerful king, now a pathetic figure, his robes torn, his face a mask of disbelief and panic, was imprisoned in the same dank, fetid cell that had once held Padmasen.

'Ensure he is not harmed,' Somadatta instructed his men. 'We must maintain the illusion of divine intervention.'

That night, a venomous snake found its way into Vidushika's cell. A silent assassin, its deadly work would appear a natural event, orchestrated by the heavens. Vidushika was dead, never to be heard from again.

Meanwhile, outside the cave, the Brahmins had begun their rituals, their fervent chants rising into the night, even as

Somadatta's masons prepared for the next stage of the plan. Wielding their nav utsa chisels, they carefully separated the idol from its newly welded base. By morning, the idol faced west, deepening the mystery and amplifying the people's unease.

'Why does the deity no longer face south?' the devotees questioned. 'Our Hanumanji always faces south.'

'Bajrangbali will only face south when the true king rules Saketa,' the Brahmins declared, their words reinforcing the carefully crafted narrative.

Seizing the opportunity, Somadatta stepped forward. 'There is only one rightful ruler … We all know this,' he proclaimed. 'Padmasen, the 157th Dvaitalingam Rakshak, the protector of Rama and Lakshmana's legacy. Let us bring him back!'

The crowd, primed for action, erupted in cheers. Somadatta's plan had worked flawlessly. Hanuman's enigmatic shift had paved the way for Padmasen's return. The sway of collective belief was a formidable force. The ancient gurus had been right: deception was the very foundation of warfare.

Somadatta surveyed Saketa with satisfaction as a thrill of excitement coursed through the city. The power of faith and the precision of their scheme had set the stage for a new era. 'What news of Padmasen?' he asked Vatsadhara.

'He is already en route,' Vatsadhara replied. 'He should be arriving any day.'

85

Geumgwan, Garak Confederacy

Present-day Gimhae, South Korea

Around 2,000 years ago

The sun beat down as Suriratna and Soju approached Kim Seok's old foundry. The gates creaked open, revealing a desolate facility. It had been operating at negligible capacity when Kim Seok began devoting more time to the Confederacy. After his death, it had fallen dormant.

A pang of sorrow struck Soju as he entered the vast space. 'It feels so much emptier without Abeoji,' he murmured.

Suriratna squeezed his shoulder reassuringly. 'We will revive it, Soju. I promise you.'

She looked around the space, taking in every detail—the large clay furnace at its heart, the bellows beside it, the slag pit nearby that was filled with the remnants of past smelting. Rows of crucibles and moulds lined the walls, whispering tales of countless hours of labour. The quenching tanks, large and rectangular, their water murky and still from months of disuse. Anvils of various sizes, mounted on sturdy blocks, awaited the blacksmith's hammer. Grinding stones, connected to foot pedals and hand cranks, stood ready to sharpen blades. Shelves and racks held an array of tools—tongs, hammers, chisels—each bearing the marks of use and time. Leather aprons and gloves dangled from hooks, waiting for the men that once wore them. Every element, from the towering furnace to the smallest chisel, spoke of quality and dedication.

Soju paused before the anvil where he had often watched his father work. 'I remember the first time he let me hold the hammer,' he said, his voice awash with nostalgia. 'He would guide my hands, teaching me the rhythm of the strikes.'

As they ventured deeper into the foundry, workers who had remained loyal to Kim Seok began to gather, drawn by news of Soju and Suriratna's arrival. Dae-Hyun, one of the older workers, stepped forward. 'Master Soju, it has been too long,' he said, bowing respectfully. 'We have maintained the foundry premises as best we could, but without your father ...'

Soju clasped Dae-Hyun's shoulder warmly. 'Thank you, Dae-Hyun. This foundry will operate again. We need you all to ensure my father's legacy endures.' He turned for a moment to look at Suriratna and continued, 'And I have brought someone who can help. Heo Hwang-ok possesses remarkable skill as an ironworker. She will guide us in restoring this foundry to its former glory.'

A chorus of acknowledgement rose from the assembled workers. Dae-Hyun bowed to Suriratna, pledging his support. But confusion lingered in his expression. The idea of a woman leading an ironworks factory was unconventional. But Suriratna knew their doubts would vanish once they witnessed her expertise.

Suriratna gave a small nod of respect to the gathered workers, her gaze sweeping over the familiar and unfamiliar faces. 'Each one of you matters,' she said, her voice calm but firm. 'This foundry carries the legacy of not just one man, but of every hand that ever worked its flame.' Then, eyes sharp and focused, she began issuing instructions.

'First, we assess the condition of our tools. Everything must be inspected. Begin with the furnace. Ensure the clay lining is intact, free of cracks. We need it to contain maximum heat.'

'You,' she directed another worker, 'take a team and inspect the bellows. Remove any debris and check the leather for wear and tear. We need a constant, powerful airflow to fuel the flames.'

She turned to the civic maintenance foreman. 'Inspect the quenching tanks. Make sure they are filled with clean water and are free of leaks. We will need them ready for tempering metal. And check our ore stockpiles. We must replenish our supplies.'

'You and I,' she said to a younger worker, 'will inspect the anvils and grinding stones. They must be free of corrosion and damage, and securely mounted. Precision work demands a solid foundation.'

As the workers dispersed, Suriratna turned to Soju. 'Mithra's ship carried more than weapons,' she said, lowering her voice. 'It also brought special stones. I need you to retrieve them. Our success hinges on it.'

Soju frowned. 'Is there anything I should know?'

'Trust me, Soju. You do not need to know. But they will help us revitalize this foundry and many more. My matalu, Kulasekara, would have sent stocks to Mithra, who would have sent some of it here. Pitaha and I discussed this plan long ago when Vidushika's agents attempted to abduct me.'

Soju nodded. 'I will speak to the captain. But Suriratna, you only just arrived. I feel terrible putting you to work immediately.'

She smiled. 'I came here for you, Soju. I will do whatever it takes to see you succeed, to see you triumph.'

Catching sight of Dae-Hyun, whose skill and experience she had noted, Suriratna called him over. 'Master Dae-Hyun, I have a special project for you,' she said, her voice confident and steady. 'I need you to create a weapon. Not a standard weapon, but a prototype based on an ancient Pandyan design. The Mrityuchakra.'

Dae-Hyun's brows rose with curiosity. 'What kind of weapon is that?'

An enigmatic smile played on Suriratna's lips. 'All will be revealed in time, Master Dae-Hyun. Trust me, it will be unlike anything you have ever forged.'

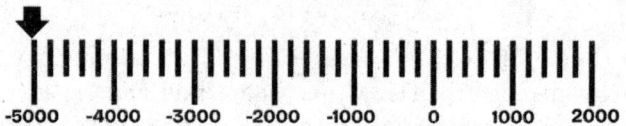

Ayodhya Nagari, Kosala Samrajya
Present-day Ayodhya, Uttar Pradesh, India
Around 7,000 years ago

On the outskirts of Ayodhya, Bharata prostrated himself before Rama, placing a pair of sandals at his brother's feet—the same sandals he had placed upon the throne as a symbol of Rama's rightful rule. Bharata had lived as an ascetic in Nandigram, governing Ayodhya in Rama's name, his devotion unwavering through the long years of his brother's exile.

Alerted by Hanuman, Bharata, joined by Shatrughna and Ayodhya's nobles, had rushed to greet Rama. Tears flowed freely as the brothers embraced, their bond unshaken by time and distance. Lakshmana had joined them, his eyes brimming.

Now, Rama's chariot moved at a measured pace through Ayodhya's streets, allowing every citizen a glimpse of their beloved prince. People lined the route, showering his entourage with flower petals. Thousands of oil lamps twinkled along the streets and in windows, draping the city in a warm glow.

Ayodhya was alive with celebration—banners and flags fluttered, drums and conch shells resounded. It was as though the entire city had returned from exile alongside their prince and princess. Rama, seated beside Sita, smiled and waved, while Sita's eyes brimmed with emotion as she took in the joyous faces of her people and the city she had longed to return to. Lakshmana walked alongside the chariot, his joy tempered by

The Ayodhya Alliance

vigilance. Hanuman, ever loyal, stood behind Rama, a steadfast guardian. Rama and Sita both gazed upon the familiar streets, landmarks, temples, gardens and homes—their hearts swelling with pleasure and relief.

As they neared the palace, Rama saw his mother, Kaushalya. He rushed to her and embraced her tightly, his eyes moist with the pain of separation. Beside him, Sita stepped forward to touch Kaushalya's feet. Next, they greeted Sumitra, her tears mingling with theirs. Happiness radiated from their faces.

When it was Kaikeyi's turn, she placed a trembling hand upon Rama's head in blessing, then turned to Sita and caressed her cheek with affection. 'I had no option but to play the villain and have you exiled,' Kaikeyi whispered to Rama. 'Without that, you could never have acquired Ravana's most prized possession.' Rama bowed low, his heart full of love and gratitude, free of any anger towards her.

'Preparations for your coronation are underway,' Kaushalya announced, leading them both inside.

The next day, Rama entered his father's court, the weight of destiny heavy upon his shoulders. A hushed reverence filled the grand hall, packed with ministers, sages and nobles, as Rama approached the throne.

Kulguru Vashishta, who had personally oversaw the preparations, began the coronation ceremony, pouring sacred water from the Ganga over Rama's head. The jewel-encrusted crown, laden with history, was placed upon his brow, a symbol of the lineage he embodied. As chants filled the air, punctuated by the sound of conch shells, a collective breath of contentment seemed to emanate from the kingdom.

Cheers erupted, cascading through the palace and spilling onto the city streets. Rama rose from the throne, raising a hand to silence the joyous assembly. 'Beloved citizens of Ayodhya,' he began, his voice strong and steady, 'this marks the dawn of a new era. Together, we will uphold dharma and ensure the prosperity of our kingdom.'

~

The rituals complete, while the city celebrated, Rama and Lakshmana retreated to a secluded garden near Kaushalya's quarters. The moon painted the path silver, guiding their steps. 'Lakshmana,' Rama said, crouching beside a chosen spot, 'this garden will house the Dvaitalingam. Let us begin.'

Together, they dug a pit, creating a fitting sanctuary. Reverently, they placed the box containing the extraordinary substance within it. It settled into its new home as if it had always belonged there, suffusing the surroundings with a subtle, sacred energy.

'Lakshmana, we must guarantee the Dvaitalingam's safety for generations,' Rama said. 'Construct a pillar that will defy time, a marker for this sacred spot. Engrave upon it the symbol of the two fish, signifying the combined powers of Vishnu and Shiva.'

Lakshmana nodded, his mind already teeming with ideas. 'Your instructions will be implemented, Brother. The Dvaitalingam will be safe.'

Rama placed a hand on his brother's shoulder. 'You will be the first Dvaitalingam Rakshak, as advised by Ravana with his dying breath. But you must establish a lineage of guardians—not of blood, but of duty. This duty transcends our time. As a serpent guards its treasure, so must you guard this, O avatar of Sheshanaga.'

Lakshmana's expression was resolute. 'I accept this responsibility, Brother. The Dvaitalingam will be protected, at all times, through all time.'

The brothers stood in silent contemplation. Around them, the city awakened. The garden, now the resting place of the Dvaitalingam, thrummed with a quiet power, a testament to the enduring connection between the divine and the mortal.

The pillar, once constructed, would stand as a symbol of their dedication. And the line of Rakshaks would ensure the Dvaitalingam's protection for eternity.

As the first light of dawn broke over Ayodhya, the Dvaitalingam settled into the earth—but in the shadows beyond, unseen forces stirred, drawn to a power they could not yet comprehend.

86

Seorabeol, Silla Kingdom
Present-day Gyeonju, South Korea
Around 2,000 years ago

Seorabeol, the grand capital of the Silla dynasty, embodied the kingdom's beauty and sophistication. Tucked into a fertile valley, surrounded by rolling hills and meandering rivers, it thrived with life—its winding streets lined with wooden houses, lively markets and centres of learning and culture that prospered under royal patronage. Artists displayed exquisite lacquerware and ceramics, rivalling the artistry of Geumgwan's ironwork.

On this day, however, a ripple of unease spread through the otherwise peaceful city as a contingent of Silla soldiers, clad in gleaming armour and bearing the insignia of the royal guard, marched through the gates, escorting a mud-splattered horseman. The rider, his hands bound, lips curled into a faint, unyielding smirk, had been captured near the tripoint—the border where Silla's, Baekje's and Talhae's territories converged. He had been en route from Talhae's court to that of Baekje until his journey was abruptly cut short by a vigilant Silla patrol.

At the head of the unit stood Captain Jang, a seasoned officer known for his sharp instincts and unyielding loyalty. He studied the prisoner intently and asked, 'Where was he apprehended?'

'Near the tripoint, sir,' a soldier replied, snapping a salute. 'He resisted, but we subdued him without casualties.'

Jang nodded, turning his attention to the horseman. 'Search him thoroughly.'

The soldiers stripped the captive, leaving him shivering in the cold. They rifled through his belongings—a pouch of coins, a water flask, a small dagger—before discarding them as mundane. Other soldiers examined his body, ensuring his humiliation was complete. Tucked within his belt, they discovered a folded, well-worn parchment.

'What is this?' Jang murmured, unfolding the parchment. His face blanched as he scanned its contents. 'This ... must be delivered to the king immediately.'

The captive's defiance wavered, his eyes betraying a trace of fear momentarily. He quickly recovered, spitting out a venomous threat. 'You will regret this. Talhae will have your heads.'

Jang ignored him. 'Transport him to the dungeon,' he ordered. 'I am taking this to King Yuri.'

∼

Captain Jang was ushered into a grand chamber where elaborate murals of Silla's past rulers stretched across the walls. At the far end of the chamber, King Yuri, Silla's fierce and volatile monarch, paced restlessly before his throne, his ornate robes billowing. Court officials and guards stood motionless, their attention fixed on the floor to avoid becoming a target of the king's wrath.

Jang bowed deeply. 'Your Majesty,' he reported. 'We have captured a messenger travelling from Talhae's northern territory in Garak to eastern Baekje. He was intercepted by our patrols near the tripoint. This parchment, addressed to King Daru, was found on his person.'

Yuri snatched the parchment, scanning it quickly. His face contorted with fury. 'That treacherous Talhae!' he roared, crushing the note in his fist. 'He dares to plot against me with King Daru of Baekje *even before* he fully controls the Garak Confederacy?'

His voice, spewing hatred, reverberated through the hall. 'Mobilize our troops, General Seon,' he said, turning to the stoic commander of Silla's royal armed forces. 'Prepare for war. Talhae and Baekje will learn that Silla is not to be underestimated. Our retribution will be swift, forceful and unmistakable. Let them reconsider their treachery.'

General Seon saluted sharply. 'As you command, Your Majesty. Our troops will be assembled and ready to march.'

'Good,' Yuri said, his anger receding. 'Talhae, that vile father-killer, will learn a lesson he will not soon forget.'

~

Several hours away, in his mother's house, Soju sat hunched over a map of the peninsula. Kim Hwa, sipping tea, watched him from her seat by the window. Suriratna was at the foundry, breathing life back into its dormant heart. Soju's mind raced, formulating plans and contingencies, his finger tracing borders and paths. A knock at the door interrupted his thoughts.

'Enter,' he called, his attention remaining on the map.

A messenger entered, bowing low. 'Master Soju, our strategy is in motion. King Yuri of Silla, reacting to the fabricated message, has ordered his forces to assemble at the tripoint.'

A smile touched Soju's lips. 'And our courier? Is he safe?'

'He is imprisoned in their dungeons near the tripoint,' the messenger assured him. 'Once deployment begins, we will extract him amidst the confusion.'

Soju nodded. 'Excellent. Ensure his safe return. He is a brave and loyal soldier who volunteered for this dangerous mission, knowing capture was inevitable. He does not realize how many lives he has saved.'

The messenger departed, leaving Soju to his thoughts. The strategy was unfolding flawlessly. Talhae's forces, preoccupied with the perceived threat from Silla, would be vulnerable. It was the perfect opportunity for the combined forces of Geumgwan, Bihwa, Bangam and Ara to strike.

Kim Hwa observed her son, a gentle smile gracing her lips—the first since Kim Seok's death. Catching her expression, Soju, overjoyed to see her spirit returning, turned to face her. 'Yes, Eomeoni?'

'I was wondering …' she began, hesitantly.

'Tell me, Eomeoni.'

'You steal away each night to be with Heo Hwang-ok. Why not make her your wife?'

Soju smiled. 'I love her, Eomeoni. But now is not the time for marriage. First, I must secure Garak and neutralize our enemies. Then, I will seek your blessing to make her my bride.'

'She is a good match for you, Soju,' Kim Hwa said, her voice filled with affection. 'The foundry workers speak of her reverence for your father, of how she commences work every day only after offering prayers to his spirit. She possesses all the qualities a mother could desire in a daughter-in-law. You have my blessing. Marry her … soon.'

Soju smiled and nodded. He did not want to wait too long either.

As Kim Hwa turned away, a flicker of unease crossed her face. Under her breath, she murmured, 'Before it is too late … Fate has a way of stealing what it envies.'

87

Ayodhya, Uttar Pradesh, India
Present day

The Ayodhya Tent City, located near the Ram Katha Park, offered a blend of rustic charm and modern convenience. The Sarayu Suite, where Aditya, Somi, Ramaswamy, Jung and Jayaraman were gathered, offered a panoramic vista of the Sarayu river, its surface reflecting the evening's golden light. The suite's elegant interior, lined with traditional Indian tapestries and artifacts, belied the tension permeating the room.

Aditya tapped his fingers impatiently on the polished teak table, his attention fixed on the laptop screen, which displayed the results from the tests they had conducted on the stone block. In 2001, the South Korean government had gifted Ayodhya a massive stone block, nearly 10 feet tall and weighing 8.2 tons. It had been installed in a corner of the Ram Katha Park, a beautiful open-air theatre where the epic Ramayana was celebrated through dance, music and poetry. Two decades later, the Queen Heo Memorial Park had been built around it by carving out some land from the Ram Katha Park.

The group's visit to the park had prompted a theory—that the stone block was a secret gift, a reciprocal gesture for an ancient favour. Over the past few days, they had been camped at Tent City, their efforts focused on analysing the stone.

'Let us begin,' Aditya said, breaking the silence. 'Dr Ramaswamy, what did the first test tell us?'

Ramaswamy adjusted his glasses and leaned forward. 'The strontium isotope analysis shows the stone comes from South Gyeongsang Province in South Korea and it is not old. It was quarried recently and does not match anything that might have been transported from India long ago.'

'That's disappointing,' Somi murmured, frustration evident in her tone. She had hoped for a meaningful link between their histories.

Jung, the metallurgist, nodded. 'The test results are clear. This stone is much newer than we thought.'

Aditya sighed and rubbed his temples. 'You mentioned another test—infrared or something?'

Ramaswamy nodded. 'Yes, we looked for chemical traces. The test found modern materials, like those used to preserve the stone, which were probably applied in recent years. It is another sign this is not ancient.'

'So, nothing from the past at all?' Somi asked, frowning.

'Nothing,' Jayaraman confirmed. 'The materials match something that is used today to protect artifacts.'

The group fell quiet, disappointment on their faces. They had hoped this stone would lead to a historical breakthrough, maybe even a clue to the secret behind nav utsa steel.

'What about the stone itself?' Aditya asked in a weary voice.

Jung flipped through the report. 'The minerals are typical of stones from South Gyeongsang Province—quartz, feldspar, biotite. There's nothing unusual that points to a different source.'

'And the crystal structure?' Somi pressed, her impatience showing.

Ramaswamy spoke carefully. 'It matches the stone's origin. There's no indication it was part of any ancient trade or connection between India and Korea.'

Aditya leaned back in his chair, the wood creaking beneath him. 'So, it's just a modern stone with no ties to the past. And no hidden compartment either.' He looked around the room. 'What are we missing?'

'Let's step back,' Somi suggested. 'Let's assume, for argument's sake, that a final additive perfected wootz—or nav utsa—steel. Ayodhya housed this additive and it was eventually moved to Korkai. Isn't it possible that portions were then transported to Damascus or Korea?'

'Then we should find evidence of this fantastical ingredient in each of these locations,' Aditya countered.

'We have,' Somi pointed out. 'The twin fish symbol appears in some form in every recipient culture—those who received either the substance itself or products made from it. But that doesn't tell us where the primary source was kept. Remember, this substance, in ancient times, would have been akin to plutonium—safeguarded with extreme care.'

She looked at Ramaswamy. 'Remind us of the Sanskrit verse you came upon at Ghaznawar's fortress, Dr Ramaswamy. The lines that spoke of something called the Dvaitalingam.'

Ramaswamy consulted his notes. 'Here it is.'

hastayo rakṣakasyāsti dvaitaliṅgaṃ pratiṣṭhitam
dṛḍhaṃ pratiṣṭhamānena balenaikena rakṣitam
ayodhyāsandhirāpnotu vardhanaṃ śauryasaṃyutam
bhāgyāni hyatra baddhāni yathāsthānaṃ yathocitam

He recited the verse flawlessly in Sanskrit. Then, referring to his translation, he read:

The Dvaitalingam in Rakshak hands,
Guarded by a force that firmly stands.
May the Ayodhya Alliance flourish strong,
With destinies bound, where they belong.

'That word before Dvaitalingam,' Somi said. 'What does "Rakshak" mean?'

Ramaswamy smiled. Somi had honed in on the crucial element. 'Guardian or protector. It seems specific individuals were entrusted with safeguarding this secret.'

'What does that tell us?' Somi asked, a knowing smile spreading across her face.

'That we need to find the guardians,' Ramaswamy said. 'If we locate the Rakshak, we increase our chances of finding the substance itself.'

'Indeed,' Somi agreed. 'But what about the phrase "Ayodhya Alliance"? What does that imply?'

'Perhaps an alliance of kingdoms possessing this technology?' Aditya ventured.

'It is possible,' Ramaswamy opined. 'Damascus, Korea and Pandya Desam may have been part of such an alliance.'

88

Pyongyang, North Korea

Present day

Khalil Ghaznawar and Choe Tok Hun arrived at the unassuming entrance of the Academy of National Defense Sciences, a vast complex hidden within the heavily guarded heart of Pyongyang. The academy, with its state-of-the-art research facilities, high-security zones and meticulously maintained gardens, served as a monument to North Korea's ambition to rival the West in science and defence prowess.

Many in the West seemed unaware of North Korea's history of aggressive post-Korean War industrialization and economic reconstruction, fuelled by significant Soviet and Chinese support. By prioritizing heavy industries—steel, coal, machinery, chemicals—North Korea had experienced rapid economic growth. By the early 1960s, it ranked among Asia's most industrialized nations, its per capita GDP surpassing that of South Korea. It was only in later years, particularly after the collapse of the USSR, that North Korea fell behind.

The subtle hum of air conditioning greeted them as they entered. A tall woman in a crisp military uniform, her face stern, bowed before Chairman Choe Tok Hun, Kim Jong Un's powerful cousin. She acknowledged Ghaznawar with a curt nod before leading them through a series of security checkpoints.

The walls were lined with photographs of the nation's scientific luminaries, each pictured alongside Kim Jong Un, his father, or his grandfather.

Ghaznawar and Choe were ushered into a small conference room where Dr Ryu Seong-Jin awaited them. Celebrated for his intellect and scientific contributions, Dr Ryu had an impressive résumé. Born into a family of academics, he had graduated top of his class from Kim Il Sung University and followed it up with advanced studies in Beijing. His work on particle physics had garnered international acclaim, his insights on quantum mechanics lauded even by Western scientists.

'Gentlemen, welcome,' Ryu greeted them in impeccable English. 'Based on the information you've provided regarding this hypothetical substance, I will present a theory that connects it to my universal duality model.'

The lights dimmed and a screen lit up at the front of the room. Ryu approached the podium, clicking a remote to bring up the first slide—a circuit diagram. 'Electricity,' he began. 'At its most basic, it is the interplay of positive and negative charges. This duality powers our world, from the smallest household appliances to the largest industrial facilities.'

Another click and the screen displayed a magnet with its north and south poles clearly marked. 'Magnetism operates on a similar principle. Like poles repel, creating instability, while opposites attract, generating a stable magnetic field. Duality is fundamental to magnetism.'

His lecture moved swiftly through various scientific disciplines, each slide introducing a new aspect of the principle. 'In quantum physics, we encounter wave–particle duality—particles exhibiting both wave-like and particle-like properties, depending on how we observe them,' Ryu explained, displaying an image of the famous double-slit experiment, demonstrating light's dual nature. 'Chemistry, too, is governed by duality—acids and bases,' he continued, transitioning to a slide depicting the pH scale.

Slide after slide, he continued his exposition. 'In cosmology, we have matter and antimatter; in physics, centrifugal and centripetal forces; in thermodynamics, exothermic and endothermic reactions; in biology, growth and decay.' He paused, his gaze sweeping across his two-person audience. 'What if I told you all these dualities are interconnected?'

Ghaznawar leaned forward. 'You suggest a link between these seemingly disparate phenomena?'

Ryu nodded. 'Precisely. My research suggests a common origin for these dualities, possibly stemming from the Big Bang. Consider the prevalence of the twin-fish and yin–yang symbols across various cultures. They may represent the two fundamental energy types underlying all dualities.'

Choe Tok Hun, who had been listening intently, finally spoke. 'And how does this relate to our work?'

Ryu's face lit up with excitement. 'If we understand these principles, we could make breakthroughs in material science, energy production and even advanced weaponry. Take the idea of opposites working together—the Law of Complementary Dualities. It is like finding balance to create something both hard and flexible, like carbon–steel.'

He clicked to the next slide, which showed an explosion. 'On the other hand, when opposites clash, the Law of Symmetrical Dualities comes into play. It causes instability and releases energy—like what happens in an explosion. Imagine this: a sword where one part is designed to be unbreakable, while another part focuses destructive energy along the blade's edge. The result? A weapon with unmatched power.'

Ghaznawar and Choe exchanged a look, grasping the implications. The potential applications of this technology were staggering—from new forms of energy and more powerful weapons to materials of unprecedented strength.

'Think about it,' Ryu said, excited. 'A material as flexible as rubber yet as strong as concrete. Or an energy source that taps into the balance of opposites to produce limitless power. The possibilities are endless.'

The lights came up as Ryu concluded his presentation. He turned to the others, his expression earnest. 'Gentlemen, this is just the beginning. Exploring these dualities could lead to breakthroughs that would establish our nation as a leader in scientific and technological advancement. The challenge lies in finding a catalyst to facilitate these extreme combinations. Think of an emulsifier—capable of binding oil and water, despite their natural tendency to repel.'

'That is it!' Ghaznawar exclaimed.

Choe, startled by the outburst, turned to him. 'What do you mean?'

'I have been trying to understand the nature of the Dvaitalingam,' Ghaznawar explained. 'It is not just any raw material, but a *catalyst*. Something that facilitates bonding.'

Ghaznawar rose, extending his hand. 'Thank you, Dr Ryu. Your presentation has been enlightening. No scientist in the West could distil so much information and insightful analysis into a single hour.'

Ryu smiled. 'I hope we can translate this theory into reality,' he said.

'We are working on it,' Choe replied, his eyes on Ghaznawar. After a pause, he added, 'And when we do, the world will never be the same again.'

89

Saketa, Kosala
Present-day Ayodhya, Uttar Pradesh, India
Around 2,000 years ago

Saketa's citizens thronged the city gates, eager to welcome the 157th Dvaitalingam Rakshak. After years of turmoil, they finally had a leader who genuinely cared for the people. Somadatta, flanked by his loyal followers, bowed low before Padmasen. 'Welcome back, Maharaj,' he said, his tone warm with respect.

Padmasen grasped his shoulders, pulling him into an embrace. 'I would not be here without you, Somadatta,' he said, overwhelmed by emotion. 'From freeing me from Vidushika's dungeon to fighting for my return, you have earned my eternal gratitude. I am forever in your debt.'

Cheers rose from the crowd as Padmasen's chariot, escorted by a procession of horses, elephants and soldiers, passed through the gates and proceeded along the wide avenues towards the palace. Petals rained down upon them, the cheers intensifying as they neared the palace. Padmasen descended from the chariot, his gaze sweeping over the grand courtyard.

His family was absent. He had not brought Indumati; she would return only once he deemed it safe. His children were far away: his son wandering the world, and his daughter possibly

The Ayodhya Alliance

in Garak. Only his trusted brother-in-law and business partner, Kulasekara, stood beside him, their joint presence reflecting the strengthening ties between the north and south. Cheliyan had remained behind in Korkai to ensure Indumati's safety.

Padmasen was ushered into the throne room, where the expectant royal court awaited him. He moved towards the throne with measured steps as royal priests chanted mantras and sprinkled him with water from sacred rivers.

'O guardians of Rama's kingdom, today marks a new beginning,' Padmasen declared. 'We have overcome many trials together and I now promise to usher in an era of peace and prosperity. I am not your king, but your servant. Three hundred years ago, Acharya Kautilya wrote, "In the happiness of his subjects lies the king's happiness; in their welfare, his welfare. He shall not consider as good only that which pleases him but treat as beneficial to him whatever pleases his subjects." I vow to live by these words.'

As applause filled the hall, Padmasen rose from his throne and walked barefoot from the palace, his hands clasped humbly. Somadatta, flanked by palace guards, formed a protective circle around him, shielding him from any potential threats. Padmasen continued until he reached a peaceful grove a short distance away.

He stopped before the Vishnu Stambha, and looked all along its 23-foot height to the Garuda perched atop. He studied the inscription extolling Rama's virtues and the symbol of two fish swimming clockwise. Together, Padmasen, Somadatta and Kulasekara bowed their heads, united in their shared purpose. A sense of calm and resolve settled over them as they stood before the Vishnu Stambha.

Padmasen prostrated himself before the pillar, his hands raised in a namaste above his head. 'In honour of Lord Rama, we bow before this sacred pillar,' he intoned reverently. 'May his blessings guide our every action.' He then chanted:

*śivāya viṣṇurūpāya śivarūpāya viṣṇave
śivasya hṛdayaṁ viṣṇuḥ viṣṇóśca hṛdayaṁ śivaḥ*

He rose, offering a silent prayer before returning to the palace, surrounded by cheering citizens.

~

Back in the palace, Padmasen sat with Kulasekara and Somadatta in the study he had often frequented during Vidushika's reign. The scent of rosewater from the basin near the entrance, the vibrant peacocks visible through the large window overlooking the garden—all of it remained unchanged. Padmasen turned to the two men who had stood by him through thick and thin.

'Somadatta, your task is far from over. In fact, the true work begins now. I need you to serve as my senapati,' Padmasen said, referring to the supreme commander of the kingdom's forces. 'There are still battles to be fought.'

Somadatta bowed. 'I will serve you to the best of my ability, Maharaj. Even at the cost of my life.'

'I have no doubt,' Padmasen replied. He turned to Kulasekara. 'I could ask for no better pradhanmantri. Help me bring prosperity to this land as my prime minister.'

Kulasekara smiled, clasping his hands. 'I am honoured, O King. I am proud to serve the 157th Dvaitalingam Rakshak, the true maharaj.'

'I wish Indumati could have been with us here today,' Padmasen murmured. 'Once we have established peace, send for her, Kulasekara. Cheliyan can accompany her.'

Kulasekara nodded.

'We must also ensure that the Dvaitalingam and the nav utsa iron reach allies who strive for peace,' Padmasen declared.

'It shall be done,' Kulasekara assured him.

'We are here in Saketa in the north,' Padmasen continued. 'The Pandyas control Korkai in the south, Mithra and his allies hold Dimašq in the west and my daughter is in Geumgwan to the east. From these four nodes, we will spread this technology, ensuring it is used for peace, progress, development and defence.'

He paused thoughtfully before speaking again. 'This must not be only about swords. The network must be used to build magnificent temples, forge alliances, expand trade and foster prosperity. A grid spanning continents. This technology should benefit all, not just a select few. This will be the enduring nature of our indomitable—*a-yuddha*—alliance. The Ayodhya Alliance.'

90

Geumgwan, Garak Confederacy
Present-day Gimhae, South Korea
Around 2,000 years ago

The moon radiated a silvery glow upon the boarding house. Inside, an oil lamp cast shifting shadows across Soju and Suriratna as they lay together, their bodies a source of comfort and security in a world that had felt perilous in recent days.

Soju's fingertips brushed Suriratna's face. 'I wish this moment could last forever,' he murmured. Her eyes closed, savouring his touch.

'But we both know it cannot,' Suriratna replied, drawing closer. He leaned in and their lips met in a kiss that sought to suspend time. The kiss deepened, passion eclipsing the worries of the outside world. Suriratna's hands moved to his chest, feeling the steady beat of his heart beneath her finger. They were lost in each other when a deafening crack split the air—the doorframe exploded inward, sending shards of wood flying like shrapnel.

Soju leaped to his feet as armed men rushed into the room—some bursting through the door, others leaping in through the open window. Talhae, flanked by his deadly assassins, swords glinting in the moonlight, stood in the doorway. 'Your time is up, Soju,' he hissed, his voice dripping with venom.

Soju barely had time to draw his sword before Talhae's soldiers attacked. The room erupted into chaos, the clash of metal and shouts of fury. 'Stay behind me, Suriratna!' Soju yelled, placing himself between her and the assailants. But he had underestimated her. She sprang into action, snatching her dagger from the table beside the bed.

The fight was brutal and uneven. Talhae's ten men swarmed them, their attacks relentless and precise. Suriratna and Soju fought valiantly, but they were outnumbered. As blades whirled, the air filled with the sounds of battle—grunts, shouts, clanging metal, and the sickening hiss of blades slashing flesh.

Four of Talhae's men surrounded Soju, their movements raptorial, their eyes cold and calculating. The first lunged, his sword aimed at Soju's heart but Soju blocked the blow and spun to his left, narrowly avoiding another attack. His sword met the third attacker's blade with a resounding clang. He kicked the fourth attacker in the groin, sending him crashing to the floor. The cramped space was a whirlwind of motion and sound, but Soju remained focused, fighting with precision.

Suriratna, meanwhile, wielding her dagger, battled three attackers at once, her movements swift and fierce. She ducked beneath a sword stroke, slashing the attacker's thigh. Another lunged, aiming for her stomach. She feinted, countering with a swift thrust to his side. A third man tried to attack her from behind. She whirled around and drove her dagger into his shoulder. She fought with the agility of a dancer, the ferocity of a cornered animal.

Some of Talhae's soldiers were fighting off the staff of the boarding house who had been drawn by the commotion. As the fight raged on, both Soju and Suriratna sustained injuries. Blood streamed from a cut above Soju's eye, blurring his vision, and a deep gash marred Suriratna's left arm. But they continued fighting, fuelled by adrenaline and the will to survive. Gradually, the odds began to turn. Talhae, who had been content to let his men do the dirty work until then, stepped into the fight.

He advanced on Soju, hatred burning in his gaze. 'You think you can defy me?' he growled, swinging his sword. It missed Soju by a hair's breadth. Undeterred, he lunged again. Soju parried the blow, their swords locking in a contest of strength. Their faces inches apart, Talhae snarled, 'Good little Soju, kind little Soju. You ruined my life; now I will end yours. And when you are gone, I will have that whore of yours begging for mercy.'

His words inflamed Soju's rage. The battle intensified. Talhae's sword whistled through the air, aimed at Soju's head. Soju ducked, feeling the blade graze his hair. Talhae grunted, shifting his attack, aiming for Soju's belly. Sparks flew as their blades connected. 'You will pay for my father's murder!' Soju roared, his face flushed in fury.

Even in the midst of the chaotic fight, Soju realized that with Silla mobilizing its forces, Talhae could not risk dividing his own. The quickest solution was to eliminate Soju, crippling the Confederacy.

Suriratna deftly reached for the device concealed beneath her bed. It was as yet untested, a mere prototype, but she knew it could turn the tide. 'Soju, down!' she cried, her voice cutting through the tumult. He reacted instantly, dropping to the floor.

The Mrityuchakra, a marvel of nav utsa metal, compact and intricate, with two swimming fish engraved in the centre, held a circular magazine of twenty-four razor-sharp miniature daggers, powered by a spring-loaded mechanism. With a practised move, Suriratna disengaged the safety and released a volley of blades in a fan-like arc. The air sang with a high-pitched whine. Each dagger, designed for maximum penetration, found its mark before Talhae's men could react. One by one, they crumpled to the ground. A dagger plunged into an eye, the attacker collapsing with a scream. Another pierced a throat, unleashing a torrent of blood.

By now, the commotion had also alerted neighbours as well as Soju's guards, who were stationed some distance away. They raced towards the boarding house. Talhae remained standing, but his face was bloodied, a deep gash carved into his cheek by one of the Mrityuchakra's daggers. Six of his men lay dead and two were grievously wounded. Only two continued to fight. The tide had turned.

Astonishment and rage contorted Talhae's features. He knew he had to escape. He jumped out the window, fleeing into the night. Driven by a thirst for vengeance, Soju leaped to his feet, giving chase. 'Talhae! Coward! You cannot run forever! Face me!' Soju's voice rang out, echoing in the darkness.

But Talhae was in no condition to fight. Desperation fuelled his flight. He raced through Geumgwan's narrow streets, Soju close behind. Others joined the pursuit, attempting to cut off Talhae's escape. The chase led them to the city's outskirts, where the terrain grew treacherous. Talhae disappeared down a narrow tunnel leading into a ravine—a path any sensible person would avoid, but he had little choice.

Soju and his men searched the tunnel, the surrounding area, even the ravine's precarious slopes, but Talhae had vanished. Soju stood there, chest heaving, drenched in sweat, his hands fisted around his sword. Frustration gnawed at him. 'I will find you, Talhae,' he vowed. 'You will pay for what you did to my father.' Exhausted and wounded, he stumbled back towards the boarding house.

He found Suriratna calmly retrieving the miniature daggers from the bodies of their attackers and reloading the Mrityuchakra. He tried to embrace her, but her focus remained on her task. 'You will give me a group of warriors,' she said, her voice quiet but firm. 'I will train them. The Iron King will have his Iron Queen.'

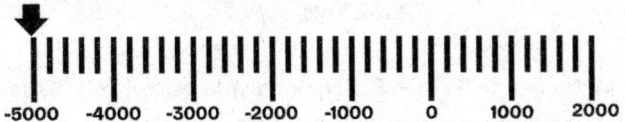

Yahangala, Lanka

Present-day Medamahanuwara, Kandy District, Sri Lanka

Around 7,000 years ago

As dust settled over Lanka's blood-soaked fields, the clamour of war gave way to a heavy silence. Bodies lay scattered, their limbs contorted in grotesque postures. Broken weapons and shattered chariots littered the ravaged landscape. This was the aftermath of a war that had torn the world asunder. At the heart of this devastation lay Ravana, king of Lanka, his body battered, his breath shallow. The smell of blood, sweat and decay mingled with acrid smoke.

Ravana had abducted Sita, Rama's wife, sparking a war that would scorch the land and test the bounds of dharma. The battle had raged across Lanka's golden shores, driven by love, honour and an unyielding sense of justice. But even justice, once served, left behind devastation.

Rama, prince of Ayodhya, stood nearby, his bow lowered, his expression sombre. He had been victorious in battle, but his triumph was shrouded in sorrow. How could this staggering loss of life ever be justified, even in the name of righteousness? Lakshmana, his younger brother, stood beside him, exhausted from the fight. Once prosperous, Lanka now lay in ruins, a stark reminder of the merciless consequences of war. Dark clouds gathered overhead, as if in mourning for the vanquished king.

'Brother,' Rama said, his voice breaking the silence. 'Go to Ravana. Even in his final moments, he has much to teach us.'

Lakshmana looked at Rama, confusion evident on his face. 'From *him*, Brother? After all that has transpired?'

Rama nodded, his gaze unwavering. 'From him. True greatness lies not only in valour but in wisdom. And despite his transgressions, Ravana possesses an intellect we may never encounter again. Go, learn what you can, for knowledge is impartial.'

With a hesitant nod, Lakshmana approached Ravana. Misinterpreting Rama's intent, he stood beside the dying king's head, an unintentional insult. Rama quickly corrected him. 'Not there, Lakshmana. Stand at his feet. That is where a student stands before his teacher.'

Lakshmana's cheeks flushed with embarrassment. He moved quickly, positioning himself respectfully at Ravana's feet. The fallen king seemed to sense the shift. His eyes, which had been half-closed in despair, fluttered open. He coughed, a grimace of pain twisting his features. His body screamed in protest, but he summoned the strength to speak.

'You seek knowledge from me ... so close to my end ... son of Dasharatha?' Ravana rasped.

Lakshmana hesitated, then spoke, his voice low but clear. 'I do not fully understand why, but my brother believes you possess wisdom worth learning—even now.'

Ravana studied him, then nodded slowly. 'Very well,' he whispered. 'Listen then, Young Prince, to the words of the greatest Shiva devotee in all of creation. And relay them to your brother, the mighty avatar of Vishnu.'

He winced as he shifted his position to look at Lakshmana. 'Vishnu and Shiva are but facets of a single soul, merging to form a whole.' He paused, each breath a struggle. 'True strength lies in the union of opposing forces. Remember that, son of Dasharatha.'

Lakshmana listened intently, absorbing every word as the dying king continued. 'Never underestimate your foes, nor overestimate your own power. Learn from my mistakes. Your greatest enemy can be your greatest teacher. Like I am to you now.'

Ravana took a deep breath. Though his body was tense with discomfort, he managed to give Lakshmana precise instructions. 'Go to Lankapura Fort. Dig beneath the Shiva temple. What you will find there holds great significance. You shall be the first Rakshak of an immense power—a power that cannot be harnessed without your brother.'

Thunder rumbled, lightning illuminated the battlefield. Ravana's life was fading. 'One last thing,' he whispered. 'Safeguard the secret I have shared. And ensure that Rama blesses it with his touch. Only then will the Atmalingam become the Dvaitalingam. May Queen Kaikeyi's wish be fulfilled.'

~

Miles away, in Ayodhya Nagari, Kaikeyi's eyes shimmered with a pain long buried. On the battlefield of Vaijayanta, Rama's father had granted her two boons—and she had not hesitated to use them. Not because they would give her power but to ensure the unfolding of the grand design. She asked for Rama to be exiled not out of envy, but because only in exile would he face Ravana. And only by defeating him could Rama retrieve the Atmalingam and awaken its potential.

Long ago, in the age of twilight between the yugas, King Ashwapati of the Kekaya clan undertook a fierce penance to invoke Lord Shiva. He did so not for kingdom, glory or power— but because his seers had foreseen a time when a shadow, born of arrogance and fed by stolen boons, would rise to challenge cosmic balance: Ravana.

Moved by Ashwapati's clarity and sacrifice, Shiva appeared before him and said, 'A force of darkness will indeed rise, shielded by the misuse of my own blessings. But through your line, balance shall be restored. Your daughter, Kaikeyi, will be the key—not by sword, but by sacrifice. Through her hands, exile shall lead to awakening. And the bearer of light shall transform the Atmalingam into the Dvaitalingam, reclaiming its purpose.'

Ashwapati had humbly accepted the prophecy, knowing his daughter would be reviled by history but cherished by dharma.

∽

Ravana's eyes closed, his head falling to the side. As the wind swept across the ravaged fields, it was as if the king's spirit was being carried away. Lakshmana remained motionless for a moment, contemplating the dying king's words. Why did he feel compelled to protect this knowledge? He pushed the doubt aside and bowed deeply to Ravana's lifeless form before returning to Rama.

'What did he say, Brother?' Rama asked softly.

'He spoke of strength in the union of opposites, and the danger of complacency,' Lakshmana replied. 'He also spoke of the Lankapura Fort, of a discovery to be made beneath the Shiva temple. Something that can transform the Atmalingam into the Dvaitalingam.'

Rama nodded thoughtfully. 'We must heed his words and act accordingly. But first, we must honour the fallen and ensure their sacrifices were not in vain.'

As night fell, the camp settled into an exhausted slumber, the weariness of battle yielding to the hope of a new dawn. Gazing up at the star-studded sky, Lakshmana contemplated the vastness of the universe and his place within it, Ravana's final words echoing in his mind like a distant drumbeat—warning, urging, reminding.

∽

The following morning, as the first rays of sunlight pierced the darkness, Rama, Lakshmana and a small band of loyal soldiers set out for Lankapura Fort.

Following Ravana's instructions, they dug beneath the Shiva temple, unearthing a massive stone block. Upon its surface was an engraving of two fish along with an inscription.

'Shiva's Atmalingam awaits Vishnu's touch to transform into the Dvaitalingam,' Lakshmana read aloud. 'Guard this as the serpent you are, O Sheshanaga.' He turned to Rama, astonishment filling his voice. 'What is this?'

'Just as I am an avatar of Vishnu, you have come into this world to aid me in my purpose, O avatar of Sheshanaga,' Rama replied. 'Guard this well. You are the first Rakshak. Ensure you choose a worthy successor.'

'But I still do not understand,' Lakshmana confessed.

Rama silenced him with a gesture. Kneeling, he placed his hand upon the stone block and chanted:

śivāya viṣṇurūpāya śivarūpāya viṣṇave
śivasya hṛdayaṁ viṣṇuḥ viṣṇóśca hṛdayaṁ śivaḥ

'Shiva is in the form of Vishnu, and Vishnu is in the form of Shiva
Vishnu resides in Shiva's heart, and Shiva resides in Vishnu's heart.'

As Rama's hand touched it, the stone block began to vibrate. Its dull grey hue changed to a vibrant purple before it fragmented. 'Gather these pieces,' Rama instructed. 'We will take them to Ayodhya Nagari, to be used for the betterment of mankind.'

91

New Delhi, India
Present day

High above the Earth's surface, an Indian satellite relayed border images to a facility in Karnataka's Hassan district. Soon after, the images, transmitted through encrypted defence channels, materialized in a subterranean command centre beneath an unassuming building on Rajaji Marg in New Delhi. The building housed the elite Integrated Defence Staff, its control room a cutting-edge space with large screens lining the curved walls. Each screen displayed a different feed from watchful satellites maintaining constant surveillance over India's sensitive borders with Pakistan, China, Bangladesh, Myanmar and the coastal waters shared with Sri Lanka.

In addition, the room had ten state-of-the-art workstations, each connected to secure communications. Three ten-person teams manned these stations 24/7. The vault-like control room, accessible only via stringent biometric security, received, analysed and disseminated high-resolution images to command posts along the volatile borders. A central archive stored all satellite imagery for interagency sharing.

In an adjacent conference room, the defence minister and the national security advisor huddled with key personnel. 'Are we certain?' the NSA asked, gesturing towards a screen displaying the Indo-Pak Line of Control. 'What is the probability of a false positive?'

The senior analyst studied the projected image. 'All indicators suggest it's the same,' he stated. 'Identical size and shape, consistent spectral signatures, matching infrared and multispectral data. There's no doubt in my mind. Before the attack on our BPBT, we detected a similar reading on the Chinese side of the LAC. Now we see it again—on the Pakistani side of the LOC. The same missile system has been deployed against us on another front.'

'The scenario we've been dreading,' the defence minister said gravely. 'China's next-generation ATGMs are finding their way into Pakistan-Occupied Kashmir. Our tank regiments along the LOC will be as vulnerable as those along the LAC.'

'Get Dr Reddy on the line,' the defence minister ordered. Within moments, the chairman of DRDO was on the conference call. 'What is Aditya Pillai's progress?' the defence minister demanded, dispensing with pleasantries.

'Minimal,' Reddy replied. 'I've been pressing for updates, but have received only vague assurances that the Pillai–GISCO joint venture is on track. No data has been shared regarding their development work. I truly wish we had a backup plan.'

'Any alternative would require significant time and resources,' the defence minister pointed out.

'My concern is the flimsiness of Pillai's entire plan,' Reddy said. 'Even if he delivers, I am not convinced he'll meet the specifications. After all this time, we might end up with nothing.'

'We pulled out all the stops to get him Dr Ramaswamy from CERN,' the NSA interjected. 'I do not believe his lack of progress stems from insufficient effort. The timeframe we imposed is nearly impossible. Only a maverick like Pillai would even dare to attempt something like this.'

'What *is* his plan?' the defence minister asked. 'Does his Korean partner possess the necessary technology?'

'Neither company does,' Reddy replied. 'Pillai believes there's an ancient type of steel with unique molecular properties, capable of both bonding and repelling. He believes amplifying those properties is possible once the catalyst is isolated. The problem is, there's no evidence to suggest this element—this catalyst—even exists, or that he is close to finding it.'

The defence minister considered the situation. 'Should we explore a parallel team working with Chobham armour?' Chobham, a composite of ceramic tiles encased within a metal framework and bonded to a backing plate, offered superior missile protection.

'We've already tried Chobham,' Reddy said. 'It's ineffective against the Chinese HJ-12E.'

'Shifting gears at this stage would be unwise,' the NSA agreed. 'But perhaps we should have our people monitor Aditya Pillai and Somi Kim.'

'Why?' the defence minister asked.

'If they will not keep us informed, we need to find another way to stay abreast of their progress. Or the lack thereof.'

92

Gimhae, South Gyeongsang Province, South Korea

Present day

Aditya, Somi, Ramaswamy and Jung stood before the tomb of Kim Suro in Gimhae. A large burial mound, roughly 72 feet in diameter and 20 feet high, dominated the site. Before it stood Kim Suro's tombstone, an altar, and stone figures of warriors. On either side, stone sculptures of horses, sheep and tigers guarded the tomb.

The group's attention was drawn to the ornate gate leading to the tomb, painted in vibrant red, blue and green. Three wooden doorways bore the Taijitu symbol. Even more intriguing were the embellishments above the two side doors—artwork depicting two fish swimming towards each other.

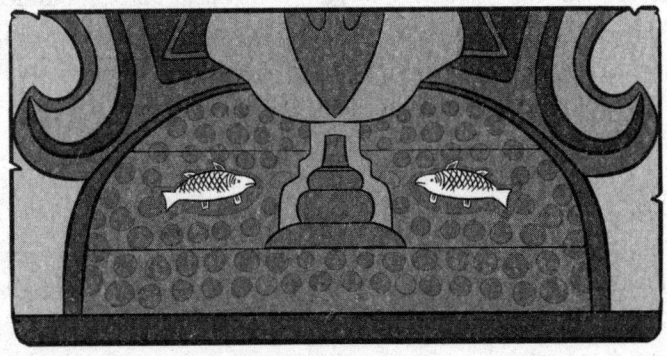

Somi gestured northward. 'Ahead lies Gujibong Peak, shaped like a turtle's head. This is likely why the turtle became the symbol of the Garak Confederacy.'

Ramaswamy shook his head in amazement. 'The first avatar of Vishnu is Matsya—the fish,' he mused. 'But the second is Kurma—the turtle. The connections are striking. Or am I overinterpreting?'

'You aren't,' said Somi. 'Look closely at the turtle's two front claws and you will see two fish built into the design.'

'Legend says six eggs in a golden box wrapped in red cloth descended from heaven onto that turtle peak,' Somi continued with a smile. 'After twelve days, the eggs hatched, revealing six boys. One of those boys became Kim Suro. Each eventually ruled different regions, but Kim Suro rose to lead the Garak Confederacy.'

'Could Suro have been a part of the Ayodhya Alliance?' Aditya wondered. 'The one mentioned in that parchment?'

'Considering his marriage to Suriratna—or Heo Hwang-ok—it's certainly possible,' Somi replied. 'But whether this site holds any clues to the substance used in wootz steel is another matter entirely.'

'Let us start with a more fundamental question,' Ramaswamy said. 'Is Kim Suro actually buried here?'

Jung had the answer. 'Records indicate that upon Suro's death, a hall was constructed northeast of the royal palace to house his coffin. That corresponds with this location. But the structures we see today—the mound, the altar, the platform—date back only to 1580. The tombstone was erected in 1647. So, while he was likely interred somewhere here, the memorial is much more recent.'

'What about Suro and Suriratna's descendants?' Aditya asked. 'Perhaps they mentioned this secret in their writings?'

'That would be a monumental undertaking,' Somi said. 'Around six million Koreans—including my own family—claim descent from this legendary couple. The Gimhae Kim, Gimhae Heo and Incheon Yi clans. They had twelve children, and Heo requested that two bear her surname. Apart from the *Samguk Yusa*, no other text mentions Kim Suro and Heo Hwang-ok.'

'How is that possible?' Aditya asked, incredulous.

'The *Samguk Yusa* primarily focuses on Goguryeo, Baekje and Silla—the Three Kingdoms,' Jung explained. 'The Garak Confederacy is rarely mentioned, and when it is, it is portrayed as a minor polity absorbed by Silla in the sixth century. For over a millennium, Garak's historical significance has been largely overlooked.'

'Has this area been LiDAR mapped?' Ramaswamy asked. 'Do we have subterranean data?'

Somi nodded. 'This site and the adjacent Daeseong-dong,' she confirmed. 'There are one hundred and thirty-six mounds here, containing stone chambers, bent weapons, iron armour, cylindrical bronze items, jasper artifacts and even evidence of horse and human sacrifices.'

'Sacrifices?' Aditya asked, a shiver running down his spine.

'Servants and horses were sometimes interred with deceased kings or nobles,' Somi explained. 'To serve their masters in the afterlife.'

'What about iron?' Ramaswamy pressed.

'They discovered Garak helmets with vertical plates and sun visors or cheek guards,' Jung replied.

'Anything else?'

'A significant amount of Gaya armour,' Jung said. 'Constructed with interlocking vertical plates, this type of armour originated in Garak, which was known for its advanced ironworking and weapon-making techniques. Gaya armour, often used to denote social status, features unique bird- and fern-shaped decorations. But there's nothing to suggest it possessed the qualities of nav utsa.'

'Those items are likely of a later period,' Ramaswamy said. 'If the Dvaitalingam was given to Suro, would it not have been buried with him? It would have been his most prized possession.'

'You're right,' Somi agreed. 'Unless …'

'Unless?' Aditya echoed.

'Unless it was considered his queen's possession, not his,' Somi suggested. 'What if Suro was meant to be the Iron King, but Suriratna became the Iron Queen?'

93

Seongsan, Garak Confederacy
Present-day Seongju County, South Korea
Around 2,000 years ago

Storm clouds gathered over Seongsang, a prelude to the impending battle. The ground trembled beneath the determined advance of the troops from Geumgwan, Bihwa, Bangam and Ara. Soju rode at the head of this formidable army, his face set, determination burning within him.

'Forward!' he roared, his voice rising above the clamour of marching feet and clanging armour. 'Today, we reclaim our honour! For the Garak Confederacy!' Flanked by the other chiefs—Jinhyeok of Bihwa, Wonsik of Bangam and Yongho of Ara—Soju knew the fate of the Garak Confederacy rested on this battle.

Talhae, having healed from the injury caused by Suriratna's Mrityuchakra, now supported by soldiers from Seongsang, Goryeong and Daegaya, watched the approaching army, his face hardened by years of warfare. 'Hold!' he commanded. 'Wait for my signal. Let them walk into our trap. We will break them.'

Tension crackled in the air as the two sides stood motionless, sizing each other up, the silence punctuated only by the distant rumble of thunder. Then, with a deafening roar, they collided, the battlefield dissolving into mayhem. The ground shook beneath the force of the clash. Arrows arched through the air, swords met shields with bone-jarring force. War cries, the clang of metal and the groans of the wounded filled the air. Neither side was prepared to yield.

Fuelled by a cold fury, Soju led the charge, his sword a blur of silver as he cut through enemy ranks. Talhae was equally ferocious, performing a deadly dance of war, his every parry flawless, each strike precise. He moved through the chaos with predatory grace.

As the battle raged, the tide began to turn against Soju's forces. Talhae's troops, disciplined and cohesive, driven by desperation and the fear of their own leader's wrath, pushed back the attackers inch by bloody inch. They were an impenetrable wall of shields and flashing blades.

Soju's soldiers faltered, their advance stalled. Every step forward met with fierce resistance. Fatigue and discouragement crept into the ranks as defeat seemed to loom over them.

Suddenly, a woman's voice rang out from the rear. '*Jugeum-ui bakwi!*' Suriratna, leading her contingent of specially trained warriors, issued the command, a Gaya term for 'wheel of death'. The specialized brigade, armed with Suriratna's deadly Mrityuchakras, charged ahead, moving with lethal precision.

Turmoil erupted within Talhae's ranks as the Mrityuchakras unleashed their deadly blades. The tiny daggers, imbued with terrifying force, ripped through flesh and armour, leaving trails of devastation in their wake. Despite their valiant efforts, Talhae's army struggled. Soldiers fell, their screams piercing the thick fog of war. Despair mounted, but Talhae remained focused on his ultimate target: Soju.

With a snarl, he cut a path through the fray, heading towards his lifelong rival. Soju, seeing Talhae approach, dismounted, his sword at the ready. 'Talhae!' he shouted. 'Face me, if you dare!' The two commanders met in the heart of the battlefield in a spectacle of skill and fury, their armies parting to create a circle around them.

Sword met sword with a deafening clamour, sparks flying from their grinding blades. Soju's muscles strained as he unleashed a flurry of blows, each seeking to bring his opponent down. Talhae countered with lightning-fast thrusts, parrying every attack with the agility of a seasoned warrior.

The battle raged, their duel becoming the focal point as the world around them seemed to shrink. Sweat poured down their faces, mingling with dirt and blood, but neither showed any sign of yielding. They pushed each other to the limits of endurance, the ferocity of their fight leaving the onlookers awestruck.

As the fight wore on, Soju felt his strength waning. His limbs grew heavy, his mind clouded by a growing fog. He shook his head, trying to clear the haze, but it was of no use. Unbeknownst to Soju, Talhae's blade was coated with a deadly poison—the same pishuan that had killed Kim Seok's trusted servant, Minjun. With every cut, minuscule doses of the toxin were seeping into Soju's bloodstream.

Suriratna watched from a distance, her keen eyes detecting something amiss. Talhae's blade seemed to absorb the sunlight, while Soju's sword sparkled. 'Talhae's blade is poisoned!' she shouted to Jinhyeok, Wonsik and Yongho. 'Get Soju out of there!'

Recognizing the danger, the chiefs intervened, pulling a protesting Soju away from the fight. Suriratna moved to confront Talhae. He greeted her with a rapacious grin. 'Ah, the lovely Heo Hwang-ok,' he said, lowering his guard. 'With you, I would rather make love, not war. Become my lover and I will show you pleasures you have never known.' He gestured lewdly.

'You talk of pleasure, yet resort to poison to fight your battles, like a coward. Is that how honourable soldiers fight in your land?'

He laughed at her words, but the sound died in his throat as Suriratna attacked. She moved with the swiftness and grace of a hunting cat. Caught off guard by her ferocity, he struggled to deflect her blows. 'You are skilled,' he grunted, scrambling to regain his footing. 'But not skilled enough.'

'We shall see,' she replied. She feinted left, drawing his attention, then spun right, her blade slicing through the air. Talhae, still overconfident, reacted a fraction too late. Her sword found its mark, making a swift, clean cut across his throat.

'You …' he choked, his eyes wide with disbelief. 'How …?'

'You underestimated me,' she said coldly, stepping back as Talhae clutched his throat, blood spilling from it like a crimson river. His knees buckled, and as he fell she leaned in, her words dripping with venom. 'Your tyranny ends here,' she whispered. 'The great Talhae, slayer of Kim Seok, undone by the woman he scorned. History will not honour you—it will erase you.'

94

Gimhae, South Gyeongsang Province, South Korea
Present day

Ramaswamy spent the night as Jung's guest, while Aditya and Somi took rooms at the Arirang, a business hotel frequented by GISCO associates in Gimhae.

Early the next morning, without a single other visitor in sight, Somi and Aditya arrived at the tomb of Queen Heo Hwang-ok—also known as Suriratna. They had visited this place weeks earlier, unaware that their journey would lead them back here. Ramaswamy and Jung planned to join them after a stop at the museum to examine the artifacts recovered from Kim Suro's tomb.

'We've discussed the linguistic similarities between Korean and Tamil,' Aditya said as they walked towards the burial mound. 'Are there other indicators?'

'Food is another major cultural export,' Somi replied. 'Consider the Korean dish called mandu—dumplings filled with meat, vegetables and tofu. It's very similar to the south Indian kozhukattai. Likewise, our dessert yakgwa resembles the south Indian athirasam. Both regions have a fondness for rice porridge—juk in Korea, kanji in south India. South India has idiyappam, nearly identical to the Korean noodles called myron. The culinary overlaps are significant.'

They followed the cobblestone path to the grassy mound. Beside it stood a gazebo with an ornate roof, housing a stack of rough-hewn stones arranged in six tiers. A placard identified it as the Pasa Stone Pagoda. Aditya had recognized them on his first visit—ballast stones used to stabilize Pandyan ships.

Then, a thought struck him, electrifying, forcing him to stop. He stared at the ballast stones, a wild idea taking root. *Could what we seek be hidden in plain sight?* His fists clenched. Every instinct screamed at him to trust his gut.

Sensing the sudden change in him, Somi asked, 'Aditya, is something wrong?'

He nodded, his focus remaining on the stones. He pulled out his phone, dialling Ramaswamy's number. 'Dr Ramaswamy, I think I've found something. If I send you a sample, can you immediately run the same tests we've done previously for other samples? We may be standing right on top of the Dvaitalingam.'

Somi's eyes widened as she listened. She looked at the stones with newfound interest. *Could Aditya be right?* The idea was incredible. How many times had she passed this pagoda without giving it a second glance?

'I see,' Aditya said, continuing his conversation with Ramaswamy. 'When will you and Dr Jung arrive?' He paused. 'We'll wait for you.'

He ended the call, turning to Somi. 'He said they found a unique chemical signature at Kailasa, Petra and Konark. They will need to examine these stones to see if they contain the same signature—but amplified. If they do, it will confirm what we are thinking.'

'Isn't that a bit of a stretch?' Somi asked, trying to temper her excitement. 'Why would such a valuable substance—something capable of transforming iron ore into superior steel—be left in plain sight? And why wouldn't it have been depleted over the years?'

Aditya grinned. 'Think about it. We declared the cow sacred to protect our cattle. We personified our rivers as goddesses—Ganga and Sarasvati—to ensure their preservation. We worshipped the peepal tree to keep forests intact. Attributing divinity is the simplest way to safeguard something. Why transform ballast stones into embellishments for a sacred pagoda? Besides, only minuscule amounts would have been needed. Irrespective of whether these stones were kept in Ayodhya, Korkai, Damascus, or Geumgwan, they would have only used small shavings for steel making.'

Excited, he did not notice the three figures emerging from the shadows behind the gazebo, their movements stealthy and coordinated. Khalil Ghaznawar, flanked by two of Choe Tok Hun's men, approached, their weapons drawn.

Catching a glimpse of the approaching men, Somi felt a jolt of fear. She grasped Aditya's arm, her grip tight. 'Aditya, we are not alone,' she whispered in a strained voice.

Aditya turned just in time to see Ghaznawar nod to his men, signalling them to close in. 'Stay calm,' Aditya murmured to Somi, though his pulse quickened. He knew they were in trouble. Outnumbered, outgunned and neither of them trained for combat.

But Somi wasn't one to give up easily. As the attackers approached, she subtly reached into her pocket, where her phone was set to speed dial. She pressed the emergency number, praying the Gyeongchal—the Korean National Police—would trace the call. Then she tucked the phone back, keeping the line open.

Ghaznawar raised his gun, his expression cold and menacing. 'You two have caused me enough problems,' he snarled with barely concealed rage. 'Time to pay the price. But thank you for leading me to the solution.'

Realizing they were sitting ducks, Aditya and Somi scrambled over the protective fence surrounding the pagoda, entering an area off-limits to visitors. One of Ghaznawar's men fired and Aditya ducked behind the pagoda, the bullet chipping a fragment from one of the stones.

The other attacker turned his gun on Somi. She huddled beside Aditya, her heart pounding. Scattered on the pagoda's base were smooth white pebbles. She grabbed one and hurled it at the gunman with all her might. It struck his arm, causing his shot to go wide, the bullet whizzing past her ear. She knew they couldn't hold out for long. 'Aditya, the pebbles!' she hissed. 'Distract them!'

Aditya understood. He grabbed a larger pebble and flung it at the second attacker. Somi followed suit, aiming for Ghaznawar's face. He dodged, but the distraction gave them an opening. They scrambled back over the fence, fleeing down the path behind the pagoda.

'Do not let them escape!' Ghaznawar roared, urging Choe's men to give chase.

Aditya and Somi sprinted down the cobblestone path, their pursuers' footsteps pounding close behind. Somi's heart leaped as she heard the distant wail of sirens. The police were coming, but would they arrive in time? As the attackers gained ground, Somi spotted a small shrine, its stone walls offering potential cover. She dove behind it, narrowly avoiding another gunshot, and called to Aditya, behind her, to join her.

Just as he reached the shrine, a searing pain ripped through Aditya's left shoulder as a bullet found its mark. He stumbled, clutching the wound, blood seeping between his fingers. The world spun; he collapsed onto the cobblestones.

'Aditya!' Somi screamed in panic. Ignoring her own safety, she rushed to his side, dropping to her knees. Her hands trembled as she pressed her scarf against his wound, trying to stanch the bleeding. 'Stay with me, Aditya,' she pleaded, her voice trembling. 'The police are coming.'

Ghaznawar and his men closed in, their guns trained on Somi and the wounded Aditya. 'You should have stayed out of this,' Ghaznawar growled, his voice laced with menace.

Somi looked up, defiance burning in her eyes. She shielded Aditya with her body, refusing to abandon him. 'You won't get away with this,' she said, forcing her voice to remain steady. 'The Gyeongchal are almost here.'

Unfazed by the approaching sirens, Ghaznawar smirked. He aimed his gun, preparing to finish them off. 'Too late,' he sneered.

Just as he was about to pull the trigger, the roar of motorcycle engines shattered the air. Police officers, sirens wailing, burst through the park gates. One of them slammed into an attacker, sending him sprawling, his gun clattering across the cobblestones. Ghaznawar and his remaining accomplice fled, their plan in ruins. Police officers, some on foot, others on motorcycles, pursued them as the park descended into chaos.

Somi watched them disappear, her breath coming in ragged gasps. She turned back to Aditya, who lay pale and bleeding on the cobblestones. She continued pressing her scarf against his wound, her efforts frantic. Moments later, Ramaswamy and Jung arrived, their faces creased with worry.

'He's been shot,' Somi said, her voice trembling. 'We need to get him to a hospital—now!'

A police officer had already radioed for an ambulance. It arrived within minutes, paramedics rushing out, taking over from Somi. They worked swiftly, stabilizing Aditya and transferring him to a stretcher. As they wheeled him towards the ambulance, Somi refused to be left behind. 'I am going with him,' she insisted. The paramedics nodded and let her in.

Somi looked out the window as the ambulance sped away, terrified—because Ghaznawar, she knew, was crouched somewhere in the shadows. He was not finished yet.

95

Seongsan, Garak Confederacy

Present-day Seongju County, South Korea

Around 2,000 years ago

Temporary tents dotted the rocky plains around the battlefield, their canvas walls flapping in the breeze. Inside these makeshift shelters, hundreds of wounded soldiers lay on thin mattresses, their bodies broken and bleeding. The air reeked with the stench of blood, sweat and suffering.

The battle between Soju's and Talhae's forces had left its mark on every combatant. But here, in this sanctuary of healing, there were no enemies, only injured souls in need of care. Bhadraketu made no distinction between friend and foe. He moved tirelessly from tent to tent, his hands stained with the juices of crushed herbs, sweat glistening on his forehead. Nurses, hastily trained in the rudiments of battlefield medicine, followed his lead, purposeful and calm. They moved among the rows of injured, offering water, cleaning wounds and administering Nadikasyapa's herbal remedies which Bhadraketu had taught them to prepare.

'I will be as gentle as I can,' Bhadraketu murmured as he replaced the bandages on a soldier's chest. The man winced, his breath catching in his throat as the dressing brushed against his wound. 'The pain will subside soon,' Bhadraketu said, his hands tireless, efficient. 'Let the healing begin.' The soldier nodded weakly, tears welling in his eyes. Bhadraketu gently squeezed his shoulder, reassuring him, before moving on to the next patient.

As he worked, he offered words of comfort and solace to those enduring unimaginable pain. 'Suffering is a part of life,' he said softly to a young soldier who had lost a leg, his face drawn and pale. 'But pain is not permanent. It will pass, just as darkness gives way to dawn. Find solace in the Buddha's wisdom.'

In the largest tent at the centre of the encampment, Soju lay unmoving, his breathing shallow, his face a canvas of wounds. The air was heavy with the scent of the various remedies Bhadraketu had concocted—garlic, milk thistle, golden seal, charcoal, turmeric and fennel—each a partial antidote to the pishuang that had coated Talhae's blade. He hoped their combined effects would be enough. Bhadraketu tended to Soju personally, entrusting the task to no one else.

Suriratna sat beside Soju, her eyes red and swollen from days of weeping, hands trembling as she reached for his face. Her own body bore the marks of battle, bandages wound around her arms and torso, but her physical pain paled in comparison to the agony of seeing Soju injured and prone. She had not left his side since they had carried him from the battlefield.

'Will he awaken?' Suriratna asked, her voice barely a whisper.

Bhadraketu knelt beside the bed, applying a thick paste of turmeric and fennel to one of Soju's wounds. 'He will,' he said, striving to pacify her, even as uncertainty shadowed his face. 'The poison was potent, but these remedies are effective. They will purify his blood and heal his wounds. We must be patient.'

Suriratna watched him work, her fingers twisting nervously in her lap. Her days had melted into an agonizing blur of fear and waiting. She had never felt so helpless, so at the mercy of fate. She was grateful he was still breathing. 'You saved him,' she whispered, her voice breaking. 'I do not know how to thank you.'

Bhadraketu paused, meeting her gaze. 'There is no need for thanks, Suriratna,' he said gently. 'Even if you were not my sister, I would care for him. Every living being deserves compassion. And let us not forget, he would not be alive were it not for your intervention in the duel.'

Suriratna nodded, though her heart remained heavy. She reached out, her fingers brushing against Soju's cold skin. She had never seen him like this—so vulnerable, so close to death. Tears welled up in her eyes, but she blinked them back, fighting the despair that threatened to consume her.

'He is strong,' Bhadraketu said, sensing her fear. 'Stronger than you realize. He possesses a fierce will to live. That will sustain him.' Bhadraketu had witnessed men in far worse condition recover—Mahidol, for instance—but a nagging worry persisted. He could not be certain Soju's fate was in his hands.

Suriratna wanted to believe him, but the sight of Soju lying so still, his chest barely rising with each shallow breath, filled her with dread. She bowed her head, tears spilling down her cheeks and whispered a prayer to Harihara, her voice trembling. Bhadraketu joined her, chanting the words they had grown up with.

śivāya viṣṇurūpāya śivarūpāya viṣṇave
śivasya hṛdayaṁ viṣṇuḥ viṣṇóśca hṛdayaṁ śivaḥ
yathā śivamayo viṣṇurevaṁ viṣṇumayaḥ śivaḥ
yathāntaraṁ na paśyāmi tathā me svastirāyuṣi

~

On the sixth day after the battle, as dusk settled over the camp, Soju's eyelids fluttered. Suriratna, who had been holding his hand, felt a tremor course through it. 'Bhadraketu!' she exclaimed, hope surging through her. 'He is waking up!'

Bhadraketu hurried to his friend's side, studying his face intently. 'Soju,' he said softly. 'Can you hear me?' For a moment, there was only the faint rasp of Soju's breath. Then, his eyes opened gradually, his gaze unfocused and distant, as though he were peering through a thick fog. He blinked repeatedly, confusion wrinkling his forehead.

'Soju,' Suriratna said, her voice trembling. 'I am here.'

His eyes shifted towards her, lingering for a moment, devoid of recognition. Then, slowly, as if emerging from a dream, his expression softened, warmth filling his face. Suriratna burst into tears. 'Suriratna,' he whispered, his voice feeble. He tried to lift his hand to touch her face, but the effort was too much and it fell back onto the bed.

She took his hand and held it gently against her heart. 'I am here, Soju,' she said. 'I am here, and I am not leaving.'

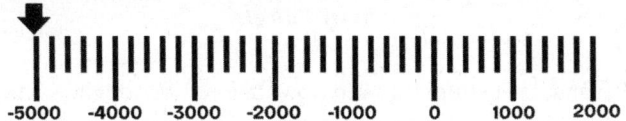

Kailasa Parvata, Manasa Sarovar
Present-day Mount Kailasa, Tibet
Around 7,000 years ago

Ravana stood at the base of Kailasa Parvata, the sacred, snow-capped peak rising against the sky. The biting air seeped into his bones, chilling him to the core. The world around him was stark and unforgiving, a landscape of jagged ice and frozen streams that glittered in the fading light. A perpetual mist clung to the mountain, lending it an ethereal aura.

For days and nights, his cries had reverberated amidst the icy cliffs, travelling on the relentless wind that howled through the crevices and mingling with the distant rumble of avalanches. By day, the sky was a vast expanse of azure; by night, it transformed into a canvas of a thousand stars, unmarred by the smoke and dust of distant kingdoms. Though harsh, his surroundings held a pervasive tranquillity, a constant reminder of the sacred presence that resided within the mountain.

After months of fasting and enduring the elements, Ravana witnessed a section of the rock face slide open. A figure emerged, powerfully built, with wild, unkempt hair cascading to his waist. He stood bare-chested against the icy winds, clad only in a tiger skin.

'Ravana,' came Shiva's voice, calm yet commanding. 'Your devotion has summoned me again. But know this—I have not forgotten your last request, when you dared to seek Parvati as your reward.'

Ravana, awestruck, bowed low before the mighty Shiva. 'Forgive my past folly, Great One,' he pleaded. 'The treacherous Narada Muni planted that wicked thought within me. I have learned from my mistake. Hear my plea.'

Shiva's gaze seemed to penetrate Ravana's soul. 'Speak,' he commanded, though he already knew the king's desire.

'I seek the Atmalingam, the ultimate source of power and transformation,' Ravana declared. 'Grant me this boon, that I may rule the world with unmatched might.'

Shiva regarded him with a knowing look. 'The Atmalingam is no mere stone. It is a divine catalyst, capable of revitalizing the fundamental building blocks of existence, of altering the very fabric of reality.'

Desire burned in Ravana's eyes. 'Grant me this gift, O Powerful One, and I will harness its power for effective rule.'

Shiva raised a hand, silencing the king's passionate plea. 'Listen closely, Ravana. The Atmalingam's true power lies in its balance. When all its particles are charged alike, they repel, causing destruction. But when the two universal forces—Shiva and Vishnu—are united in it, they create a bond as strong as the universe itself.'

Ravana listened, captivated, forgetting the biting cold altogether as Shiva continued. 'I will bestow the Atmalingam upon you. But know this: its full potential can only be unlocked through a connection with Vishnu. The Atmalingam will then become the Dvaitalingam—the lingam of dual energy. Seek balance, not domination. The pursuit of domination will lead to imbalance and, ultimately, your ruin.'

With a wave of his hand, Shiva summoned an enormous stone, a massive cylindrical block that seemed to blot out the sky as it rolled forward. The earth shook violently beneath its crushing weight, its energy pulsating in waves that reverberated through the air. It came to a thunderous halt near Ravana, its sheer magnitude dwarfing him.

Marvelling at its immense power, Ravana stepped closer, his fingers trembling as they traced the intricate engravings on the Atmalingam. The symbol of two fish, carved on it with divine precision, seemed almost alive against the polished surface. Upon its surface was an inscription.

'What is this, O Powerful One?' he asked, awed.

'Shiva's Atmalingam awaits Vishnu's touch to transform into the Dvaitalingam, and will also need to be guarded by Sheshanaga. The two fish represent two energies—my own and Vishnu's,' Shiva replied. 'You will need both energies to activate the Atmalingam. Without that balance, you risk your own destruction.' With that, Shiva turned and vanished into the swirling snow.

Ravana remained alone at the base of Kailasa, both hands placed firmly on the stone. His mind raced. How could he compel the Vishnu avatar to imbue the Atmalingam with his power? Why would Vishnu even consider such a thing?

An idea took root, a cunning smile spreading across his face. What if he could lure the Vishnu avatar to Lanka through a series of strategic manoeuvres? What if he left Vishnu with no choice but to come to him?

As snow continued to fall around him, Ravana began his descent from Kailasa, pulling the heavy Atmalingam behind him with ropes, a task that would have been impossible for any ordinary man. Desire burned within him, driving his ambition. He envisioned the armies he would raise, the kingdoms he would conquer and the absolute power he would wield.

96

Gimhae, South Gyeongsang Province, South Korea
Present day

Khalil Ghaznawar ran through the undergrowth, his breaths falling in rapid, controlled bursts. The dense woodland surrounding Queen Heo's tomb was eerily silent. He could feel the pressure of the pursuit—the insistent drone of police motorbikes and distant shouts filtering through the trees. With each stride, the damp earth squelched beneath his boots, but he moved with a predator's precision, his senses honed through years of experience.

Behind him, his accomplice struggled to keep pace, hampered by a leg injury sustained during their escape. But Ghaznawar remained focused, his instincts geared towards survival. He snatched the satellite phone from his pocket, the screen flashing to life as he punched in Choe Tok Hun's number in Pyongyang. The line crackled with static until the North Korean's icy voice answered. 'Report,' he demanded curtly.

'We're compromised. I need extraction—immediately,' Ghaznawar hissed, his eyes darting around for any sign of approaching officers.

There was a pause, pregnant with suppressed fury. 'You imbecile!' Choe Tok Hun's voice was a low growl, bitter with censure. 'Using that phone now will lead them straight to me! You've jeopardized everything!'

Ghaznawar wanted to retort, but he bit back the words. He needed the North Korean's help. 'Then tell me what to do,' he said, forcing his voice to remain respectful.

'Dispose of the phone and disappear,' Choe ordered, his tone clipped and precise. 'You understand the stakes. Do not fail me again.'

The line went dead. Ghaznawar stared at the phone for a moment, then flung it into a nearby pond, stopping long enough to watch it sink beneath the surface.

He did not have time to dwell on the North Korean's anger. The police were converging on them, their shouts echoing through the trees. He scanned the woods, his eyes searching for an escape route. A ravine cut through the forest—he would lead them there, into the treacherous depths where the terrain would work to his advantage.

'We need him alive!' Inspector Moon's voice crackled over the police radios as he directed the search. 'Orders from the top. Close in!'

Ghaznawar's accomplice, winded and injured, tripped over an exposed root, falling heavily. He scrambled to his feet, but he knew he could not match Ghaznawar's unrelenting pace. Despair gripped him but he pushed himself onward despite his fading strength.

Ghaznawar did not slow down. He never did. Weakness had no place in his world. The trees thinned as he approached the ravine. He could hear the police motorbikes, their engines roaring as they navigated the wooded paths. At the ravine's edge, Ghaznawar paused, his breath steady despite the adrenaline coursing through him. He surveyed the jagged rocks below, the precipitous drop. A dangerous fall, but it would buy him time. Glancing back, he saw his partner struggling to catch up. There was no time for hesitation. He raised his gun, his gaze cold and calculating.

Two officers emerged from the trees. Ghaznawar fired twice, the shots echoing through the woods. One officer fell, the other dove for cover. Ghaznawar retreated behind a tree as the police returned fire, bullets splintering the air. His accomplice, limping towards the ravine, was caught in the crossfire. He crumpled to the ground with a cry, his blood staining the earth. By the time the police reached him, he was too weak to resist. They swiftly apprehended him, their attention shifting to their primary target—Ghaznawar.

He was already moving, scrambling down the steep slope of the ravine. He could hear the officers shouting above, and the distant barking of dogs, but he was in his element, his movements fluid and surefooted as he navigated the treacherous terrain.

The pursuit continued. The police, recognizing Ghaznawar's skill, pressed forward, their numbers giving them an advantage. They followed him down the twisting paths of the ravine. Then came the sound Ghaznawar had been dreading—the sharp crack of a sniper rifle. He barely had time to react before a searing pain ripped through his thigh. He stumbled, but managed to remain upright, his hands clutching the bleeding wound. Gritting his teeth against the pain, he pushed onward, each step a battle against his weakening body. Above, the sniper adjusted his aim, tracking Ghaznawar's movements with chilling precision. There was no room for error. The next shot had to be the last.

Ghaznawar reached a narrow ledge, his breath coming in ragged gasps as he looked down. The void beckoned—a possible escape, but at what cost? To leap was to surrender, to die on someone else's terms. And Ghaznawar had never bowed to fear. Far away, the sniper's crosshairs settled on his left knee.

Time seemed to stand still. Ghaznawar gazed down at the path—the faces of those he had served, the causes he had fought for, flashing before his eyes. In that final moment, he saw the image of his ancestor, Mahmud of Ghazni, looming above him, silent, judging. 'I am sorry,' Ghaznawar whispered, his words lost on the wind. The advice of the Kekaya tribe leader, Ibn al-Kaqaya, to Ghazni, had been in vain. The Dvaitalingam ... so close, yet so far ... Queen Kaikeyi's secret unattainable.

As he dizzily swayed, the sniper fired. The bullet found its mark, piercing Ghaznawar's knee. The impact shattered his leg and he tumbled over the edge, disappearing into the darkness below. Rifles trained on the spot where he had last been seen, Inspector Moon, accompanied by dogs, cautiously approached the edge.

As the void consumed Ghaznawar, it carried no sound—only the weight of a legacy undone.

97

Gimhae, South Gyeongsang Province, South Korea
Present day

'He's fortunate the bullet didn't cause more extensive damage,' the doctor said to Somi as Aditya emerged from surgery. 'It missed the brachial and subclavian arteries. It passed through muscle tissue without striking any major structures, minimizing the risk of complications. While there's no significant organ or vascular damage, we must monitor for infection and ensure proper healing.'

Two hours later, Aditya's eyes opened. He smiled weakly when he saw Somi seated beside his bed. 'Somi, are you all right?' he asked, his voice scratchy.

His concern touched her. Reaching for his hand, she smiled. 'I should be asking *you* that,' she said. Though fatigued, he was eager to hear what had happened. She filled him in.

'What about Ghaznawar?' he asked. 'Where is he?'

'He was killed in the shootout,' she said. 'One of his accomplices is in custody. His interrogation will likely reveal more.' Somi Kim was no ordinary citizen and the directive to discover the truth had come to the police from the highest levels of the government.

'And the pagoda stones?' Aditya asked.

'Dr Ramaswamy and Dr Jung have got permission to analyse some fragments,' Somi told him. 'They're working at Jung's lab at GISCO. They'll contact us when they have something.'

Aditya wanted to talk more, but Somi urged him to rest. He ate dinner under the nurse's watchful eye, and took his antibiotics and a sleeping pill. Somi remained by his side.

For the next two days, she stayed in a nearby room until he was cleared for release. As they headed towards the waiting car, he asked, 'Where are we going?'

'Back to the Arirang Hotel,' she replied. 'The surgeon said you can travel in a couple of days. I considered inviting you to my home in Seoul, but perhaps we should remain in Gimhae until the scientists finish their analysis.'

'Any news from Jung or Ramaswamy?' he asked as they settled into the car.

'I spoke with Jung,' Somi said. 'The pagoda contains six boulders, stacked from largest to smallest. The bottom four are ordinary carbonate rock.'

'And the top two?'

She sighed. 'Unlike anything they've ever seen. They believe they might be meteoric in origin.'

Aditya drew a deep breath. 'If they share a chemical signature with Kailasa or Konark, this could be it,' he murmured. Somi nodded, trying to contain her excitement. It was best to remain cautious, to avoid unrealistic expectations. Their journey had been marked by too many false starts.

~

They returned to their rooms at the Arirang, located within the GISCO complex, seeking respite from the relentless pace of recent days. Despite their comfort, the rooms felt impersonal, lacking the warmth of familiarity. Aditya stood by the window, gazing out at the lights of the GISCO facility, his mind replaying the latest events. A soft knock interrupted his thoughts. He opened the door to find Somi standing there, looking exhausted.

'Room service,' she said. 'Shall we dine together?'

Aditya nodded, stepping aside to allow her to enter. A waiter followed, pushing a dinner trolley laden with fragrant ramyeon, noodles in a characteristically Korean spicy broth. The aroma was enticing, stirring his appetite. They settled at the small table, the clinking of silverware the only sound in the room. The comfort food was satisfying, but they ate in silence, each lost in thought. The meal brought a brief moment of solace amidst the turmoil.

After dinner, while the waiter cleared the dishes, Aditya moved to the sofa. Somi joined him, switching on the television. Thanks to GISCO's PR team, news of the incident had been suppressed, the details minimized. The public knew only that an arrest had been made after an incident at the memorial park.

'We've been through a lot together in a short time,' Aditya said, turning to face her.

Somi nodded, meeting his gaze. 'It's been quite a whirlwind. But I am glad we are facing it together. By the way, Mr Thakural called. He was aware of what happened before I could tell him.'

'How?' Aditya frowned. 'I thought the information was contained.'

'Your guess is as good as mine, but he was possibly tracking us for our own security,' she replied with a shrug, switching off the television after flipping through a few channels.

'Fat good his security did us,' Aditya said. 'More likely he wanted to keep tabs on our progress.'

As the moments passed, the awkward silences and hesitant conversation that had characterized their lone date in Chicago resurfaced. An unspoken tension filled the room. They sat close together, their proximity amplifying the unspoken feelings that had been simmering between them. Aditya reached out, gently brushing a stray strand of hair from her forehead. The gesture was unexpectedly intimate, electrifying. He withdrew his hand embarrassedly. 'Somi,' he began, his voice hoarse with emotion. 'I—'

She didn't let him finish. Closing the distance between them, she kissed him, her lips pressing against his, tender and urgent. The world outside was forgotten; they were aware only of the connection that flared between them. The kiss deepened, fanned by a passion that had been smouldering for weeks, perhaps even years. Somi's fingers tangled in his hair, holding him as if he might disappear.

They lost themselves in each other.

98

Gimhae, South Gyeongsang Province, South Korea
Present day

They were in Dr Jung Tae-hyun's domain—his laboratory. Furnaces, ovens, specialized equipment were everywhere. Jung had access to virtually any solvent or reagent imaginable. Metal tables, gleaming under fluorescent lights, were covered with tools, microscopes and samples at various stages of analysis. GISCO's computer servers stored a vast library of test data, accumulated through years of research and development. As GISCO's chief metallurgist, Jung reigned supreme.

The stone fragments from the pagoda, carefully labelled and arranged in sequence, sat in dishes on a table in the middle of the room. The fragments from the two upper stones seemed to display a subtle iridescence under the lights, absent in the lower stones.

Jung donned a pair of gloves and carefully selected a fragment from the lower stones, placing it under a high-powered microscope. The monitor flickered to life, revealing the stone's intricate matrix. Ramaswamy watched as Jung adjusted the focus, sharpening the image.

'This,' Jung began, 'is a classic carbonate breccia. Nothing remarkable at first glance ... except for its origin.' He tapped a few keys, bringing up a map on a secondary screen. 'Large deposits of this breccia are found in the Tirunelveli district of Tamil Nadu, particularly around Korkai. Sedimentary rock from the Proterozoic era—over a billion years old. Interesting how these stones ended up in a pagoda in Gimhae.'

'Proof that the legend of Suriratna arriving here on a ship is true?' Ramaswamy suggested, leaning closer. 'They seem ordinary, yet their placement within the structure is ... curious. Almost like a foundation, supporting the more enigmatic upper stones.'

Jung moved to the next fragment—one of the upper stones. He hesitated, then lifted it with a reverence typically reserved for something far more precious. The microscope revealed a complex, almost alien structure. The crystalline formations defied all documented geological processes.

'These upper stones,' Jung said, his voice hushed, 'are unlike any known terrestrial mineral. Their composition defies conventional geological understanding. Silicon, sulphur, manganese, phosphorus, nickel, chromium ... all are present, but there's something else.'

'As I've mentioned earlier, silicon was known to the ancients,' Ramaswamy pointed out. 'They called it "ayah samsraya". Sulphur was "gandhaka"; manganese, "manikya"; phosphorus, "agnidharaka"; nickel, "pindarajata"; chromium, "chitraka". But what is this additional element you're detecting?'

Jung switched to another monitor, where a 3D model of the stone's molecular structure rotated slowly. 'There's an unknown element here. It does not correspond to anything on the periodic table. Not yet, at least.'

Ramaswamy felt a shiver run down his spine. 'Are you suggesting—'

'Yes,' Jung interrupted, his voice charged with excitement. 'These stones may be remnants of a lost advanced technology. Or, even more intriguing, they may be extra-terrestrial.'

Jung initiated a chemical signature comparison. Graphs appeared on the screen, each representing a trace element found within the stone.

'This is where it gets even more peculiar,' he continued. 'The chemical signature of these stones bears a striking resemblance to traces your teams found at Kailasa, Konark and Petra.'

'But not identical,' Ramaswamy observed, his analytical mind processing the implications.

'Precisely,' Jung confirmed. 'The differences could be because the traces at those sites were from metal tools used on them—tools produced using this element—not the ingredient itself. Imagine finding fingerprints from the same hand but with slight variations depending on the surface touched.'

Jung moved to another station where a sleek machine with multiple nozzles stood ready. 'Let's begin with X-ray fluorescence analysis,' he said, positioning the fragment beneath the instrument. 'This will determine the elemental composition non-destructively.'

The machine hummed to life, directing a beam of X-rays into the stone. A spectrum began to form on a nearby screen, each peak representing a different element. Ramaswamy watched as familiar elements appeared—silicon, phosphorus, manganese—but then a new peak emerged, one that corresponded to no known element.

'There it is,' Jung said, pointing to the anomaly. 'The unknown element. Present in substantial quantities, yet unidentified.'

'And its role in these stones?' Ramaswamy asked, his mind buzzing with possibilities.

'Further testing is required to get an answer to that,' Jung replied. 'Shall we see how it reacts to extreme conditions?'

He led Ramaswamy to a furnace capable of reaching thousands of degrees Celsius. 'Let's test its thermal stability,' he said, placing a small fragment inside. The furnace roared to life, the temperature display climbing rapidly. Ramaswamy and Jung watched as it passed 500°C, 1000°C, then 1500°C. 'Astonishing,' Jung murmured. 'Most materials would have begun to degrade by now. This is nearly impervious to heat.'

He switched off the furnace, carefully retrieved the fragment and placed it in a cooling chamber. 'Let's see if it retains its properties after such stress.'

Ramaswamy peered into the chamber as the stone cooled. 'Any change?'

'None that I can detect,' Jung replied. He moved the fragment to a laser ablation device. 'Let's try laser-induced breakdown spectroscopy.'

The laser fired, vaporizing the stone's surface into a plasma cloud. The spectrometer analysed the emissions, generating another graph. As expected, the familiar elements were present, but the unknown element remained prominent, unaffected by the laser.

'This material seems designed to withstand extreme conditions,' Jung mused. 'Or perhaps it is a natural anomaly that ancient civilizations somehow harnessed.'

The two men stood in contemplative silence, grappling with the import of their discovery. The lower stones were clearly terrestrial, ancient remnants of southern India's geology, anchoring the structure in known history. But the upper stones ... Their composition, their resilience and their presence in sacred sites across continents all pointed to something deliberately obscured, yet profoundly connected. These were not just materials—they were artifacts, perhaps components of a forgotten science, or relics of a technology misunderstood as magic.

How had they come to be placed with such precision atop the humble breccia? Who had known enough to do it? The fusion of the two—the plausible and the inexplicable—was no accident. It was a cipher, waiting for the right mind to decode it.

'I do believe we have found the missing link,' Ramaswamy said, his voice hushed with wonder. 'A convergence of myth and matter. If we understand how they interact, we may finally unlock what the ancients hinted at—and what they sought to conceal.'

99

Geumgwan, Garak Confederacy
Present-day Gimhae, South Korea
Around 2,000 years ago

The sun reflected off the placid Nakdong river, its amber rays catching the ornate clothing of the nobles gathered in Geumgwan. The city prepared for a momentous occasion—the marriage of Soju and Suriratna. The union of Kim Suro and Heo Hwang-ok would irrevocably alter the course of the Garak Confederacy.

Kim Hwa's courtyard was transformed into a canvas of colour, with silk banners billowing in the breeze. The scent of incense mingled with the aroma of pine and flowers as Soju, dressed in a fine blue hanbok, waited for his bride.

Wearing an elegant crimson sari, Suriratna entered, each step measured and graceful, reflecting the poise and dignity that had captured the hearts of Geumgwan. Her hair, interwoven with delicate gold threads, glittered as it caught the fading sunlight. She was keenly aware of the significance of this moment—not just the union of two souls, but also the forging of an alliance between her homeland and this distant kingdom.

Soju's mother stood beside him, emotions surging in her heart. As Suriratna approached, she extended her hand, her voice trembling as she offered a blessing. 'May the heavens bless your marriage, my daughter, Heo Hwang-ok.'

Bhadraketu stood beside a group of shaman monks. Nearby, a priest from Korkai, who had sailed with Cheliyan, awaited the commencement of the ceremony. The wedding rites would be a fusion of Hindu, Buddhist and Shamanic traditions. The couple bowed before the elders as priests chanted in multiple languages. They sealed their union by drinking from a shared cup of wine.

The assembled guests, including the allied chiefs—Jinhyeok of Bihwa, Wonsik of Bangam and Yongho of Ara—erupted in cheers as the bride and groom clasped hands.

Kadalan Cheliyan stepped forward, his inherent grace belying his rugged appearance. He presented a silk-lined box containing two exquisite Korkai pearl necklaces, their lustrous orbs catching the light. 'These are but mere tokens of my respect and admiration,' he declared, his voice resonant. 'One for Soju, a leader of men, and one for Suriratna, a conqueror of hearts.'

Suriratna accepted the gift with a grateful nod, her eyes meeting Cheliyan's. Her father, Padmasen, had gifted them a magnificent Harihara statue from Saketa, encrusted with sparkling diamonds, that Cheliyan had transported on his Pandyan vessel. From distant Dimašq, Mithradates had sent an elaborate chest filled with frankincense, myrrh and fragrant oils.

Once the wedding rites concluded, the gathering proceeded to the Great Hall of the Confederacy. Soju was invited to stand at its centre, flanked by the leaders of Bihwa, Bangam and Ara. Yongho, the eldest chieftain, presented Soju with a golden sceptre. 'You are now formally the head of the Garak Confederacy,' he proclaimed. 'May you rule wisely and may the gods guide you.'

Soju took his place at the head of the table, his posture humble. He requested a moment of silence to honour his departed father, Kim Seok, and the chiefs and warriors lost in recent battles. Then he rose to address the assembly. 'Honoured leaders and elders,' he began, 'the Garak Confederacy stands at a crossroads. Today marks not only a consolidation of our strength, but also a call to action for the wellbeing of our people.' The audience applauded.

'I propose a careful reallocation of the territories formerly under Talhae's control—Seongsang, Goryeong and Daegaya. They have suffered under his tyranny. It is time for them to be governed wisely, with a renewed sense of purpose.'

The chiefs deliberated, ultimately deciding to appoint three individuals of integrity and knowledge from those regions to govern under the Confederacy's supervision. 'Let us pray that these honourable men will uphold the strength, unity and justice of our Confederacy, with each province working towards the common good.'

Jinhyeok of Bihwa rose, his voice carrying the weight of experience and respect. 'Honoured chiefs, as we look to a prosperous future under Kim Suro's leadership, we must acknowledge the invaluable contributions of Suriratna, now our own Heo Hwang-ok. Without her exceptional work at the foundry, where she transformed our weapon production capabilities, we would have struggled to overcome Talhae's forces.'

'Indeed,' Wonsik agreed. 'Her expertise in metallurgy and forging has been crucial to our success. The outcome might have been very different without her innovations.'

'I propose that she be formally recognized for her achievements,' Jinhyeok continued, 'and bestowed the title of Cheol-ui Yeowang—the Iron Queen. She should be tasked with overseeing the construction of new furnaces, foundries and forges throughout our Confederacy. Her skills will ensure we remain well-equipped.'

Soju gazed at his wife with admiration. 'The chiefs speak wisely. Your vision and dedication have been invaluable. The title of Iron Queen is most fitting.'

Suriratna bowed her head humbly. 'I am honoured by your trust. I accept this role and vow to perform it with the utmost dedication. But I must acknowledge that without the assistance of Saketa, Korkai and Dimašq, my efforts would have been in vain. Many of our friends and allies could not be here today—but one among them is.' She looked towards the entrance. 'Let us summon Kadalan Cheliyan and honour him.'

As Kadalan Cheliyan entered the hall, the chiefs turned to face him. The merchant bowed respectfully. Soju rose, his face alight with gratitude. 'Your efforts, along with those of my father-in-law, Padmasen, and Suriratna's matalu, Kulasekara, have been instrumental in our success. The timely arrival of armaments from my dear friend Mithradates was also invaluable. I am deeply indebted to each of you. I offer my personal gratitude, and that of the Garak Confederacy. And how can I forget the day you carried me across the seas to Korkai, at my father's behest?'

'I am proud of the man you have become, Kim Suro,' Cheliyan replied, his humility evident in his demeanour. 'Serving you remains a privilege. I also bring a proposal from Padmasen, Suriratna's esteemed father, now the king of Kosala.'

'Tell us,' Soju urged.

'He envisions a collaboration between Saketa, Korkai, Dimašq and Geumgwan,' Cheliyan explained. 'Partners working together to expand trade, enhance production, develop new products and refine existing techniques and knowledge. We will establish trade routes for our raw materials and finished goods. More importantly, we will support each other with resources and weaponry in times of need. He wishes to call it the indomitable alliance—the Ayodhya Alliance.'

Murmurs of agreement filled the chamber as the chiefs and elders exchanged glances, recognizing the wisdom of the proposal. Soju surveyed the council, and was pleased to see their expressions mirroring his own. Turning to Cheliyan, he said, 'My father-in-law's proposal is both sensible and progressive. The chiefs, Suriratna and I endorse this alliance. Let this mark the beginning of a new era of collaboration and industry.'

Soju's gaze shifted to Bhadraketu, who was observing the proceedings quietly from a corner. 'My dear friend,' Soju addressed him, 'I cannot allow you to return to Ayutthaya just yet. Your presence here is invaluable. The Garak Confederacy needs your spiritual guidance. I envision our people enlightened by the teachings of Harihara, our ancient shamanic traditions and the wisdom of the Buddha. Remain with us yet and guide us.'

Bhadraketu glanced at Suriratna. Her expression too seemed to plead with him to stay.

'There is more,' Soju continued. 'I ask that you serve as our envoy of peace to the Three Kingdoms—Silla, Baekje and Goguryeo. You will be our ambassador, ensuring peace in our region. For peace is the only path to progress.'

Bhadraketu bowed. 'It would be an honour, my friend,' he replied. 'I will do everything in my power to help you realize this vision.'

100

Biliya, Thar Desert, Rajasthan

Present day

The Thar Desert stretched endlessly, its dunes shimmering beneath the harsh midday sun. A swirling dust cloud in the distance heralded the arrival of India's newest military marvel, the upgraded Bharat Primary Battle Tank—the BPBT-2—as it thundered across the parched landscape, leaving deep furrows in the sand, its engine roaring.

Unlike its military-green predecessors, this tank was unpainted. Its steel surface bore a distinctive wavy pattern, reminiscent of a Damascus blade. Closer inspection revealed microblades projecting outward, tiny chisel heads designed to maximize the absorption area of any impact. The Ashoka Chakra, the emblem of India's national flag, was emblazoned on the tank's front.

Several miles away, in a state-of-the-art control room, Aditya and Somi waited with bated breath. Engineers and military personnel hunched over their consoles, monitoring every aspect of the tank's performance. The far wall was dominated by a massive screen, displaying the live feeds from multiple drones circling overhead. Every angle showcased the tank's unique design, a powerful statement of the collaboration between GISCO–Pillai and the DRDO.

Dr V.K. Reddy, chairman of DRDO, stood at the front of the room, his eyes fixed on the screen. Beside him stood General

Upendra Tripathi, India's army chief, flanked by Vinay Kamat, the project's director general. They were surrounded by top engineers, their faces a mixture of hope and apprehension. A voice crackled over the intercom, cutting through the tension. 'All systems nominal.'

'Good,' Reddy murmured, his eyes never leaving the screen. The BPBT-2 was approaching the first testing zone. The tank came to a halt, its massive frame settling into the sand.

'Driver, disembark,' Kamat instructed, his voice calm but edged with tension. The stakes were too high. The tank's hatch swung open and a soldier emerged, saluting smartly before climbing onto a waiting all-terrain vehicle that sped away to a safe distance.

Aditya leaned towards Somi. 'This is it,' he whispered. 'They're about to switch to remote control.' Somi nodded, her attention fixed on the tank. The DRDO crew initiated the remote operation sequence and the BPBT-2 rumbled back to life, now under their command. It swivelled gracefully, ready for the trials.

'Commence small arms test,' Kamat announced.

A barrage of gunfire erupted, targeting the tank from multiple directions. Bullets of .30 and .50 calibre ricocheted off its hull, producing a cacophony of metallic clangs. The tank's most vulnerable points—its sides, rear and external equipment—were subjected to intense scrutiny. On a secondary screen, close-up views of the tank's surface, captured by hovering drones, showed the impact of each hit.

'Looking good so far,' Aditya murmured, scanning the screen for damage. Somi said nothing, her hands clasped tightly. The BPBT-2 moved with an almost defiant grace, the small arms fire bouncing harmlessly off its surface.

'Initiate heavy machine guns.' Kamat's voice cut through the nerve-wracking silence.

The noise in the desert would have been deafening, but in the control room it was muted by sound filters. Autocannons and heavy machine guns unleashed a torrent of high-calibre rounds. The BPBT-2 shuddered as its armour absorbed the continuous impact. As the dust settled, the drones moved in for closer inspection. The zoomed-in images revealed minor dents and scratches, but remarkably, the tank's exterior remained intact.

'Those were just the preliminary tests,' Aditya said, his voice tight. 'The real challenge is yet to come.' Somi nodded, her eyes glued to the screen.

'Prepare for kinetic energy penetrators,' Kamat ordered.

A high-velocity round designed to pierce the tank's armour was fired directly at the BPBT-2. The screen displayed the projectile's path, culminating in a violent impact, followed by slow-motion replays. Silence gripped the control room, followed by a collective exhale of relief. The BPBT-2 stood firm. Its armour had withstood the force of the kinetic energy penetrator, the projectile now embedded in the hull, unable to penetrate.

'Let's see how it holds up,' Somi said, no less anxious than before.

The tank was then subjected to a barrage of increasingly powerful weapons—tandem warheads, high-explosive anti-tank rounds, even IED simulators. Each test, intended to push the BPBT-2 to its limit, was more demanding than the last. The screen showed the tank weathering wave after wave of assault, its structural integrity intact.

Finally, the room fell silent as they prepared for the ultimate test. The screen displayed images of a helicopter, armed with India's third-generation ATGM, the Nag. Equipped with an infrared imaging seeker and fire-and-forget capability, the Nag was designed to defeat even the most heavily armoured targets. The air-launched variant, the Dhruvastra, had been modified to mimic the capabilities of the Chinese HJ-12E.

Aditya and Somi exchanged a look. This was the moment of truth.

'Fire the Nag,' Kamat instructed.

The missile streaked towards the BPBT-2, a blur of deadly intent. A massive explosion rocked the desert, sending a plume of dust and smoke billowing skyward. The screen was obscured momentarily, the tank completely hidden. Somi's heart hammered against her ribs as she waited for the dust to clear.

As the smoke dissipated, jubilant shouts erupted in the control room. The BPBT-2 stood unscathed, with only a large, crater-like impression on the tank's surface. Not only had the missile failed to penetrate, but, astonishingly, it seemed to have partially crumpled upon impact.

'The microblades ...' Aditya whispered, his eyes wide with amazement. Until this moment, he had been unsure if the design would work.

Realization dawned, a grin spreading across his face. 'It worked!' he exclaimed. 'It bloody worked!'

The microblade surface, a ground-breaking innovation inspired by Damascus steel, had not only protected the tank but also compromised the missile's structural integrity upon contact. And now, on closer inspection, the microblade surface appeared to have absorbed and redistributed the impact damage—like a dense, reactive skin, subtly shifting and reforming at a microscopic level.

A rare smile touched Dr Reddy's face. 'We've done it,' he announced, giving a thumbs up. His voice reflected the shared elation of the entire room. 'We have created a tank capable of withstanding the most formidable threats. And you—GISCO–Pillai—have developed a revolutionary material that will result in countless new patents.' Somi and Aditya exchanged a triumphant look.

One of the drones zoomed in on the tank's front. The Ashoka Chakra remained untouched. 'A symbol of peace—the Dharma Chakra—on a weapon of war,' Dr Reddy remarked. 'Ironic, wouldn't you say?'

Aditya shook his head. 'We romanticize Ashoka as a pacifist. But Ashoka had enemies. He murdered ninety-nine brothers to secure the throne. He was sometimes known as Chandasoka—Ashoka the Cruel. He massacred eighteen thousand Ajivikas in Bengal. Two hundred and fifty thousand perished in Kalinga—*after* he became a Buddhist. His use of the tiger and the chakra on his pillars was a demonstration of power, not weakness. We now know of a weapon called the Mrityuchakra. Isn't it surprising that our Dharma Chakra and an ancient weapon can be so similar?'

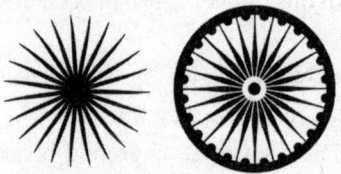

Dr Reddy smiled. 'Krishna's Sudarshan Chakra was also a lethal weapon. I suppose the lesson is that peace demands demonstration of strength first.'

The room thrummed with a new energy as doubt was replaced by confidence. They had witnessed a turning point in India's defence capabilities, a moment where history's lessons had forged the foundation of a powerful future.

-2.5 M   -5000

EPILOGUE

Kumari Kandam
Present-day Indian Ocean
Around 2.5 million years ago

The two men sat within an opulent crystalline chamber, a sanctum reserved for the most significant deliberations in Kumari Kandam.

Hari was dressed in a pale gold uttariya and antariya that complemented his bluish complexion. His long, dark hair framed his handsome face, his eyes holding a steady, penetrating focus. Opposite him, Hara sat clad in a tiger skin antariya, his matted locks cascading to his waist, a crescent moon adorning his head.

The crystalline chamber shimmered—an exquisite fusion of primordial geometry and transcendent technology. It exuded a sense of serene power and enlightened purpose. At the centre stood a monumental obsidian slab—its mirror-smooth surface glinting with shifting patterns of thought and a display of mantras reflecting the mood and tenor of the conversation. The chamber's walls, sculpted from sentient crystals, could veil or unveil their clarity in harmony with intention. Hovering thrones of woven ginkgo and luminous alloy adapted wordlessly to the will of those who sat in them. Overhead, a vaulted dome shimmered, depicting the constellations in motion—an ever-shifting cartography of the cosmos. A holographic wall pulsed with projected forms—glyphs and visions summoned from the deeper strata of knowledge. In the background, the Nasadiya Sukta, a hymn from what would later come to be known as the Rig Veda, resonated—not spoken or written, but simply conveyed.

Who really knows, and who can swear,
How Creation came, when or where!
Even gods came after creation's day,
Who really knows, who can truly say
When and how did creation start?
Did He will it? Or did He not?
Only He, up there, knows, maybe;
Or perhaps, not even He.

The chant served as a reminder that even the gods had emerged eons after creation—including powerful beings like Hari and Hara.

Kumari Kandam was a civilization unlike any other. Its political system was a diarchy, with Hari and Hara sharing equal authority. It was a vast and flourishing land, spanning 7 million square miles. But distance was irrelevant, for its citizens possessed the ability to teleport. Medicine was unnecessary; its inhabitants were immune to disease. They subsisted on minimal food, deriving energy primarily from sunlight and the atmosphere. Their average lifespan was a thousand years. They possessed intuitive knowledge that rendered language, writing and calculations obsolete.

EPILOGUE

Kumari Kandam represented the pinnacle of human evolution—pristine rivers, lush forests, verdant meadows bathed in pure air and blessed with a perfect climate, and teeming with wildlife. Nature and technology coexisted in perfect harmony. Temples, palaces, homes and work spaces, crafted from intricately carved materials, pulsed with glyphs, holograms and liquid light. The hum of sacred mantras, attuned to each individual's frequency, permeated the air.

But Hari and Hara knew that their paradise was imperilled. Kumari Kandam was changing, a slow deterioration that would eventually lead to shorter lifespans, increased susceptibility to disease, negativity and materialism.

The crystalline sanctum at the heart of the complex was encircled by four monumental quadrants—each representing a pillar of governance and harmony: the Hall of Accord, the Tribunal of Balance, the Circle of Counsel and the Chamber of Resonance. Of these, the Chamber of Resonance was paramount, its sacred duty to sustain the equilibrium between the two primal forces that powered Kumari Kandam.

The two opposing forces had been unleashed at the moment of creation. The first, a force driving the expansion of planets and galaxies, was known as Hari—or dark energy. The second, a contractive force binding planets to their suns and solar systems into galaxies, was called Hara—gravity. Both were essential, but balance was paramount. These forces shaped all duality—male and female, positive and negative charges, heat and cold, the magnetic north and south, and countless others. The two men in the room had mastered the science of harnessing and regulating these forces, their collaboration creating the utopia that was Kumari Kandam.

But today a shadow of concern clouded their meeting. The oceans surrounding Kumari Kandam—in all directions—were experiencing rising temperatures, disrupting currents and wind patterns. The source of this disruption resided in an undersea cave, a man exiled from Kumari Kandam—Guhasura. This was a rare occurrence in their history. Guhasura had created a pulse capable of disrupting the equilibrium between the two primary energy forms, using it to destabilize Kumari Kandam.

Hari turned to Hara, his serene composure undiminished. 'The balance must be preserved,' he communicated without words. 'Guhasura could undo all we have so carefully cultivated. The evolution from Matsya to Kurma to Varaha, Narasimha and beyond will have been for naught.'

Hari was referring to his ten avatars, each corresponding to a stage of life's evolution. First, the aquatic forms, represented by Matsya, the fish; then the amphibians, embodied by Kurma, the turtle; followed by terrestrial mammals, represented by Varaha, the boar; then the emergence of humanoid forms, symbolized by Narasimha, half man, half lion; next, primitive man, embodied by Vamana, the dwarf; and so on.

Hara inclined his head. 'Call forth the Keeper of Constructs,' he conveyed. 'We must find a way to neutralize this disturbance. Do you recall the era of fading light, when lifespans waned and ambient energy thinned? That, too, bore Guhasura's mark. His interference stretches across eons.'

In response to their summons, the Keeper materialized in the sanctum—tall, luminous and serene.

'Your guidance has shaped the lifeblood of Kumari Kandam,' Hari transmitted. 'Hara and I are merely the sources. It is you, Brahma, who has woven that essence into civilization.'

Brahma inclined his head in silent assent. For countless cycles, he had devoted himself to channelling and harmonizing the energies of Hari and Hara, cultivating the evolution of Kumari

Epilogue

Kandam. Now, Guhasura's interference threatened to unravel the delicate weave of their creation.

'I have conducted a series of deep calibrations to identify a counterpulse,' he conveyed. 'Until now, we have regarded your energies as complementary yet contraposed, forever in balance. But this disruption calls for a new paradigm—one of synthesis, not separation.'

'What is your solution?' Hara inquired.

'Oil and water, though naturally immiscible, can be combined using an emulsifier,' Brahma explained. 'While your energies typically resist integration, we have successfully created a harmonic binder that functions similarly. We have tentatively named it Harihara.'

'Why not Harahari?' Hara joked, momentarily breaking the sombre mood.

'Hari appointed me,' Brahma replied. 'The mural in the Hall of Accord depicts me emerging from a lotus in his navel. I owe him that much.'

A ripple of telepathic laughter passed between them.

'Will it be effective?' Hari transmitted, returning to the pressing matter at hand.

'It will,' Brahma said. 'But the signs are clear. Our civilization will continue to degenerate. Lifespans will dwindle; we will become dependent on food for sustenance; our forms will grow denser; our ability to teleport will weaken; we will require spoken language for communication; spirituality will give way to materialism. Our species will become but a shadow of its former self. These are the hallmarks of the Satya Yuga's decline.'

'And our energies?' Hara asked. 'Will they endure?'

'They will,' Brahma assured him. 'Each individual will possess varying degrees of one or the other. In future ages, beings with heightened levels of these energies will emerge and be revered. Avatars of Vishnu, imbued with Hari, and avatars of Shiva, imbued with Hara ... they will periodically manifest on Earth, guiding and assisting humanity, whose capabilities will have diminished greatly.'

'And Harihara?' Hari inquired.

'It will be fossilized within a rock,' Brahma replied. 'At the northernmost point of Kumari Kandam, there stands a mountain called Kailasa. When humanity requires its power, it can be activated. But it will require both Vishnu and Shiva to do so.'

In the Chamber of Resonance beyond—a sanctified space visible to both Hara and Hari—technicians moved with serene precision, preparing for the release of Harihara, the counterpulse crafted to neutralize Guhasura's disruption. Their translucent robes shimmered in the ambient glow as they calibrated radiant instruments and aligned themselves to the harmonic currents rippling through the chamber. Runes thrummed across the walls, syncing with the gathering energy.

Above the core pedestal, a sphere of liquid light began to form, swirling with both dark and luminous strands—Hari and Hara in potential union. The room reverberated with resonance, as if the universe itself was holding its breath.

'All systems are aligned,' one intoned, eyes fixed on the readings. 'The synthesis can begin. But to deliver it to the undersea nexus of the disruption, we require a vessel—one capable of enduring, guiding and destabilizing the pulse.'

A silence followed, brief but expectant.

'Have you considered using two fish?' Hari suggested, a trace of timeless mischief in his tone.

ACKNOWLEDGEMENTS

It would be impossible to write the books that I do without the assistance, input, guidance, love and support of so many. Here are some of those without whom this book—and the Bharat Collection—may not have happened.

My publishers, HarperCollins Publishers India—in particular, Ananth Padmanabhan and Udayan Mitra, who have ensured that books reach my readers quickly and efficiently; also my wonderful executive publisher and editor Poulomi Chatterjee, ably assisted by Kartik Chauhan and Shatarupa Ghoshal.

I would be remiss in forgetting the late Prita Maitra, my first editor of the Bharat Collection; Ashok Rajani, my perfectly ruthless fact-checker; and Swati Daftuar, Karthika V.K., Deepthi Talwar, Aparna Gupta and Meru Gokhale—individuals who helped polish one or more books in this collection. Also, Gautam Padmanabhan, my friend, philosopher and guide who gave me my first publishing break and has encouraged me through several stories including most in the Bharat Collection.

My gratitude to Rupesh Talaskar—my illustrator, who has meticulously executed internal images in several books; Ameya Naik—the versatile composer who conceived the haunting tracks used in the Collection's video trailers; Ramnika Sehrawat—the talented cover designer for this series; and the team at Oktobuzz for their social media support. I am also indebted to Vishwajeet

Sapan and Nityananda Misra who have assisted me with some of the Sanskrit elements in my text from time to time.

My thanks to Ashoo Naik at Collective Artists, Sidharth Jain at The Story Ink, Anuj Bahri at RedInk, and Fareen Dossani at SpeakIn for representing me and my work to the world.

Then there are my parents—Mahendra and Manju, and my siblings—Vidhi and Vaibhav, who have always encouraged me to follow my dreams. My wife, Anushika, and son, Raghuvir, have been my constant support in my writing endeavours. Had it not been for their unconditional love, none of my books would have been possible. Also, my little rakhi-sister Farah, who has taught me that not everything in life can be explained and that some things are better left unexplained.

And the late Ramprasad and Ramgopal Gupta, my maternal grandfather and maternal granduncle, who inspired me with their stories and books. Their blessings prevent the ink in my pen from running dry.

Finally, Ma Shakti, the One who puts power in my pen. I thank you, Ma, for your abundant blessings—forever.

REFERENCES

The books in the Bharat Collection are fictionalized narratives based on some elements of fact. Readers often ask me, 'How much of your book is fact and how much is fiction? Which parts are fiction and which parts are fact?' I always say that my reader should treat the entire novel as pure fiction. But for those who are interested in learning more, I try to provide a comprehensive list of books, papers, journals, videos and websites that I have referred to while developing my fictional narrative. Some of these sources may even express views that run contrary to the story. The idea of any book within the collection is to provide a starting point for further exploration. I am hopeful that my readers will use this list of sources for additional reading and discovery.

Books
- *A Concise History of South India*, Noboru Karashima, Oxford University Press, 2014
- *Ancient Delhi*, Upinder Singh, Oxford India Paperbacks, 2006
- *Angkor and the Khmer Civilization*, Michael D. Coe and Damian Evans, Thames and Hudson Limited, 2024
- *Ayodhya—The Land of Shree Ram*, *Outlook Traveller Getaways*, Outlook Publishing India, 2021
- *Damascus: A History* (Cities of the Ancient World), Ross Burns, Routledge, 2019
- *Evidence for the Ram Janmabhoomi Mandir*, Vishwa Hindu Parishad, 1990

- *History of Korea*, Captivating History, 2020
- *History of Kosala upto the Rise of the Mauryas*, Vishuddhanand Pathak, Motilal Banarsidas, 1963
- *Imperial Rome, Indian Ocean Regions and Muziris*, K.S. Mathew, Routledge, 2017
- *India's Legendary Wootz Steel*, Srinivasa Ranganathan and Sharada Srinivasan, Universities Press India Private Limited, 2013
- *Petra: The History of Jordan's Rose City*, History Titans, Creek Ridge Publishing, 2023
- *Indian Traces in Korean Culture: The Legend and Beyond*, Renata Czekalska, Routledge, 2025
- *Rama and Ayodhya*, Meenakshi Jain, Aryan Books International, 2013
- *Samguk Yusa: Legends and History of the Three Kingdoms of Ancient Korea*, Ilyon, Olympia Press, 2016
- *Sri Ratna Kim Suro: The Legend of an Indian Princess in Korea*, N. Parthasarathi, National Book Trust India, 2015
- *Suvarnabhumi: The Golden Land*, Bunchar Pongpanich and Somchet Thinapong, Geo-Informatics and Space Technology Development Agency, 2019
- *The Battle of Hattin, 1187*, Eric W. Olson, Georgetown University, 1983
- *The Christianity of Constantine the Great*, T.G. Elliott, Fordham University Press, 1996
- *The Mahabharata*, Dr Bibek Debroy, Penguin Random House India, 2024
- *The Pandyan Kingdom: From the Earliest Times to the Sixteenth Century*, K.A. Nilakanta Sastri, Luzac and Co., 1929
- *The Rustless Wonder: A Study of the Iron Pillar at Delhi*, T.R. Anantharaman, Vigyan Prasar, 1996

- *Valmiki Ramayana*, Dr Bibek Debroy, Penguin Random House India, 2017

Academic Papers
- 'A Phonetic Comparison of Korean and Tamil', Uthayanan Thanabalasingam, *Open Journal of Modern Linguistics*, 2023
- 'A Tale of Wootz Steel', Srinivasa Ranganathan, *Resonance*, 2006
- 'Archaeology for the Courtroom: The Ayodhya Case and the Fashioning of a Hybrid Episteme', Rachel A. Varghese, *Journal of Social Archaeology* Vol. 24(2), 2024
- 'Ayodhya: Archaeology and Identity', Reinhard Bernbeck and Susan Pollock, *Current Anthropology* Vol. 37, 1996
- 'Emergence of Iron in India: Archaeological Perspective', V. Tripathi, *Metallurgy in India—A Retrospective*, National Metallurgical Laboratory, 2001
- 'Fish Symbolism in Indus Valley Epigraphy and Protohistoric Accounts', Shamashish Sengupta, *Studia Orientalia Electronica* 11(1), 2023
- 'Gaya History and Culture', Kim Taesik, *Journal of Korean Art and Archaeology*, Vol. 15, 2021
- 'India and Korea in Ancient Times', Byung Mo Kim, Korea Institute of Heritage, 2021
- 'Interfacing Cultural Landscapes between India and Korea: Illustrating the Memorial of Korean Queen Heo in Ayodhya', Rana P.B. Singh and Sarvesh Kumar, *The Geographer* Vol. 66 (2), 2019
- 'Kailasa: The Stylistic Development and Chronology', M.K. Dhavalikar, *Bulletin of the Deccan College Post-Graduate and Research Institute* Vol. 41, 1982
- 'Korkai: An Emporium of Pearl Trade of the Ancient Tamil Country', S. Jeyaparvathi, Thanga Selvam R., Shunmuga D., *International Journal of Creative Research Thoughts*, 2018

- 'Mahmud Ghazni's Failure to Loot the Treasure of Somnath and Stratagem of Gujarat's Jain Minister Vimal Shah', Bipin Shah, Researchgate, 2020
- 'Muchiri: In Ancient Tamil Texts and Tamil Tradition', Dr V. Selvakumar, Ekalokam Trust for Photography, 2016
- 'On Technical Analysis of Cannon Shot Crater on Delhi Iron Pillar,' R. Balasubramaniam, V.N. Prabhakar, Manish Shankar, *Indian Journal of History of Science* 44.1, 2009
- 'The Ancient Korean Tamil Connection via Heo Hwang-Ok Alias Chempavalam', Kannan Narayanan, *DIS Journal*, 2020
- 'The Dipole View on the Mystery of Kumari-Kandam', K.M. Anitha Sheryl and Sr. P. Rajakumari, *Journal of Emerging Technologies and Innovative Research* Vol. 5 Issue 12, 2018
- 'The Glory of Meenakshi Amman Temple Madurai', Inder Janakarajan and Priyaranjan Behera, *International Journal of Multidisciplinary Research and Growth Evaluation*, 2022
- 'The Key Role of Impurities in Ancient Damascus Steel Blades', J.D. Verhoeven, A.H. Pendray and W.E. Dauksch, *Journal of the Minerals, Metals and Materials Society* 50 (9), 1998
- 'The Lost Tamil Continent of Kumari Kandam', Dr Uday Dokras, Indo Nordic Author's Collective, 2021
- 'Why Do Hundreds of Koreans Throng to Ayodhya Every Year', Dr Uday Dokras, Indo Nordic Author's Collective, 2020

Articles

- 'A Walk around the Qutb Complex', https://wmf-production.nyc3.digitaloceanspaces.com/documents/9c_A20Walk20around20the20Qutb20Complex.pdf
- 'Ancient Indian Metallurgy', https://vedicheritage.gov.in/vedic-heritage-in-present-context/metallurgy/

References

- 'Design Resource: Sun Temple Konark Orissa', Prof. Bibhudutta Baral, Divyadarshan C.S., Rakshitha, NID, Bengaluru, http://www.dsource.in/resource/sun-temple-konark-orissa/introduction
- 'Historical Tour Gimhae Tomb of King Suro and Others', Korea Tourism Organization, https://kto.visitkorea.or.kr/file/download/bd/18ddb0fc-73a8-11e5-b596-5311eaaaa337.pdf.kto
- 'Kailasa: The Majestic Temple of Ellora', Ministry of Culture and Indian Institute of Technology, Bombay, https://indianculture.gov.in/stories/kailasa-majestic-temple-ellora
- 'Shri Ram Janmabhoomi Mandir Project Brief', Tata Consulting Engineers Limited, https://www.vhpsa.org.au/images/events/Ram_Mandir_2022.pdf
- 'The Legend of the Indian Princess in Korea', Akshay Chavan, Live History India, https://www.peepultree.world/livehistoryindia/story/people/the-legend-of-the-indian-princess-in-korea?srslti d=AfmBOopMwnQ9URQMIAnSzqzE63GjJGch7p83zGBrLnP ZSElHVSjHQMnb
- 'Words That Speak of an Enduring Link between Tamil and Korean' by D. Madhavan, https://www.thehindu.com/news/cities/chennai/words-that-speak-of-an-enduring-link-between-tamil-and-korean/article7853212.ece

Video Resources

- Ayodhya Queen Huh Memorial Park, https://www.youtube.com/watch?v=-kReY_mkEmc
- Heo Hwang-ok Korean Queen and Tamil Princess, https://www.youtube.com/watch?v=XQLfV2fvgN4
- Kim Su-Ro: The Iron King (Korean TV Series), https://www.youtube.com/watch?v=u0yZRrlVFMs
- Princess Suriratna India (Heo Hwang-ok): Indian Queen Married Korean King, https://www.youtube.com/watch?v=CEw9yt6Xvpk

- Royal Tomb of Queen Heo, W.D. Walker, https://www.youtube.com/watch?v=L_CK82yLpEA
- Surprising Similarities between Tamil Nadu and Korea: Story of a Legendary Indian Princess, https://www.youtube.com/watch?v=cAeLh-seSK8&t=102s
- The Lost Technology of Steel Making in Ancient India (Project Shivoham), https://www.youtube.com/watch?v=VX8EOlOO7Ek
- Wootz Steel from South India: Film by Prof. Sharada, https://www.youtube.com/watch?v=pVCUYqa9kos&t=742s

ABOUT THE AUTHOR

Ashwin Sanghi is among India's highest-selling English fiction authors. He has written several bestsellers in the Bharat Collection (*The Rozabal Line*, *Chanakya's Chant*, *The Krishna Key*, *The Sialkot Saga*, *Keepers of the Kalachakra*, *The Vault of Vishnu*, *The Magicians of Mazda* and *The Ayodhya Alliance*) and two *New York Times* and *Sunday Times UK* bestselling crime thrillers with James Patterson, *Private India* (sold in the U.S. as *City on Fire*) and *Private Delhi* (sold in the U.S. as *Count to Ten*). His novel *Razor Sharp*, the first book in the Kutta Kadam thriller series conceptualized by Ashwin, became a national bestseller. He mentors, collaborates and edits several non-fiction titles in the 13 Steps Series on Luck, Wealth, Marks, Health and Parenting. He contributes to the opinion page of *The Times of India*.

Ashwin has been included by *Forbes India* in their Celebrity 100 and by *The New Indian Express* in their Culture Power List. He has won the Crossword Popular Choice Award 2012, Atta Galatta Popular Choice Award 2018, WBR Iconic Achievers Award 2018, the Lit-O-Fest Literature Legend Award 2018, the Kalinga Popular Choice Award 2021, and the Deendayal Upadhyaya Recognition 2023. He has also been awarded an Honorary Doctorate by JECRC University, Rajasthan.

He was educated at Cathedral and John Connon School, Mumbai, and St. Xavier's College, Mumbai. He holds an MBA from Yale University. Ashwin lives in Mumbai with his wife, Anushika, and son, Raghuvir.

You can connect with Ashwin via the following channels:
Website: www.sanghi.in
X: @ashwinsanghi
Instagram: @ashwin.sanghi
Facebook: fb.com/ashwinsanghi
YouTube: youtube.com/ashwinsanghi
LinkedIn: linkedin.com/in/ashwinsanghi

WELCOME TO THE SHADOWY AND ADDICTIVE WORLD OF INDIA'S MASTER STORYTELLER

THE ROZABAL LINE

Shadowed by a clandestine society, which would rather wipe out creation than allow an ancient secret to be disclosed, Father Vincent Sinclair must uncover the secret of a tomb called Rozabal in the heart of strife-torn Kashmir. The tomb holds the key to an ancient riddle, but is time running out for Father Sinclair?

CHANAKYA'S CHANT

Having once averted the threat of invasion by Alexander the Great, the calculating and ruthless Mauryan kingmaker Chanakya emerges two and a half millennia later in small-town India. Will he be able to unite a broken nation once more against the rot that consumes it?

THE KRISHNA KEY

The arrival of a murderer who executes his gruesome and brilliantly thought-out schemes in the name of God is the first clue to a sinister conspiracy to expose an ancient secret—Krishna's priceless legacy to mankind. Historian Ravi Mohan Saini must dash from the submerged remains of Dwarka and the mysterious lingam of Somnath to the icy Mount Kailash in a quest to discover the cryptic location of Krishna's most prized possession.

THE SIALKOT SAGA

The lives of two businessmen, Arvind and Arbaaz, are inadvertently intertwined as they ricochet off one another, playing out their sinister and murderous plots of personal and professional one-upmanship.

KEEPERS OF THE KALACHAKRA

When unsuspecting scientist Vijay Sundaram uncovers a primordial clue to a galactic secret that could accelerate the downward spiral of humankind, he finds himself trapped in a labyrinth, chased by unnamed killers who work with the clinical efficiency of butchers. Can he save humanity—and himself?

THE VAULT OF VISHNU

A young investigator with a complex past races against time to maintain the balance of power in the new world. Across the borders of time and space, from the empire of the Pallavas to the battlefields of the Indo-China wars, myth and history blend into edge-of-the-seat action in another Ashwin Sanghi masterpiece.

THE MAGICIANS OF MAZDA

In this gripping and provocative novel, Ashwin Sanghi travels through epochs of Islamic jihad, Macedonian revenge, Achaemenid glory, messianic birth and Aryan schism—to the Vedic fount from where it all began.

HarperCollins *Publishers* India

At HarperCollins India, we believe in telling the best stories and finding the widest readership for our books in every format possible. We started publishing in 1992; a great deal has changed since then, but what has remained constant is the passion with which our authors write their books, the love with which readers receive them, and the sheer joy and excitement that we as publishers feel in being a part of the publishing process.

Over the years, we've had the pleasure of publishing some of the finest writing from the subcontinent and around the world, including several award-winning titles and some of the biggest bestsellers in India's publishing history. But nothing has meant more to us than the fact that millions of people have read the books we published, and that somewhere, a book of ours might have made a difference.

As we look to the future, we go back to that one word— a word which has been a driving force for us all these years.

Read.